Chakra Kong part 1: Birth
or
The Exquisite Sound of One Hand Falling Off a Turnip Truck
By
S.T. Gulik

Published by Sausage Press
Second Edition
Copyright © 2020 S.T. Gulik
All rights reserved
Front Cover by Roman Dirge
Cover art by Justin Talarski
ISBN 978-0-9977095-5-1

The following prophesy takes place far in the future. Nothing/no entity referred to in these texts will exist for well over one-hundred years from the date published (except for the immortal/eternal ones who are not litigious). This is exactly how shit goes down as revealed by extradimensional beings.

Notes on the second edition

When I wrote the first edition, I wanted to try something a little different. I wrote a bunch of optional, short articles that built out the history of our future and put them all in an appendix at the back. The eBook was full of hyperlinks so you could go down a wiki-hole if you wanted to. For instance, not everyone cares to know the full details of how the Iiites organize their educational system to create hyperintelligent children. Those who do can read all about it in the appendix entry titled Project Prometheus.

It was a fun idea, but a lot of people hated all the jumping back and forth. I tweaked this second edition for a smoother user experience. The appendix is still in the back, but the main text has a few more details.

Intelligence– A measure of capacity for harmonious organization.

WHAT'S UP, OCTOPUSSY?

When Max was eleven, the government collapsed.

It started with a fistfight during a State of the Union. The opposition leader sucker-punched the president mid-speech, and it quickly escalated into a full-scale riot. Right, left, politician, press, everyone joined in. It was a national catharsis long overdue.

Everyone hated politics. They bitched about being overtaxed and overregulated. They joked about how nothing got done and ranted when something did. It was bad reality television targeted at masochists and rage addicts. So when it was canceled, the only real surprise was that they'd been doing an okay job.

Historically, governments fell because revolutionaries overthrew them. This was more like a breakup. Everyone agreed it wasn't working and they didn't want to see each other anymore. The two major parties dissolved into hundreds of factions, each with their own manifesto and charismatic podium-thumper. None were moderate enough to secure more than a tiny fraction of the vote. People had been settling for years. Now everybody wanted it their way.

While the politicians were slap-fighting for votes, society came apart in their hands like overcooked salmon. The problems weren't that serious at first. With the right solutions, they could have made a tasty croquette. Instead, they tried to put it back together with glue and nails, making the product unpalatable.

The police stopped coming to work because nobody paid them. Crime spiked until the mutants pouring from the sewers made it too dangerous to leave the house. Their wrath was justified. Max would have cheered them on if not for his legitimate fear of dismemberment.

Several generations ago, a popular video game console dubbed the Iii used radioactive materials in the batteries for their nunchuck-style controllers. The batteries leaked, causing a lot of cancer and death, but also a genetic mutation known as Iiitis (pronounced E-Itis), which caused the muscles of the right arm to create mass at several times the standard rate. Those afflicted looked like they spent all their time lifting weights, but only with one arm. They were frequently referred to as lobsters until the word was deemed hate-speech and replaced with Iiite.

The Iiite's superior strength made them popular for a little while. They were a symbol of strength and human adaptability. Within a generation, they were dominant in every sport, the military, and every other industry where muscle was a factor. Before long, they got paid more than regular folks. That caused resentment, which developed into racism, oppression, and violence. Eventually, it got so bad Iiites had to go underground, literally.

They created new towns in abandoned sewer systems. Unable to earn money or grow food, they had to raid for the things they needed. The military tried to take them out, but the Iiites always managed to survive. Over time, the war petered out. Raids grew infrequent. It became one of those things that happened to other people.

This was all way before Max was born. When he was a kid, Iiites were assumed to be a few stragglers of a dying species eking out a sorry existence in the shadows. They were more pitied than hated. A few groups even attempted reconciliation, but their ambassadors rarely returned.

When the cops disappeared, Iiites reappeared everywhere. Angsty teens came up in groups of eight to ten and roamed the streets, ripping the right arms off everyone they encountered. They laid the arms out to spell messages, usually short ones like "Retribution."

That seemed like a big deal until God manifested in Bryant Park. It turned out, thirty years ago, he'd split himself into four humans and started a shitty metal band called Poison Candy. Since everyone was worried about dying, Poison Candy's big reunion tour wasn't selling many tickets. Not wanting to be upstaged, they stopped pretending to be awful crotch-rockers and merged into a single divine being, breaking reality in the process. All kinds of shit went haywire after that. It was like living in a comic book.

That got old fast.

A few corporations saw opportunities in new markets and stepped in to provide missing essentials. Rather than taxing for things like schools and police, subscriptions popped up at various price points. Instead of toll-roads, they paved McRoads with mandatory drive-throughs. The result was horrible traffic, a spike in diabetes, and three distinct classes living side by side but divided by a cultural gulf so broad the passage from one street to the next sometimes felt like time-travel.

The most forward-thinking corporations created synergistic systems with other companies that catered to clientele in specific income brackets. Eventually, three conglomerates managed everything. K. Co. managed middle-class areas known as K-Districts and provided security through their world-famous K-Squad. Security for high-end I-Districts was seen to by I-Force (a division of IMD, a.k.a. International Monetary Divestitures, a.k.a. The Bank). Low-end S-Districts were stuck with Sav-Cops (a division of Sav-Mart). A Savanian could hire I-Force if they had the money, but if they had that kind of money, they'd be Klipsch.

S-districts had service-based economies and provided unskilled labor to the other districts. Most Savanians live in Smart Homes, large tenements designed to house as many people as possible without creating a health risk. The Valucational school system has six grades focused on vocational training and sales tactics.

Sonyans were middle class and generally had fourteen years of liberal arts education. They lived comfortably and enjoyed access to quality healthcare.

Inhabitants of I-Districts were called Klipsch. Unlike Savanians and Sonians, that name was foisted upon them by the lower classes. They refer to themselves simply as People.

People are the economy. They own all the businesses and make all the decisions. Instead of going to school, Klipsch kids have a small army of tutors to groom them for their roles as world leaders.

Things went right back to normal, proving once and for all that humans can't resist organizing into arbitrary casts with no concept of merit or empathy.

Max grew up Sonyan, but never applied himself. He'd been managing Savanians at shitty jobs since high school. Some of his employees were smarter than him, but they couldn't afford a real diploma, so they would always be poor. He saw what their life was like and always felt guilty for how much easier he had it. Over the years, the steady drip of guilt, tragedy, and disappointment in humanity eroded Max's soul. Reality became a disease he treated with a variety of over and under the counter medications, some with unfortunate side effects.

✳✳✳✳✳

Max gasped and flailed, splashing icy water over the edge of the tub. The black flame of freezer-burn played around his every cell. Trembling, he pulled himself over the edge and landed hard on his side.

It felt like he landed on a hunting knife.

"Fuck!" He growled through chattering teeth.

Reaching back, he found crude stitches running from his ass to the center of his spine in the shape of a heart. They tingled and drooled thick rivulets of various hues as he ran his fingers over them.

"Is that dental floss?" He swatted away the clinging ice then grabbed the splotchy old robe he used for a bathmat. It smelled like mildew and feet, but it was warm.

Max curled up in a ball and cocooned himself in dirty laundry until the shivering subsided. His heart was racing, pumping his remaining blood so fast he could feel ice crystals scratching up his veins.

The room went black then snapped back into focus.

His mouth felt like rotten leather. His eyelids stuck to his corneas as his gaze shifted to the sink.

It was far away. Looking at it made him want to go to sleep. His eyes slowly rolled to the ice cubes that lay melting on the tile. It took every speck of his remaining energy to lean over, but that moisture on his tongue was glorious. He sucked that puddle dry then wiggled a few inches to the next. Several pools later, he crawled back to the vent.

Max liked his little cocoon. When he was a kid, his parents kept their dirty laundry on the floor of a small closet in the hall. Tiny Max liked to go inside, close the door, bury himself in it, and toss it around. All those exciting textures, its weight, and the smell of his parents were all so comforting.

He hoped the heat would kick on soon. The thermostat was on 67, so it never stayed on for long.

As his mind cleared, a few blurry images flitted around the corners of his memory: hands in the air, people in ugly suits, chanting, a drag queen putting a little pink pill in his hand.

"Damn it! I knew there was something off about that guy."

Rage gave him the boost he needed to reach for the sink. "Fucking turtle dick cunt swapping son of a whore!"

It felt like somebody replaced his kidneys with hungry rats. The room went monochrome, and the pitch of the ringing in his ears felt like it might shatter his skull. Luckily, his many overdoses had made him good at powering through.

He held onto the counter with one hand and used the other to drag his foot into a position where he could rock onto it. He did the same on the other side, then grabbed the counter with both hands and used every muscle in his body to lunge. He hit his head on the faucet but didn't fall over.

"I'm going to kill everyone for this."

He turned on the faucet and filled his toothbrush cup with water, chugging glass after glass until he noticed the black crud floating up from the bottom. He realized he was drinking five years of congealed toothbrush water.

"Oh, God." Feeling like he was going to hurl, he turned to the little green trashcan and found two glistening lumps that smelled like Freon.

Max laughed and sprayed his kidneys with minty scum-water. "Joke's on you, asshole."

He stuck his head in the sink and sucked fresh water directly from the stream. With his mouth rinsed and his belly full, he returned to the can and fished out one of the kidneys.

It was black and covered in little ridges that looked like ears. Imagining the look on the harvester's face made Max feel a bit better. The more he stared at them, the more he wondered if the thief had done him a favor.

The first time he should have died, he'd drank an embarrassment of liquor and taken a header down a flight of stairs. His skull cracked in seven places, and his head swole up so big it looked like a rubber mask. He never figured out how he made it to that Savanian ER.

When he woke up, the doctors told him he was more or less dead; not quite as dead as the living dead but in that general vicinity. It was shortly after the "Divine Disturbance," so doctors were still trying to figure out why and how things had changed.

His doctor had said, "It's like Poison Candy tied Death's shoelaces together. Anything beyond that is speculation."

They didn't even know if his face would heal. Thankfully it did. He later learned that his body repaired itself extremely fast.

Max was one of the lucky few to get the "alive-plus" upgrade when Poison Candy momentarily expanded the chemical world, stretching the fabric of reality. Now, instead of being either alive or dead, people could also be zombies or alive-plus. "God" said that alive-plus was "a special gift so partiers of a certain caliber could keep rocking forever."

Max hated parties. The prospect of immortality was horrifying, but he could do all the Krokodil he wanted, so yay?

At least real zombies weren't hungry like in the movies. They mostly just moped around smelling bad until they either crumbled or gelled, depending on the weather. Max preferred them to the zealous idiots who migrated to Bryant Park to make offerings of cocaine and cheap liquor.

Max waddled to the hallway and cranked his thermostat to 73, then returned to the bathroom.

He frowned at his reflection. "What the fuck, Max? You know better than to go around other people."

Morbid curiosity had driven him to the Baptastic Revivalicious Cavalcade of Christianity. He could never resist a good freak show. Ironically, in that sea of fundamentalist sociopaths, it was the friendly drag queen who did him in.

"Who knew free pills from a stranger could be a bad thing?" He wanted to slap himself, but he didn't feel up to it.

The air hung like green-gray mold, couching everything in a sticky film. The seeping humidity was making the wallpaper sweat and squirm like a fat boy on a blind date. Outside his bathroom window, the sky had been turned a hideous plaid of greens and browns to warn of potential terrorist activity. Even the zombies looked depressed.

His stomach gurgled. The only solid food he'd eaten in the last twenty-four hours was the breading of a burnt corndog.

"God, I feel like shit."

He scoured the bathroom for narcotics but couldn't find so much as a headache powder.

He'd been living off his savings for the last several weeks, ever since the zoo fired him over an incident that led to the zombification of three turtles, two penguins, one debutante, and a small group of Klipsch perverts. Now he was broke and out of everything. Even if he got a job today, he didn't know how he'd afford food to last until his first check.

In no condition to go on interviews, Max put the thought out of his mind and shuffled to the kitchen. He guzzled the last of his herbally fortified juice-drink on the way to his liquor cabinet.

"Goddammit!"

His urinary jowls weren't the only things the paunchy poacher had plundered. Max kicked the door shut.

"Fuck!" He braced himself against the wall until his toes stopped throbbing. His wounds would heal, but now he would have to spend the rest of his money restocking his bar, which meant he would have to find a job. Then it dawned on him.

"Shit! It's Sunday. I can't even buy booze. Fucking Baptastics ruin everything!"

"Mroowr?" Spooky meowed inquisitively.

Max walked to the bedroom, where his Bio-Bed nestled in several inches of dirty laundry. She liked it that way. Every time he washed clothes, she acted like he was destroying her natural habitat. He used that as an excuse to buy new clothes every time he found something cheap and cool.

"Hi, Spooky." Max ran his fingers through her soft, black-and-grey striped cheek. "I bet you're wondering what was going on last night. Just a little organ theft. Nothing to worry your big squishy head about."

Spooky purred and rubbed against his hand.

He glanced at the lines pumping the sedatives in and the waste out to make sure everything was normal. He took good care of Spooky. Being genetically engineered as an immobile blob of fat for humans to sleep on was indignity enough for one lifetime. She was the nicest thing he had and the only living being that loved him.

Max was morally opposed to Bio-Beds, but she'd come with the apartment. His options were to maintain her or put her down. She was way too sweet and comfortable to kill. Whoever came up with the idea of harnessing the oozy squish of cat-fat for furniture was an evil genius.

He plopped onto Spooky's belly and burst a stitch.

"Ahh!" The pain triggered a coughing fit that triggered more pain. He rolled onto his belly and screamed into her fat.

"Mroooww?"

Max wanted to cry, but he was too dehydrated. It was all getting too vivid. With nothing to dull his senses, he couldn't help but notice the filth. The glassware on his nightstand was stuck in a mass of tissues and allergy medicine that had gotten wet and dried out so many times it turned into paper-mâché.

He thought of the sign by the kitchen door. 'Abandon soap all ye who enter here.' It was cute when he got it, but less so in light of his having run out of soap weeks ago. How had he let it get this bad?

"I gotta get some fresh air."

He snatched a T-shirt out of the closet, found his pants, and made sure his phone, keys, and hammer were still in them. He hadn't left the house without a hammer since a brief but unpleasant encounter with a feisty undead lady. He was pretty sure a couple of whacks to the head would put anybody down, but he'd never tried it. The National Association for the Advancement of Dead People paid the cops to arrest zombie bashers.

When the dead first woke up, there were a lot of hate crimes against them. People expected them to be like they were in the movies, so every jackass with a shotgun decided they were going to save the world. A few people who were too sentimental to splatter grandma's skull discovered zombies were mostly harmless. They just moped around, looking confused. Every so often, one would flip out. Nobody knew why.

He opened the door and scanned the hallway for crackheads. Seeing none, he hurried down the stairs to the street. He stopped to stare at a zombie who was hunched over with his forehead pressed against the bricks of the complex adjacent. Black saliva dripped from his dangling jaw to pool in front of his mildewed oxfords.

"What's up with you?"

A passing woman mistook his words for a quasi-friendly salutation. She forced a weak smile, shrugged, and quickened her pace.

Max blushed. He hated it when strangers talked to him.

What kind of creep goes around talking to random people? She probably thought I was hitting on her, and homeless. Fuck, I look like I just crawled out of a grave.

Max made a mental note that he was no longer at home and walked briskly towards S-District. He'd chosen an apartment at the edge of a K-district so he could have middle-class amenities while still within walking distance of slum pricing. The previous tenant as murdered, so he'd gotten a great deal.

His heart palpitated as he remembered rent was due in a week. He pulled out his phone and checked his balance, sixty-three dollars and fourteen cents left. If he didn't find some money soon, he'd lose his place, and Spooky. That couldn't happen.

Maybe he'd check out the gr app. He'd heard a lot of Klipsch hipsters were collecting Savainians like trading cards. All he needed was a tragic story to get their attention. That bubble was due to burst, but it might get him through the end of the month.

Neo-Catholistics were handing out pamphlets up ahead, so he shoved his hands in his pockets and crossed the street. Organized panhandling pissed him off on a good day, and he was more than usually in the mood to curb someone. His aptitude for repression had kept him from killing anyone so far, but it was an inevitability he preferred to avoid as long as possible.

Two blocks from the Mega Sav-mart, he noticed an unusual movement out of the corner of his eye. His eyes darted reflexively after it just in time to catch a glimpse of something pink and lumpy slithering behind a snack-cake display. It looked like an amputee had dragged his boneless stump out of view, but there wasn't room for a person back there.

7

The display was in front of a small market, the kind where the register is outside so the proprietor could bark deals at people as they passed. Max respected Savanian chutzpah but hated their pushy bullshit. They all reminded him of W.C. Fields.

Still, it would haunt him for days if he didn't find out what that was.

He forced a smile and walked over to the produce table to get a better view without being rude. The barrel-chested merchant smirked beneath a thick walrus mustache.

"Can I help you with anything, sir? We have a special on porcupine kabobs, only $7.99 a pound."

"Nah, just browsing. I'll let you know."

Max snuck around the display for a closer look. A sliver of something fleshy peeked out from behind the box. Before Max could come any closer, a giant worm-like thing scuttled toward the merchant, clambered up his leg, and wrapped around his head.

Max jumped back and grabbed a handful of snack cakes to defend himself. "What the fuck is that?"

The worm was about the size of a large man's arm and covered in little fleshy lumps. Its head looked kind of like a hairless beaver with big black eyes and a mouthful of long needle-like teeth.

The merchant was off-kilter, his curses muffled by the creature's midsection.

Max hurled cakes at it, wincing as the floss chomped his side.

The creature caught one of the snack cakes in its mouth and unwrapped it with its nubby under-thingies. It made a cute nom-nom noise as it chomped through the cake and relaxed around the merchant's head like a scarf.

The man smiled and scratched the sucker marks on his face.

There was a conspicuous absence of blood and screaming.

"No need to be frightened, sir. This is my cheekworm, Cat." He unwrapped another cake and handed it to Cat.

The worm was horrifically cute, adorably monstrous. It nibbled the little bar like a contented toddler with long pointy fangs.

"I named her Cat because I had a cat named Cat when I was a kid. He was a good cat. I've named every pet that came after in honor of him. My name, incidentally, is Cecil."

"It certainly is different." Max's eyebrow twitched.

"They're something new. My brother discovered them a few short weeks ago. He was on an expedition to a sunken city off the coast of Cobya. He went under, and they came up. The whole area was crawling with them."

Max stepped forward to examine the creature.

Cat was hairless and ruddy. It looked like somebody sewed a bunch of baby cheeks onto a fat snake. Her underside had lines of little plungers that could protrude on stalks like fingers or contract to barely perceptible ridges. Her feline mouth and the big black eyes near the top of her face gave her a cute, cartoonish quality.

Max reached out his hand but quickly jerked it back when she dropped the cake and hissed, propelling sticky saliva in and around his eyes. A guttural howl swelled in her throat as she bared six rows of teeth.

Max stepped back, and the growling slowly subsided.

The merchant gained Cat's attention by humming what sounded like polka. Cecil locked eyes with her and blinked until she smiled and licked his face.

He wiped a smear of icing drool from his cheek. "Unfortunately, they tend to be a touch territorial. They bond instantly with the first human they see and protect them from anything they perceive as dangerous. My brother learned that the hard way." He pulled the thing down and cradled it in his arms like a baby.

"The first mate tried to pick one up that had already bonded. The little guy felt threatened. Took his head clean off like he was a chocolate bunny."

Max looked skeptically at the creature. "Shouldn't it be on a leash or something?"

"No. We know enough about them now to avoid further incidents."

Max arched an eyebrow.

"Pretty soon, they'll be as common as cats or dogs. In many ways, they're superior to both. They are sweeter, smarter, and more loyal than any other household pet. One hundred times more effective than guard dogs. They don't claw the furniture. They eat almost anything, but nothing they're not supposed to, and you don't even have to worry about having them fixed. Watch this."

He placed Cat on the table, pulled a butcher's knife out of his apron, and placed it about six inches from her tail. Cat coiled in ecstasy as he sawed through her with smooth, even strokes. She trilled as though in the throes of passion. When the blade hit the cutting board, Cat curled away from it, giggling and oozing thick yellow goo.

The merchant slid the blade under the segment and flung it like a teppanyaki chef.

Max was too shocked to do anything but catch it.

Its jiggly warmth spread through his hand, tingling up his arm and throughout his body, filling him with peace. It felt like falling into a hot tub.

Taking hold with all its suckers, the peppy lump squirmed and dripped yellow custard onto his shoes. He tried to drop it, to shake it off, but the suckers had fused to his flesh.

It was growing about a centimeter every second, winding around his arm until a head bloomed cooing on Max's shoulder. It opened its big black eyes, and all the shock and disgust melted into fatherly pride. It wasn't long before Max was cooing back.

"Amazing, isn't it?" the merchant asked proudly. "You now have a friend who would kill or die for you. He's a part of you, built from your own DNA. That's why he looks like you. He's your son."

"Did you just rape me?"

"I did nothing of the sort. If you don't want it, just put it on the ground and stomp its head. It'll let you. They're that sweet."

"Right."

The cheekworm snuffled around Max's ear.

"I guess this is where you tell me how much he costs."

"Oh, no. I couldn't take him away from you now if I wanted to. He's yours for life. If you'd like to show your gratitude by purchasing something from my store, that's up to you. They love snack cakes. How about a treat for your new friend?"

The creature rested its head on top of Max's.

"Sure, why not? Do you carry Juicetastic XXX by any chance?"

"What flavor?"

"Mango ecstasy?"

"I'll just go get it for you." The merchant waddled through the doorway.

Cat poured off the table and followed close behind.

Max tossed a few snack cakes on the counter and called after him, "Two gallons."

The merchant came back and bagged everything up. "What do you think you'll call him?"

"I don't know. Cakey?"

The worm trilled in his ear.

"That's just adorable. I think he likes it."

Max didn't care that Cecil was patronizing him. He placed his phone near the sensor and watched his funds roll back to forty-nine dollars and fifteen cents. "Is it a he?"

"Call it whatever you want, but it's neither. No genitalia, you see? These little guys just latch onto the first DNA they come into contact with. You might say you played the role of the father, making Cat here the mother, so I suppose they're metaphorically female. I don't see what it matters, though. You aren't going to fuck it, are you?"

"Eww, no. Of course not. I was just curious."

"Only joking, sir, only joking. Be good to the little guy, and he'll be good to you. Now, if his feathers get ruffled, and you need to calm him down, do as I did earlier. They seem to enjoy polka the most. Blinking at them conveys love and trust and puts them at ease. If you have any problems or questions, feel free to come back any time."

The merchant handed him his bags with a big smile that said Max was free to fuck off. "You have a nice day now."

Max smiled politely, "You too." Not quite sure what had just transpired, he quickly returned home before anything else could mate with him.

THE 39 WHELPS

The idea of fatherhood had always terrified Max. Children were loud, selfish vectors of disease. Parenting was the business of keeping a parasite alive long enough for it to move out, generate many tons of garbage, take up housing, and generally be a nuisance until something made it stop. One in a million might be entertaining. One in a billion might make a real contribution to the world. The rest of them basically existed to circulate currency. Pets were cuter, and you didn't have to worry about them launching nuclear weapons. No cat ever paid to masturbate in a stranger's septic tank.

Misanthropy aside, how could anyone live knowing that every mistake in word or deed could cause a psychological scar in a developing mind? Giving them the wrong toy could initiate a string of perceptions resulting in a tyrant or a whiner. The wrong amount of candy might create a rapist or a crackhead? How could anyone navigate that?

Max would have sooner teabagged a garbage disposal than reproduce, but Cakey was pretty awesome. If he was honest, Cakey was the best thing that ever happened to him. Luckily, he didn't have any friends, so nobody had to know he'd become a lame cliché. Even if he had, what was he going to do, put Cakey to sleep so he could retain his nihilism?

His face was sore from smiling all the time. Apparently, years of being a miserable bastard had atrophied his smiling muscles so much he could barely hold a smirk for twenty seconds without getting a cramp. He'd timed it in the mirror.

With the help of a new friend and a healthy Begr profile, he was relearning how to be happy. Cakey wormed deeper into his heart every day. He was smarter than a baby and more emotive than a pet. He immediately understood toilets and could get up and down all by himself. Max taught him to play Chess and lost their first game.

He also lost all subsequent games. It was getting frustrating.

"Again? Fuck!" Max tipped over his king for the third time in under an hour. He reached across the couch and put his finger in Cakey's sucker. "Good game, you little bastard. I'm going to beat you one of these days."

Cakey giggled.

"Don't laugh." Max grabbed Cakey's scruff and gave him a playful shake.

Cakey moved to reset the board.

"Nope. That's enough for today." Max snatched the board and looked for a steady place to set it.

The coffee table was a thriving ecosystem where all forms of garbage were free to return to their primordial roots and eventually re-imagine themselves as new forms of life. He transferred the set from the middle cushion to a small plateau of old magazines, which accepted its weight with minimal sliding. All the king's horsemen and all the king's men mingled happily with their new neighbors.

Cakey surged into Max's lap, curling inside out and upside down to peer up from a position of blissful vulnerability.

Max beamed with almost romantic love. He wondered how an animal could validate him so thoroughly. Could a human and a worm to be soulmates?

The doorbell chimed, reminding him he had a date.

"Shit."

He'd meant to clean, but realistically it would have taken days or weeks of hard labor to make his place presentable. He'd never worried about it before, but Diana was Klipsch. This might be her first time in a home that didn't have a housekeeping staff.

Cakey snorted and crawled to his spot on the couch.

"I know. I'm sorry, but it's time for daddy to get laid."

Max rushed to the door and opened it.

"Hey, come in."

Diana's designer outfit was modeled after Sonian street clothes. They looked as inauthentic on her as they did in general, accentuating that sexy alien quality she'd gotten from growing up in Society. Every ringlet of her hair hung like polished mahogany some artist had crafted to encode ancient secrets. She was well out of his league in every way.

A lot of People got off on screwing below their station, but her booty call seemed more pragmatic than bestial. She had noticed Cakey a few days ago in the park. After Max answered all her questions about cheekworms, she had asked him if he would like to copulate. Just like that. "Would you like to copulate with me this weekend?"

He imagined she had "casual sex" marked on her calendar, and he was in the right place with the right worm.

Max ushered her in and sat her next to Cakey. "Can I get you a drink or something? I've got just about everything; beer, wine, a full bar..."

She frowned. "No, thank you." She glanced at the strange lifeform beside her and debated petting him.

Max took Cakey's "Really? Her?" expression to mean it was bathroom time. He opened the door and snapped his fingers, ignoring his friend's pleading eyes and silent promises to be good. Cakey hopped down and began his walk of shame but stopped as a second chime sounded.

Max smiled apologetically. "Sorry. I'll get rid of them."

Max returned to the door to find Scarlet decked out in green leather and fuck-me pumps. She had little pins over her nipples. One said, "Stop looking at me," the other "Pervert." Her immoderate accessories sounded like jingling keys as she brushed him aside and let her steampunk handbag clatter to the floor.

"What's up, Maxie-pad?" She noticed the woman on the couch and smiled. "Ooh, somebody's been busy. I like her!" She pressed her body against him and bit his cheek affectionately.

Diana hovered an inch above the couch, wavering between hurt and angry. Her cold blue eyes darted between Scarlet's bountiful bouncing baubles trying to define what phylum to file her in. Her face hardened into a mask of disgust. She must have pegged her as a Savanian.

Max panicked. Being a Sonian, he was immune to most of the tension between classes, but the Klipsch and Savanians reacted to each other like bleach and ammonia.

"Hi, Scarlet. What are you doing here?"

"I thought I'd surprise you. I didn't know you had a guest. Fine with me, though." Her voice sounded even more like a phone sex worker than usual. "Well, are ya surprised?"

"Uh...yeah."

"Good." Scarlet strode over to Diana, pushed her back, and straddled her. "What's your name, sweetie?"

Diana had a hole she'd hoped to fit a peg into, but brazen gutter-slut was the wrong shape, and the force with which Scarlet was attempting to insert herself was threatening to break the frame. She shoved Scarlet to the side, stood, and sputtered a jumble of apologies and outrage on her way to the door.

"Hey, I'm really sorry." "Max tried to intercept her, but she shrugged him off. "Don't go."

"Yeah, don't go." Scarlet's plea was slightly exaggerated.

Diana slammed the door behind her, but the doorknob didn't catch.

Max watched it slowly creaked open. "Dammit."

Scarlet laughed. "That was rude as fuck. What'd a girl like that want with you, anyway?"

"I think she wanted to borrow my penis."

Scarlet walked over and wrapped her arms around his waist. "Sorry about that, I guess it's just you and me tonight."

"You really should call before you come."

"But you can usually tell when I'm about to cum." She wrapped herself around him like an octopus. "Come on, don't be mad. Let's make the most of a sorry situation."

As Scarlet peeled his clothes away, Max noticed the crowd of voyeurs gathering in the hall. Cakey slammed the door before any of them could make off with his TV.

Max removed his tongue from her throat. "Good boy! Now go to the bathroom."

Cakey did a sarcastic little poop dance.

"Now!"

Cakey moped to the bathroom and nuzzled the door shut.

Cakey hissed as loud as he could, then made himself comfortable in a nest of mildewing underwear. Every time a female came around, he was tossed in the bathroom faster than an inflatable party sheep. The girls made Max happy, so Cakey tried not to be offended.

It didn't work.

He took a deep breath of bathroom air, letting the familiar sickly-sweet chocolaty funk coat his lungs. There was nothing to do but curl up and endure the groans of the chalky usurper while she played with Max in ways he never could.

Cakey hates sharing! Why monkeys need squishy time with other monkeys? Use Cakey to get phone numbers then lock Cakey in the bathroom. Stupid monkey! Cakey should go toss bitch-monkey like wet confetti.

He rested his chin on a wadded-up shirt. What so special about shedding skins and writhing monkeys in the squishy place without Cakey. Why always without Cakey? Cakey squishy too. Why Cakey's fleshy squish not as good as top-heavy money-pit?

Cakey knows how treacherous monkeys can be. Need to protect Max. He fantasized about busting through the door and eating Scarlet's face.

Rejection sours Cakey's inner goo.

Deep down, Cakey knew bathroom-time was his punishment for interfering. The door couldn't stop him if he decided to come out, but he was held at bay by an impenetrable barrier of shame.

Girls rarely came around more than once. Dozens had come and gone, but none had formed a bond deeper than the length of Max's penis-- until now. This one, with her tattoos and her corsets and her ridiculous raspberry-colored hair, was here for the third time.

Max didn't seem to mind that she showed up uninvited and chased away the sexy librarian. Very worrisome, indeed.

When the door finally opened, he was alarmed to find the woman was still there. Instead of being gone as was right and proper, she sat defiantly in his spot, sipping beer from a green bottle and slowly dragging her fingernails across the upholstery in an insulting attempt to lure him to her.

This was too much. A line had been crossed, and Cakey was now burdened with restoring the natural order. He made himself as large as possible, displayed his teeth prominently, and issued a warning hiss.

Maybe Max like squishy time with Cakey more once Cakey makes head and butt warmers out of monkey chest-flaps.

The woman laughed. "I don't think the little guy likes me anymore."

Max hum-paed and moved in to intercept him. He was blinking hard and fast, but Cakey was beyond the reach of such simple offerings.

Cakey sprang forward, but Max's arms intercepted him. He climbed around Max's back and wrapped himself around his head. Cakey took hold of his monkey and made a clear declaration of ownership. Max yelped in pain as the suckers latched on.

Max stroked him gently and scratched behind his ears. Cakey wanted to melt into his arms and have his belly rubbed, but he'd gone too far to turn back.

The enemy remained seated but shifted forward, looking equally amused and horrified. She was obviously considering some sort of intervention. Cakey continued to growl at the transgressor as he rode his stumbling steed into the kitchen.

Max's plan was obvious. Cakey is a jealous God! Cakey's altar is vast and barren, and all the snack cakes at Sav-Mart cannot fill it. No cake, no icing, no fluffy cream will satiate my wrath!

While groping the countertop, Max accidentally slapped the box, scattering his last resort amongst the garbage and groceries at his feet. He stumbled under Cakey's shifting weight. Packaging popped, and icing squished between his toes as he danced awkwardly in the pastries. The room was filling with the dizzying bouquet of Polysorbate 60, diglycerides, and whey.

Scarlet's laughter was almost as loud as Cakey growl as she snatched the last untrampled cake and offered it up in all its artificial glory.

Cakey's jaw, which had been dropped in a gesture of aggression, gently masticated the air as he chewed over his options. The subtle aromas of intertwined chemicals sang with a sophisticated harmony more beautiful and overwhelming than any composer's dream.

The red velvet Tookie bar was far and away the most splendid of its kind. In all the world of chemically modified FÜD products, nothing was so like reading a poem in God's own language. The synthetic lard reached out for him, beckoning, caressing his nasal cavities with lascivious precision. It called to him incessantly as though it were in heat, coiling around his brain, tightening its grip, refusing to be ignored.

Powerless, he folded. Bitterly snatching the peace offering, he tore into it the way he wished he could the redhead and fantasized it was her tasty white goo trickling down his esophagus.

Cakey swallowed the last of his bribe and loosened his grip, only then noticing the warm tack of blood on his suckers. He slithered around to get a better look and began to cry. Max's face was now covered in oozing hickeys the color and shape of large rotten grapes. It was the first time he'd seen Max angry.

Max carried him to the bathroom and hurled him into the tub. Cakey was so ashamed the impact felt good. He wanted Max to give him the beating he deserved.

Instead, he stepped away.

The click of the lock once again rattled his dank prison.

✳✳✳✳✳

Scarlet gave Max a much-needed hug. "What the fuck was that all about?" She playfully licked a drop of blood from his chin.

"I don't know. You were in his spot on the couch? He's never done that before." Max walked to the mirror to see how bad it was. "Holy fuck, I look like an alien."

Scarlet laughed. "You totally do."

"That sucked!"

"Aww, don't be a pussy. It's only meat. You still wanna go out?"

"I look like I have the plague, like an alien with the plague."

"It's not that bad. You're just a little polka-dotted. It's kind of cute in a pitiful way." She slowly and lovingly kissed each sore starting with his neck and working around to the top of his head, ending at his mouth.

The metallic tinge of blood on her lips was like MDMA. Soon they were naked on the floor, and she was making the rest of his body match his face.

At first, Cakey's whimpering was drowned out by the panting thump of flesh on flesh. As their energy waned, the pathetic sounds of self-abomination became more and more audible. Eventually, the wailing of his wounded friend was all he could hear. The mood was lost.

He rolled off of her and rested his face in his hands. "I'm sorry. I just can't ignore him while he's making that noise. All I can think about is how hard I threw him. Do you think he's okay?"

"Does he have bones?"

"I don't think so."

"He'll be fine. Finish fuckin' me." She grabbed his cock, but he jerked away.

"I'm not in the mood anymore."

"Don't beat yourself up. He deserved it. I'm all for the ethical treatment of animals, but you got to let them know who's in charge."

"I know, but I still feel like a bastard. I'm going to go check on him." He walked to the bathroom.

"You're really not going to finish fucking me?"

"I can't concentrate while he's whining like that. Did you not get off?"

"I'm starting to go numb down there. I just thought you might want to cum before I go. I have to work tomorrow, so I don't have all night to make your worm happy."

"I'll be fine. My worm is quite happy. I think I'm still depleted from last time."

"Suit yourself. I'll just find my clothes and get out of your hair." She got up and gathered her things.

"Don't be like that. You understand, don't you?" he asked, not really caring.

She did a lousy job of pretending to shrug it off. "Yeah, I'm just giving you shit. Fair warning, he ever does something like that to me, I'll do more than throw his ass in the bathroom."

Max laughed and felt a little better about his reaction. She had a point. Cakey had to learn about boundaries, and this was as good a time as any.

When Scarlet had finished buckling on her various garments, he escorted her to the door and kissed her goodbye. He shut the door behind her, confident she would return despite Cakey's temper tantrum. If she didn't, that was okay, too.

He retrieved his emergency snack cake and approached the bathroom door cautiously. He took a deep breath and collected himself before opening it.

Cakey was puffy-eyed and pitiful, shivering in the corner of the ceiling. Instead of the usual two black marbles, his friend stared through darkened slits set like scars in the swollen tear-stained flubber of his face. A steady stream of sorrow dripped down his forehead, pooling on the counter around the sink.

Max raised his hands to help his friend down. "It's okay. Come here."

Cakey squirmed away in shame, crawling in irregular circles to communicate his sorrow.

"Really, I'm not mad anymore. You can come down now. Come on." He pulled the snack cake from his pocket and peeled the wrapper back. "See, it's cool. Come on down."

Cakey forced his eyes open. Their gazes collided like atomic subs, exploding in the water of their faces. Cakey read like the thesaurus entry for regret. Unable to bear being away from him any longer, he gently dropped into Max's hands, careful not to use his suckers.

Max snuggled him gently, running his lips over the poofy folds of his head. He promised himself that he would never again use violence when Cakey got out of hand. They spent the rest of the night cuddling under a blanket and watching TV, secure in the knowledge that nothing could ever come between them.

BUY ANOTHER DAY

Max could smell the delicate musk of Fall as soon as he opened his door. Cakey ran between his legs and ricocheted down the hall sniffing his neighbor's doorframes in search of the source.

"Chill out, man. That's just pumpkin spice."

Cakey stopped and turned.

"It's a nonlocal olfactory stimulant that means nature is going to stop being a bastard for the next two months."

Cakey sniffed the air and let out a little noise that sounded like, "Liar!"

"It's also a flavor, but don't get too excited. Everything is going to taste like that for a while. You'll be sick of it in no time."

Doubt sat heavy on Cakey's brow.

"You'll see. The yogurt place will probably have ten different versions. Come on." He patted his leg, and Cakey followed.

They ambled toward the Froyo Palace, enjoying the contemplative glow of nature coming to terms with mortality. "So, are cheekworms related to tardigrades?"

Cakey looked up, unsure if he should be insulted. He decided to let it go. It was too nice a day to be bothered by racism, and the froyo was so close he could almost taste it.

"It's a valid question. Both of you steal DNA. If a nautilus and an octopus are related, you could be part water bear.

"Anyway, they found these huge tardigrades in a lake about fifty miles from here. They were almost an inch long. The Nrrds are all freaking out, saying the Iiites did something to the water. I didn't read the whole article. Nrrds are a bunch of racist wackadoos. Every time somebody sneezes, they scream, 'Iiites are genetically engineering plants to produce super-pollen!' Isn't it bad enough their ancestors were mutated and banished to the fucking sewers? Do we really need to scapegoat them too? I mean, their right arms are big. Get over it."

He noticed Cakey was no longer walking beside him and turned to find him mesmerized by the cornucopia of colors in the window of a Costume Boo-tique.

Max crouched to look at the picture of the Oscar Brayer Wiener costume for dachshunds.

The Boo-tique specialized in unimaginative, overpriced, flimsy costumes for people with no souls. Max hated the chain, but Cakey was too cute to deny. "You want a costume?"

Cakey scurried over to the door and whined.

"Fine, Halloween is coming up." He pulled the door open and ushered Cakey inside. They strode past light-up gravestones, party favors, and balloons to a small beige display of pet costumes in the front corner. There weren't a lot of options, so the hotdog was easy to find.

Max unsnapped the package and pulled it out. The thin tube of red felt was surrounded by a foam bun with holes for a head, a tail, and four legs. The zipper was a wavy yellow line that ran the length of the wiener. It looked like a cute way to give your pet heatstroke, but there was no harm in letting him try it on. He held it next Cakey to check the size. "It might be a little short."

Cakey shook his head. He was determined to fit.

"You want to try it on?"

Cakey nodded vigorously. The syrupy smell from the fog machines was making him drool.

"All right, but don't slobber on it. It's probably cheaper online." He unzipped the mustard and laid it open so Cakey could snuffle in.

Cakey the hotdog couldn't walk, but it was adorable watching him try. Max posted a video to Begr before helping him wriggle free. Cakey huffed and stared daggers at the floppy foam.

"I'm definitely buying this."

Max was stuffing it back into the bag when the wall on the far side of the store exploded. A fist-sized clump of drywall glanced off his arm.

"Ow, what the fuck?"

Everything got very loud. Behind a thinning veil of smoke and dust, a small band of Iiites wreaked havoc in the electronics store next door. Most people ran for the exits, but a few were transfixed by the carnage. They watched silently as the mutants beat people to death with their own limbs. Max's instinct was to stay very still and hope he wasn't noticed. Surely they had no reason to raid a costume shop? Why steal rubber masks when there are perfectly good computers? Right?

One Iiite wrapped his massive hand around a cashier's head and swung him around like a lasso until inertia detached his body. It arced over a table of clearance makeup and splatted right in front of Max. A jet of blood sprayed his shoes so hard it shot straight up into his face. He stumbled backward, slipped, and landed hard on his tailbone.

"Fuck!" He rolled to his feet, but the Iiite was already between him and the door.

The Iiite winked and crushed the cashier's skull like a piece of rotten fruit.

The news showed clips from Iiite attacks almost every day, but he'd never seen one in person. They looked way freakier than they did on TV. Max tried not to stare at the disproportionally massive right arm.

Eyes filled with murderous glee, the Iiite slung the pulp to the ground and advanced. More Iiites were spilling into the Bootique. There was no way Max could get past all of them.

"Hey, I'm a friend, man. Take whatever you want. I'll help you carry some shit."

The Iiite laughed. "You saying you want to give me a hand?" He stalked closer, savoring Max's fear.

Max had always defended the Iiites. Going militant seemed a reasonable response to being downgraded from superhuman to freak and banished from society. However, in light of his current situation, he was forced to acknowledge that his stance was naïve and that murder is fundamentally not-cool.

"Come on, man."

Cakey lunged, latched on to the Iiite's chest with all his suckers, chomped his throat and twisted, ripping flesh like tissue paper. The Iiite grabbed him and pulled, peeling away a four-inch hangnail that ripped through his shirt. The pressure of blood leaving his body forced him to the ground. He was not getting back up.

"Goddamn Cakey. Good boy!"

Max's first taste of pure adrenaline was a lot like PCP. His thoughts were moving faster than time. His body was running on all cylinders. All those murderous thoughts he'd had as a teenager came rushing back. This seemed like a great time to tick something off his bucket list.

An Iiite was pulling the legs off an attractive young cashier a few feet away. Max pulled a pole out of a nearby dummy torso and brained him with it. The mutant's skull flopped open like a purse.

"That was easy!"

The exsanguinated cashier smiled gratefully, then slid off the counter and landed on top of her murderer. She died spooning him.

Cakey snapped the spine of a third.

Max hadn't grinned so big since his first blowjob. Running at number four, he thrust the pole straight through attacker and prey, pinning them to a rack of prosthetic wounds.

He turned to find number five right behind him.

Suddenly the room was a wash of bleeding stripes as he spun over the toppled racks of masks and makeup and landed in the rubble of the fallen wall. The taste of blood and the sound of muffled screaming trickled through the cracks of his dazed nervous system. He hoped the Iiite would squish his skull before he ripped off his limbs.

The Iiite grabbed his ankle and lifted him a couple inches off the ground.

Someone was screaming close by. Max drunkenly scanned the room for survivors. Finding none, he realized with a great deal of embarrassment that the voice was his own. He stopped and smiled with flaming cheeks.

"Sorry about your friends. Just trying not to die."

"No worries." The Iiite paused, considering how to inflict the most pain. He put the tip of his thumb just above Max's ankle.

"Please don't?"

He heard a crack as his foot flopped to the side. Max's eyes shifted nervously between the man's eyes and his ankle, anticipating the moment the signal would reach his brain.

The Iiite's eyes bugged out. His head disappeared behind his chest and reappeared, dangling from his spine, between his legs. They hit the ground together.

He could feel Cakey sniffing his wounds as he tried to blink the blood away. When he eventually succeeded, he saw that Cakey had taken the last two out all by himself.

He patted his friend on the head and said, "That's a good boy," in the patronizing tone reserved for the cute and cuddly.

Cakey tried to nuzzle the bone back into his leg.

Thank god for shock.

As the adrenaline drained from his body, the damage began to register. Several broken bones, a cracked skull, missing teeth, and several compound fractures were too much for his mind to take in all at once. A white wall of pain short-circuited his brain like a blinding flash from Satan's camera.

THE MAN FROM OWL

A nagging ache slowly dragged Max out of the drug-induced womb of tingly comfort and slapped him like an ugly baby. His eyes fluttered open but refused to focus. He smelled bleach and flowers.

Am I dead?

Displeasure rattled in his chest as he tried to roll over.

"Fuck!" His IV twisted out with a spurt.

Suddenly wide awake and bleeding, Max realized he was in a private hospital room surrounded by an absurd amount of flowers.

"Who the fuck sent me flowers? I hate flowers."

Everything hurt. His leg cast felt like it was full of poison ivy, and the TV was blaring the annoying milk song that got stuck in his head every time he heard it.

God? You win. I hate life. I'm sorry I think your music sucks. If you can hear my prayers over your tinnitus, please take me now.

Max noticed two Sav-Cops gawking at him from the doorway.

Please?

Sav-Cops were the one security firm that sucked worse than pre-privatized police. Their recruiters were notorious for headhunting any idiot who wanted a license to kill. Max's Freon-huffing cousin joined and made Lieutenant in three months.

The cops approached squeamishly, trying not to look at the oozing vein.

The fatter of the two addressed him shyly. "Mr. Quick? We have a few questions we need to ask you about Wednesday the 18th."

"The 18th? What day is it now?"

"It's Friday the 27th, sir. We've been waiting for you to wake up for nine days. Not that we mind. This is the longest I haven't been shot at in a while. So, you know, it's cool if you're not up to it."

"Nine days?" The Iiite attack came rushing back to him. "Shit! Where's Cakey?"

"What's Cakey?" The fat cop nervously tried to sip his coffee, but his stomach was doing cartwheels. He was growing paler by the second.

"My pet cheekworm. He was with me when we were attacked. What the fuck have you idiots done with him?!"

The cop grimaced and swallowed a wet burp. "Oh, you mean the thing they found sitting on you." He poured the remainder of his coffee into a synthetic rubber tree plant, which excreted the unwanted substance and sat defiantly in its mess like a rebellious toddler.

Skinny cop didn't seem to notice. He was chewing his unkempt mustache with his bottom teeth and staring out the window, high as fuck.

Fat cop tossed his cup at the garbage and missed. "I wasn't there, but I heard about it. Dude, that was your pet? It killed like five K-Squad guys and three paramedics that were trying to save your ass. Lucky for you, they got some tranq darts into it before you bled to death. Nobody knew what it was, so they sent it down to Bio-Corp."

Max remembered the PITA-4 propaganda video his ex had shown him. Terrified kittens with their guts laid out on the table, staring straight ahead, rasping mews while scientists probed their empty chests with needles. He'd tried to forget, to drink away those haunted eyes, but it all came flooding back. Hellish images bubbled from every crevice of his brain: A puppy with its exposed brain full of pins. Masked men spraying hairspray in its eyes. Chickens with cigarettes stuffed down their throats. Monkeys vomiting toothpaste.

"I'm going to fucking kill you assholes!" Max shoved his cast off the bed and dragged it towards them.

Skinny ran out the door while Fatty slowly backed away. "Now sir, we didn't have anything to do with that. Like I said, we weren't even there. K-Squad had the contract for that strip. The only reason we're here is they're pissed off about your pet killing a bunch of their friends. They subcontracted us to handle this mess after Cakey or whatever was sent to Bio-Corp. If you want to kill somebody, try the paramedics who saved you. It was their decision."

Max's energy bottomed out before he could throw a punch. He plopped into a nearby chair. "Damn it, they're probably vivisecting him right now, if he's still alive. Fucking Iiites! I never did shit to them."

"So, can I ask you those questions now?"

"Whatever." Max grabbed a handful of tissues and tried to stop the bleeding.

"And could you stop calling us names and stuff? We're officers of the law."

"Just ask your fucking questions and fuck off!"

"Fine, be a jerk. That'll make your leg feel better." The cop crossed his arms. "You're really lucky, you know. You were the only person who's survived an Iiite attack. They're calling you a hero on the news."

"Oh yeah? I feel downright fucking blessed."

"You need Jesus." Fatty pushed the record button on his chest camera. "The testimony of Maxwell Quick. September 28th, 2135. What happened at the Bootique on September18th of his year?"

"We were buying Halloween costumes when the fucking wall exploded. The Iiites came in and started killing everybody. We tried to defend ourselves. I only killed two of them. Cakey got the rest. He's a strong little fucker. Tore them open like Christmas presents. One of them got a hold of me, but Cakey killed him before he could finish me off. He saved my life."

"Did any of the Iiites get away?"

"No. I don't think so."

"Did they say anything about why they were killing everybody or make any threats about future attacks?"

"One of them gave me a recipe for carrot soufflé, but that was about it. Are we done?"

The cop shook his head. "Anything else we should know?"

"No! Now, will you please leave?"

"Fine. Have a nice day, Jerk." The portly patrolman waddled out the door.

Max put his head in his hands and sighed, wondering why everything in life had to be such a big stupid motherfucker of a bitch.

He wanted pants. This was too much for him to deal with open-assed. Luckily his cast was the spray-on kind, so he got them on without much trouble.

Someone knocked on his door. Without waiting for a response, a tall man with a pointy beard came into the room wearing an eighteenth-century tuxedo that made him look like a magician.

Max furrowed his eyebrows and waited for the stranger to introduce himself, or pull a rabbit out of his hat, maybe both.

"Maxwell Quick, I presume?"

"Yeah. Who're you?"

"Count Vladimir Greystoke, actor extraordinaire and Order of the Owl twenty-seventh degree, at your service." He offered his hand effeminately.

Max stared at it, unsure if he was supposed to shake or kiss the three-carat emerald. He did neither.

Greystoke continued, unperturbed. "Good name, Maxwell Quick. It is quite befitting both a hero and an entertainer. I know quite a few who have changed their names for show-business and still fail to possess such a vibrant moniker. As you may have surmised, I'm here on behalf of the Order. We believe you have a great deal of potential."

He propped his cane against the wall. "You see, we are a group of artists who have come together to bear the brunt of the harshest and most treacherous occupation in the world today: Media©. Your run-in with the Iiites has made you a Media© darling, so we would like to help you achieve your full potential.

"Why is everybody acting like I'm a superhero? Look at me. Cakey killed most of 'em. If it weren't for him, they'd still be scrubbing me off the walls of that costume shop. He's the real hero, and you know what they did? They sent him to fucking Bio-Corp. Assholes!"

Greystoke laughed. "Dear fellow, whatever actually transpired on that day, you have been embraced by the Media©, which has the final say on all historical events. If we say you are a hero, you are one."

"I don't want to be famous."

"Don't be silly. Fame is wonderful. For instance, you can throw your newfound weight around on your friend's behalf. If you address the public now and thank Bio-Corp for caring for him during your convalescence, they will have no choice but to hand him over. Unlike us, they tend to shy away from publicity."

Max shook his head. "I appreciate the advice, but me in front of a camera is a bad idea. I have a long history of bad first impressions."

"You have an opportunity here that very few will ever enjoy."

"I'm not enjoying it, either. Please go away. I'm getting a headache."

Greystoke tutted his disapproval and produced a black business card from his inside coat pocket. "Should you require assistance." He placed it on the nightstand and snatched up his cane. "Fame is coming for you. You would do well to prepare."

"I'm having a bad day, and I don't need your bombastic bullshit. Please be so kind as to fuck off!"

"Very well." He turned and walked out with magnificent poise. "Be seeing you."

Finally alone, Max was able to collect his thoughts. He had to get out of this hospital and save Cakey. There was no way going on the news would scare Bio-Corp into handing him over. That's not how things worked for someone like him. Even if it were, Cakey would be stuck there in the meantime. Every second he was there was another chance to be vivisected.

He scooched his chair over to the bed and paged a nurse to stitch up his arm. She said she would be there in two and a half hours and to 'sit tight,' whatever the hell that meant. He didn't feel like bleeding out, so he called Scarlet and asked her to bring him a sewing kit and a bottle of vodka.

Next, he called Bio-Corp and tried to convince them to give his pet back. They were monumentally unhelpful. After thirteen transfers, he spoke to a manager who suggested he insert his protests into his rectum and use them to violently copulate with himself.

Thirty-five minutes later, Scarlet showed up. She helped him Rambo his arm back together, then stole a wheelchair, and smuggled him out a side door.

"Did you really kill all those Iiites like they said on TV?"

"It was mostly Cakey, but yeah. It was surprisingly easy except for the last guy. He was a dick."

"Wow, I'm fucking a real-life hero."

He smiled. "Not yet. We've got to rescue Cakey first."

"What are you gonna do, kick the door in with your cast? I know! You can show 'em your arm, and I can sneak behind 'em and rescue Cakey while they're pukin' their guts out." She patted him on the head. "You've played action hero enough for this month. How about I take you to my place, put on my Chokey the clown outfit, and heal you up with the power of laughter?"

Max fought away a smile. "No, we have to get Cakey. Just take me to Bio-Corp, and we'll figure something out."

"He really means that much to you, huh?"

"He saved my life, and he's my Cakey. I'm not going to let him spend one more minute in that fucking hellhole. Do you know what they do there? They like, sew a pregnant female to another female, cunt to cunt, to see what happens when the baby comes to term."

Scarlet smiled. "Kinky."

"Is there anything that doesn't make you horny?"

"No."

He pounded on his wheelchair. "Damnit, this is serious. I have to get him out before they turn him into medicine or makeup or something."

"All right, fine, we'll do it your way. I know a secretary there. She's more of an acquaintance than a friend, but she owes me a favor."

"Hell yeah, call her."

"You mind if I get you in the car first? The hospital probably isn't going to be too happy about you leaving before you've been discharged."

She opened the door for him, and he executed a heroic lunge and twist move that would have been more impressive had he not caught his leg cast on the door and screamed like a little girl.

"Way to go, Mr. Smashington. Let me get that for you." She chuckled and moved the wheelchair out of the way.

The designers of the Supercar had failed to take leg casts into consideration when designing their 'perfect automobile.'

"Tiny piece of shit!" Max wondered what other people did in this situation. Ever since gas shot past twenty dollars a gallon, Supercars were all most people could afford to drive.

"Fuck this." Max pulled the hammer out of his coat and shattered the cast. It hurt like hell, but it was easier than strapping himself to the roof.

Scarlet smacked him in the back of the head. "What are you doing? You need that thing. Your leg's broken, remember?"

Max shook the chips out of his pants and moved his leg to make sure everything was in working order. It was stiff but sturdy enough to stand on. He lifted his leg into the car and shut the door.

"I'll be fine. Ever since the Divine Disturbance, I heal really fast. I've learned to get by without functioning organs. Do you really think I'm going to let a few broken bones slow me down?"

"Huh?"

"What?"

"What do you mean, 'without functioning organs'?"

"Well, I don't have kidneys anymore, and my liver looks like a salted slug."

"Everybody has kidneys."

"Not me. Organ theft is a real problem in this city."

"Bullshit. But you need kidneys to take toxins out of you, or something like that. They're important."

"Look, I drink a lot of booze. A couple of years ago, I went in for my first real checkup since I was a kid. The doctor said he was amazed I wasn't dead. This was just before the side effects of the Divine Disturbance started coming to light."

"Yeah, I heard about that, but I never really believed it."

"You've seen the zombies, right"?

"Yeah."

"So, you believe the dead walk the Earth, but you don't believe a guy can live without kidneys?"

"I don't know. I guess I didn't put that much thought into it. Wait, if you heal really fast, why's your liver all fucked up?"

"No idea. Anyway, a few weeks ago, somebody drugged me and harvested my kidneys. I wish I could have seen that fucker's face when he cut me open and pulled out two black, worthless lumps. It must have been hysterical."

"God, you're weird." Scarlet started the car.

"You gonna call that chick or not?"

"All right, calm down, it's all gonna be okay." She pulled out her little pink phone and dialed the number.

MISSION: IMPROBABLE

Max ground his teeth and stared at the building where his best friend was being held. At a mere ten stories, the Bio-Corp facility was the frumpy child of K-District. It was designed to look drab so passersby would be less inclined to think about the horrors inside. Despite billions of dollar's worth of data and equipment, there were no barbed-wire fences, no armed guards patrolling the perimeter, and only one oscillating camera between them and the back door.

"I'm glad Bio-Corp likes to keep a low profile," Max whispered once he and Scarlet were safely hidden behind the dumpster.

"Yeah, otherwise this might be stupid." Scarlet checked the time on her phone. "Okay, let's go. The cameras should be unmanned for the next twenty minutes."

Max adjusted his fake beard. "I still can't believe our luck. What are the chances you would know the chick who's fucking the head of security?"

Scarlet smiled smugly and poked him in the side. "Just don't get us caught. She's kind of hot. I'll kick your ass if ya ruin my chances with her."

"I'll do my best."

When the camera swiveled away, they crept over to the door, cracked it, and peered in. The hallway was empty, so they slipped inside and stood perfectly still. The faint buzzing of the fluorescent lights was all they heard.

The brown granite floors and neutral earth tones were surprisingly tasteful. Not Max's tastes, but nice. Aside from the stink of industrial cleaners, these offices could have passed for a law firm.

Scarlet's pointed to the second office on the right. "The stuff's in there."

They tiptoed toward the door and cautiously peered inside. The walls were covered with Gertrude Johansen's awards and diplomas. Max had never heard of her, but she was obviously a star biologist. He burned her name into his brain. Maybe he could pay her a visit someday.

Max wanted to tie her down and starve her until she was almost dead. When she was out of her mind with hunger, he'd cut open her stomach and pull her small intestine out just far enough to reach her mouth.

Scarlet's sneeze stopped both their hearts. They ducked behind the desk and listened again. When nobody came to investigate, they relaxed a little.

Scarlet laughed. "God, I hate hospital smell."

"It's fucking awful. It's a special cleaner only used in prisons, hospitals, and other places where people have to work around suffering. A while back, I read a theory that it eases the sadists' consciences, makes them feel like they're suffering along with their victims. It's also a psychological trigger that helps switch back and forth between versions of themselves."

"Focus." Scarlet smeared her nose around with her palm. "We're down to seventeen minutes, and that's assuming she can draw it out."

"Or, that he can hold it in."

"Dude, we could die here. Be less fun." She pointed to the closet.

They found the lab coats and ID cards right where her friend said they would be.

"So far, so good." He shrugged his coat on and fumbled with the buttons.

"So, what do you think?" Scarlet posed like a stripper about to start a set.

Max grabbed her lapels and kissed her. "Evil looks good on you. We should do some celebratory role-playing when we get back."

"I'm way ahead of ya, but lose the beard." She spit little bits of fuzz into the trash.

"But what about the cameras?"

"The cameras won't matter if the specimen room guard shoots us. It looks like you taped roadkill to your mouth."

"Fine." Max peeled it off and stuffed it in his pocket. Noticing how deep the pockets were, he pulled the hammer out of his belt and dropped it in the other one. It was okay if somebody called him out. He was in the mood to hurt somebody.

"Let's get this over with." Max walked to the elevator and hit the call button. It opened immediately.

They stepped inside and hit 7. The doors slid closed, and Max felt a little pressure in his legs. This was really happening.

He took a deep breath and fought the urge to pull out his hammer. He kept thinking about those Iiites and how good it felt to swing a heavy piece of metal at an enemy. He couldn't wait for something to go wrong. They were getting close.

Floor 5.

Floor 6.

Max's fist was so tight around his hammer that the hard rubber squished. He was ready for anything.

Floor 7.

The door slid open, and he made eye contact with the largest, scariest man he'd ever seen. This guard was so beefy Max got hungry. He couldn't remember the last time he ate a big juicy steak. His stomach growled so loud the guard looked at it.

Shit, I haven't eaten in over a week.

The guard smiled, happy to finally have something to do.

Tiny pinpricks of sweat broke out on Max's back as he nodded hello.

The guard eyed them suspiciously. "Hey, Doc, what can I do for ya?"

Scarlet cranked her sexuality up to ten and took the lead. "I can think of a few things. How are you today, my fearless protector?"

"Good. How are you?" He lay his machinegun on the desk and smiled.

"I'd be doing better if I wasn't in this hellhole. God, I could use a drink. Deadlines, you know? Hate 'em. We have to run some more tests on 436."

"More? I'm surprised there's anything left to test."

Max's knuckles tightened around the hammer.

"Would you mind swiping me?"

"Yeah, one second." The guard dug around in his desk drawer for the key card. He swiped the lock then followed her inside. Scarlet's sex appeal was working too well.

All around them, pitiful animals of all shapes and sizes whimpered, bleeding through their gauze. The numbers on the cages were the only system of organization. The cats were mixed in with the dogs, big with small, old with young, nearly dead with the fresh and playful. One kitten stuck its paws through the grate vying for his affection. Max's heart stopped. Nobody had come for it yet. It could still be somebody's friend.

Poor thing, probably thinks it's in a pet shop.

Tears boiled in Max's eyes. He hoped the guard would give him an excuse to break his cover.

A couple of orangutans were holding hands through the bars of their cages. The bandage over the male's eye was leaking thick yellow tears. The female had tubes hanging out of her brain. She was tapping her foot against the cage like she was listening to a jaunty tune.

Max picked up the pace. His soul shrank a little for every sad, abused creature he passed. He would put an end to this if it meant killing every scientist on the planet.

Max spotted Cakey in a small wire cage at the end of the row.

Scarlet walked slower, delaying the guard. "You must get lonely up here all by yourself."

The guard ran his fingers over his buzz cut and responded, "Yeah, it's kind of boring. Since I work night shift, I only see about four people a month, and none of them are as nice as you. Usually, they just ignore me and go on in. How'd a sweet thing like you end up at Bio-Corp?"

Scarlet choked for a second, unsure what to say. She made a thoughtful noise in the meantime and eventually gave up. "Curiosity, I guess."

He wasn't going to press any further. The air was getting thicker with flirtation by the second. "Where are my manners, I didn't introduce myself properly. My name's Jack, Jack Harper. What's yours?"

She miraculously remembered the name on her ID badge. "My name's Gertrude, but you can call me Gurdy. Nice to make your acquaintance."

The guard blinked twice, and his smile faded. He glanced down at her ID badge and puffed up with authority. "That's interesting. I was hired by a Gertrude Johansen. She was a tall old lady with the personality of a praying mantis. What have you been doing up there, makin' the fountain of youth?

"We ain't making waffles."

"That's a hell of a breakthrough. I'm sure you'll understand why I need to see some picture ID."

The corner of her eye began to twitch. "Yeah, I'm kidding. That's my mom. If you ask me, that lady spends way too much time cutting up animals. She needs to get laid. I mean, who names her daughter after herself?"

Officer Harper smiled. It was clear he wanted to believe her so he could ask her out. Unfortunately, K-Squad's seppuku clause made them take their jobs very seriously.

"Yeah, I got that impression. I hate to be a bother, but I really should see some picture ID. You know, just a technicality."

Scarlet searched her pockets for her imaginary wallet.

Bang, bang Maxwell's small red hammer came down on his head. Bang, bang Maxwell's small red hammer made sure that he was dead. It was rapturous. He stopped when the guard's head looked like cube steak.

Scarlet was stippled with blood and hyperventilating. This was probably the first time she'd seen someone beaten to death.

Max smiled and dropped the hammer in his pocket. "It's okay. He can't hurt you now." His gummy eyed, red toothed grin failed to reassure her.

Cakey smelled her ankle and hissed.

"Aww, he remembers you." Max hummed and stroked his head, eliciting a flubbery pooky noise.

"Fuck, it's good to see you." Max scooped him up for a hug, but Cakey struggled free.

"Ow, don't be mad. I was in a coma. I came as soon as I woke up."

Cakey pounded the floor with his tail as if asking what the hell they were still doing there. He looked like shit. His eyes were drunken slits, and his hiss was slurred.

No wonder he was grumpy. The bastards had installed a 4" vinyl window in his side so they could watch him digest things. Someone had fed him a bottle opener.

"Poor baby. Let's get you home."

Cakey stopped hissing and looked around, confused. He saw Max's smiling face and cried with joy. He jumped into Max's arms and snuggled with every ounce of his being.

Max carried him to the stack of pet carriers and opened one of the doors. Cakey didn't want to get into the handbasket that had taken him to hell so many times. He struggled and hissed until Max tossed in a snack cake.

Cakey stared at it like a little boy seeing boobs for the first time.

"Go on."

When Cakey dove in, Max locked the door and picked it up. "Let's get the fuck out of here."

Scarlet didn't respond.

"Scarlet, come on!"

Hearing her name snapped her out of it. She crouched and stared into the splattered meat like there was an answer in there somewhere.

"Scarlet!"

She shook her head. "We're so fucked!"

"It'll be fine. Screw him. You see where he works."

"We are going to fucking jail. And Marcy's never going to speak to me again."

"Look, I'm sorry, but I didn't have a choice. One more second and we'd have been busted."

"For trespassing, not murder! What the fuck are we going to do now? The cameras are still rolling. It'll take 'em about two seconds to figure out who we are. We are so very fucked."

"Relax. We just have to destroy the footage. You said the security room is on the bottom floor, right?"

"Yeah."

"We'll just pop in and delete it on the way out."

"That's fucking crazy. There's an armed guard. We're covered with blood. He's gonna shoot us on sight."

"Not if we surprise him." Max set the carrier down and took the guard's pistol from its holster. "You know, this would be a lot less connected to us if we opened all the cages. It'll look like a PITA raid."

Scarlet looked doubtful.

"Any chance is better than no chance."

"I guess."

They went from cage to cage, opening every door that didn't have a monster behind it. When he reached the frisky little tabby, he couldn't resist stuffing it into the pocket of his lab coat. It was too young and innocent to be left to fend for itself in a place like this.

Max felt so good about what they were doing, he was downright perky. "All right, time to meet Marcy." He snatched Cakey's carrier and headed for the door.

Scarlet followed him, growling. "Max, don't? Somebody's going to get killed."

"Hopefully not, but if it's him or us, I vote him."

"You don't get to vote. He's a trained security guy. Have you even held a gun before?"

"Guns are easy. Bullets come out this end. You stand on this side and squeeze this trigger." He handed Scarlet the pistol and snatched the machinegun off the guard's desk.

"It's actually perfect. We've been here for fifteen minutes, right? She said she would be fucking him for about twenty, so by the time we get to the room, she'll be about to leave. When the door opens, we rush in while his pants are still around his ankles. We tie them up, wipe the drives, and scream some PITA slogans. They'll take the blame. Hell, they'll probably claim responsibility."

"But what about Marcy?" She looked at the pistol as if she expected it to answer. "She's going to get fired. And you know how K-Squad works. Her boyfriend's going to have to seppuku."

They stepped into the elevator. "Yeah. That part sucks. I don't like fucking people over. On the other hand, she kind of deserve's something bad to happen to her for working here."

"It's not her fault. The job market sucks."

"That may be, but would you rather she lose her job, or us get killed?"

"There's got to be another way."

"Got anything better? Didn't think so. Look, she'll be fine. Without the surveillance footage, they won't know what order everything happened in. They'll probably assume we took her hostage before we went upstairs. Now put this on." He pulled two pairs of pantyhose out of his pocket and handed her one. He pulled the other over his face and grinned.

"Where the hell did you get these?"

"Costume shop, same as the beard. This way, they won't be able to tell them what we look like."

"Marcy knows what I look like."

"Yeah, we're going to have to feel that one out while we're down there."

"I'm not wearing this." She stuck them in her pocket.

The doors slid open, and they carefully walked into the empty hallway. They checked the map on the wall to get their bearings, then swiftly traversed the right corridor. There was a camera mounted just outside the door. Max twisted it to point down the hall.

Scarlet put her ear to the door.

Max whispered, "Are they still at it?"

She nodded and pantomimed an orgasm.

Max set Cakey's carrier down and watched him lick at the little window in his side. His friend was never going to be the same.

Max couldn't wait to get inside that room. Fuck Marcy! Everyone involved in this place is going to suffer.

A minute later, the lock clicked, and the door cracked open, seeping sappiness as they said her goodbyes. Max kicked it hard, sending Marcy flying backward into her dressing lover.

"Remain calm, and you'll live." He trained the rifle on them while Scarlet took his pistol and positioned herself between him and the gun rack.

On the floor, Marcy and her boyfriend stared at Max with wide, confounded eyes. She realized what was happening and shot Scarlet a furious what-the-hell look.

"What do you want?" The guard pushed Marcy off and sat up.

"Just the surveillance footage. Give me the drives."

"I don't have access to the drives."

"Bullshit."

"The computer's behind a four-inch-thick steel door, and I don't have the key. It's kept off-site, in case something like this happens."

"Sure it is." Max smiled and propelled the butt of his rifle into the man's pearly whites, transforming them into a twisted array of splinters to be choked up in red piles. It felt good to hit him. Really good! Max felt stronger than ever. He wanted to keep going, but first, he needed those drives.

"You're the head of security. You have the key." Max hit him again. "Give it!"

The guard's mouth was pouring thick driblets of blood down the front of his uniform. "Can't fuckin' help you. Hit me as many times as..."

Max kicked him in the stomach.

Meanwhile, Marcy crawled over to Scarlet and whispered through clenched teeth. "What the fuck are you guys doing?"

Scarlet held the gun on her and whispered, "I am so sorry about this. Really. Things got out of hand upstairs. I'll make it up to you somehow."

"How the fuck are you gonna do that? You gonna pay for Jimmy's funeral?"

"Look, we were gonna be on the video anyway. As soon as they noticed Cakey was missing, they would have watched the footage. We would've all been busted. We didn't think this through. Max was just so fucking gung ho. I'm really sorry." Scarlet crouched and put her hand on Marcy's thigh. "Please don't be mad at me. I got dragged into this, same as you."

"We're both victims here, huh? I guess we're even, then. We can just forget about the whole thing. Fuck you!" She grabbed the pistol and kicked Scarlet hard in the chest, rolling her backward into a filing cabinet.

Marcy leaped to her feet and charged over to Max just in time to see her lover's left eye float away on a stream of blood. She jabbed the gun sharply into Max's side and screamed through her tears, "Stop it, you fucking bastard. You fucking killed him. Why did you have to kill him?" She jabbed him again. "Asshole!" She screamed so hard, she drooled.

He dropped his weapon, raised his arms, and turned to face her. The red eyeliner made her look like she was crying blood. Her crooked beehive jiggled with every sob. If this were a movie, he would have laughed, but the effect was very different in person. The absurdity of the image made it all the more terrifying.

"He was a good man! I was gonna marry him. He was a really good man, and you killed him! It's not fair!"

She raised the gun to Max's head and closed her eyes. Max closed his as well and wondered what the afterlife would be like. Had it been worth it? What would happen to Cakey now? And what about the kitten in his pocket? It would probably go right back into the cage if he didn't crush it when he fell.

Everything was silent except for Marcy's sobs.

Three shots shattered the air.

Max didn't feel the bullets hit him. He didn't feel his body hitting the ground. His heartbeat pulsed in his ears so loudly he could barely feel the kitten trying to climb out of his coat.

Max opened his eyes and saw Marcy lying on the ground in front of him.

Scarlet dropped her rifle and ran over to him to give him a hug. "We need to get the hell out of here. Somebody probably heard that."

"Why couldn't you have just given me the goddamned key?" Max kicked the guard's body and heard a metallic tinkle. Looking closer, he saw a thin chain around his neck. Max pulled on it, and a little silver key slid out from under the man's cheek.

"There we go." He jammed it into the lock and swung the door open to reveal a massive server.

He yanked out all the cords, ejected the drives, and shot the motherboards a few times to be on the safe side. Scarlet stuffed the drives in her pockets, and they ran out the door just as the elevator doors dinged open. They were in the car and gone before anyone could follow.

He zigzagged through a dozen side streets then jumped on the highway heading away from home. He expected drones or helicopters to appear in his rearview any second.

Scarlet was slumped down, using a small mirror to see outside the car. "Did we get away?"

"I think so." He saw a sign advertising a park, so he took the next exit.

"Where are you going?"

"There's a park over here. Parks have Crap Cookers all over the place. I figure it's hard to pull data off a drive that's been atomized."

"True."

He pulled into the park and immediately saw a Crap Cooker over by a picnic area. Nobody was around, so he drove right up to it.

"Gimme those drives."

She handed them over. There were ten fifty-petabyte discs. PITA would pay a fortune for them, but he preferred peace of mind.

"What are you waiting for? Hurry up so we can celebrate."

He got out, piled the drives on the disposal platform, inserted the coins, and closed the door. There was a rumbling like a giant bong being hit. Moments later, the evidence was gone.

"Hey, you mind driving so Cakey can lay in my lap?"

"There is no end to your selfishness, is there?" She gave him her don't-ask-me-stupid-questions smile.

"Oh yeah." He pulled the kitten out of his pocket. "By the way, you want a cat? I couldn't leave him there. He's still frisky. Look at that cute little face. You know you want him." He made the kitten dance on the sill of the open window.

Scarlet grimaced. "Aww, he's adorable, but my apartment won't allow pets."

"I was afraid you'd say that. I can't keep it, either. Cakey would eat him." He carried the kitten over to the edge of the park and let it go. "He's better off than he was before."

Max climbed into the passenger seat and ran his fingers through the ruby ruffles of Scarlet's hair. "You were so fucking hot back there."

Cheeky snorted.

"I saved your life, and all it did was make you horny. You could at least say thanks."

"Oh, I'm going to thank you properly when we get home. I'm going to thank you so hard you can't see straight."

THUNDERBALLS

That night crawled by for Cakey.

He'd been rescued from the lab's torments only to be excluded from his own victory celebration. They hadn't even had the decency to put him in the bathroom this time. As soon as they'd entered Scarlet's apartment, Max dropped him at the foot of the Bio-Bed and started ripping off Scarlet's clothes. They'd been at it for hours now, despite the growling from Scarlet's bed.

Grinding and grunting, they wallowed in each other's dirt, showing everything but consideration to their captive audience. Cakey buried his face deep in his coils, but the sound pursued him even within the folds of his own flesh.

Why they even bother to rescue Cakey? Monkey obviously doesn't miss Cakey. All monkey wants is squishy, squirty, fun time with rancid dumpster slut.

Cakey let out a baleful howl as the can opener caught in his intestines. His bowels spasmed, tearing a hangnail in his guts. His side alternated between burning and freezing as yellow liquid pooled in the front of his cage.

Cakey tried to remember a time when jealousy was the worst of his troubles. The tiny pet carrier reeked of cleaning agents and the blood of hundreds of his less-fortunate predecessors. Beyond the dusty veil of bleach, blood screamed through the walls like a child bricked up and left to die.

Cakey peered through the steel grid, hoping to find something less upsetting to focus on. The small studio's key lime walls were hung with black-and-white photographs of naked females with makeup-streaked faces doing various household chores. The floor was carpeted in a beige shag, which, judging by the number of mites he could hear teeming within its fibers, had never been vacuumed. Her furniture was all faux Victorian Futurist; the kind Sav-Mart manufactured when retro-steampunk was in.

A hair kitschier and it might have been cool, but it suffered the fatal flaw of not being intended ironically.

Max crescendoed again and flopped onto his back.

Cakey turned around and gazed through the grid, hoping Max would finally let him out. Instead, Scarlet fired up a joint and recounted the day's events like a kid coming down from her first acid trip. Cakey stared at her smooth white throat and salivated.

When the joint was all gone, and there was nothing left to rehash, Scarlet was the first to acknowledge him. She squinted at him from across the room then leaned forward on all fours. "Hey, look who's awake."

She crossed the room and crouched before the cage, choking Cakey with her musty stench. "Hey, little guy. how you feeling?"

Scarlet's smile was dunked in pity. Her attempt to make nice was the cinnamon sprinkle of insult on the cupcake of his injury. He wanted to eat her face and said so, in so many growls.

"Whatcha growlin' at? You remember me, don't ya? You're safe now. Nobody's gonna hurt you ever again. Be sweet, and we'll let you out of the cage."

Max hauled his big stupid grin across the room and hummed their favorite song, but Cakey continued to growl.

"I don't think it's a good idea to let him out right now. He's impossible when he gets like this." He sat before the cage Indian style. "I should probably get him home. He'll calm down once he's in familiar territory. We should have gone there instead."

"I seem to remember a certain somebody saying he couldn't wait that long." Scarlet gave his deflated love siphon a playful tug.

Max grinned as lust sprouted yet again. "You're the one who suggested we come here. I got the impression you couldn't wait, either."

"Waiting Sucks." Scarlet crawled on top of him and pinned his hands to the floor.

Cakey was forced to watch them go again, this time mere inches from his cage. His sobs were drowned out by the schlorping of their sticky flesh.

Cakey's steam sputtered out long before Max's.

✳✳✳✳✳

Trying to cum a fifth time in a row was like trying to get water from a dry well. Max could pump all he wanted, but nothing was going to come out. His cock was raw and numb at the same time, and his mind couldn't come up with anything kinky enough to put him over the top.

Just when he was about to give up, Scarlet pushed him onto his back and commenced pounding his cock with her asshole. She was like some kind of sex-hulk in berserker mode trying to cave in his pelvis.

"Cum, or I'm gonna break it off and shit it out on your tits."

40

Something finally rattled loose, but it hurt. "Oww, fuck, I think I broke something." He curled onto his side in the fetal position.

Scarlet rolled off of him, laughing. "Having problems?"

"I feel like a string of razor wire was stuck in my ass, wrapped around my balls, and then jerked out through my belly button."

"Are you going to be okay?"

"Yeah, I think so. I hope you appreciate how lucky you are to be a chick."

Scarlet laughed and ruffled his hair. "Aww, poor baby's hoo hoo's all used up. Let mamma kiss it better." She dropped her face into his lap.

Max jerked away and rose to his feet. "Cut it out. I'm in serious pain here. I think I pulled my prostate."

She laughed sadistically. "Okay, fine, I'll be good. So, now what? You want to spend the night?"

"I'd love to. I'm tired as fuck, but it wouldn't be fair to Cakey. He deserves some quality time."

She peered through the grid at Cakey's hateful expression. "Why doesn't he like me? I've never been anything but nice to him."

Max pulled on his pants. "He's just jealous. He'll get used to having you around eventually."

"Is that a proposal?"

"You know what I'm saying. Eventually, he's got to figure out he doesn't have to compete with you."

"Aww, you like me. That's so sweet."

Max sighed, realizing he was getting sick of her. She was sweet and fun, but kind of annoying. Maybe it was just his lack of energy. "I'm really tired. We should get going."

"Oh, I see how it is." She slipped into a brown leather dress that made him think of Roman gladiators. "You needed me to break you out of the hospital and into a heavily guarded facility, rescue your pet, commit a few murders, give you a few rides, and fuck your brains out, but now that we're done you can't wait to get away from me."

He didn't have the energy for a proper response. "No. I'm just tired."

His tone had revealed there was more truth in her words than she'd thought. He felt bad enough that his feelings for her were all in his pants, but the look creeping into her eyes made him feel like something Humwawa would step in and go, "Eww!"

On the way out, he took her hand. "Hey, sorry for being short with you. I'm just really exhausted."

She forced a smile. "I get it. Between the injuries, the caper, and the sex, you've burned a lot of calories today."

"I don't mean that as an excuse. It's taking every spark of remaining energy I have to keep the particles that make up my body from dissipating into a cloud. You helped me in a way no sane person would. There are no words that can express my gratitude."

"Don't worry about it. I'm always up for doing something stupid." She locked the door.

Max noticed a zombie lumbering up the stairs. He looked fresh. If not for the stiffness of his movements, he might have passed for a drunk.

"Seriously, you're my hero." Max leaned in to kiss her but was interrupted by a thunderous cacophony of screaming and metallic clangs.

Not far from her apartment building, in what used to be a soccer field, a giant Jengist structure continued to collapse. Huge beams of metal and wood slid out of the towering lattice to rain on the reveling devout.

The dust from the impact made it hard to see how many had died.

Max shook his head in disbelief. "Damn, how did I not notice that on the way in?"

"You were horny. You probably wouldn't have noticed it anyway. Those wackos are everywhere now. I hardly notice them myself unless it looks like their church is going to fall on me. I'm glad it finally came down. It was getting too big and wobbly for comfort."

"I don't know how you can live next to one of those. It would drive me crazy."

"They showed up right after I renewed my lease. You get used to it, though. It's like living next to an airport."

"I don't know if I could ever get used to that," Max kicked the zombie down the stairs and watched his head splatter on the pavement. "I miss my bed."

"I'm sure she misses you too. Let's get going before the cops block us in. They park here so shit doesn't fall on their car."

Max nodded and hurried down the stairs.

✶✶✶✶✶

Max was relieved to find his apartment's parking lot devoid of police and paparazzi. "It doesn't look like anybody leaked my address to the press yet."

Scarlet pulled into a space and turned off the car. "You think they will?"

"I don't know. Some dude said he wanted to give me a TV show, or something." Max opened his door.

"Wait. What? When?"

"At the hospital. I told him to fuck off."

Scarlet followed him to his door. "Why are you just now telling me this?"

"Priorities? My friend was being tortured."

"Yeah, but I picked you up six hours ago."

"It doesn't matter. I'm not doing it. I fucking hate attention."

"Yeah, but—You know you should really—You know what, nevermind. It's a good thing you have a sweet dick because you're real fucking weird."

"Admittedly, but at least I'm not boring."

42

"I can't argue with that."

He set the pet carrier down and kissed her goodbye. "I'm sorry. It just slipped my mind."

She shook her head. "You're a piece of fucking work."

Max leaned in and whispered in his sexiest voice, "And a mass murderer."

She shoved him playfully. "Go get some rest, and try not to kill anybody."

"I'll do my best."

Walking to her car, she said, "It's okay if you get famous. I always wanted to be in a tabloid."

"I'll take that into consideration."

"See ya."

"Thanks again!"

Max picked up the carrier and hurried to his door. He turned on the light and found a scrawny teenager with thick glasses and an overbite eating nachos in his living room.

The kid dropped his snack and stretched his arm out dramatically, revealing a surprising number of tattoos. "Come with me if you want to live." He was doing his best to make his squeaky voice sound compelling. It didn't work.

"For fuck's sake. Who the hell are you? You know what? I don't even care. I don't have anything worth stealing, but feel free to look around. I'm going to bed."

"There's no time. I'll explain everything once you're safe. Now come with me if you want to live." He took a puff from his inhaler and twitched his outstretched hand for emphasis.

"Man, just fucking leave. The last thing I need right now is a goofy asshole breaking into my house and quoting the Terminator at me."

The kid rolled his eyes and pointed at the door. "Look, guys are coming to—"

"Get the fuck out of my house, or I'll feed you to Cakey." He picked up the pet carrier and fingered the latch like a trigger.

The intruder's voice was shrill, "Iiites are coming to kill you, you fucking idiot! I can help. I'm a Riot Nrrd. They're our enemies. You're their enemy, so we thought it would be nice to save your life. I've been waiting in this shithole for five hours."

He jabbed his finger toward the parking lot. "There are cops staked out across the street. They just told their boss you're home. Now the commissioner is calling the Iiites to let them know they can come kill you. The Iiites are massed at the nearest manhole waiting for the go-ahead. I'm leaving before they get here. I suggest you do the same. Call me if you live to change your mind."

The Riot Nrrd handed him a small black business card and ran out the door. The card read Pope, Super Scientist above a phone number. Max could see the glowing green eyes of his Bio-Bed staring at him from the darkness of his bedroom. He wanted to sleep so bad he almost started to cry.

Nothing the Nrrd said made any sense. Why would the Iiites bother getting revenge on someone so insignificant? Why would the police tip-off terrorists? Why would the Riot Nrrds, also terrorists, bother to save his life?

Max glanced out the window and saw the manhole cover sliding open about half a block away.

"Fuck."

Scarlet was just backing out of the parking space.

"Shit, shit, shit, fuck, shit, goddamn stupid motherfucking shit," he said as he fumbled with his phone. It rang just as Scarlet was pulling out of the parking lot.

"Hey, you change your mind?" she asked, stopping the car.

"No, I mean yes, but don't stop. Turn right and meet me around back by the subway." He hung up, picked up the pet carrier, and ran. He rounded the corner of the hallway and flew down the steps, hugging the pet carrier and humming to calm the pissed off creature beating around inside. He hit the pavement just as Scarlet's car was coming to a stop.

He jerked open the door and jumped in. Scarlet looked furious.

"What the fuck? You hung up on me. I fucking hate it when people hang up on me!"

"Drive! Drive, goddammit!"

"I'm not doing anything till I get a fucking apology," she said, turning off the ignition.

"I'm sorry, now fucking drive!"

"You don't sound sorry."

"There are Iiites coming to kill me! I promise to sound more apologetic when I'm done shitting myself! Please drive!?"

"Seriously?"

"Yes, fucking seriously!"

"You could have told me that on the phone instead of hanging up." She started the car and pulled away from the curb. "I'm sorry. I didn't know people were after you."

"Why the hell did you think I was calling you frantically, telling you to pick me up around the corner? Wasn't it pretty fucking obvious something was wrong?"

She took a deep breath and exhaled through her nose. "Probably. Look, I really hate being hung up on. My dad used to do that all the time. He was a businessman, always on the phone. He talked to me the same way he did his employees. I think his customers and his boss were the only people he ever said bye to. It always made me feel really unimportant. Now, every time somebody hangs up on me, it brings back all that childhood bullshit." She sighed. "Anyway, Iiites?"

"So, I unlock the door, flip on the light, and there's this scrawny little shit saying, 'Come with me if you want to live. Iiites are coming to kill you, blah, blah, blah.' I tell him to fuck off. He does. I look out the window, and sure enough, fuckers are pouring out of the sewer." Max rubbed his burning eyes. "I hate today."

An Iiite ran out in front of the car, but she easily zipped around him.

"Shit, he's writing down my license number. Wait, why is he writing down my license number?"

"Fuck if I know. The guy gave me this card and ran off. I'll ask him what's going on."

He dialed the number. As soon as he heard a click, he asked, "Why did an Iiite write down my girlfriend's license plate number?"

"Oh hey, look who pulled their head out of their ass."

"I guess so. You want to answer my question?"

"Obviously, he is going to run her plates so that they can come to her apartment and kill you both."

"How can an Iiite do that? They live in the fucking sewer."

"I will explain everything when you get here. I don't like talking on the phone."

"You think they bugged my phone?"

"No, I just don't like talking on the phone. It gives me a headache. Also, cell phone signals can be triangulated. Also, they cause brain cancer. I hate these things."

"Who doesn't?"

"On the corner of 29th Street and Electra Avenue, you will find a gaming store called The Cartridge Which Cannot Be Named. Go in and ask for an old Bleem game called Jiminy Snippet. The cashier will ask you whether it is a gift or not, and you will reply that it is a birthday gift for your sister's boyfriend. You will be led to safety only after saying those exact words. Do you need me to repeat them?"

"Old Bleem game, Jiminy Snippet, birthday present for my sister's boyfriend, right?"

"Yes, you might want to write it down in case you forget. However, please refrain from writing it down uncoded. And don't forget to destroy the code afterward. We don't want our secret base compromised."

"Whatever, we're on our way. Bye." He disconnected and rubbed his throbbing temples with his thumb and index finger.

"Bad news?"

"The worst. Your place isn't safe now, either. We get to go to some Nrrd compound and use secret codes to meet some James Bond wannabe who says he can keep us safe."

Scarlet laughed. "No, really, what did he say?"

Max raised his eyebrows apologetically. "Maybe this is hell. We died at Bio-Corp, and this the beginning of our eternal punishment."

DR. POPE AND THE BELLINI MACHINE

The Cartridge Which Cannot Be Named was the last business left in a shitty little strip-mall you'd barely register if you were leaning against it. The large panel windows were covered in old flyers, mostly gaming conventions and free comic book day. Max found a small gap and peered inside.

Small groups of misfits brooded over cheap folding tables heaped with chits. They placed meeples, referenced manuals, and dropped dice into towers. All around them were shelves full of every kind of game and covered in vintage action figures. It was about what he expected from a group whose best efforts at formulating an intimidating name had resulted in 'Riot Nrrds.'

Max hung his head and held the door for Scarlet and Cakey, partially to ensure they wouldn't run off and make him deal with this alone.

The Nrrds' stopped talking and narrowed their eyes at him. He felt like a frog in a seventh-grade classroom. Luckily, the mix of stale pizza fumes and plastic gave Cakey a sneezing fit that sliced through the tension like a lightsaber. The dungeon-master nodded toward the counter, and everyone went back to their respective quests.

The smug twit at the counter glared over his manga with the intensity of a chess grandmaster. His shirt had a nametag printed on it that said, "My name is Earl."

"I'm looking for Jimminy Snippet. It's an old Bleem game."

"You have a Bleem system?"

"No, it's a birthday gift for my sister's boyfriend."

"You sure you want that one? All sales are final."

"I don't think I have a choice."

"All right. It's over here." He walked them to a back room filled Hentai in every conceivable format. "You're going to love this."

Earl pulled a copy of La Blue Girl 14 and held it above his head. The shelf clicked and swung backward. What Max saw smacked him right in the gob.

"Holy fuck!"

The whole mall had been converted into a bunker and packed with alien-looking tech. It looked like the set of Star Trek: Hoarders. To the left, were countless nerd caves cluttered with computers, toys, and garbage. The roar of the processors sounded like an idling jet engine. The right side of the room was full of strange metal objects bejeweled with a cornucopia of blinking lights of all shapes and sizes. The back of the room was lined with guns; some traditional, others could have been sci-fi movie props.

As Earl slid the door closed behind them, Pope's words suddenly seemed plausible. If this was real, so was the threat.

Some days it just doesn't pay to wake up from a coma.

Five Nrrds worked at various stations, each so absorbed they didn't notice Max and Scarlet gawking. After clearing his throat several times and saying, "Hello," he realized the Nrrds knew he was there, but didn't care.

Max approached a pixieish female with short green hair who was playing a first-person shooter on her PC. Her cave was a shrine to B-rate horror flicks, so he liked her already. He put his hand on the back of her chair and came in close to address her without bothering the other Nrrds.

"Hey, is Pope around?"

The girl's body stiffened. She rounded the corner in her game and came upon an opening full of Iiites. She opened fire, but her focus was gone. Soon the screen was tinted red and filled with happy Iiites who danced around waving bits of her avatar. She slowly swiveled her chair to face him, pointed her dainty finger, and screamed, "Interloper!"

Max tripped over his own feet and fell into a stack of Big Robot magazines. The other Nrrds stopped what they were doing.

Cakey giggled.

The girl left her chair and kicked him hard in the side. "You know how much work I just lost because of you?"

"Chill out! It's just a game."

She screamed through gritted teeth. "It's not a game! I was testing a battle scenario. I created a digital model of the sewer system and populated it with Iiites. I've been testing variations on our battle strategy, commanding six squadrons simultaneously. Each squadron has ten guys who have to be outfitted with specific body armor and weapons and positioned strategically. The setup process alone takes ten hours of work."

"Just restart from the last checkpoint.'

"I don't code checkpoints. Usually, if a mission fails, it fails because it's flawed. I didn't expect to be interrupted at a crucial moment by one of Pope's idiot friends." She kicked him again and returned to her cave.

Scarlet helped him up. "You want me to stab her?"

A bird-faced man in a red lab coat stepped forward. "You must be Max and Scarlet. Pope will return shortly. I asked him to replenish our supply of chocolate milk. You can wait over there in the welcome area." He pointed to a couch in the corner. "You will find an assortment of informative magazines on the table, and should you feel parched, there is a mini-fridge in the arm. It opens away from you." The Nrrd gestured with his hand to illustrate the functionality.

"All right, thanks. I could use a drink. You wouldn't believe the day I've had."

"Cool." The Nrrd gave a little nod and went back to his cave before Max had a chance to expound.

Too tired to take offense, Max plopped on the couch and opened the arm. He was hoping for beer, but Juicetastic was acceptable. *Well, they might be a bunch of cunts, but at least they have good juice.* He selected a strawberry goji colada and let the compartment slam shut.

A Nrrd who had been soldering in a nearby station jerked his head up and shushed him angrily. Max mouthed, "sorry" and opened his drink.

Cakey curled up in his lap and flipped over for a belly rub.

Max ran his fingers across the folds but jerked his hand back when he felt the plastic. He gave halfhearted scritches until Cakey pretended to fall asleep.

"Poor little shit, he must be bored to death. You should try to be more exciting." She stroked Cakey's back. He twitched and looked at her through a tiny slit before resettling himself.

In his stodgiest voice, Max said, "Perhaps I can find an interesting article to discuss." Max flipped through the magazines. They were all about science, science fiction, or manga. He grabbed one at random and flipped it open.

"How delightful! This pornographic, gay zombie movie used real gay zombies as actors. What will they think of next?"

Scarlet played along. "How provocative."

"Honestly, I'm sick of all these wannabe artists trying to make zombies out to be real people with rights and feelings. They're braindead, nothing going on in their heads. And the zombies aren't much better. The NAADP was almost as delusional as The Cult of Abel with their 'a nude horse is a rude horse' bullshit."

"Okay, grandpa. Simmer down before your suspenders melt."

Max tossed the magazine on the table, leaned his head back, and closed his eyes. He'd been serious about the try-hard edginess getting on his nerves, but saying so made him feel like an old fart.

Ten minutes later, Pope came in with a hand-truck loaded with small milk cartons. He nodded to Max on his way to the fridge. He gasped, "Hello." and took a puff from his inhaler. "I need to get these in the fridge. Be right back." He seemed more like an office-bitch than a terrorist.

When all the cartons were lined neatly in the fridge, Pope returned. "You made it. That's good. I believe you had some questions for me?"

"Question one: What the fuck?"

The soldering Nrrd came over with a big fake smile, "Hey, would you guys mind taking this to the quiet room? I am trying to micro-solder an m990 processor into a living g30 nano-chip, and I need complete silence." His jaw clenched on 'complete silence.'

Pope explained. "The larger of the two of those is one-tenth the size of the point on a needle. That type of soldering is very delicate, and even the sound of a human voice can affect the drying solder. That's the main reason that he is by himself over here by the waiting room. We don't have many visitors. The other reason is that no one likes him."

"What's that? I can't hear you over the roar of those computers over there."

The soldering Nrrd looked like he might throw a punch.

Pope stepped between them. "I apologize. I was unaware that you were working. I would be happy to take them to the quiet room so that you may handle your minuscule thingamajig in peace.

"Right this way." He led them to the back corner by the bathroom, where he ushered them through a large red door. The quiet room was a ten-foot square insulated with foam. Apart from the walls, it looked like the bedroom of a broke college student. There was an old single bed, a heavily worn couch, and a coffee table laden with pizza boxes. The fallout from a month's worth of meals and snacks blanked every surface. It was almost as bad as his apartment used to be. Aside from The Bellini machine and Storm Trooper armor, there was nothing to offset the bleak aesthetic of communal misery.

"This is where we come when the hustle and bustle of terrorist life become overwhelming. It's soundproof, hence the name."

Max headed straight for the Bellini machine and filled two plastic cups with thick yellow slush.

Pope clasped his hands and squinted his eyes. "I have important things to do. So, let's get through this as quickly as possible." He pointed at the couch.

Max handed one of the drinks to Scarlet and sucked the other until brain-freeze made him stop. It tasted like gummy bear cum. He sucked through the pain until he hit bottom, then got himself a refill.

Pope's fingers drummed his cheek while Max moved to the couch. "Okay, the complete history of everything you never wanted to know. Riot Nrrds formed as a response to the weaponization of idiocy. Like every other group that formed to beat back the primal darkness, we have been misunderstood, ridiculed, and demonized by the ruling class because they don't want to give up their power."

Max yawned.

"I know it's a cliche, but that's what happened."

"I'm just really sleepy. Keep going."

Pope snorted. "We are a primarily nonviolent group of revolutionaries who wage meme warfare on the establishment in the hopes of saving humanity from a clandestine shadow-government. These past few months, we've been working on a more direct approach, but I'll get to that a little later. Now tell me, what do you know about the Iiites?"

50

Max and Scarlet shared a pitying glance. "Well, they're mutants who moved to the sewers because people were shitty to them, and now they're a bunch of vengeful idiots."

Pope shook his head. "Nobody reads the literature.

"That is where they came from, but the real reason they act out as they did at the Bootique is to make people think they're just bands of violent idiots. An occasional, random act of violence is just scary enough to make people malleable. If anybody read the literature, they'd know that Iiites are more advanced than we are. They've been creating a complex power structure with hundreds of long-term anti-surface programs that have been eating away at our minds and bodies for decades."

"Somebody's gotta do it."

"Don't make light of this. The Iiites colluded with several major corporations to collapse the government and then coached them as they stepped in to restore order. They have deals with all of the major string-pullers. They work with the global elite to keep the masses too terrified to think for themselves, and you just pissed them off."

Max finished his second drink and got up for another. Ice crystals were forming on his brainstem, but he needed more alcohol.

"Your kerfuffle was the first time they've looked weak."

"So, I bruised their egos. They'll get over it."

"This isn't about the event so much as the implication. People will ask themselves, 'If one guy and a worm can kill a whole unit, why isn't anyone doing anything to stop them?

"Imagine that all the lies keeping that power structure in place are playing cards. The Iiites carefully balanced those cards over many years." He mimed building a house of cards.

"That house is sitting on a table in an old RV driving dangerously fast down a bumpy road," he wiggled the imaginary house, "and you just opened a window in that RV." The imaginary house blew away. Pope looked pleased with himself.

Max wanted to say something snarky. Instead, he reclaimed his seat.

Pope clasped his hands together. "We would like very much for you to use your notoriety to open more windows. Go before the Media© and tell them how easy it was to stand up to the Iiites and win. Make them look pathetic and weak. In return, we will keep you safe and comfortable. We have a lot of resources."

There were so many smart-assed responses fighting to get out Max's mouth that Pope had time to add, "You're free to try your luck on your own, but you have about as much chance of survival as a can of cheeseburger flavored baby FÜD in a Smart House."

"That's classist."

"It's also accurate."

Max sucked down another half a glass. If he stopped, the previous drinks would slingshot back up his esophagus. He wanted to pound the table and scream that this wasn't his problem. He wanted to reach out and strangle the arrogant little fuck. Instead, he asked, "What did you mean by a more direct approach?"

"That is a bit more complicated. We tried viral internet campaigns, flyers, and public speaking, all to no effect. Every time we find an audience, the Iiites show up and kill everyone. Then talking heads read the cue cards provided by the Iiite's business partners, and we get blamed. We have hundreds of websites full of documented proof of what's going on, but most of our traffic comes from people who want to laugh at us. The truth is so weird and extreme that it sounds insane."

The more Pope ranted, the larger the vein in his temple grew. "And the Media© says we're nuts who want to destabilize society. We are not anti-society. We are anti-oligarchy and anti-fascist."

Pope's voice was growing hoarse. "Do you remember when the Divine Disturbance stripped the lies away, laying reality bare before us in all her voluptuous glory. The masses acted like it was all just a wild night at the bar."

Max rested his face in his palms. "I thought you had things to do."

Pope crossed his arms, pursed his lips, and narrowed his eyes. "The Iiite government has two branches; the elite intellectual branch known as the Meta-Intellectual Liberation Front or M.I.L.F. and the militaristic branch known as the Iron Fist. Their leaders, Felix and Xavier Mitton, are genetically-engineered super-mutants, or at least that's what they want us to think. I want to call shenanigans on that. It sounds silly."

"Naw."

Pope used his +10 eyes of sternness. "We are failing because we are all brains and no brawn. What you interrupted earlier was a simulation we use to calculate variables in attack strategies for neutralizing Iiite nerve centers. The time for pacifism has passed."

"We developed lightweight, quantum-friction pulse-cannons. They don't kick or run out of ammunition. With one of those, a little kid could take out a hundred soldiers before they got close enough to read his T-shirt.

"Unfortunately, we're having trouble finding Nrrds willing to use them. We need someone like you to recruit and inspire us to be heroes. If you lead the charge with our technology, we can expose them. We just have to provoke them enough to show their hand, pardon the pun.

"So, what do you say? Will you be our god of death?"

Max raised his head, looked him directly in the eye, and replied. "No."

The Nrrd showed no sign he'd heard Max's response. He and Max sat in silent expectation, each waiting for the other to say something. Finally, the Nrrd cocked his head and asked, "What do you mean, no? You have the opportunity to drag humanity out of the oppressive muck it's been wallowing in for thousands of years. You can be the key to a new golden age, a new era fueled by science and philosophy. The greatest living minds have calculated every variable to ensure success."

"I don't want to."

The Nrrd's eyes widened incredulously. "You don't want to be the most influential person since Jesus?"

"Nope. You do it."

Pope narrowed his eyes. "May I ask why?"

"Because being dead isn't going to make my life any better. Even if you have calculated a perfect offense where I am completely safe, I don't want to save the world. I don't like attention, and I don't like people. We're not worth saving."

Max's voice kept getting louder. "We did this to ourselves, you know. Nobody can make us dumb. They can only make us so comfortable that we don't think we need to know stuff. And, even if we deserved saving and I felt up to it, what's the point? Every new regime promises to fix things. Thousands or millions of people die so these assholes can replace those assholes, and these problems get replaced with those problems. It's all just drama we manufacture because peace is boring. You can go to war, or you can get fucked up and watch TV. Who saves more lives? Fucking TV guy, that's who. They're the real heroes."

"Incorrect." Pope's eyes burned with enough grandiose delusion to light a cigar. "It's not people's fault that they are terrible. We are computers, complex input-output machines. Our society is garbage, so we are garbage. A better society makes better people."

"I'm way too tired for a philosophical debate about the word better. I just don't want to, okay?"

"Look at me." He held out his arm to demonstrate that his elbow was thicker than his bicep. "I'm not big on physical altercations, but we're out of options. The Iiites have some heinous plans."

"So do you. I know what your pun meant."

"There has only been one instance of government based on science, and it worked wonders for the people they governed."

"When was that?"

"The Iiites are doing it now. They use science, philosophy, and art to synthesize a balanced culture. Their cities are charming. The people are like Canadians before they got nuked in the second American Revolution, but it's all built on the subjugation of the surface.

He paused to dispense himself a Bellini. "Let me give you an example of the sort of thing the Iiites do. The majority of the Riot Nrrd strongholds used to be along the Eastern seaboard. When the Iiites found that out, they used one of their companies to build an oil rig off the coast and then blew it up so they could pump a highly toxic dispersant into the ocean. Dispersant killed everything for fifty miles, then evaporated and killed everything for one-hundred miles inland."

Pope paced furiously. "Thousands of people came forward with solutions to the spill, but New Petroleum ignored them all. The Media© painted a picture of hope and triumph of the human spirit while everyone on the coast got cancer. Have you seen the images of children covered in necrotic tissue?

Max had. It was nasty.

"The M.I.L.F. held the majority stock in the companies that built the rig, owned the rig, and formulated the dispersant. The heads of all those companies sold the majority of their stock a few weeks before the supposed spill, then repurchased it all a week later for pennies on the dollar. They made money on this!

"I could rattle off hundreds of similar stories. Do you want to know what makes us different? They assassinate people who try to make the world a better place. We run interference and save those people's lives. They are why private schools are the only option for people who want a job outside of fast FÜD. We spread information freely and encourage people to achieve their potential. Iiites are poison, and we are the antidote. Don't you want to be a part of that?"

Max laughed bitterly. "I just want things to go back to normal."

"The Media© will hound you day and night until you talk to them. The Iiites will kill you the second they know where you are. Helping us is the only way you can get your life back to normal."

"I'll leave the country for a while. They'll forget about me eventually, and I'll come back. Or maybe I'll stay there."

Pope looked as though he might spit on him. "My God, you're stupid. Iiites are everywhere. You would just be making it easier for them. At least if you die here, you'd be a martyr.

"Maybe you don't care about anyone but yourself, and maybe you don't want your name in history books, but surely you want to avoid a slow and painful death. When the Iiites catch you, they won't put a bullet in your head. They will drag you underground, torture you on film, and play it on the news so everybody remembers why they were afraid."

Pope turned his attention to Scarlet. "What is your reaction to all this?"

She had been watching passively as though this were all a bad TV drama. "Me? I want to pound a bottle of vodka and pass out."

"Well, they're after you now as well. Your apartment complex is crawling with Iiites. If you go home without Max, they'll take you underground and use you as bait. Then they'll kill you whether he comes or not, which he obviously wouldn't."

Max weighed his options. He had neither the money to disappear comfortably nor the energy to be a hobo. He was screwed.

He'd enjoyed killing all those people, partially because they deserved it. It was terrifying and exhausting, but he felt more alive than he had in years. Killing bad guys might be fun.

Pope wasn't going to let him sleep until he agreed. "Fine, I'll do it on one condition. I want your people to take down Bio-Corp. Rescue the healthy animals. Put the rest out of their misery. Kill all the employees, and burn it to the ground."

Scarlet's eyes widened with shock, and Pope grinned like Hitler after being accepted into the Thule Society. "There's the little soldier our calculations predicted. Done. The Iiites own Bio-Corp. We'll take care of them tonight while you rest up. How's that?"

"It's shit, but I suppose it's the best I'm going to get."

"You can sleep here tonight. We will have better accommodations for you tomorrow. I took the liberty of collecting some of your things while I was at your place earlier, so you should have everything you need."

"You stole from my apartment?"

"No, we performed a service for you before you knew you needed it. We pride ourselves on our foresight."

"What if I hadn't agreed to join you?"

"You would have been dead before you noticed."

Max sighed, stumbled over to the mattress, and flopped face down on it. His nose made an unpleasant cracking noise. He'd forgotten how hard beds were. His body sank in well enough and soon began to tingle with the effervescence of sleep. He was snoring before the Nrrd left the room.

Max woke with a start as he hit the floor. Scarlet had turned over and bumped him off the side of the tiny mattress. He'd forgotten that was even possible. Bio-beds gripped like a hammock.

There were no windows or clocks, so he couldn't tell how long he'd been asleep. Was he rested, or did his adrenaline spike when he realized where he was?

What the fuck have I gotten myself into?

He crawled to his feet.

Scarlet was sound asleep. She would probably murder him when she woke up, justifiably. He thought about jumping off a tall building to save her the trouble

Hunger nudged his ribs to remind him he'd soon have to leave the quiet room and learn how to be a terrorist. Hoping to put it off as long as possible, he crawled onto the couch and rifled through the snack bags lying in various states of crumpledness on and around the coffee table.

Careful as he was to be quiet, the crinkling of the bags reanimated his star-crossed fuck buddy.

Scarlet sat up and surveyed her surroundings. Sheet-marks zigzagged across malachite eyes still dull and heavy with sleep. She stretched lasciviously. Even rumpled, she dripped sex.

"Shit," she said as she dangled her legs off the mattress, "that stuff happened, didn't it?"

"Yeah, sorry about that."

"It's not your fault. Who knows? This might even be fun. Last night I dreamed I was a secret agent working in a mall. Somebody was sneaking around a big department store ripping all the tags off the clothes. I had a lot of cool gadgets, but I couldn't find the guy. I eventually found out it was a kid who was crawling underneath the racks of clothes. That's why nobody ever saw him do it. The salespeople and I threw all the untagged clothes in a big pile in the parking lot and set them on fire with the kid buried inside. Everybody was wearing grass skirts. I guess it was a luau-themed witch-burning kind of thing. Anyway, it was fun."

Not one to try to interpret dreams, Max laughed lightly and resumed his search. He found a bag of rice crackers underneath the stack of pizza boxes. Whoever had been eating them shared his distaste for wasabi peas. Even starving, they were disgusting.

"Wasabi pea?" he offered, extending the bag.

She accepted them and dumped a few directly into her mouth. "I'm starving." She crunched them loudly. "Got anything to drink?"

"Just that." He gestured to the Bellini machine. "The Nrrds are going to expect us to do stuff when we leave this room. I was hoping to put it off."

"What's the point? The sooner we get started, the sooner we'll be done. After you passed out, I talked to Pope a little more, and he said this shouldn't be all that hard. They've been doing this sort of thing for a long time, and they know their stuff."

"I hope you're right, but I'm no commando. I'm not even good at video games. I'm going to die the second I hit the sewer."

"You don't give yourself enough credit. You and Cakey took six of them out by yourselves with your bare hands."

His stomach jumped upon hearing Cakey's name, "Shit, where is Cakey? Did anybody let him out of his cage?"

He scanned the room for the pet carrier. It was gone. Remembering that the Riot Nrrds were scientists was all the motivation he needed. He jumped up and ran out the door half expecting to find Cakey strapped down somewhere with needles in his brain. He was pleasantly surprised to see everyone, including Cakey, sitting on the floor, stuffing their faces with Chinese takeout.

Pope beckoned Max over. "I was beginning to wonder if you passed in your sleep. Have a seat. We got one of everything, so whatever you like is probably here somewhere."

Max quickly walked over and stroked Cakey's head. Cakey looked at him with angry, questioning eyes. The poor guy had been living like a veal since the day of the massacre.

"I am so sorry. I meant to let you out last night, but I was so tired my brain wasn't working."

Cakey narrowed his eyes and turned back to his food.

The gesture was so spicy, Max's eyes watered. "So, how's he been? Who let him out?"

"I did," said the green-haired girl from the day before. "I came in last night to find my extra pair of glasses and heard him crying, so I let him out."

"And he didn't try to kill you?"

"Kill me? He's a sweet little burrito of love." She scratched him behind the ears.

Cakey trilled and smacked his lo mein.

"He usually doesn't do well with strangers. Plus, he was in a bad mood. I'm surprised he didn't react to the lab coats some of you guys are wearing. I just rescued him from Bio-Corp."

"Oh, that's why he didn't want Spaz to come near him. I thought he was just a good judge of character."

The asshole who had shooed them into the quiet room choked on his Mongolian beef. Nobody tried to help him. After a few seconds, he coughed it back into his mouth and swallowed it properly. "Fuck you."

The girl scratched Cakey's chin lovingly. "Everybody loves Cakey. He's the cute little mascot we've always wanted. I guess he picked up on that, cuz he's been a little angel. Haven't you?" She rubbed noses with him.

Max was taken aback. Was it possible for a cheekworm's loyalty to shift? He'd never shown anyone else affection before.

"Come on, don't be mad at me. You know I love you." He traced the ticklish folds of Cakey's flesh with his finger. Cakey fell backward, giggling and squirming adorably. Within seconds everyone in the room was laughing and babbling in baby talk. Eventually, he rolled over on his stomach to signal he'd had enough. Still giggling, the odd little creature smiled at him with a classic, "Oh, I can't stay mad at you" expression. Again, Max swore he'd never let anything else come between them.

Pope put down his plate and butted in, "I suppose that I should introduce you to everybody. You already met Spaztastic over there. Most people call him Spaz. He is our resident drama queen and engineer. The woman who liberated your little friend is Asphyxia. She is a software expert, logistical genius, and the resident tease. The short one over there is Yoda. He's our tactician and dungeon master."

The little guy picked a piece of egg foo young off of his Spiderman T-shirt, gave a short bow, and said, "Pleased I am to meet you."

Pope continued, gesturing to the conjoined twins. "Then we have the brilliant particle physicists, Marvin and Arthur Dent. Talk to them for thirty seconds, and it will become painfully obvious which is who. And this is Hedorah. We call him that because he chain-smokes. It plays hell on the equipment, but nobody in the world has a better grasp of theoretical mathematics."

Hedorah's eyes rolled behind greasy black tangles. "I wanted to be called Maximum Modulus, but these assholes won't let anybody pick their name. In case you haven't figured it out yet, Pope is the gopher. He mainly runs errands and flips switches when we need him to."

"Fuck you, smog monster. I have four master's degrees from MIT."

Everyone had a good laugh and pelted Pope with bits of food. When there was no more joy to be gained from tormenting him, Max asked, "So, what's my code name going to be? Pope was calling me The One last night. Am I stuck with that?"

"Too big for his britches, his head already is." Yoda shook his head.

After another round of cruel laughter, Spaz was the first to speak, "Well, you are an inept goof. That's how chosen ones are in the beginning, but I believe that we can come up with something less on-the-nose."

Pope cracked a smile. "Yeah, The One would be kind of fitting in that respect, but I was leaning more toward Fubar. It works, whether he works out or not."

Asphyxia raised her hand. "Fubar seconded!"

The twins raised their hands and shouted, "Fubar!"

Spaz and Hedorah nodded.

Scarlet tousled his greasy hair and grinned in his ear. "Aww, my little Fubar. I like it."

"My name is Max. Wouldn't Maximum Modulus be more fitting?"

Pope got a mischievous look in his eyes. "Max does have a point. Let's take another vote, shall we?"

Hedorah glowered over his bowl of rice. "If I'm not Maximum Modulus, nobody is. Do you even know what it means?"

Judging by their expressions Pope and Hedorah had some sort of rivalry going on. Everyone said Fubar in unison.

Pope smiled with the grace of the frequently defeated. "Fubar it is. Well, Fubar, grab yourself some cold Chinese. Have you given any thought as to your plan of action? We don't expect you to do anything yet, but it would be helpful if you had some idea of where you would like to start."

"I have to plan everything?"

"No, but we all more or less run our own show around here. We work together as needed, but retain complete control over our project. Would you rather be a puppet controlled by the whims of strangers?"

Max pulled out the card the Count had given him the day before, "There is this. It might be helpful."

"What is it?" Spaz jerked the card out of his hand. "How fortunate, he already has an in with the Order of the Owl."

Max snatched the card back and asked, "Some goofy, pretentious, magician-looking motherfucker gave me this and said I was going to be famous. I don't want to be famous, but I guess it would help me to sway public opinion or whatever. What the hell is the Order of the Owl?"

Pope set down his plate and assumed his 'I'm going to be long-winded and boring now' posture. "The Order of the Owl is a secret society masquerading as a publicity firm that's masquerading as a secret society. On the surface, they seem to be a bunch of ass hats, but they employ the kind of sleazy birthday-party-magician sleight-of-hand that gets the job done. They have a massive amount of power and connections, but you should know their history before getting involved with them."

Max half-listened while heaping various candied meats onto a paper plate.

"The Order was founded in 1984 by a group of inept entertainers who were struggling in the seedy underbelly of New York's entertainment industry. Tired of failing, they worked together to change what people perceived as good entertainment. By suppressing the acts with talent and promoting the crap, they eventually convinced the public that crap was what they wanted."

Pope nibbled a nugget from his poo-poo platter. "The entertainment community was so flooded with hacks that people thought bad performances were a bold new style of comedy. They laughed at jokes because they weren't funny. What was amazingly bad was now so bad it's amazing. It was a brilliant marketing coup.

"The Order made a deal with the thirteen families to forward their agenda of commercializing art completely. Everyone started writing jingles instead of songs and incorporating commercial art into their comedy. Now there's nothing else on the market. The Order single-handedly murdered art."

"That explains a lot." He comforted himself with a mouthful of squid salad.

"On the upside, all the good old stuff is public domain now that nobody wants it. We have a massive P2P archive for anyone interested. It's legal as long as nobody logs in with a Popsy Cola jingle on their hard drive."

Max glanced over at the cache of weapons. "Yeah, wouldn't want to break the law."

"You should keep all this in mind when dealing with the Order. They completely control the Media©. The Iiites mostly control them. They undoubtedly want to groom you into a salesperson before you turn into an activist. Why not use your fifteen-minute flash in the pan to shove more of their crap down the public's throats, right?"

Max shrugged. It sounded like a good idea.

Pope swigged his milk. "The dumber you come off, the more they'll support you. If you seem to have a mind of your own, they'll feel threatened and shut you out.

"I see that look. Don't try to use them to make yourself useless to us. The Iiites will kill you as soon as you're unprotected."

Max twirled up a big ball of Lo Mein and stuffed it in his mouth.

"Write some speeches and practice them in front of a mirror to make sure you don't deliver them too well. Also, think about how to put your proposal to the Order so they will approve anti-Iiite propaganda. It shouldn't be too hard. Killing Iiites is what you're famous for.

"Plan on contacting the Order and putting your plans into effect this time next week. We will stay in contact with you throughout the process. Let us know if you need anything."

I'm not doing any of that. "Where am I staying, anyway?" Max asked around a mouthful of sesame chicken.

"Have you ever heard of Rusty Nails?"

"No."

"My uncle Rusty has a nail salon with a big apartment upstairs. He's agreed to let you use it for as long as you need to. He's not affiliated with the Riot Nrrds in any way, so you should be safe as long as you stay in the apartment. The Order will provide security when you make appearances, but we will take you to the rendezvous point and smuggle you back out.

Hedorah pointed at Max with his chopsticks. "Do not let them know where you live. Iiites have spies everywhere."

"That makes me feel real safe."

Pope shook his head. "Never feel safe. It'll get you killed. Let us know before you do anything. We'll try to give you all the information you need, but it would take years to fill you in on everything."

Scarlet set her chow mein in her lap. "What about me? Am I going to be stuck in an apartment until this is over?"

"That's up to you. You would be safer in hiding, but a strong, likable woman standing behind him would make him seem more mature and broaden his market. Some people have trouble accepting a leader who can't net a girlfriend."

Asphyxia winced at the misogyny. "You don't have to be his Jackie O. We have a really broad approach, so it'll be easy to fit you into whatever role you're comfortable with."

Hedorah whispered loudly to Scarlet. "Be careful what this broad tries to fit you in. She's hot, but she has the VD."

Spaz shook his head. "Feelgood cured that a few months ago."

Asphyxia frowned and threw a soy sauce packet at Spaz. "Excuse them. They were raised by a pack of feral 12-year-olds." Her smile was vaguely flirtatious. "So, what are you good at?"

"I don't know. I used to make my toys out of yarn and bent up hangers."

Asphyxia waited for a few moments to see if Scarlet was joking. "So, engineering?"

"I'll think about it."

"We'll figure it out later."

"Definitely. So, what's my code name going to be?"

The group pondered the question in silence for a few moments before Hedorah spoke up. "Heinlein's Lugubrious Phantom? Or HLP for short?"

Pope looked jealous. "I like it, but how about Phantom, for short. It has a nice ominous feel to it, and it sounds better than HLP in casual conversation. Hey, HLP, would you like to help me solve the Schleingensief Paradox? Hey, Phantom, would you like to help me solve the Schleingensief Paradox? See, it flows better."

"Agreed. All in favor of Phantom?"

Everyone except Max and Scarlet raised their hands in the Vulcan' live long and prosper' gesture.

It was decided.

Pope took Scarlet's hand and kissed it. "I dub thee Phantom."

She socked him in the nose then leaned back in the overstuffed position.

Hedorah laughed. "Man, you've got less game than a syphilitic tree stump."

Pope twisted napkins into his bleeding nostrils. "This is why chivalry is dead."

Asphyxia set her plate down. "Aww, I think Cakey wants a code name, too."

Pope ignored the expectant look on Cakey's face. "Mascots don't need code names."

Cakey growled, but Max calmed him with scritches. "No need to take your emasculation out on Cakey. He's the biggest badass in this room. Don't make him show you."

"Well, if you guys are finished eating, we should be on our way. Rusty's expecting us."

"I guess I'm good." Max tossed his plate in the big garbage can behind him and stood.

Scarlet reached for his hand, and he helped her up.

Having filled their quota for human contact, the Nrrds scattered to their workstations. No one bothered to throw the cartons away. No one said goodbye as Fubar and Phantom passed through the secret doorway into the parking lot. No one noticed the tears in Cakey's eyes as he moped behind them.

A VIEW TO A SPILL

The façade of Rusty Nails was a jumble of antique iconography overgrown with tangles of iron latticework and glittery barbed wire. Vintage industrial music seeped out through the cracks. Max stood at the edge of the sidewalk, waiting for the uneasy feeling in his stomach to abate.

"Who the fuck buys antique church doors and covers them with glitter?"

Cakey shrugged his eyes apathetically. He'd been downright Emo since Max had put him in the carrier.

"This place looks awesome." Scarlet opened the door, releasing a cloud of hairspray and acetone.

Max followed her inside, trying not to gag. Years of huffing freon had conditioned his lungs to breath just about anything, but he could feel his brain cells trying to hide under piles of their dead compatriots. A warm blanket of fog draped over his mind as he breathed in deep.

Nothing like a chemical lobotomy after a long day, or a short one. Oh God, it's still early.

The front room looked like what you'd get if you tossed a black cat and a rainbow into a woodchipper. The left and right walls were hung with large broken mirrors and lined with swiveling chairs where hair was being sculpted into figments from Georges Braque's nightmares. The center was a labyrinth of steampunk hairdryers and gypsiesque manicurists who were painting tarot readings onto people's nails. There was a standing sign to the right announcing 25% off bad news.

A drag queen spotted them in the doorway and smiled. The candy canes protruding from his enormous crayon-red wig scraped the ceiling as he wound his way towards them, arms outstretched in an exaggerated pantomime of salutation.

"Welcome, welcome to Rusty Nails. Do you have an appointment?" He shot Max a look that said, You must be the loser boyfriend who will be paying. He noticed Cakey and fell to his knees, baby-talking.

Max was impressed. It must have taken years to develop the poise necessary to move quickly in a four-foot wig. "We have an appointment with Rusty for a Julia set."

The stylist withdrew his fingers from the carrier and cocked his head. "Oh, um, I'm not familiar with that one. I'll be right back." He strode over to the co-worker in the peach, bouffant hairpiece and held his hand so Max couldn't read his lips. After a few seconds, they both glanced over and giggled.

Max shielded his lips with his hand and whispered to Scarlet. "There sure are a lot of wigs for a place that cuts hair."

She arched her eyebrows.

A short, gothic teenager walked up. "Can I help you?" He asked as though he'd caught Max peeping in his bathroom window. He wore nipple shields on the outside of his fishnet-shirt and a pink armband with a black X on it.

This time Scarlet tried her luck. "Yeah, we're here for a Julia set. I was told to ask for Rusty."

The kid tongued his lip ring knowingly. "Kinky."

Max wasn't sure he wanted to know what this guy thought was kinky. "A dude named Pope sent us."

He busted out laughing. "God, the look on your face. Follow me. There's no need to shit yourself, unless that's your thing."

He led them around the manicurists and past the tattoo stations to a beaded curtain, then pulled it back to reveal two topless men standing chest to chest in a small kitchen. The buff one was wearing leather chaps, a Nazi officer's cap, and a couple bottles of baby oil. The pudgy one wore a maroon codpiece, a pirate hat with cherries, and too much makeup. They were going back and forth, tugging on each other's nipples, saying, "Who's a hunky donkey?" To which the other would bashfully reply, "I'm a hunky donkey."

It had been years since homophobia had been anything more than a sad footnote in the history books, but Max felt an emotional wormhole opening to suck him back to the nineteen-fifties. They must have enjoyed having an audience because they repeated the ritual eight times before acknowledging their guests.

Suddenly the chubby one turned and gaily inquired, "And who is this hunky donkey?"

The buff man looked as though he might cry as he pushed past and disappeared behind a velvet curtain beside the stairway to their left. Max's mind went momentarily out of order. Mallowy freak or not, he didn't want to offend the man who was possibly saving his life. Luckily his fear of making a bad impression released a wave of adrenaline, which kick-started his brain and reestablished the link between it and his lips.

Forcing a smile, he replied, "I'm Max. I'm a friend of your nephew. He told me to ask for the Julia set."

"Of course, I should have known. Please follow me to the boudoir." Rusty winked. His four-inch prosthetic eyelash stirred the air like a naughty eunuch, blushing Max's cheek with a kiss of wind. Scarlet giggled at Max's terror-stricken expression and playfully pushed him up the stairs.

At the top was a hallway with five doors. Starting with the farthest, Rusty pointed to each one, saying, "Storage, den, bathroom, fuck palace, your room." Rusty opened the door to their right. "Where is little Orville, anyway? I thought he would be with you."

Scarlet gasped at the tawdry cluster-fuck. "Wow, this place is kick-ass! Where did you get all this stuff?"

Max was afraid any comments about his new home would come out sounding sarcastic. "He's parking the car."

"Oh, I'm so happy you like it. We're going to have so much fun. I just love having guests. The Nrrds sent your stuff over earlier. It's all in the closet, the armoire, or the dresser. There are fresh toothbrushes and plenty of toiletries in the bathroom down the hall. If there's anything else you need, just let me know."

Max looked over the eccentric jumble of clowns, religious iconography, gay-porn, crypto-taxidermy, and black lace and tried to imagine why anyone would want to surround himself with so much cheesy garbage. The wall opposite the bed sported a huge airbrushed painting of Rusty hanging from a cross, sporting a massive erection. A little plaque on the bottom read, "Heavenly Host."

That's the first thing I'll see every morning for the foreseeable future. Yay.

He was too high on fumes to actually care about the décor, but the people worried him. He liked to be left alone, and Rusty was chatty. All the drag queens he'd known were boring, catty gossips, or organ thieves, and this place was crawling with them. It would be hard to maintain his curmudgeonly persona without seeming like a complete asshole.

Overly friendly people had a tendency to misinterpret his antisocial behavior as personal dislike. Max always tried to explain that he was merely misanthropic, but that always led to a definition of misanthropy, which rarely won him any friends. Because of this tendency, he found it easier to get along with assholes, which eventually led him to withdraw from society altogether. As he stood staring at an antique gas-powered fuck-bench, one thought echoed around in the cavern of his mind. This is what I get for leaving the house.

Pope bounded up the steps, puffing his inhaler as he went. "Sorry, no parking."

"Orville!" Rusty gave him a big hug. "It's been too long. Why don't you ever come to visit me? I was starting to think you didn't love me anymore."

Pope twisted his face out of Rusty's rubbery bosom and apologized, "Sorry, I've been kind of busy trying to save the world."

"Well, you don't have an excuse anymore. I have your pet Rambo right here, and anyone who wants him will have to get through me first, including you." Rusty laughed jovially and gave Pope's head another squeeze before letting him go.

"Well, I'm sure you kids have lots of secret plans to discuss and code words to code, so I'll leave you to it." He walked towards the door, then stopped and turned. "Oh, I should go over the rules real quick before I go. There aren't many, but they are firm. One: this isn't a sleazy motel, it's a sleazy nail boutique, so clean whatever you cum on. Two: don't break any of my stuff. Many of these things are one-of-a-kind and irreplaceable. I'm very materialistic, so all broken items will be forced through your digestive tract backwards. Three: I'm hell to live with, but I own the place, so you have to put up with me. And four: absolutely no pets. I don't know what that thing is, but honey, it has to go. The last thing I need is some wriggly thing pissing all over my stuff."

Max turned to Pope. "What the fuck, man?"

Pope shrugged.

Rusty cracked a big smile and chortled. "I'm just fuckin' with you. I love big wriggly things that piss all over my stuff."

"I went out earlier and bought enough snack cakes to build a house. Do you think he'd like one now?"

"Thanks, but he just ate."

"Alrighty then. I'll pop my head in later to see you need anything. Play nice now." Rusty backed out the door and closed it gently.

Pope motioned for Max and Scarlet to take a seat on the bed. "Actually, I can't stick around. Let us know when you come up with a plan. We need to get things rolling as soon as possible."

"I'll get right on that."

"You should be safe here as long as you stay inside and keep us informed. Deviate from that, and you'll probably die. Do you understand?"

Max nodded.

"I need you to say you understand that. It's important."

"I get it. I'm stuck here until I've saved the world."

"Good. Enjoy tonight. It's probably the last peaceful night you'll see for a long time. There are several pressing matters to which I must attend, so I'm going to head out."

"Cool, later." Scarlet flopped backward into the squishy folds of the purring black Bio-Bed.

Pope nodded and slipped out with the nonchalance of a roommate.

Finally alone, Max threw his leg over Scarlet and squeezed her tight. "Well, agent Phantom, you heard the man. We should enjoy ourselves while we can."

"Sir, yes, sir." She pulled his head back and bit his cheek.

The pain tripped his floodgates of adrenaline and testosterone. He made a face like a bat, and ripped her clothes off, flinging them in all directions. By some miracle, the only thing knocked over was an eight-inch framed photograph of a fat, nude, Korean Elvis impersonator with a stain of greasy lips in the bottom right corner.

While the ecstasy of flesh on flesh momentarily delivered Max and Scarlet from their circumstances, Cakey languished in his carrier.

Forgotten once again, the toilet in the bathroom of his mind began to bubble and overflow with thick, chunky rage. It pooled and spread across the floor, seeping through to spoil the rooms below. The walls were bleeding. The drains bubbled, and soon the furniture was stained with the acrid stench of hate. With damage this extensive, it was unlikely the full equity would ever be regained.

✶✶✶✶✶

Max woke to the sound of Rusty's distant cursing. The sun glaring through the gap in the curtains had the confident glow of early afternoon.

He groaned and buried his face in the pillow.

The torrent of profanity stopped just long enough for him to slip halfway back into his dream, then grumbled closer, accompanied by the clomping of angry feet.

The wall by the door had a cock-themed clock with swinging balls. It had dicks for hands and buttholes in place of numbers, so it took a few seconds to register that it was 10 A.M.

Max tensed. He had a moral conviction that waking a person before noon constituted assault. He considered pushing Rusty back down the stairs in self-defense.

The door slammed open, almost rattling the clock off the wall as Rusty burst in. He stomped and crossed his arms. "Okay, fuckers, time to get up. I need my beauty sleep." His wife-beater and Speedo cutoffs accentuated the withering lump of his morning erection.

Typically, Max would have responded with threats and projectiles, but Rusty was too adorable to hate with his mud-mask, and giant, plushy house shoes shaped like high heels. Max wanted to call him a cantankerous fruit but figured it was early in their relationship for jovial name-calling. "Dude, it's early as fuck."

Rusty kept getting louder. "Get up, get up, get up, get up."

"Fuck off."

Rusty stalked toward him. "I want to go back to bed, goddammit!"

"Me too! Let's both do that."

"It's too early for this shit!"

"Exactly!"

Rusty's lower jaw jutted out, further crumbling the mud around his mouth. "Orville just called and said you need to get your shit together. I can't kill him because he's family, but you are fair game. Up now, or I'm gonna take my morning piss on your face and charge you to have the bed cleaned."

"Fine." Max sat up, swung his feet to the floor, and rested his face in his palms. "I'm up."

"Nope. I know that trick. I do that trick. Now, get the fuck up."

Max forced himself up and balanced precariously on his feet until Rusty was satisfied.

Rusty left the room, grumbling, "Stay away from that bed. You have work to do, or something. I'm going back to sleep."

Max sat down next to Scarlet and gently squeezed her ass. She groaned and dug deeper under the covers, mumbling, "Five more minutes. Sleepy."

"Cute. I'll come back when I've got this spy shit out of the way."

He ground his palms into his eyes and spoke in tongues, but nothing changed. The air still stank of acetone, the odd glow of morning played lightly on the faces of clowns and crucifixes, and somewhere out there were a bunch of terrorists who expected him to do the impossible.

How the fuck did this happen?

On his way to the door, he noticed Cakey snoring loudly in his cage. He was curled up using his body as a pillow. His mouth hung open, dribbling little rivulets through the valleys in his side. He looked so peaceful, so adorably ridiculous with his big, wet tongue draped over those horrific little teeth. It was too perfect to exist in this world.

Max opened the door and gently traced the folds of his flab with an index finger. Cakey rolled over with the sweet surprise of a one-night stand who'd expected to be expelled the night before.

"Hey, buddy." He scooped Cakey up and kissed him on the forehead. Cakey stretched, vibrated for a few seconds, then sneezed in his face.

"Gah!" Max spat on the floor and wiped his mouth on his shoulders. "Fuck you too, man. So rude."

Cakey nuzzled his face in Max's armpit. He was heavier than usual, firmer.

Max snuggled him tight and rubbed his little earlike thingies. He held Cakey up and buried his face in tender lumplings. This was the gooey center of his emotional succor. How could this sensation exist in a world so packed with fuckery?

Cakey squirmed a little like he wanted to be let down.

"What? You're hungry? Let's go get some breakfast."

Of course, Cakey was hungry. Max and Scarlet had fucked each other unconscious and forgot to feed him.

Cakey stared hatefully over Max's shoulder at the woman who had replaced him in Max's heart. Max would only pay him attention when Scarlet was unavailable. Still, Cakey decided it was better to have the crumbs of Max's affection than nothing at all.

Yawning, Max carried Cakey down the stairs and found the bag of snack cakes sitting on the antique redwood median. He piled five red velvet bars on the black marble countertop and let Cakey gorge himself.

"I wonder if Rusty has anything for me. I need meat." He ransacked the kitchen in search of something edible. The navy-blue cabinets were packed with every spice, sauce, and garnish known to man. The refrigerator was full of white wine, beer, sauces, salsa, and cheese, but no meat or legitimate sides.

"How is it possible to have so much food and nothing to eat?" He closed the door of the last cabinet and unwrapped a chocolate cupcake. He'd loved them as a child, but nostalgia tasted like fat and chemicals.

His grandmother used to bring him a family pack every time she came to visit. Eventually, he got fat, which got him bullied, which led to a general dislike of people. Being a loner, he wasn't shaped by the same experiences as the other kids. Being weird and fat got him bullied more and created a feedback loop of negative social interaction, plunging him ever deeper into a rage-filled mental cesspit. He'd never thought about it before, but snack cakes had probably played a bigger role in his early development than any other factor in his young life.

"Dammit, Nana."

The sticky brown paste slid down his esophagus and coated his stomach like wax. He could feel the chemicals radiating out of it, seeping into his blood, poisoning his cells. He set the remainder in front of Cakey. At least his appetite was gone.

"I guess I should get this over with." He pulled out his phone and dialed the number on Greystoke's card.

A woman answered. "Greystoke Enterprises. Hold, please." Her voice was replaced by soft muzik compelling him to take advantage of the Free Hot Wax Fridays at Handy Dan's Mega Wash. "He's your friend when you need a hand."

Max thought of the friendly Iiite they used as a mascot and wondered if he might be giving himself up to the enemy. All this cloak and dagger shit was making him paranoid.

The jingle was interrupted by a different woman. "Greystoke Enterprises. How may I direct your call?"

"This is Max Quick. I'm calling for Vlad."

She whispered, "Never call him that."

"Okay, is he around?"

"One moment, please."

The jingle returned.

Max sighed and hoisted himself onto the marble countertop so he could rest his head on Cakey. Cakey was a great pillow, and the smooth stone was oddly comfortable. He was afraid he might doze off before his call was connected.

Greystoke answered. "Mister Quick, how are you? Healing well?" His voice was full of self-satisfaction.

"Well enough. Sorry about yesterday. It was a bad time."

"I completely understand. I hope you'll forgive me for the intrusion. Strike while the iron is hot and all that."

"I get it."

"I take it you've reconsidered?"

"I'm willing to listen to your pitch."

"I pitched to you yesterday. If you want fame and fortune, we can provide it. If not, I have other calls."

"Fine, I'll do it. I just need to know how it works."

"We will see how you do and the press conference and go from there. Ultimately the plan is to market you as a plainclothes superhero, someone inspirational but relatable."

"I'm neither. What else you got?"

Greystoke laughed. "Just be at Igor Stanislavski Commemorative Park tomorrow at noon and stick to the script. There will be seven major TV networks and twenty-five periodicals in attendance. The masses will come slavering like pigs to a trough."

Max never felt more like slop. "That's a nice image."

"The public is going to eat you up."

"Or eat me alive."

"There's no need to be nervous. I have an embarrassing amount of experience with these things."

"That's not what I mean. The Iiites are apparently trying to kill me. I'm a little worried about dying."

"No need to worry. We have a contract with I-Squad. If you die on stage, it won't be from a bullet."

"That's cool, but I'd be more comfortable if my guys were there too."

Cakey licked the creme filling from his lips and bumped Max's phone with his head to get his attention. Max rubbed his knuckles on the bottom of Cakey's chin while he waited for a response.

Greystoke asked, "You have people?"

"You heard of the Riot Nrrds?"

"Oh, god."

"I know what you mean. They're annoying, but I'll take all the protection I can get."

"The Nrrds are Media© poison. Everyone hates them, and for good reason."

"I'm not saying put them on camera. I just want them there for supplemental security. It's a sticking point. Just say, yes."

"That is a terrible idea."

"Probably, but I've made up my mind."

Greystoke's smirk was audible. "You will give up everything if we don't humor you?"

"Man, I'm not taking any risks I don't have to. These guys have tech and intel. I want them there. That's it."

Greystoke snorted. "Very well. It will be amusing to see how I-Squad reacts. There may be another show here, a gameshow where viewers bet on when you will die and which of your security teams will be responsible."

"We're not doing that."

Greystoke laughed. "The hell we're not. This is a much better concept than the one we had."

"Dude, if you kill me for ratings, I will haunt you in the most embarrassing ways imaginable. I'll float around you, making fart noises all day every day until you die."

"What a wonderful idea for a sitcom. I've already thought of two seasons of material."

"Focus."

"On a more serious note, professionals are accustomed to a degree of respect. I know how I would react if you demanded I work with an amateur publicist. You should consider the long-term effects that this offense might have. If everything goes swimmingly and the Nrrds get whatever it is they want, they will move on. I-Squad will be there as long as we pay them."

"Good point, but I-Squad will have to get over it."

"Very well, I'll make the arrangements. There are a number of documents you will need to sign before the conference. Is this a good number to send them to?"

"Yeah."

Max's phone beeped.

"Got 'em."

"Excellent! It's all standard. For your convenience, there is a link at the beginning of each document that will take you to the place you need to sign. Is there anything else?"

"No, I'll let you know if anything comes up."

"I look forward to your debut. Good day."

Max lay his phone on the counter and rubbed his burning eyelids. Cakey nuzzled him and licked his face until he sat up.

Max knew he should look over the documents, but it was too early in the morning to sign away his soul. He could go back to bed, but this was the first time he's had alone with Cakey for several days, weeks if he counted the coma. Cakey-time was infinitely more seductive than anything upstairs.

Scarlet thought his relationship with Cakey was unnaturally intense and a little creepy. He always felt goofy and lame when he showed Cakey affection in front of her. It was nice to relax and have fun the way they used to.

He felt terrible for resenting her. She was a really good person. He cared deeply for her, but it wasn't love. He knew he should end it before they got codependent and ended up with a gaggle of children. But how could he dump a hot nympho who'd risked her life to help him? It would be insane and make him the biggest asshole in the history of boyfriends. In lieu of Cupid's arrows, fate had bound them together with barbed wire.

Max jiggled Cakey's blubber lumps to get him excited. "Want to go explore? There's no telling what crazy shit they have around here."

Cakey went wild, wagging his butt and squeaking happily. Together they frolicked through the empty boutique rummaging through the drawers, trying on the wigs, spinning in the chairs, grinning, and laughing like crazed children.

Max appreciated the opportunity to break character and embrace his silly maniacal side. Scarlet was far too gothic to tolerate such behavior. He half-worried half-hoped she would walk in on their frivolity and leave him because of it.

Hours passed before the newness of their playground wore away. When their energy was running out, Cakey unearthed a gargoyle chess set and insisted they play.

"Can't I just concede? You always win, anyway."

Cakey hung out his tongue, panting expectantly.

"One of these days I'm going to swap you for a dog. They're less needy." He brought the board to the kitchen table and took a seat.

Forty-five minutes later, he was ready to throw his king out the window. "I'm just going to say it. One of these days, you need to let me win, so I'll have some tiny amount of hope or self-respect. Damn. This is really hard on my ego."

Cakey was setting up for another game when the telephone rang. It was now two o'clock, and Pope was annoyed he hadn't checked in. "What part of keep me updated do you not understand?"

"Chill, it's okay. I set up a news conference for tomorrow. There's nothing else to do right now."

"No, jackass, we need to know what's going on, before it is going on. Information is our best weapon, so stop being a douche bag and keep me in the loop."

"Fine, sorry."

"Today was a test. I knew what you were going to do, so I pricked up my ears in the Order. I found out the information has already been leaked to K-Squad and the Iiites, and both are planning to take you out tomorrow. If I hadn't known what you were planning to do, you would probably have died tomorrow and taken a few of us with you. It's time to grow up and start taking shit seriously."

"Somebody's got their grumpy pants on."

"You made my pants grumpy when you fucked up. That being said, I apologize if I seem overly harsh. The alertness drug I'm testing makes me feel like my brain is going to shoot out through my eyes. It does the job, though. I've invented three things today.

"Granted, none of them are practical. Maybe the ray gun. It uses microwaves to make people itchy. It might be a good torture device. The Riot Nrrds are all opposed to torture because the surrendered information is rarely reliable. So, I don't know. What are you going to say at the conference?"

Max had been doing all he could not to think about it. "Haven't we already gone over this?"

"But have you written anything yet?"

"The public is rarely moved by scripted speeches. They're moved by emotion, and emotion can't be practiced. It'll come off as a lot more authentic if it's on the spot."

"True. Maybe you will be better at this than I had initially estimated. Anyway, I have shit to do. If anything comes up, let me know, or I'll make you itchy. Agreed?"

"Yeah, sure. Sorry about that. I didn't think it mattered."

"Well, it does."

"Now, I know."

"Indeed, you do. Goodbye."

"Toodles." Max yawned and hung up the phone.

Max's stomach dropped when he heard a door creak in the other room. Scarlet wasn't awake to divert Rusty's torrential friendliness. It seemed like a good time to fix that, so he scooped Cakey into his arms and headed up the stairs.

For the first time ever, Cakey squirmed to get away. Being much stronger and more agile, Cakey quickly escaped and tore down the steps like he was fleeing from an ax-wielding maniac. At the bottom, he stopped and turned defiantly before climbing onto the table and reclaiming his spot by the chessboard.

"Come on, I'm tired of chess." Max made his way back down. "Maybe Scarlet will play with you."

Cakey bristled upon hearing her name. He gazed intensely into Max's eyes and pushed the board a few inches towards him with his nose. Max approached the table but refused to sit.

"Maybe later, okay?"

Cakey nudged the board again, this time harder. The board slid halfway off the table and stopped just short of sending squadrons of tiny gargoyles plummeting to their deaths. Max worried rule number two was about to be broken, so he carefully lifted the board out of Cakey's reach.

Cakey hissed defiantly and stood up tall as if to say, "Don't even think about it?"

"That's adorable." Max set the board on the stove and started up the steps.

Cakey panicked, knowing Scarlet would soon be awake, and he would once again be stuffed in his cage to rot while the two of them indulged themselves for hours on end. He didn't understand. Max liked rolling around and cuddling with each of them, but never at the same time. Maybe he wouldn't have been so jealous if Max had let him join in, but he never did. He was sick of feeling like an old toy at the bottom of a closet.

Cakey scrambled up the stairs, but he was too late. Max was on the bed, leaning in for a kiss. Their morning ritual was already starting. Kisses would lead to heavy petting, clothes would be discarded, and the rest of the day would be spent grunting in each other's arms.

Cakey jumped onto the bed and tried to get between them, but as usual, Max pushed him away.

Scarlet woke up, giggling. She grabbed Cakey and kissed him good morning.

Cakey jerked free and growled, baring his teeth.

Max sat next to Scarlet. "Aww, pissy little baby."

Cakey jumped between them and flailed so hard he knocked Max off the bed.

The cuteness of his tenacity faded quickly. The Bio-Bed growled and farted foully beneath them as they struggled to wrangle him.

"Fine! Come here, you're going back in the carrier. I'll let you out when you're ready to behave."

Max dove for him, but Cakey narrowly escaped by climbing the wall, leaving a trail of sucker holes along the length of a vintage Bauhaus poster.

As far as Cakey was concerned, Scarlet had declared war on him. In times of war, anything is permissible, even going against the wishes of a friend. He skittered along the ceiling until he was directly above Scarlet's giggling head.

Max tried to snatch him down, but Cakey maneuvered out of reach. For all his efforts, he only succeeded in trampling his lover and evoking the most insistent growl he had ever heard from a feline. He saw Cakey look him in the eye, almost apologetically, before dropping suddenly onto his lover's face.

It took him a few seconds to comprehend what was happening. He saw Cakey fall, he heard Scarlet scream, and he saw the fur begin to mat with blood, but it didn't make sense. He almost laughed, thinking, I guess that's what it must have looked like when Cakey was on my head that time.

Scarlet's cries reached a crescendo as he tried to tear the little beast from her face. Max begged, hummed, and blinked, but Cakey wouldn't stop. In desperation, Max grabbed a large marble crucifix and swatted him in the butt.

Scarlet screamed like he's hit her in the face, which he sort-of had.

Cakey didn't let go, so Max hit him harder. Cakey dug in. Tears streamed down his face as he hissed with the ferocity of a wild beast. He was almost unrecognizable.

Max was getting scared Cakey might seriously hurt her. She was doing her best to remain still, but her sobs were gut-wrenching. Max swung again, this time in a panic.

As the cross glanced off, Jesus's hand wedged beneath the plastic window in his side and ripped it off like a Band-Aid. Cakey fell away and rolled off the bed, yelping and writhing like a skinned snake.

"Oh, fuck!"

Scarlet's face, once silky and dripping with sex, was now--gone, her emerald eyes reduced to gory craters left in the battlement of her skull. She gasped through bare teeth, trying futilely to speak despite the absence of vocal cords, lips, or a tongue. Her hands flailed wildly in search of her lover. Finally, catching hold of his shirt, she touched him tenderly on the chest and died.

Max made a pitiful noise of disbelief and began to cry. He turned to scream at Cakey but stopped short, vomiting instead. The hole in Cakey's stomach was oozing a generous assortment of exotic sweetmeats all over Rusty's oriental rug. Cakey tried to plug the hole by doubling over, but the agony of disembowelment triggered a convulsive fit, which emptied him out like a vigorously shaken can of soda.

"I'm so sorry! I love you. Please don't die." Max rushed over and tried to scoop Cakey's innards back inside, but the flimsy tissue shredded in his fingers. The writhing stopped. Cakey blinked at him one last time and died, his lips crusted with a weak smile of forgiveness.

"Fuck! Why did you do that?" Bawling like an Italian widow, Max buried his face in the husk. "You can't die. You're all I have!"

He sat up and snatched the big, curvy, sacrificial blade from the altar and commenced sawing the ass off of his little friend.

"What's all this racket? Some of us are trying to..." Rusty opened the door and planted one of his overstuffed kittens in a puddle of red and yellow bodily fluids. "Holy shit! What have you done to my guest room?" His head jerked around, trying to take it all in, finally coming to rest on Max and his knife, "What the fuck are you doing? Are you crazy? You're killing him." His knees landed in the entrails just as Max was lifting the hunk in his palms.

"I...I'm saving him." Max sputtered.

The severed lump lay in his hands like a flabby Cornish hen. He had almost given up hope when he felt the pinch of one little sucker taking hold. One by one, the suckers latched on, saturating his body and soul with tingly warmth. He knew the sensation was life flowing out of him, but this time he gave it willingly. He hugged the lump close as it grew, ignoring the confused whimpering of his host.

"Aah! It's growing! That's freaky! Somebody tell me what's going on." Rusty crawled backward until his back hit the dresser. Something slimy had tangled around his hand as it slid through the goo. At first, it looked like a swath of fabric. Upon closer inspection, he saw tiny hairs surrounding the hole that had caught his ring finger. He opened it up and screamed like a little girl.

Max had just finished birthing the bouncing baby cheekworm when Scarlet's face splatted across his own like a wet rag. The newborn snatched it in its teeth and tried to eat it. Max tried to get it away from him before he could swallow, but only got a cheek.

He imagined Cakey with a taste for human flesh, the trouble that would cause. If he had half of Cakey's appetite, there wouldn't be a living human left this time next year. Max was relieved when the adorable little critter made an ick face and spit up all over his shoulder.

Meanwhile, Rusty was shrieking so loud Max could barely hear the strange banging noises coming from below. After all of that, he had to calm someone else down. At least it stopped his brain from imploding.

"Calm the fuck down, geez" Max walked over to the dresser. "It's all over now."

"What's over?! This room is over, that's for sure. Is she dead?" Rusty looked over his shoulder at the ruined form of his houseguest.

"What do you think?" Max's eyes twitched at the ruins of his former lover and then quickly to the floor.

"Why did you do it? You two made a nice couple."

"I didn't do it. Cakey freaked out. I was trying to save her, and I accidentally bashed in his window. He died, but I grew a new one. See? I'm going to call him Cheeky."

Max held the baby out. Cheeky's cold, wet nose tickled Rusty's chin and made him giggle. Everything momentarily seemed all right. The three strangers now shared the most profound bond there is; a deep psychological scar.

Now that things were calming down, the banging became more noticeable. They heard it once. Twice. The third was followed by a crash and the cadence of a large man running through the house at top speed.

"Crap." Rusty sounded annoyed as he called to his lover, "It's okay, honey. I'm upstairs."

The beefy man from the day before burst through the door wearing nothing but a gimp hood and a broken leash around his neck. His muscles rippled as he shrieked through his fingertips and ran downstairs, mumbling through the thick leather ball-gag.

"What did he say?"

"He said, 'Oh my God, I'm calling the police.' Billy's such a drama queen. Let me go get him." Rusty grunted as he climbed to his feet.

Cheeky nuzzled Max's chin. He didn't seem to care that his father had just killed his mother. Max tried to block out his surroundings and focus on the sweet little creature in his lap. Cheeky looked a little more like him than Cakey had, thinner features, bluer eyes. The change was barely noticeable, but it made him wonder if cheekworms might eventually evolve to be humanoid.

He hoped Bio-Corp would never discover the cheekworm's reproductive process. This thought dragged him kicking and screaming into the reality that he was sitting in a puddle of his lover's blood; the same lover who had rescued her murderer only a couple of days before. He swore to keep his lovers at arm's length for their sake as well as Cheeky's.

He heard the slow, heavy thump of feet on stairs. Rusty and his partner emerged from the door, their arms full of cleaning supplies and their faces full of unease. Rusty was angry and his lover a bit scared, but both bore masks of resentful disgust. The worst wasn't over, but at least the beefy guy had put on some pants.

They searched for a dry spot to set the cleaning instruments, but there wasn't one. Rusty growled like a Pomeranian and dropped everything in the center of the floor. "Ugh, I am not cleaning this up. This may not have been your doing, but it is your fault. You are confined to your room until it looks the way it did before you came."

Max flicked his eyes at the bed again and gagged. Was Rusty really going to make him scrub his loved ones out of the carpet? He wasn't even sure it was possible. Not that it was fair to ask his host to help. He'd been enough of a burden to Rusty already.

Why can't Billy do it? He is a gimp.

"Incidentally, I called Orville for you. He said he would send a cleaner over to get the big stuff out of the way. You're welcome.

"He's not happy. I gather that he liked her and Cakey a lot more than he liked you. He said something about a horrible waste of an alias, whatever that means. Anywho, I'm going to watch my stories. Keep in

76

mind what I said about my stuff. If you break anything or if anything is permanently damaged, I'm going to let Billy here keep you as a pet. And let me tell you, if you think I'm kinky, well..."

Billy was terrified of Cheeky. He tossed a mop at Max's feet from across the room. Rusty looked at his anxious boy toy and shook his head, slightly ashamed.

"Okay, Billy, let's get you a little drinky-poo. I could use one myself."

Cheeky could smell Billy's fear from across the room, but he couldn't understand it. Because of genetic memory, he knew what happened, but he hadn't had anything to do with it. All he'd done since he was born was love and cuddle. Wanting to show the man he only wanted to be friends, he slowly slithered out of Max's arms and blinked his way over to him.

Billy shrieked and tried to scale the dresser for safety. Max could tell Cheeky was being friendly but feared for the safety of the artfully crafted Fiji mermaid, which hung halfway-off the dresser by one spindly little arm.

"Chill, man. He just wants to say hello. He won't hurt you. He's a newborn baby."

"I think he's hungry!" cried the panicking gimp as he leaped from the dresser onto the bed. He landed face-first in the hole where Scarlet's throat used to be and rolled over, wearing her head like an expensive Japanese hat. The scream coming from her mouth would have made any professional ventriloquist green with envy and nausea.

Rusty was the first to laugh. Seconds later, all three spectators were cackling uncontrollably.

Billy grabbed her hair and tried to pull himself free. Without a face to hold it on, her scalp peeled back like a hoodie. His screaming grew shriller as he pushed against her shoulders. The little band of flesh left around the bottom of her chin snapped, and with a sucking pop like a cartoon sound effect, his face was finally freed.

Billy glared around the room at his ecstatic audience as they howled and gasped for breath with bulging eyes and burning cheeks. "I hate you." He ran down the stairs screaming, "I hate all of you!"

The others were rendered impotent by fits of laughter. Any time it would die down, someone would remember the look on Billy's face and begin the cycle anew. Eventually, the glee was all used up, and the pain of their cramping faces overwhelmed the cycle of hilarity.

Rusty sat up and sighed. "We're all going to Hell. In the meantime, I have a lot of making up to do. You have fun with this." He stood and toddled out of the room.

Max's sadness swelled in his chest as he remembered he would spend the rest of the day scrubbing his lover out of the bed. Earlier, he'd thought about dumping her, now he'd have to figure out where to dump her body. The upside was she could now take her place on a special pedestal in the back of his mind to be ignored or venerated at his convenience.

Something felt off about those thoughts. They had the false ring of a catchphrase, like his brain was just spitting out words that sounded like something he would say.

She and Cakey were the best things to ever happen to him, and now they were dead. Why did he feel hopeful?

Cheeky crawled up in his lap and sneezed in his face. "Dammit, Cakey."

Cheeky's face sagged.

"Sorry Cheeky. I'm probably going to do that a lot."

Cheeky unrolled his long, forked tongue and licked the snot off Max's chin.

"You are disgusting, but I love you." Max gave him a big hug and took a deep breath of the freshly-laundered-baby smell.

Max felt like a part of him had died with his friends, but it was the part that used to feel dead. The rest of him felt more alive than he had in years. If Cakey could be reborn as Cheeky, maybe he could be reborn, too.

He had willingly sacrificed years of his life to bring another into the world. A year ago, that wouldn't have even occurred to him. It may have been for selfish reasons, but he felt good about it. He even began to look forward to saving the world from the Iiites.

A warm tingle wound up the base of his spine. It felt like the opposite of a pinched nerve.

Smiling at Cheeky, he picked up the mop and said, "You should go watch TV, try to forget all this happened."

Cheeky pulled a rag out of the bundle with his teeth, transferred it into his top right sucker, and made a scrubbing motion in the air.

"Thanks, but nobody should have to mop up their parent's goo. Are you sure?"

Cheeky bit Cakey's neck and flung him into the wastebasket.

That should have been unnerving, but looking into Cheeky's eyes, he could see Cakey looking back at him. A third of Cakey was still alive.

"Okay, then. Let's get to it."

YOU ONLY DIE TWICE

Max sat on a park bench, enjoying his falafel and his last few moments of anonymity. It was a rare day in the city, not too warm, not too cool, and the sky was set to yellow—the lowest terror alert in ages. Even the Media© Circus was beautiful and serene in its golden glow.

Too bad the yellow sky was a red herring. The powers that be wanted him lulled into a false sense of security before their attack. He watched the masses crawl over each other as they went about their business. Of the thousand or so people, he'd been warned that at least a third were spies or assassins. He was told to assume that they were all there to kill him.

Somehow he wasn't worried. It was a nice day. Even the laughter from the children at the dunking booth flitted across the soundscape as benignly as a kaleidoscope of butterflies.

Zombies were out in force as well, outnumbering the Nrrds two to one. They milled about gawking at the bright colors and sniffing at the FÜD stands as though some tiny part of them remembered the fun they'd had in the past. No one was sure why zombies were attracted to large gatherings. It had been postulated by a leader in the field that, since their nervous systems were entirely autonomic, they were naturally inclined to go with the flow of pedestrian traffic.

For every zombie security dragged away, four more would appear in their place. Zombies broke in lines, stared rudely, and their smell was diminishing FÜD sales, which legally constituted a menace to society. Some of the cops were losing patience. Max could hear them talking about the good old days when they could simply shoot them and haul away the bodies. They hated zombies almost as much as they hated the NAADP for securing them the right to pursue whatever life, liberty, and happiness they could without the benefit of will or intellect.

The park seemed greener than usual, like somebody had been messing with the contrast in his head. The stage would have looked better if they had put it there, but the rides had taken precedence. Instead, he would be making his first impression on the masses standing on a yellow plastic stage in front of the Media© Office, which towered over the surrounding buildings like a giant granite dildo. The buildings in this area were mismatched, like someone had taken downtown and yuppie-town and shuffled them together. Max had always wondered why, but not enough to ask his phone.

The stage was the least exciting thing there. It was a cheap pop up with mounted corporate flags as the only decoration. Most of these people didn't even know who was speaking. They came for the thrill of having something to do.

There were a lot of people, though.

It would have been terrifying if the crowd hadn't been more interested in the bouncy castle than him. Luckily the Ferris wheel, teacup ride, and cotton candy machine were all above his name on the marquees. For all his audience cared, he could read from the phonebook.

The crowd by the dunking booth erupted with applause as a ginger kid hit the target, liberating a thrashing convict from the enclosure by way of the chipper below. Everyone cheered as the hapless criminal sprayed over the line of waiting inmates.

Max chuckled and took a swig from his flask. Shoplifters.

Max hardly noticed the barker slide up beside him. "Salutations, Max! Are you ready for your big debut?"

Max crumpled the falafel wrapper and tossed it in a nearby trashcan. "Ready as I'll ever be." He shook the ice in his thirty-dollar margarita. He tried for one last sip, but there was none to be had. He tossed it in as well.

The barker handed him a list of names and notes on how they could be slipped into his speech. First was Brock Smashington, star of a long list of bad mid-budget action movies. Easy but humiliating. Second was Chaz Lightbeard, the prop comic whose magnificent chin had made him a big-shit political pundit. He was best known for his strong support of various PITA organizations, which somehow remained Media© darlings despite being violent fundamentalists. They'd lost a lot of support when PITA -4 came out in support of cannibalism, but they had enough money to last them until people stopped caring.

He crumpled it in his pocket without reading the rest. "I'll do what I can. When do we start?"

The barker nodded to a bearish man by the soundboard who whispered into the ear of another who pushed a button to change the jovial carnival muzik into the jarring dance beat of the Allbright toothpaste ad. Anchorman Walter Hannity, a.k.a. the Hann, stipulated it be played every time he appeared in public. It was his biggest hit and one of the only reminders of his previous career as a prominent rapper.

The walking forehead took the stage pumping his fist and screaming, "Yeeeeaaahhhhh! Han-dog's in the house y'all."

"God, I hate that guy."

The barker smiled. As they walked to the stage, he leaned in, saying. "That guy is going to be the next president." He winked and strutted back to his perch.

When the Han finished running around the stage, the sound guy backed the beats down a few decibels.

"Yeah, Yeah, Yeeeeaaahhhh! I'm back again, and I'm bringin' you the freshest new face in the history books. Y'all heard his name a lot a few weeks ago, but this the first time he actually gonna talk about what happened.

"Lest you forget, lemme bust a recap in yo ass. This boy did the impossible. He took out a whole crew of Lobsters by his self. Imagine that shit. This dude's just chilling in a store, right, and all a sudden, the wall blows up, and all these crazy-ass monsters run in and start rippin' everythin' to shit.

"Everybody else is just freakin' out, but this dude, Max, he says, "Fuck y'all, I'm tryin' to buy my ass a Halloween costume. Y'all done fucked-up now." Then this nigga kills every last one o'm with his bare hands.

"This year everybody gonna be goin' as him for Halloween. It's my great pleasure to introduce to you the great, the mighty, Max Motherfuckin' Quiiiiiiiiik."

Everyone clapped and cheered.

Bidding adieu to his self-respect, Max ran onto the stage, screaming like an idiot just as he had been instructed. It was what the masses demanded from a Media© personality.

No matter how hard he tried, he still sounded sarcastic.

"Yeah, thanks, everybody! Woooo!" he screamed over the toothpaste ad. The muzik stopped, and he almost lost himself in the sudden silence. He felt like the crowd might start hurling things at him any second.

Terror brought the feeling back to his lips. His scream had been pitiful, debasing, and short; like an orgasm he'd forced himself to have to end bad sex.

"Fuck the Iiites!" This time he sounded as raw and meaningful as a drill sergeant who had been accidentally shot in the nuts.

Yay for adrenaline.

"How's everybody doing tonight?! Y'all havin' fun?"

The crowd raised their beers and let out a mechanical, "Wooooo!"

"All right! I'm here to tell you about the most fucked-up thing that ever happened to me. It's some crazy shit. Y'all wanna hear it?"

The crowd went off again, adding half an exclamation point to their Wooooo! Some of them started recording video on their phones.

"So, let me start by saying I'm no Brock Smashington. I don't work out. Hell, I hardly ever go out. Fact is, I'm kind of a pussy. At least that's what I thought. All of a sudden, in that costume shop, I was in an action movie. Shit's blowing up, everybody's screaming, there's blood everywhere, and I see one of those fuckers coming at me. He was walking slow and confident, like he owned me, like he was just strolling over to fuck my head like a tiny dog, not because he wanted to, but because he could.

"Now, I don't know about you guys, but I'm sick of all this terrorist shit. I want to be able to go out and have a good time without some asshole trying to blow me up or tear my head off. Time kind of stopped, and I thought to myself, 'am I going to die like a little bitch, or am I going to nut up and take some of these bastards with me?' I thought of Chaz Lightbeard, how he gave up a successful career as a comic to fight for what he believes in. That shit's powerful. If I was going to die, I wasn't going to make it easy.

"I said, 'Fuck you, you Lobster piece of shit,' and Pow! I rammed a mannequin stand through his head. I'm not gonna lie. I was shocked as shit that it worked. Holding that bloody pole, I felt more alive than I had in years! Do ya hear me, people? I was alive! Fuck being a victim!"

The crowd cheered and whooped and pumped their fists. A couple of drunk girls flashed their breasts. As the cameras turned on them, they seemed to forget what they were doing. Their blank stares returned before they had a chance to roll their shirts back down.

The blond threw up on the brunette. Neither seemed to notice.

Max had seen them shotgunning malt liquor behind the port-o-lettes earlier. He had done the same thing at their age, but he never thought to appear naked in front of the Media© covered in vomit. A few Order initiates were already breaking cover to offer them contracts.

He continued, "I have a crucial message for you. Listen closely to what I'm about to say. The Iiites are a bunch of little bitches. You don't have to be afraid of them. If I can kill a whole squad of them by myself with a metal stick, you can beat them too. If you see them starting some shit, don't run away. Run towards them and kick their asses back to the fucking sewers."

Their ferocious screams were pouring energy into him. He wondered if this was how Hitler felt his first time. God, I'm not being Hitler, am I? Crap, I kind of am.

The ghost of Hitler executed his buzz. Luckily the crowd was too frothy to notice. "Everybody who ran away was chased down and killed. I fought back. I'm alive. Think about it."

He felt terrible leaving Cakey out of the story, but some higher-ups had decided it would be best. It wouldn't be good for his image if he choked up on live TV admitting he'd killed his adorable pet, so he put it out of his mind and stuck to the plan.

"Now I'm not the only one that's stood up to them. I know they've gotten a lot of bad press, but the Riot Nrrds are leading the fight against the Iiites. So stop givin' them shit. I don't even think they're responsible for all the stuff that's been pinned on them. Have you ever seen any actual video of them doing any terrorist stuff? I haven't. Weird right? There's video of everything."

The crowd screamed louder and began to mosh.

Wow, I'm doing really well.

Max squinted deep into the reddening thrall and saw zombies treating his audience like an all you can eat buffet. Pursued by slavering zombies, they rushed the stage, trampling security and each other as they tried to scramble to safety. Max braced himself against the podium as the stage lurched down the street, propelled by the crush of fleeing fans.

"Fucking lightweight plastic stage!" He turned to the Hann and asked, "What the fuck happened?"

"Probably all that shit about the Riot Nrrds. Everybody hates those mo'fuckers."

One of the fans almost made it onto the stage. Max moved to help, but a flag fell from its mount and knocked her back into the mob.

The Han sucked his teeth. "See, never get political."

"This piece of shit's about to tip over. Any ideas?"

"I was a mo'fuckin' scout. My contract covers everything, and I mean everything." He opened the door at the bottom of the podium, pulled a yellow jetpack.

"Cool! Would you pass—" Max stared into the empty compartment.

Han rocketed into the inappropriately cheery sky.

"Fuck you, too!" Max flipped him off with both hands.

Where was all that security he'd been promised? It had been almost a minute since the carnage started, and the ride was getting rougher by the second. If he didn't get off this stage soon, he would end up on the wrong side of a zombie's intestinal wall.

The stage was nearing a building with a rooftop low enough that he might be able to jump to it from the rail. Help had to be on the way. He had been carried away by a zombie attack on live television. Surely the Order was scrambling to save their new cash cow. Or, maybe, they were enjoying the ratings boost. They might even be behind the attack.

He could hear Greystoke encouraging him to be true to his image. "Jump into the fray and heroically bash a path to freedom."

There was no point, though. His audience was dying, and the cameras weren't on him. Then again, Greystoke mentioned hidden cameras. This could be a live-stream event.

The cheap plastic structure continued its bumpy grind toward the rooftop, but a side-street relieved a bit of pressure, causing the course to drift. One of the legs was now on a collision course with a potted tree.

At the rate the stage was moving, he had about a minute to climb to the roof before the stage would flip and scrape him off like an unwanted condiment. He pulled out his trusty hammer and put it between his teeth, just in case.

Max steadied himself on Handy Dan's corporate flag as he climbed the rail. When he was as close as he was going to get, he launched himself at the wall and barely managed to catch the ledge with both hands. As he tried to scramble over the top, his right shoe came off, subjecting his bare toes to the building's unaccommodating facade.

He scrambled to regain his footing, but ripped his big toenail off instead. "Fuck!" The hammer fell, kissed his boo-boo, and disappeared into the throng. He tried again to pull himself up, but the tipping stage caught his pants and jerked him to the ground.

"Goddammit!" His hammer lay fifty zombies deep on the other side of the tumped-over stage. The groaning, groping dead surrounded him.

"Shit!"

He narrowly avoided a clacking jaw. An enthusiastic uppercut shattered the zombie's head like rotten wood. How do they bite through skin without losing their jaws?

They were slow and light, but goddamn there were a lot of them. Max punched another head off, but it every one that fell only made room for the one behind it.

"Fuck off." He swung again, hitting a tall female in the chest. Her slimy ribs slid around his hand and contracted like a finger trap. Invoking his inner berserker, he grabbed her crotch with his left hand, picked her up, and spun around smacking other zombies with her until she fell apart.

His inner geezer came out shortly after he dropped her torso. Out of breath, muscles aching, his mouth and lungs full of zombie-dirt, he wheezed, "You assholes are destroying my sinuses."

One zombie got its mouth around his right hand. Max ripped off its jaw before he could apply pressure and slammed it into the side of its head. A cloud of dust spewed in Max's face as its skull split open.

"Fuck you, too!"

Eyes full of corpse dust, he smashed, kicked, and punched in a blind rage until his fists stopped finding targets. He spit and wiped the dust from his eyes.

From atop a ziggurat of mangled bodies, he saw hundreds of zombies standing still. They looked confused, like neutered cats that started to hump then forgot what they were doing.

"If you're going to eat me, bring it. If not, get the fuck out of my way. I'm thirsty."

Pain exploded in Max's neck.

It felt like a wasp.

The zombies shimmered.

He tasted pavement.

There was just enough time to register he was dying before the void swallowed him.

At first, the hum was dull and distant—the way politics used to be. Easing ever closer, its developing harmonies fractured into counterbalanced choruses filtering through the haze on the horizon of his consciousness, gaining momentum until it slammed on the brakes and hunkered down to taunt him from the darkness.

Angels? No, angels would sing better.

His limbs seemed spongy and noncorporeal.

He tasted dirty socks and assholes.

This definitely isn't heaven. Shit.

Something moved in the darkness. It hovered vast and ominous, just this side of the strange choir. Gumming the darkness, he tried to ask if this was hell. All that came out was garbled gibberish. The thing in the darkness drew closer. Max could feel its breath on his face. He braced himself for the torments of the damned. He knew he deserved it, but shouldn't he have been a zombie? Was his body wandering around the city without him in it?

A voice reeking of sulfur came from the blackness. "Well, well, look who's awake."

Reeling with horror, Max barely registered the voice was that of a child. The darkness exploded, loosing all the conflagrations of hell upon his eyes and the contents of his bowels into his pants. Soon after, the fire died down and came into focus. It was a single one-hundred-watt light bulb.

His eyelids flapped furiously, his mind like a tiny bird trying to fly in a hurricane. Continuing to blink, he coerced patches of color into solid form; first a table, then a digital alarm clock, a minifridge, and an Iiite child of roughly six years smiling innocently as he folded the blindfold and set it on the table. Max looked down past the bridge of his nose and saw a dingy brown sock bulging between his teeth. Further down his torso, he saw the duct tape that held him in his chair.

He wasn't dead.

He wasn't that lucky.

His flight to Hell had been interrupted by a layover in a tiny Iiite interrogation room. He'd get there in good time, but not before he experienced all the suffering life had to offer.

Max laughed so hard he nearly swallowed the sock. He had survived zombie attacks, a raid on a heavily guarded laboratory, and an Iiite death squad. Still, it was all nothing compared to the psychological torture implemented by this six-year-old kid.

The child removed the gag, poured some water into Max's mouth, and smiled innocently—as though he didn't have him strapped to a chair and hadn't used advanced psychological torture to make him soil himself.

Max had always assumed shit-scared was just a euphemism. Somehow he didn't feel it necessary to thank the child for correcting him.

Unfortunately, the gritty squish in his pants was the least of his problems. This was probably the child of one of the raiders he had killed. The whole Hell thing was probably a trick designed to bring about a momentary feeling of euphoria, making it hurt so much more when they jabbed paperclips into his eyes. Once he'd told them everything about the Nrrds, they would send him to hell for real.

Max was disappointed to find himself terrified once again. He wondered when and if he would finally get past this frequent, obstinate emotion. He blinked questioningly at the boy, wiggled his tongue around to distribute the moisture, and attempted to play it cool, "Hey, kid? You mind untying me? This is kind of uncomfortable, and I need to pee."

"Sorry, mister, I'm just supposed to keep an eye on you until you wake up. The grown-ups really want to talk to ya about something. If I let you go, they'll probably spank me."

Max pictured an Iiite spanking their child, "You get spanked? Dude, that's brutal. With arms like that, I'm surprised any of you live to puberty, let alone through it. I'll wait."

The loblet giggled behind his massive right hand, "You're funny. You act like you have a choice."

Max knew the child's comment came off a lot more sinister than intended, but it still fed the horror that grew in his belly like hairworm larva. Knowing kids rarely approve of their friends being tortured, he forced a crooked smile and tried to break the ice, "So, nice place you have here. The cement really complements the cinderblocks."

The Iiite giggled again.

"What's your name, kid?"

"Andy."

"Nice to meet you, Andy. What's up with the choir?"

"Choir practice, it's right next door. I don't like it much, though."

"And what kind of muzik do you like? What's your favorite song?"

Andy perked up immediately and grinned from ear to ear, "I like the one that's all like, 'Wrenchy's best, when your cars a mess.' and the one with the cowbell."

"Cowbell? You mean the Winkie Burger theme?"

"Yeah, that one. I want a Winkie Burger so bad, but dad says I can't eat them because they're made of pig fat and ground-up zombies. He says he knows the guy that runs the company, and he set it all up and paid a lot of money for a cool theme song to trick surface dwellers into eating lots of carcinogens and pesticides."

Max raised an eyebrow. "Carcinogens and pesticides?"

"Yeah."

"Well, Winkie Burgers aren't as good as they sound. You really aren't missing much."

"You sound like daddy."

Max cursed himself for being so bad with children. He was losing the kid fast. "So, what do you want to be when you grow up?"

"Why do adults always ask kids that question? I don't want to grow up. Adults define themselves by their work and get all boring. I mean, every time daddy introduces somebody to somebody else he says, "So and so, this is so and so, he's a so and so,' like none of them have anything better to talk about than their jobs. I don't want a job. I want to play video games and eat ice cream. And here's another thing, why is it adults can talk forever about stocks and business and stuff and hang on every word, but when I try to tell them how I saved the universe from destruction, they act all bored?"

Max didn't know how he hadn't seen it sooner, but something was off about this kid. "You're kind of bitter for a little kid." How much of that childlike innocence was an act? For all he knew, this was a genetically engineered baby man they used to make people lower their guard.

"I'm just sayin'.."

"I see your point, though. How'd you get to be so smart?"

"I'm normal for my age group."

"You seem smarter than any kid I've met."

"That's because, up there, kids have No Child Left Behind, and, down here, we have Project Prometheus."

"What's Project Prometheus?"

"It was one of the first things the founding fathers did when they moved to the sewers. It started as a Pavlovian reinforcement system to get kids interested in learning, but now it's a combination of advanced eugenics, imprinting technology, and other stuff. It kinda sucks because I'll never get to be in a position of power."

"Why not?"

"Every generation is engineered to be smarter than the one before. Project Prometheus made me about seventeen times smarter than daddy, but the kids that are being born right now are gonna be somethin' like twenty-six times smarter than me. It'd make sense for my generation to take charge now and get a demotion every year as the next generation took our place, but the adults aren't smart enough to see that. It's gonna happen, but by the time it does, I'll be obsolete. It's not a big deal, though. I'll get to retire with all the adults and never have to take on any responsibility. I'm probably going to be happier this way, but it doesn't seem fair."

"You're right. That definitely doesn't seem fair. Grown-ups do tend to suck. I'm cool, though. I'm a bit of an adventurer. You want to hear about the time I broke into a heavily guarded facility to rescue my pet cheekworm from a bunch of sadistic jerks who were torturing him?"

Andy's eyes lit up like a pair of sparklers. He finally had the kid, assuming he was a kid, right where he wanted him. Unfortunately, Max's tenacity was once again superseded by his luck. The door opened, and two Iiites swaggered in looking like they had wandered off the set of a Dick Tracey movie. The first was sleek, with reptilian features. He wore a tailored pinstripe suit, which didn't quite manage to make his massive right arm or pencil mustache look any less ridiculous. The second was a seven-foot-tall wall of beef with more grit than a Winkie Burger that fell on the floor. His stubble was thicker and longer than his buzz cut, and his tattoos all looked like he'd done them himself with an ashtray and a rusty knife. He wore biker boots, tight jeans, and a muscle shirt that said, "Kill 'em all and while God's sorting them out sneak around the back and slit his fuckin' throat."

The men walked past him to the minifridge and selected two wine coolers. He watched silently as they approached, festively colored beverages in hand, eyeing him menacingly as though they were about to jam them in his eyes or force him to drink a whole case and then spin him in a chair until he passed out.

They walked right past him. The big one turned and winked at him before shutting the door.

"Why do you look so scared, mister? I thought you were going to tell me a story about how you beat up the bad guys and saved your pet."

"Yeah, in a minute, who were those guys?"

"That's Percy and Darryl. They're special friends. Daddy says Percy tries to look extra tough because he has a girly name."

"Special friends, huh?" Max couldn't help picturing Darryl giving Percy the reach around with that massive fist and inadvertently tearing his cock off.

"What's so funny?"

"Nothin,' man. You want to hear that story?"

"I'm still waiting." Andy sat Indian style on the floor.

All he needed was some product placement and a camera. "Okay, it all started when I was at the costume shop with Cakey, that's my pet's name, by the way. He's a cheekworm, a flubbery little tube of love with suckers on the bottom, little black eyes, and a catlike mouth." He didn't feel like explaining the past tense.

"Cute, keep going."

"Well, we were trying on costumes when the wall caved in. A bunch of Ii...diots came in and started killing everybody, so I grabbed a pole and started wailing on them. Meanwhile, Cakey was running around, ripping them to shreds like they were nothing. It was insane. I killed two, and he killed like six or eight or something, I forget. The last one was a big tough guy. He wiped the floor with me, smashing me all over the place, breaking all my bones. I thought I was about to die. Then, from out of nowhere, Cakey tears out his spinal cord."

"Cool, Cakey sounds awesome. Can I play with him sometime?"

"Uh, maybe, we'll see."

"Are you making this stuff up? I thought that this was an invasion story."

"I wish. Don't worry, we're getting there. So, Cakey saved my life, but I was still all smashed up on the floor. I passed out. When I woke up, they told me Cakey had done some bad things. See, he was still trying to protect me when the paramedics got there. Apparently, he killed a bunch of the people that came to take me to the hospital. His heart was in the right place, but try telling that to a dead guy's friends.

"Anyway, he was taken to a big building full of mad scientists who did experiments on him while I was asleep for a couple of weeks."

"Why didn't you wake up and go get him? Mom says lazy and stupid are the two worst things you can be."

Max laughed. He was starting to like this kid. "I was in a coma."

"What's a coma?"

"It means you can't wake up. My body was, like, resetting itself, or something. I don't know. Anyway, when I found out what had happened, I smashed my cast and got a friend to give me a ride to the bad guy's lair.

"This is where the story gets good. We knew Cakey was being guarded by an ex-soldier on the seventh floor, and I didn't have a gun. So, with the help of one of my friend's acquaintances, I snuck in and disguised myself as a bad guy. She disabled the guy who was watching the cameras while I snuck to the elevator and...."

The door opened, and in walked the male equivalent of a soccer mom. If 1950s sexual norms were reversed, this guy could have been the househusband in nuclear family propaganda films. He wore a baby blue sweater vest, Easter yellow turtleneck, and Khakis with pleats sharp enough to cut your finger on. His hair was short and spiked with gel in a way that made metrosexuals look like vagrants. He had tiny wire-rimmed glasses, penny loafers, and a huge fucking arm.

Max could feel his testosterone levels waning. If he didn't say something soon, he was going to start laughing uncontrollably. "Goddamn, you're neat."

The Iiite looked confused by that statement. Instead of responding, he addressed the child, "Hey, whatcha doin' kiddo?"

"He's tellin' me a story about rescuing his pet from mad scientists."

"Oh, really? What else did he tell you?" From the tone of the question, Max could tell this was daddy, and daddy was on the verge of being extremely pissed off.

"He had to rescue his pet because he was put into a coma while beating up a bunch of bad guys who were killing people, and the scientists kidnapped his pet and performed experiments on him."

"Sounds like a great story, but I'm afraid that he'll have to tell you the rest later. Mommy wants you to clean up for dinner."

"No, I want to hear the story now. It was just getting to the good part."

"What did I tell you about the n-word? Now go upstairs and get cleaned up, or I'm going to tell Mommy that you've been a bad boy."

"I want to hear the story. Pleeeease?"

"No, you run along now. One..., two..., three."

"Okay, fine, but one of these days, I'm going to stop loving you over something like this." Andy got up and ran out the door in a huff.

Daddy Iiite was stupefied. He opened his mouth like he was going to say something, but his tongue was tied tighter than Max.

"Oh, snap. That kid's a fucking firecracker. I like him. Yours?"

"Yes, he is. And what makes you think you can come in here and fill his head with a bunch of violent garbage like that?"

"I'm sorry. I can see I've outstayed my welcome. If you'd be so kind as to untie me, I'll be on my way."

"Haha, funnyman, we'll see how funny you are after Percival works you over with a pair of pliers."

"Do you mean Percy, Darryl's special friend? We already met. He seemed nice enough," Max added smugly.

"You should thank me. The others wanted to kill you or torture you and then kill you, but I made them wait. See, there are many anti-Normalists down here, and their answer to everything is 'maim him,' 'kill him,' 'make an example of him.' Not me, though. Their grudge is justified, but I don't agree with the way they're handling it."

"So, what, you're a pacifist?"

"Well, yes and no. I'm an ideological pacifist, but at this point, we're too deep in this war to pull out. We've got to stay the course and deal with the babies."

"Was that a naughty joke?"

"What do you think I am, a monster?" he said in an exaggeratedly angry voice as he wrapped his enormous hand around Max's throat, but started to giggle before the word monster formed on his lips. "I'm not above the odd tongue in cheek."

Max smiled, and Daddy let go. "So, what do you want, exactly? They want me dead, you don't. I get that, but what the hell am I doing here? How did I even get here? Last thing I remember I was fighting a horde of zombies. Did you rescue me or something?"

"No. It would be easier if you thought that, but I believe in complete honesty. Lies never did anyone any good. Before we get into that, my name is Yakov, but you can call me Jacob or Yak. I prefer Jacob. I have no idea why my parents went with the Russian version. My mom smoked a lot of pot, which is probably the reason for my high IQ and low testosterone. In school, kids used to tease me about being gay all the time because I'm kind of effeminate."

"You don't say."

"Well, I'm not gay, and it doesn't bother me one bit if people think I am. It's childish to make fun of people for their mannerisms. I do have a wife and son, after all."

"Yeah, I don't mean this in any offensive way, and I'm certainly not calling you a liar, but lots of gay men have families. The wives are traditionally called beards. It's pretty common."

"I can't tell if you're an idiot or a genius. I mean, you're taped to a chair, and I'm the only thing standing between you and death, and you're messing with me."

"I thought you said it didn't bother you."

"It doesn't. I'm past all that." Every muscle in his face rippled in contradiction.

"Look, I give zero fucks about your sex life. You seem like a decent guy. I'm sorry I was facetious. I can't help it. I'm kind of an asshole. I just want to know why and how I came to be taped to this chair.

"Just a few weeks ago, I was a normal guy who drank my weight in alcohol every week. Now, except for you and that kid, all the Iiites want me dead. For fuck sake, man, I was just trying to buy a Halloween costume."

Jacob's demeanor regained its previous level of pleasantness, "I totally understand where you're coming from. I wanted to be a school teacher, but Daddy wanted to make a man out of me, so he put me smack dab in the middle of the Iron Fist." He sighed. "We're here. Let's make the most of it. Okay?"

"Sure, whatever, spill. Start with the zombies."

"Very well, that was us."

"You were the zombies?"

"No, but we did put them there, and we used our gadgets to make them violent. We did it to get you away from the Nrrds. You weren't supposed to be in any real danger, but Jimmy spilled grape soda on the zombie machine and didn't tell anyone, so the button got stuck. You should have seen us banging away at it, trying to turn it off. We ended up having to take out the batteries. I was horrified, but everything turned out just fine, didn't it? Now we have a colorful story to tell at dinner parties."

"Maybe it's a cultural thing, but I would expect to get some really weird looks if I told a story like that at a dinner party. Then again, maybe not. I can't say I've ever been to one, and I really don't have any friends or family, so I could be out of touch."

"Sadly, that is the sort of thing people talk about at dinner parties around here. That and professional sports. I detest them both."

Max bit his tongue and asked him to continue.

"When the zombies reverted to being docile, we shot you with a sleepy dart and brought you here."

"That's what that was! I thought a zombie got me. So, why am I here?"

"The others wanted you dead for what you did to our friends in the costume shop, but I could see that you were only trying to survive. What you did was quite impressive, by the way, valiant even. Too many people just lie back and let things happen. It did my heart good to see someone rise up against such great odds and triumph over evil. Not that we're really evil. Times like these make monsters of us all.

"Getting back to why you're here, I got them to spare your life on the condition that you work for us. You can never have too many spies. Now, I'm sure that the Nrrds told you all sorts of horrible things about us, and most of them are probably true, but you know that there are three sides to every story."

"Three?"

"Yours, mine, and the truth. I hoped that you would listen to our side of things and decide the truth for yourself. The Riot Nrrds are hardly a bunch of do-gooders out to save the world. They are a group of highly intelligent anarchists who want to bring society to its knees so that they can create their own version of utopia with an intellectual elite at the top and everyone else living like cattle at the bottom. Anyone with an IQ less than one hundred and fifty would have no rights whatsoever. On top of that, they want to purge the world of Iiites. That's ethnic cleansing.

Jacob removed his glasses and polished his already immaculate lenses with a little blue cloth. "I'm not trying to say that all Nrrds are Nazis. They started out with good intentions, but since then, they have been taken over by a megalomaniacal genius with plans for world domination. The funny thing is that most Iiites and Riot Nrrds would get along really well if it weren't for the ones in charge screwing things up for everybody. At first, we were only trying to survive against the violent actions and oppressive sanctions that were forced upon us because we were different. It wasn't our fault that the Japanese mutated us, and it wasn't our fault that it made us stronger. All we did wrong was evolve instead of dying. We're no guiltier than you are."

Max suppressed the urge to rattle off a list of things he'd never done.

"The Iiites have done a lot of terrible things. Our forefathers got extremely pissed about not being able to stick their heads above ground without being attacked, so they decided to go on the offensive. I strongly disagree with the population control programs and the dumbing down of the populace, but those tactics have been used for thousands of years. That doesn't make it right, and my sincerest wish is that one day I will rise to a position where I can put a stop to it.

"That is where you come in. You become a double agent and do an outstanding job. Then I can get promoted and put an end to all of the unnecessary ugliness. You have a chance to save the whole world from both Nrrdist and Iiite dystopia. What do you say?"

Max exhaled deeply. "Why does everybody want me to save the world? I'm nobody. The Nrrds say you're evil, and you say they're evil. The truth is you're both probably right. Forcing your will on others is inherently evil. If everybody stayed out of each other's business, ninety percent of the world's problems would go away."

Jacob came in close and whispered, "Don't say anything else. The room might be bugged. Not everybody in the Fist likes me. But, that's what I'm saying. I am part of a small group within the Iiite government that is working to dismantle it from the inside. You won't really be working for them or the Nrrds. You will work for us. You don't have to decide anything now, but I would strongly advise you to agree to be a double agent. If you refuse, they will probably kill you before you have a chance to change your mind."

He backed off. "You may be right about that. In a perfect world, everybody would get along and do what was best for mankind, but this isn't an ideal world. Most people are idiots who have to be kept in line by the government. It's tough to keep everybody from running amok, so the government occasionally has to use morally grey tactics to pull it off. It's sad but true.

"Take population control, for example. You have billions of people breeding like rabbits all over the world. They require food and housing, so they need jobs to earn money to pay for that stuff. To have jobs, you need a thriving economy. Therefore, it was necessary to create a consumer culture that requires a massive amount of goods and services, but the products create massive pollution that could kill the planet. To save the planet, we need fewer people.

"There are two ways to make that happen. You can either stop people from having babies, or you can cause death. People get mad if you tell them they can't reproduce, and anything that could covertly sterilize that many people could backfire and sterilize everyone, thereby wiping out the human race. On the other hand, you have the death machine, which uses war, famine, disease, and poison to kill off the living so that people can have as many babies as they want. The war option creates jobs, so it's the more popular of the two."

Jacob leaned against the table. "It got a lot more complicated after the Divine Disturbance. Now, people rarely die of natural causes, and even when they do, they won't say dead. It's a mess, let me tell you. I don't see why anybody wants to be in charge. If there is a hell or something similar, you can be sure that every politician who has ever lived and died is there along with everybody else who ever tried to make a difference."

"So, if there has to be somebody in control, it might as well be you. If you were in charge, you would try to make things easier on the little people because you're a great guy. Is that about it?"

"In so many words."

"Sounds like a load of shit. On the other hand, the Nrrds are a bunch of assholes. They're so focused on the details they can't see the big picture. They're so smart they don't have common sense. I'd hate to see what would happen if they had to figure out a solution to overpopulation. We're talking some serious sci-fi nightmare shit." He shook his head sadly. "I'll help you for the same reason I signed up with them. I don't have a choice."

"I had hoped that you would be slightly more enthused." Jacob pulled a switchblade out of his pocket and cut the tape around Max's hands.

Max rubbed his hands together to get the circulation back while the Iiite removed the tape around his ankles. "It's hard to be enthusiastic about a job where your new boss ties you to a chair and tells you he'll kill you if you don't take it. What? You did say you liked honesty."

"Understood, and I do. Furthermore, I am fully confident that you will be completely won over once you get to know us."

Max shrugged his eyebrows. "Nrrds aren't really known for their success in popularity contests."

"True dat. Are you hungry? I know a great little restaurant right around the corner. You'd never know you were eating in a sewer."

"I'm actually kind of nauseous. I think I'll take a rain check on that."

93

"That's probably from the sleepy dart. It should go away in about twenty minutes or so."

Max stood, feeling the gritty squish in his nether regions, and followed Jacob out the door with his butt cheeks clenched as tight as a Catholic schoolgirl who had just had sex for the first time. He never imagined he would be so grateful for the stink of the sewer. "It could also have something to do with the stench of human feces."

"You'll get used to it. I was born down here, so it doesn't really bother me, but even noobs get used to it after a couple of hours. Your nose learns to tune it out."

"I could do with a bath and a change of clothes. I've still got zombie all over me. Maybe I'll feel more like eating when I'm not covered in death."

"That's not a problem. I had a feeling that you would accept our offer, so I took the liberty of arranging a room. You should find everything you need in the closet."

"It was an offer I couldn't refuse."

They laughed uneasily, delighted with each other's sense of humor, but knowing dark comedy is only funny at a distance. Max was aware of the long strange road ahead. He wondered with a mixture of anxiety and excitement where it would take him.

Max was highly skeptical about the Iiite's good intentions. This was most likely a good cop bad cop routine that petered out before the bad cop was brought in, but Max was happy to leave it that way. He tried to keep up the friendly conversation as he wobbled like a penguin behind his new boss.

THE M.I.L.F. WHO LOVED ME

Max smirked at the print of Dali's "Soft Construction with Boiled Beans" above the bed. Of all the things he expected to find in the mutant terrorist's underground base, a sense of humor wasn't one. Honestly, nothing here was what he'd expected.

He could almost see himself being happy here. The room they had given him was surprisingly pleasant. It was larger than his old apartment and had a king-sized bed, cushy blue shag, a Jacuzzi, and a big TV with surround sound. Aside from the faint stench of feces, he never would have guessed it was in the sewer.

His skin tingled fresh and exfoliated from his shower. Steam was still billowing from the bathroom. He smelled like cucumbers and felt like a cool glass of milk, a marked improvement over the shit-and-zombie-smeared wretch that had waddled through the door thirty minutes ago.

He emptied the pockets of his previous outfit before stuffing it in a garbage bag, which he double-knotted and placed at the bottom of the brushed silver trash can in his kitchen. His closet was stocked with an assortment of high-quality attire ranging from jeans and T-shirts to eveningwear and tuxedos. He'd never had a tux before, and until that moment, he never knew he wanted one. It was a silly impulse, but he couldn't resist trying it on.

Standing before the full-length mirror, Max finally felt like the secret agent everyone expected him to be. He blamed all those late-night James Bond marathons he had watched in his previous life while he was too drunk to bother changing channels.

Startled by a knock at his door, he scrambled to change into something less humiliating. After the third knock, the door opened.

Max scowled as Jacob entered. Even with his tie off, shirt unbuttoned, and beltless, the tux made Max feel cocky and untouchable.

"Not big on privacy down here, huh?"

Jacob smiled, "Well, don't you just look like a hundred-dollar bill. Practicing in front of the mirror, are we?"

"Fuck you and the downtrodden masses you rode in on. Can't you give me a moment of peace?"

Still smiling, Jacob closed the door gently. "I'm just stopping by to make sure you have everything you need. I see that our tailor did an excellent job, as usual."

"Yeah, I'm cool. The room's a lot nicer than I'd expected. Definitely nicer than where the Nrrds stuck me."

"And where was that?"

"Look, I don't mind informing on the Nrrds. They're a bunch of dicks. But where I was staying before doesn't have any connection to them, and my presence already caused enough trouble. Is that going to be a problem?"

"No, I don't think so. Any bit of information on the Nrrds is extremely helpful, but their safe houses are of little consequence. We would much rather know where their bases are. You will be expected to give us information, of course, but that can wait. Are you hungry yet? I have a table booked at La Panache and an extra chair with your name on it. You are already dressed for it."

"I guess I could eat. Are you serious about the tux? You really have places that nice down here?"

"Oh yes, we have everything down here that you have up there. In many cases, what we have is better. We have to entertain some of the most prominent members of the global elite and, trust me, those guys are picky."

"All right, just a second." Max buttoned his shirt and ineffectively fumbled with his bow tie.

"Here, let me help you." Jacob walked around behind him and loosed the jumbled mess.

"I got it right a minute ago," Max said as he marveled at how nimbly Jacob's mismatched mitts manipulated the little strip around his throat. The fingers on Jacob's right hand were like bony bratwursts while his left hand sported the slender, delicate digits of a pianist. Yet, somehow they worked together harmoniously. Max thought about how often he messed up tying his shoes and tasted the jealousy that created this debacle.

Physiological transgressions were to be tolerated with sympathy, but never envied. The Iiites' physical prowess made Normals feel like last year's MP3 player. He'd like to think he wouldn't have supported society's latest PR debacle, but he probably would have been too lazy to act against it.

"There you go." Jacob stepped back and turned him around. "Well, look at you. Someone cleans up nicely."

Max furrowed his brow and smiled painfully.

Jacob patted him a little too hard on the cheek and spoke crisply through his teeth. "Someone needs to learn how to take compliments. Come now. We mustn't be late. They only hold tables for fifteen minutes."

Max followed him out the door and down the long stinky hallway. It had been furnished like a fancy hotel, but, despite their best efforts, the sewer's feculence continued to make itself known. The red carpet was beginning to show signs of mildew around the edges. The polished silver door handles were coated in something akin to dew. Even the framed prints lining the hallway were beginning to bubble and warp behind the glass.

"How often do you guys replace this stuff?" Max asked, swirling his finger nonspecifically.

"What? Oh, well, more often than we'd like. The moisture gets in, no matter what we do. It's quite irritating. This carpet is only a month old, the paintings six, and everything else is about a year.

"The carpet is the worst. We have to replace it every month and a half, or we start getting bronchial infections. It's quite laborious and expensive, but we have systems in place that make it manageable. We have our own carpet factories and a small army of carpeting technicians that work every day in one section or another simply rolling up the old and rolling out the new."

They passed through a doorway into a vast business district. Max followed his new boss down a line of shops and restaurants, which stretched as far as he could see in both directions. He was shocked to see each shop and restaurant was different from the others. The windows displayed all sorts of products he had never seen before. It would take years to browse them all. A shopaholic with a decent line of credit could get lost in here forever. Luckily Max didn't like shopping and didn't have any credit.

"Damn, that's a lot of commerce."

"I told you."

"I haven't seen small stores like these since I was a kid. I didn't think they existed anymore."

"That would be our fault. One of the first things the founders of the revolution did was take over the big four and systematically eradicate small businesses. Controlling the populace is easier when you can control their experience, and limiting the items a person encounters limits the variety of their experiences to a great degree. Variety fosters imagination and free thought, which are two things that you don't want the enemy to have.

"We thrive on variety. You wouldn't believe the flavors of ice cream we have. We also have a wonderful non-commercial art culture. You should go to Gigapoodle.com and listen to some of our music. It's quite unlike anything you have up there."

"I'll do that. I remember when music was about more than where you should shop or how often you should have your car waxed. It was a lot better than the crap people listen to today."

"Here we are." Jacob gestured grandly to a dimly elegant dining room flickering faintly behind tinted glass.

Upon entering, they were received by a tuxedoed Iiite whose snooty air was almost as cliché as his pencil mustache. The look of profound disgust with which he scrutinized Max grew sharper with each step as they approached. He couldn't have been more displeased if Jacob had walked in with a monkey wearing fetish gear. Still, the maitre d' knew his place. He led the men to a table in the corner and bid them good riddance as politely as was required.

Jacob took a seat with his back to the wall. Max sat across from him. He didn't like sitting with his back exposed, especially among so many enemies, but it was better than being near his supposed friend. Something about Jacob made his skin crawl.

When the host was out of hearing range, Max inquired, "What was his problem?"

"Not everyone approves of unnecessary interaction between Iiites and Normals. It's petty reverse racism, nothing personal."

"They aren't going to spit in our food, are they?"

"Oh God no, they hold their food in far too high regard to tamper with it. McDougle's, on the other hand, is not so safe."

"I'll keep that in mind."

"Bigotry aside, what do you think of the place?"

"It's nice. I've never been to a fine dining restaurant before. I never considered food worth a hundred bucks a plate. The art's an odd choice, though. You'd think a place like this would have real paintings instead of reproductions."

Jacob smiled knowingly. "Well now you can see what you have been missing. There is a reason that the prices are so high. Order whatever you like. It's on me."

"We'll see," Max said skeptically as the server approached.

The server may have had similar reservations about serving Normals, but his demeanor hid them well. His snootiness was limited to what one would expect from a Normal in the same position. Jacob ordered a bottle of 1994 Chateau Lafite and three glasses and sent him on his merry way.

"Is somebody joining us?"

"My friend Adhra wanted to meet you, but she's running late." He leaned in close and quietly added, "She is a friend of our cause."

"Great, so this is a business thing."

"No. Not really. We were hoping to discuss our plans in greater detail, but this is primarily a meet and greet. I suspect you two will get on swimmingly. Everyone just loves her.

"In the meantime, I'd love to hear your take on the Riot Nrrds. I've never had the pleasure of speaking to one of them when their mood hadn't been adversely influenced by unfortunate circumstances."

"Well, the cliché pretty much nails it, smart as fuck, no people skills."

"What about their cause?"

Max fiddled nervously with his salad fork. "I think most of them get off more on the spy/mad scientist thing than helping people. It's like a game to them. That's not to say they don't believe in what they're doing.

They're really pissed about you dumbing people down and enslaving them, and they have a right to be. You guys turned the surface world into a fucking slaughterhouse."

"I understand completely, but have they considered the benefits of a gilded cage?"

"Not so much. No."

"We have more creature comforts than any other time in history, and even the poorest can acquire them with a minimal amount of effort. Anything you can think of is available at a superstore right down the street. Old-timey royalty would have given their legs for that. How would life be better in an anarchistic anti-society with complete freedom."

"Anarchy doesn't mean unruly conduct. We can have TV without mind-control. Okay, not the best example. I should say, TV doesn't have to be used for mind-control."

"Laws exist so people can go about their lives without worrying that some rando will impulsively murder them or burn their car. Without laws, that's what people do. Why? Because it's fun. Right now, I wish I was naked and high on PCP, jumping up and down on the roof of a flaming car. Deep down, everyone does."

"No, they don't."

"Figuratively, they do." Jacob gestured to the wine room, where a rope-dancer spun up and down the wall on a long strip of indigo cloth retrieving rare vintages. "Look around. This sort of place exists to offer that level of wanton abandon in a way that doesn't hinder or destroy. All these comforts are made possible by the social contract. Society is compromise. If you have to compromise, you are not free. So, which is better, freedom or comfort?"

"They both suck." Max dropped the fork in disgust. "The Nrrds aren't trying to free anybody. They just think they can rule the world better than you. Maybe they could. Who knows? There is a huge difference between knowingly trading work for conveniences and going through life manipulated through drugs, brainwashing, and terror. You seem to have struck a pretty good balance for yourselves down here. Why not share it with us?"

Jacob leaned in confidentially, "That is what we are trying to do, but we can't do it while the Mittons are in charge. Oh look, there's Adhra now."

Max followed Jacob's gaze and saw the personification of pulchritude moving towards him with all the power and grandeur of an electrical storm. Her slender frame was hung with purple velvet, which clung seductively to ample, perky breasts, but left most of her opalescent skin to glow in the meager candlelight. Even her freakishly large right arm turned him on. He imagined her shoving those extra-large fingers into his mouth while she came.

Her blue-black hair was short and parted on the side with red baby berets holding the longest part just above her right eye. Their eyes met, and he was frozen. Her eyes were circuits of electric blue, which instantly and permanently burned into his dreams. He looked away, trying not to

99

stare, but her image remained, drifting translucent and ghostlike across the restaurant walls.

He had been with quite a few women in recent months, but none had rendered him half as helpless as he found himself then. An icicle of panic grew in his stomach as she approached. She sat down casually as though she was a mere human and not a goddess whose DNA was woven from poetry and satin.

She offered her ethereal left hand and greeted him warmly, "Hey, thanks for coming. I've been hoping to meet you for some time. My name is Adhra, but you can call me Addy."

Max took her hand but forgot what to do with it. The strip of flesh between her breasts induced an almost Zen-like state in him. He felt at one with the universe. Everything swirled harmoniously around her, vibrating in radiant perfection. His tongue was affected similarly, becoming at one with the desert. He opened his mouth to respond, but all that came out was a warm breeze. Addy took back her hand and smiled gracefully with nary a hint of amusement.

"See?" Jacob said. "I told you that you would like her. Simply everyone does. The older members of the board jokingly refer to her as Viagra."

"Jacob!" she protested with reddening cheeks.

"I'm sorry, but he was going to find out eventually."

She slapped Jacob on the shoulder, then turned her attention to Max. "So, how do you like our little subterranean Utopia?"

Max was beginning to regain his higher brain functions, but hadn't reached one hundred percent, "I think Viagra's a pretty name."

Jacob and Addy's raucous laughter sent ripples of outrage ricocheting through the restaurant. Realizing his folly, Max receded as far into his tuxedo as possible and stared at the ceiling. The laughter continued until the waiter returned with the wine and poured a taste for Jacob, who collected himself and performed the expected ritual.

"It will do." He waved the server on.

When the glasses were all full, the server went over the specials for the night and thoroughly described a few of the more expensive items. Max had never heard of most it and feared that more cachinnation would result from any attempt to re-form the syllables the server had so effortlessly articulated. He avoided displaying his ignorance by ordering the Lamb special and a cup of lobster bisque, but his nerves made the order sound a bit like a racial slur.

When everyone had ordered, Jacob picked up his glass and quietly leered through the swirling ruby nectar. Max took a forty-five-dollar gulp and tried not to stare at the goddess beside him. Her face was young and sweet, but she had the eyes of a Spanish prostitute turned freedom fighter. He repeatedly shifted his eyes to Jacob only to have them snap back against his will. Before the nervous tension could build any further, Addy set them both at ease by giggling innocently and shifting in a way that made her breasts look like they might fall out onto the table.

Her voice was casual but quiet. "I bet you never thought you'd be eating five-star cuisine in the sewer as a double agent working for a small revolutionary sect within a mutant shadow government."

Jacob's smile widened sardonically. "Isn't life funny?"

Max wasn't sure if it was her tone or the pricy alcohol, but his nervousness left as fast as a conservative grandmother at a John Waters film. Life was funny. Maybe he was in an impossible situation with no options and a high likelihood he would be killed soon, but at least it wasn't dull. More immediately, there was the small issue of the beautiful double agent he hoped to take to bed. It was probably a bad idea, but no more idiotic than the other items on his agenda.

He sat up straight, summoned his inner spy, and looked her in the eyes for the first time without breaking into a sweat. "With company like yours, I can only consider it serendipity."

"Aww, shucks." His smile was too wide to be patronizing.

"So, what exactly is it you want me to do? I'm really not the type to steal microfiche or jump out of helicopters, but who knows? I've learned to do a lot of things over the last few days."

Jacob shook his head. "Nothing so dramatic. Just keep us informed and do us a little favor here and there. We want to keep you as far out of harm's way as possible, but we can only do that if you let us know exactly what's going on."

"That's comforting. The Riot Nrrds seem to expect me to be their own private Rambo and lead sieges based on the outcome of a video game. It's fucking ridiculous."

Addy leaned forward, grinning. "I love that thing. It'll never give them accurate results, but it's fun."

"You know about that?"

"Of course. We keep tabs on everything they do. We hacked their computers a long time ago, so it's easy."

"So, what do you need me for?"

Addy lowered her voice and continued, "We don't really need you. Every little bit helps, but we mainly just didn't want to see you killed for defending yourself. All we need from you is to occasionally make them zig instead of zag. Tiny decisions on timing can make a big difference."

"And how do I do that? They want me as their spokesperson and personal badass, but they think I'm an idiot. They aren't going to listen to me."

"Sure they will. First, we're going to help you escape so you can go back a hero. Then you can lead a couple of successful raids on sparsely populated areas that are already in need of repair. When things heat up, we'll direct you to the nerve center of our military. Once you are in a position of power, you can help us bring down the whole organization. You provide us with similar information on the Nrrds and hopefully rid ourselves of megalomaniacs altogether. We just have to keep it balanced, so both armies are shrinking at the same rate, and neither can win."

Again, he wasn't sure if it was the wine or the skin between Addy's breasts, but Max was beginning to believe them. "So, you really are trying to overthrow yourselves?"

"Shhh, whisper if you're going to talk about that." Jacob's eyes tore around the room conspicuously making Max wonder if he was really cut out for this sort of thing.

A long time ago, Max had figured out that a person's will to power was inversely proportional to that person's degree of wisdom, so anyone who should govern doesn't want to and vice versa. Stupid people consistently made things worse by trying to get things done.

"Don't worry about it," Addy said, patting him on the knee. "He's just a little paranoid. Everybody here is stuck so far up their own ass they can only hear their own voice. If I climbed on this table and screamed something at them, everybody would turn and scowl at the interruption, but nobody would know what I said."

Max glanced around at the bloated egos bursting from the seams of their suits, then nodded and took another sip of his wine. Shortly thereafter, the soup arrived, and the conversation drifted to more pleasant topics. Addy told a few of her favorite anecdotes about horny politicians, what they had done for her, and what she had done to them. Jacob told Max a few of the more interesting conspiracies. He also dismissed a few as disinformation the M.I.L.F. had leaked to discredit the theorists and/or make themselves seem more in control than they actually were. Max recounted the events of the past few days in great detail and surprised himself by having the most interesting anecdotes of all. He was even more surprised to find he was charming Addy's pants off. Sure she was a political prostitute, but unless she automatically reverted to work mode when she got drunk, there was a chance she actually liked him.

After dinner, Jacob paid with his expense account and left Addy and Max to amuse themselves. They sat for hours discussing amusing cultural differences and annoying the restaurant staff. One of the things they discovered was their mutual addiction to Juicetastic. Max became giddy upon hearing she had a new flavor back at her place.

On the way to her room, Addy was unusually forthcoming with personal information, and Max was surprised at how interested he was to hear it. In just a few hours, they'd developed the connection that was missing between him and Scarlet. They were barely in the door when the foreplay of conversation bubbled over into intense physical displays of acceptance.

While engaged in tender, violent, juicy sex, Max learned the benefits of being with a partner of superior strength. His mind was so thoroughly blown that he wasn't bothered when she produced a vial of white powder.

Max had a few rules about drugs that had always kept him out of trouble. As a child, he had always been curious about mind-altering substances. Knowing he would one day partake, he decided to make some guidelines to keep himself from getting hurt. At the tender age of six, he promised himself never to snort or shoot anything since those methods were most common with hardcore drug addicts. Though his rules had served him well all his life, he was so enthralled and impatient for more that he partook in a drug known to lead to dependency and assholism.

Round two was even more intense than the first. During round three, Addy taught him things about himself he had never suspected. After round four, they were exhausted, chafed, and extremely sticky.

As Max's dopamine waned, it was replaced by paranoia. "Please tell me that wasn't just a trick to win me over for the Iiites."

She took another bump and rubbed a little on her gums while she responded, "Please, let's not ruin this with work stuff."

"Sorry. I had to ask." His penis was a shining oasis in the syrupy wasteland of reddened flesh and matted hair. "I need a shower."

Addy smiled and led him into the bathroom. Under the showerhead's warm caress, they took turns cleaning each other and making each other dirty again. When the water ran cold, they returned to the bedroom to cuddle on a fresh set of sheets.

Exhausted though he was, he laid awake entwined and smiling on sheets that smelled like the woods in winter, his mind atwirl with a vast menagerie of uncharacteristically optimistic thoughts. He was looking forward to tomorrow for the first time since he was a kid. Everything seemed perfect in the dim glow of her accent lighting. He wondered if things might work out after all. Hopefully, Cheeky wouldn't fuck this one up. With any luck, the two would never meet.

After an hour of blissful entanglement, Addy noticed the clock and groaned, "Damn it, I can't sleep. I've got to work early tomorrow. You want a Seconal?"

"You government types sure do a lot of drugs."

"Very funny. I have to do lots of powder while I'm entertaining. A lot of these guys can snort their own weight. I have to keep up. The Fist gives me an unlimited supply, so I can keep my tolerance up. The pills are so I can sleep."

"Aren't you worried about the physical effects?"

"Nah, we have excellent healthcare down here. I'm in a program that repairs the damage the powder does to me every two months. It's not as bad as it seems. You aren't going to get all judgmental on me, are you?"

"I was just kidding. I'm wired, but I think it's more your fault than the drugs."

"Aww, sweet."

She was smiling, but something strange flickered in her eyes. If Max hadn't known better, he would have thought it was fear, but he didn't have the energy to be paranoid. She kissed him on the cheek, popped the pill into his mouth, then rolled over. Seconal immediately took hold of his mind, tucking it in tight with a big fluffy comforter. His last thought before he fell asleep was a mental note to see what Iiite acid was like.

OMEGA OF SOLACE

Max glanced at the clock on the nightstand. It was 4:29. How had two months gone by so fast? A better question might have been, "How sad is it that the best two months of my life were the ones I spent in the sewer with mutants?" But he was way too nervous for introspection. The Iiite statisticians estimated it would take about thirteen minutes to squash the Nrrd's 4:34 P.M. rescue attempt, so he had about eighteen minutes before he would be expelled from the compound. He felt like these were his last few minutes on death row.

Addy gave him an encouraging smile and checked over his costume one more time. He sat anxiously on the corner of his bed naked from the waist down. The cuts and bruises Addy had taken so much pleasure in inflicting over the past few nights, showed nicely through the tears in his grimy white T-shirt. They'd taken a pint of his blood and used it to paint weeks of torture on the canvas of his flesh. The masterstroke, a pair of shit-caked boxers, sat waiting by the door. He stared at his ash-and-mud-smeared feet currently shod in his favorite pair of sandals.

"I don't want to go to work," he said for the sixty-third time that day.

Addy leaned over and kissed him on the forehead. "I know. I don't want you to go either, but you've been trained for over a month. The last thing you need is for the powers-that-be to decide you're a freeloader. Just remember how important what you're doing is. You're one of the most important people who ever lived. You're going to free the normals from the forces responsible for most of their suffering. You'll be the father of the new utopia, and I'll be your queen."

"Yeah, I know I have to go. I miss Cheeky, anyway. This whole espionage thing'll probably be fun once I get started, but I'm still dreading it.

"It's safe down here, and people are nice to me. Well, some of them. More than up there. And I know you told me to stop saying it, but I'm going to miss the shit out of you. Why can't you come with me? It would be easier to say you helped me escape than it was to leak information and set up a trap for the rescue party."

Addy laughed and pinched his cheek, "You are so cute, but that wouldn't work."

"Why not?"

"Lots of reasons."

"Like what?"

Addy grew impatient. "For starters, the Nrrds wouldn't trust me. They're even more paranoid than the Fist. Since they wouldn't believe me, they would probably assume you were a double agent and kill us both. Plus, you need Jacob and me down here making sure the Fist doesn't change its mind. To them, you're a pawn they would rather sacrifice than have to move. Are you satisfied, or do you want to waste our last few minutes together on work stuff?"

"I guess you're right. Being a spy is too damned complicated."

"Yeah, but you'll get used to it." She glanced at the clock. It was 4:35. The Nrrds were late.

Maybe they're not coming. That would be nice.

Max heard the first distant shots of the attack. They sounded more like fireworks than bullets.

"There they go. You about ready?"

Max glanced at the shitty boxers. "No."

Jacob burst in like an annoying sitcom neighbor. If anybody ever deserved a laugh track, it was him. "Hey guys, how are we looking?"

Max shot him an angry look and pulled a jacket over his lap.

"Well, we should probably start walking. It seems the Nrrds fed us that strategy, or maybe they got lost. You never know with them. Anywho, they're pretty close."

Addy furrowed her brow. "How close?"

Jacob raised his walkie-talkie. "Where are they now? Over."

They heard the same shots through the wall they heard over the walkie. "Sector four, moving east. We're trying to push them back into sector three before they hit the business district. They have some kind of pulse cannon that's blowing everything to shit. Damn it, there they go again. They're in the business district. Hope you weren't a big fan of Das Waffle. Over."

"We need to go. Put on your shorts," Jacob demanded urgently.

"Are you sure this is necessary?" Max whined.

Jacob slapped him in the face, leaving a cleanish spot. "This is not the time to argue about fashion. Now come on!"

Max gritted his teeth. "Eww." He stepped out of his sandals and into a pair of boxers designed to look like he'd worn them for months while tied to a chair and denied bathroom privileges. "Happy?"

Jacob and Addy each took one of his hands and dragged him into the hall. Addy quizzed him one last time as they ran toward the exit. "How did you escape?"

"When the attack started, they tried to move me. My guards thought I was too weak to fight back, so they didn't drug me or put me in handcuffs. When the tunnel exploded, I hit them in the head with a fire extinguisher and ran."

"Good, now up you go," Addy said as they arrived at the manhole cover. She kissed him deeply and tenderly, like she would never see him again and then punched him hard in the nose.

"What the fuck?" Max asked as he fell back against the ladder, blood bubbling from his broken schnoz.

"For luck."

Jacob stepped around the corner to give them some privacy and check in with the troops. They could all hear the good news as they said their goodbyes. "It's over; we got all but one of them. He ran to the nearest manhole as soon as we took out the pulse cannon. We have scouts tracking him down as we speak. Over."

"Finally! What took you so long? Over."

"I told you, they had a fucking pulse cannon. Nobody could get near them. They even collapsed the roof in several places so people can see us from the street. The police are supposed to cordon off the area, but they haven't got here yet. I got to give it to those Nrrds. We underestimated the shit out of them. On the upside, we got their pulse cannon. Over."

"Get this straightened out fast. This could turn into a nightmare. Over."

"Sir, yes sir. We're on it. Over."

Jacob came back around the corner just as Max placed his foot on the first rung, "S'all good. Max, have a wonderful time and good luck. Just remember your training. You'll be fine."

"I better be. I plan to do a lot of haunting if this shit gets me killed. I'll be in touch." Max stopped halfway up the ladder to smile at Addy one last time. She wiped away an imaginary tear and waved goodbye as he climbed into the sunlight.

"Good god, I had completely forgotten what fresh air smells like." He hoisted the manhole into place and took a deep breath of surfacy goodness.

He was in the center of the banking district, but the street was almost empty. Everybody was probably off gawking down one of the holes the Nrrds had blown in the sewer. The few people there were pretended not to see him. They probably thought he was homeless.

"Oh well, works for me." He jogged to the sidewalk.

He was too busy looking for a taxi to notice the broken figure, dead-eyed and dragging a rifle, slowly ambling towards him from the far end of the street. He heard metal scraping concrete and turned to see the escaped Nrrd soldier. His features had been chiseled by a lifetime of pain and disappointment. If eyes were windows, he found himself staring into a condemned building where someone squatted for lack of anywhere else to go. He'd wondered how a Nrrd would react to battle. Apparently, not well.

They locked eyes. The Nrrd raised his weapon to Max's face. Did he know Max was working for the other team, or had he just snapped? For all

Max knew, the guy was melting every face he saw. Max screwed his eyes shut and prepared to die.

He heard an odd noise like an electrical arc followed by a splash-sizzle-clank, so he opened his eyes. The gun's barrel was once again scraping concrete. Turning towards the smell of bacon, he saw half an Iiite soldier sizzling in the dirt around a tree. He turned to the Nrrd and smiled a big I'm-so-happy-you-didn't-just-kill-me smile, but the Nrrd's eyes remained hollow and dispassionate as he ambled past.

"Come on, we've got to get out of here before more of those guys show up." Max tried to hail a cab, but nobody wanted to stop for a bloody guy with no pants. The crazy guy with a weapon probably wasn't helping.

He gave up on a cab and decided to put some of his Iiite training to good use. He dragged his would-be rescuer into the middle of the street and commanded him to lie down, then took his gun and hid it behind a garbage can. Unfortunately, the next person to come down the road was a sixteen-year-old girl having a screaming fight with her boyfriend. If she had noticed him a few moments later, the Nrrd's head would have cracked like an egg under the wheel of her car. Fortunately, she jerked the wheel and only ran over his feet. Judging by the Nrrd's reaction, he would have preferred it the other way around.

The girl slammed on her brakes and jumped out of the car, screaming like it was her ankles on backward. The boyfriend was also screaming, but more with rage than panic.

"What the fuck is wrong with you? This is a street, not a fucking park bench," the boyfriend screamed as the erstwhile speed bump fell unconscious under the anesthetic blows that punctuated every other word.

The girl screamed louder and attempted to pull him off, taking an elbow to the face in the process. "Oww! Bastard! This is what I'm talking about. Why do you always have to pummel everybody? You're beating a handicapped person. Do you even know how fucked-up that is?"

Max was enjoying the show but felt he should intervene. The guy had just tried to rescue him. He retrieved the gun and stalked forward with the boyfriend in his sights. "Excuse me. Over here. Hi, please stop beating on my friend. I need to borrow your car."

The girl shrieked and ran away, but the boyfriend was too full of adrenaline to back down. Much to Max's surprise, he rushed forward and took a swing at him. Max ducked, accidentally vaporizing the boyfriend's midsection in the process. "Shit," he said as he watched the girl scream again and rush back to her steaming hunk of an abusive boyfriend.

"Sorry. It just went off."

"You killed him! You bastard, you fucking killed him! What the fuck? He was an asshole, but he didn't deserve this! I'm going to have you put away for this. My brother's a K-Squad trooper!"

Max had enough problems. He raised the gun and vaporized her and looked over at his ruined rescuer.

"Sorry about your legs, man. They'll give a license to anybody these days. You okay? Should I take you to a hospital, or do you have your own medical facility?"

No response. Max couldn't tell if he was in shock or comatose, but it didn't look like he would be coming around any time soon. His legs would probably heal, but his mind was another matter. The merciful thing would have been to put him out of his misery, but it didn't seem right to kill the guy who just tried to save him.

Still surprised no one was around to witness this debacle, Max dragged the Nrrd into the passenger seat and drove away. With the windows down, he took a deep breath of fresh air into his lungs and smiled, barely resisting the urge to hang his head out the window like an excited puppy.

He wanted a shower more than anything, but this might be his only chance to grab stuff from his apartment. A few more minutes weren't going to kill either of them. He was a hero now. He deserved something other than nail-polish-fumes to help pass the time between battles.

He hadn't expected to see his place again. Bounding up the steps two at a time, Max felt like a kid at Christmas. Unfortunately, the most festive thing he saw was police tape hung like streamers across his boarded windows. Someone had been very naughty.

The stench of death pushed him back as he opened the door. From the hall, he could see everything had been destroyed, but he couldn't help himself. He had to go inside.

His apartment had never been homey. The concept of home was alien to him. All he wanted was a roof and walls to keep other people away. He hadn't even managed that.

Who knew it was possible to wreck an apartment that had been furnished out of dumpsters and never cleaned? He had to admire the Iiites' dedication. They had reduced every scrap of usable material to a dismal hodge-podge of splinters and fluff. Every stick of furniture, every bit of FÜD, every piece of garbage had been smashed or ripped and distributed methodically around the room.

He found his computer smashed in half and stuffed into his overturned refrigerator. The fridge door had been torn off and shoved through the wall, half in the living room and half in the bedroom. He followed the smell of death around the corner.

"Spooky! What the fuck?"

The bastards had even slit the throat of his Bio-Bed and decorated the room with its insides. Throbbing pools of larvae dripped from its eyes and mouth, tumbling through the fur to pool in its gut hole. The stench was unbearable, but he felt drawn by something more powerful than will or instinct.

Choking on his tears, Max stroked its big, silky ear for the last time. "What kind of sick fuck can cut the throat of a big friendly kitty? Assholes!"

It struck him that he was working for the people who had done this. That he was mostly working against them was little comfort. He wanted to march right back there with every Nrrd in the city and show the bastards what real destruction was. But then he thought of Addy; her sweet voice, her delicious breasts, her coy smile, the way her cheek twitched when she came. No, he wasn't doing this for the Iiites. He was doing it for her. He was doing it for himself. He was doing it so ordinary people could once again buy Halloween costumes without the fear of being torn to pieces by megalomaniacal monsters.

He would have his revenge. He had the resources of every major organization at his disposal now. It would take an act of God to keep him from achieving his goal.

The time for mourning had passed. Everything that mattered was gone. Life as he knew it was over. His new life had afforded him replacements, but he knew they too would dissolve if he failed to act quickly.

Cursing, he kicked a pile of bloody debris and said goodbye to everything that once defined his life. He took one of the ears to remind him of the cruelty his adversaries were capable of. That triangle of flesh would justify any action necessary to achieve his goal, and if there came a time when he stood before a higher being to be judged, he would place it on the scale along with the feather. He wouldn't want to share an afterlife with any God who would condemn him in the face of such compelling evidence.

TATTOOS ARE FOREVER

Max felt like the sheriff in a bad western as he walked into Rusty Nails for the second time. The gay cacophony of giggles fell silent as all heads turned to gawk.

"What?" he demanded as he hurried toward the back. Any second now, ripples of sniggers would grow into a tsunami of gossip. He had to get to a safe altitude before it hit.

He was halfway to safety when the slap of flesh on flesh made him jump. He turned to rail at his first antagonist but stopped short.

In the left-hand corner, against the wall, a bleach-blond stylist grinned and clapped. "Fuck yeah, bitches. That's what I'm talking about. That is a fresh fucking look."

Max was caught in a full-blown storm of accolades.

Why didn't I move faster? And how the fuck can anybody describe being caked with blood and feces as fresh? At least they aren't laughing at me.

Max went along with it, bowing and waving as he continued on. Several times he was stopped for hugs and photos with various employees and clients. By this time tomorrow, he would probably be on the cover of every fashion magazine in the city. Next week, every dance club in Japan would stink with the secretions of its clientele. This was not the best way to stay low key.

Before ducking into the back, he addressed his fans. "Hey, everybody chill for a minute. I have something to say."

The crowd quieted down except for a hipster who chanted, "Speech, speech, speech!"

When someone shut him up with an elbow to the stomach, Max continued, "I just want to thank you for your support and ask a small favor. I'm not ready to unveil myself yet, so I would appreciate it if you wouldn't tell anyone about this. You know how people are. You come up with something new, and fifty people will rip you off before you have a chance to take credit for it. The last thing I need is for this to get out into the Media© before I do.

I'm sure you understand. Thanks again. I'm going to go back here for a bit. You guys have fun."

He smiled and waved one more time before ducking behind the curtain and high-tailing it to the bathroom.

Damn, I hope that did the trick.

He'd underestimated their lack of taste. Hopefully, he hadn't overestimated their aptitude for treachery. With any luck, every one of them would want to pretend they had come up with it themselves, and those pictures would never see the light of day.

He was halfway up the stairs when Rusty shrieked. His coffee mug shattered on the linoleum.

"Max?! Jumping June bugs on a fuck machine, I thought you were dead. And here you are fresh from the set of an extreme makeover show. You could have called."

"What is wrong with you people? This isn't an outfit. I just escaped from the Iiite's dungeon, where they've been torturing me and pumping me for information for the last two months. Didn't Pope tell you about that?"

"No. The last thing I heard was that you'd disappeared. I was supposed to call him if you turned up, but that was a while ago. Poor baby, they tortured you? Are you okay?"

"I've been beaten, starved, and forced to sit in my own shit. What do you think?"

Rusty grinned salaciously. "They did all that for free? Where do I sign up?"

Max cocked an eyebrow. He was too tired to act offended by Rusty's flippancy.

"Well, I suppose you'll want a shower. You know where it is. Should I call Orville and let him know you're here, or would you rather I wait until you've freshened up?"

"Go ahead. I need to talk to him. Also, there's a car outside with a hypoperfusional Nrrd in it. You should probably call an ambulance for him."

"Huh? You mean he overdosed or something? I don't want anybody OD-ing on my property. It's bad luck."

"No, he's in shock. His feet got crushed."

"Why didn't you just say that?"

"What good is it to know big medical words if you never get to use them?"

"Why do you know that word? You're so weird."

"I don't know. I just do. I'm going to take a shower." Max scratched at the smut beneath his eye. "By the way, where's Cheeky? I kind of expected him to tackle me as soon as I walked in."

"Oh. Well, when you didn't come back, Orville came and got him. Probably still has the little guy. I kind of miss him despite what he did to my rug."

"Cheeky didn't do anything to your rug. That was Cakey, remember? You were there when Cheeky was born."

"Whatever. You know what I meant. Go take your shower. You're stinking up my kitchen."

Max ran to the bathroom and stripped away the feculent rags. It was a waste to throw them away. Soon trendy clothing stores would be selling knock-offs for hundreds of bucks apiece. It was like throwing away a designer original.

God, fashion is fucked-up.

It wasn't easy to scrub away the kind of stink the Iiites had prepared for him, but he finally succeeded by putting to use every sponge, scented body wash and cologne in Rusty's impressive arsenal. He was left wearing pungent flowery musk as irritating to the eyes as it was confusing to the nose.

He wrapped himself in a fluffy pink robe and exited the bathroom only to be accosted by Pope and two other Nrrds he'd never seen before. Pope and the one who looked like the rape child of Takashi Miike and Sylvester Stallone dragged him into the bedroom without salutation. The tall, bald, super-villainy one followed a few steps behind, giving Max the stink-eye. This was not the reception he had hoped for.

"Hey guys, you know I can walk by myself." They threw him face-first onto the bed, which hissed in protest.

He spit out a puff of fur and added, "I thought you'd be happy to see me."

The rape-baby screamed, "What the fuck happened down there?"

"Fuck if I know. I assume it was a rescue attempt."

"We were in constant communication, and nobody ever found you. How did you manage to escape when our entire squad was wiped out?"

"Shit started blowing up. I ran away. I was damn lucky it worked."

Baldie grimaced. "You expect us to believe that you simply scampered away while the Iiite's backs were turned?"

Max glared defiantly. "It wasn't that fucking easy. When the fireworks started, the Iiites got antsy and tried to move me. Something exploded along the way, so while the guard was distracted, I whacked him in the head with a fire extinguisher and ran. I guess they were all hiding or fighting at that point because I didn't see anybody till I was on the surface. That's where I found your guy. He shot an Iiite that was running up behind me. You should give him a medal or something. In any case, mission accomplished. I'm back."

Pope came forward and sat on the bed beside him. "Don't misunderstand our frustration. We are happy to have you back. We just don't understand how we were trounced so thoroughly when we had greater firepower, intelligence, and a computer formulated plan with an eighty percent probability of success. This rescue was a debacle. We lost fifteen men, and the Iiites have our pulse cannons.

"So, what he means to ask is, how can one unarmed civilian escape from the heart of a highly guarded underground base when a team of our best men was all wiped out? Your story is plausible, but it sounds too good to be true."

"Look, that's the way shit works. No amount of planning or intelligence can guarantee the outcome you want, especially in battle. All hell broke loose down there. The Iiites were scared shitless, so they probably weren't making the same super-rational decisions your computers thought they should. If you guys are ever going to have a chance to win this war, you're going to have to stop depending entirely on your formulas and learn to use your instincts."

The Nrrds were agitated, but they seemed to buy it. The strangers' expressions mellowed into thoughtful irritation. Baldie stopped himself just short of a speculative coma and addressed him, "I apologize. We do not usually fall prey to our emotions. None of us is accustomed to losing strategy games."

"You have to stop thinking of war as Chess. It's more like Risk. Every squeeze of a trigger is a dice roll."

Baldie forced a smile and continued. "It is my honor to make your acquaintance. My name is Dr. Manhattan. I am the leader of the Riot Nrrds. The man who screamed at you a moment ago is Newton, my right-hand man. What you did today was highly impressive. You have proven yourself a valuable asset. I can only imagine the horrors you must have endured, and yet it seems you didn't even tell them about this place. Quite impressive considering your lack of training and low interest in the cause. You have certainly earned your pilcrow.

"I hope that you won't hold the initial tone of our meeting against us. You are obviously quite important to our cause, as evidenced by my presence here. I rarely see to things myself. You know how it is, wheels within wheels and all that."

Max smiled politely. Addy had shown him a picture of Dr. Manhattan. This wasn't him. Max's paranoia flew into high gear.

Is this a trick to find out if I changed sides? Do they know I saw the picture? If so, a failure to say anything proves me a spy. On the other hand, interrogators don't usually give out information. The Iiites could even have bad intel.

Spies want to ingratiate themselves to the people they spy on. I've already established myself as a difficult asshole, so it's less conspicuous to call him out.

"That's interesting, you don't look like Dr. Manhattan," Max said matter-of-factly.

The Nrrd was taken aback. "Excuse me?"

"Iiites showed me pictures while they were interrogating me. They hooked me to a machine that was supposed to tell them if I recognized any of the names or pictures they showed me. The guy they told me was Dr.

Manhattan had sharper features, a full head of hair, and a small birthmark on his shin in the shape of a dolphin. You're not him."

Pope narrowed his eyes and stepped away as if the two might launch into a martial arts extravaganza.

Baldie laughed nasally and sat in a nearby velvet chair. "And I'd been told you were slow. You're right. I'm not Dr. Manhattan, but neither is the man in the picture. The man they showed you is a composite of Lee Harvey Oswald, John Wilkes Booth, and Igor Stanislavski. We doctored and leaked them all the pictures they have."

"How would you know what pictures they have?"

"We're the Riot Nrrds! We fucking hacked them. Then we watched them hack us and rerouted them to a whole server full of disinformation."

"So, who are you, and why did you lie to me?"

"And me." Pope's brow was smeared with hurt.

"I wanted to make you feel important while providing you with information, which were it to be extracted, would confuse the enemy. We do everything we can to mess with the enemy's head, including telling our own agents white lies that won't affect their performance. I do apologize for the dishonesty."

Max shrugged. "I get it."

The Nrrd gestured at the rape baby. "His name is General Hawk, and I am Newton. The Doctor never appears in person. Losing him would be far too damaging to the cause.

"Nifty. Before, you said I earned something?"

"Earned? Oh, you earned your pilcrow."

"What the fuck is a pilcrow?"

Newton rolled up his sleeve to reveal a black typographical symbol. "Don't you have one yet?"

Pope sputtered. "We didn't have time to mark him yet. Inky was at ComiCon."

Newton crossed his arms. "The convention was only three days. You had him for a week."

"We didn't expect him to be kidnapped on his first mission."

"So that's why you had so much trouble finding him. What if he had escaped and needed protection? Nobody would have believed he was one of us."

"I know; I'm sorry. We'll get it done today."

"Could somebody please tell me what the fuck you're talking about? I don't want a tattoo. Some booze would be nice, maybe some money?"

Newton exhaled deeply and pointed at the symbol on his arm. "In editing, a pilcrow is the symbol for a new paragraph. It symbolizes a new train of thought, which is what we hope to inspire in the masses. It also includes a tracking chip, which could have saved you two months of torture. All the Nrrds have them. It isn't up for debate. If you're worried about the discomfort, don't. We have a special painless technique that only takes a few minutes."

"Fine, I guess it's not the worst thing you assholes have made me do. One more question: Why isn't Cheeky here?"

Pope unzipped his backpack and pulled out a thick file. "We thought he would be a distraction. Don't worry, he's safe and happy. You'll see him tonight when you get your pilcrow."

Newton rolled his sleeve back down. "Max, is there anything that you need or any questions you would like answered? I should be going."

"No, not that I can think of. Actually, could you get me a computer? It's kind of boring sitting here waiting for you guys to send me to my death."

"Pope will get you one tonight. Anything else?"

"No, I don't think so. You can go."

"I'll be off then. Good work today. You are already our most effective military agent. I look forward to seeing you in action. Come, General Hawk, we have things to do."

The general glared at Max as he followed Newton down the stairs. He had obviously not made a good first impression. When they were a safe distance away, Pope relaxed and handed Max the file.

"I need you to look through these pictures and tell me who you saw while you were down there and what you saw them doing."

Max opened the folder and thumbed through the first five pictures seeing no one familiar. The fifth page was a picture of Percy and Darryl, "These two did most of the ouchie-making. I gathered they were a couple, but that's it."

"Ouchie-making. I like that. It's good that you've retained your sense of humor through all this. Most people would have cracked in your position. Their names are Percy and Darryl Handson. They are married, and ouchie-making is the family business."

He flipped to the next page and saw a wasp-faced little man with a pencil mustache. "I think I saw this guy somewhere. Who is he?"

"We're not sure, he pops up in a lot of these pictures, but no one has been able to figure him out yet. He sits in on important meetings, never saying anything. He's everywhere something big is going down, but we can't figure out his connection.

"There are several theories. One is that he's the PA for somebody important, and is there to take notes and report back. But he doesn't take notes, and nobody can figure out who he reports to, so that's probably not it. A lot of people believe him to be the Iiite leader, but I really doubt that. He isn't an Iiite, and even if he was, they're too smart to use such an obvious tactic as hiding their leader out in the open. They wouldn't risk us figuring out their reverse psychology, let alone risk him being killed in some lesser attack. In any case, if you see him on a mission, go ahead and kill him."

He continued on and came to one of Jacob shaking hands with the CEO of Bio-Corp. "I saw this guy. He seemed to be in charge."

"What can you tell us about him?"

"Well, I can confirm he's a douche bag. He has an evil little hell-spawn that's already as good at torturing as he is. That's about it. He mostly asked me questions and told people to hurt me." He felt terrible for dragging Andy into this. He was a good kid. It wasn't his fault his dad was in the Fist. He hoped the Nrrds wouldn't have enough to go on to figure out which kid was Jacob's.

"All right, that's good. We didn't know he had a kid. That might be useful. His name is Yakov Palmer, the director of eugenics for the Iron Fist. Among other things, he determines the levels of poison and sedatives that go into our FÜD and water. We know how he works, but that's about it."

Pope pulled out a large photo of Jacob and three women. "He frequently uses these three to manipulate people. Do you recognize any of them?"

Max tried not to smile too big as he pointed to Addy. "I wish I'd run into her down there. She could pump me for information any day."

"Be careful what you wish for. She's probably the most dangerous operative they have. Her name is Adhra Duke, and she's got more pull than the M.I.L.F. and the Iron Fist put together.

"Her title is ambassador, but she's really a political hooker who seduces people and gets them addicted to a mind-control drug called Victory. It's a nightmarish concoction of the worst elements of cocaine, heroin, crystal meth, PCP, oxytocin, and pure adrenaline. It feels like you're doing great coke, but its purpose is to make the user more susceptible to brainwashing. The parts of the brain involved with decision-making are shut down, essentially destroying the person's will and making it easy to imprint her own.

"She has all the major power brokers on a leash. She's beautiful, intelligent, and chaotic neutral. She could charm a religious fundamentalist into raping and eating his own children in about three minutes, so be sure to shoot her before she gets her hooks into you. She gives me nightmares."

More like wet dreams. Max barely managed to suppress a grin.

Of course Pope would say something like that. Newton admitted they told strategic white lies from time to time. On the other hand, she did seduce him and get him to snort some white powder, and it would explain how he'd fallen for her so fast. Addy had turned him into a double agent, but she never discussed business after drugs. If she was manipulating him, she was damn good at it. But, what about the plan to remove all megalomaniacs? Was it all bullshit, or was she one herself?

Every new bit of information contradicted something he'd been told before. Which Adhra was real? The bunny-loving sweetheart that grew up wanting to be a jazz singer or the ruthless seductress preying on men's weakness? Probably both. In any case, he was sick of being the communal pawn. It was time for him to take control of the situation.

Flipping through the rest of the photographs, he saw a few more people he recognized but was too preoccupied to care who they were. When he came to the end, he handed the folder back and shrugged.

"Sorry, man, they had me tied to a chair in a room the whole time. I didn't have a chance to go out and rub elbows."

"Nobody else came in the room for the entire time?"

"Well yeah. People were in and out all the time, but you know how it is. All Iiites look the same."

"Max, that's not cool. We may be at war with them, but that's no excuse for bigotry."

Max laughed bitterly and rubbed his burning eyes. "That was a joke. I was tied up, starved, and tortured. They barely let me sleep. I'm sorry if I didn't make a mental note every time somebody came in to deliver coffee or electrocute my nipples. I tell you what; go get kidnapped by the Iiites, stay for a couple months, then escape. If you can do a better job than me, I'll buy you dinner at your favorite restaurant."

"Fine, I get it, you were tortured. No need to get testy. Did you overhear anything that might be useful?"

"Well, they did bring me to their strategy meetings. Xavier Mitton and I hit it off. Sometimes we would bounce ideas off each other. I helped pick new wallpaper for Felix's office. Don't tell him though, it's a surprise."

Pope removed his glasses and scrunched up his face. "Perhaps it would be more productive to do this tomorrow. Over such a long period, someone probably said something to your torturer or maybe in the hallway with the door cracked? Think about it. Sometimes they might tell you things to intimidate you or brag because they don't think you'll escape."

"But wouldn't you discount anything I heard as seeded disinformation?"

"Probably."

"So, why does it matter?"

"In case what you heard was true."

"But how would you know?"

"We would decide."

"What if you were wrong?"

"We're rarely wrong."

"I'm not being a smartass this time. I'm asking you a question. How do you tell the shit from the shinola? I need to know so I can do my job."

"We do it the same as anybody else. Do you believe everything you see on TV or read in a book?"

"No."

"Well, what system of logic do you currently use?"

"I don't know. Some stuff seems to be true. Other stuff sounds like bullshit."

"Exactly. Based on the information you have taken in over the years, your brain automatically checks each new meme to see how well it fits with the other memes that it has decided are true. If it fits, you believe it. If not, it's kicked out. Some are so outlandish that it doesn't even register."

"So, how do you know when something's true? I mean, if you get something wrong, people die. What if you have some basic fundamental concept wrong that taints your whole system of beliefs? You won't know until it's too late?"

"When geniuses debate an issue, the majority decision is almost always correct. All our brains together are like a super-supercomputer with a system of checks and balances. What more do you want?"

"Never mind. Can we go now?"

"Yeah, we'll deal with this work stuff later. You could probably use a drink."

"Fuck yeah, I could use a drink."

"Well then, tally ho."

The Pins and Needles tattoo parlor was located two blocks from the local community college dorms. Its main functions were stamping tramps and marking frat boys with the names of soon-to-be ex-girlfriends. The Nrrds had a speakeasy in the back for when their baser instincts became distracting. Even if there weren't other Nrrds looking for an immediate physical release, there was always a steady flow of drunken college sluts into whom one could blow a little steam. It was a practical mechanism for keeping their physical urges in check without wasting valuable time or money on coupling rituals.

The front room looked like every other tattoo parlor Max had ever seen; small and square with rows of sample books and a glass display case featuring a menagerie of overpriced bars and plugs to suit the taste of any rebellious neophyte. The walls were covered with graffiti and the whole place stank of pizza and rubbing alcohol. A single, heavily inked barbarian stood behind the case ignoring the customers in favor of his sketchbook.

Pope rolled up his sleeve to display his pilcrow and sauntered over to the barbarian, "Hey, what's the haps Paps?"

The barbarian nodded towards the back without missing a single pen stroke.

"Is Inky around? I got a noob for him."

The barbarian's shoulders tensed, and he jerked his head angrily. "He's with a customer. Go on back." It sounded like a threat.

Pope nodded casually and motioned for Max to follow him as he walked behind a thick curtain to the right of the register.

"Nice guy," Max said as they journeyed down the row of grimacing patrons, "One of yours?"

"That's Porkchop. He's just there for security. I think his brother is one of our biomechanical engineers. Inky's the guy down there on the end. He's the owner of this fine establishment and one of the most ingenious masters of body modification in the world. He invented the retinal camera, electro-magnetic fingertips, and a long list of other useful items that make our job a lot easier. I'll show you the catalog later. You might want to modify yourself for a mission sometime. Anything you want would be free, so why not, right?"

"Yeah, elective surgery isn't really my thing."

"You might change your mind when you see what he can do."

They walked past Inky without saying hello. He was preoccupied tattooing 'bitch' in italics on a girl's left breast. Pope ushered him through another door marked private, then stopped a moment to drool.

Max was used to finding bizarre things behind inconspicuous doorways, so he barely blinked as he stepped into an exact replica of the Star Wars Cantina. There were a few differences. Instead of aliens and Jedi, he was surrounded by hackers and scientists. Instead of glowing or bubbling beverages, they served gourmet beer, wine, absinthe, and a signature beverage called Bliss.

Cheeky was dancing for a few Riot Nrrds on a large round table to the right. Their eyes locked. Seconds later, Cheeky was affectionately cuddling him on the floor. He was nuzzling so hard it seemed his cheeks might come off, but Max didn't mind. He was home, kind of, and things felt right again.

When Cheeky didn't stop flailing, Max hugged him tightly, rolled over onto his knees, and stood. He recognized Hedorah and Asphyxia from the secret base, but the other three at the table were new. Asphyxia was obviously drunk and making out with the two women he didn't recognize. She acknowledged him with a glance but didn't bother to pull her tongue out of the other girl's mouth. The unidentified male was staring blankly at his half-empty glass of Bliss. Hedorah was sandwiched between them, looking horny and agitated.

Hedorah's eyes were even creepier and more intense when he was drunk. He stared through the twisted tendrils of his hair, bit his cigarette, and grinned. "Hey, look who's not dead. Somebody buy Fubar a drink." He seemed genuinely happy to see him, but he was probably just bored.

Pope staggered in as though he'd been shoved through the doorway, but acted as if nothing had happened. "Good, you found our table. Name your poison."

"Bourbon, neat; something good."

Hedorah picked up his bottle of Optimizer and shook it to demonstrate its emptiness. Everyone else ignored him, so he clapped Max on the back and went to the bar.

Max and Hedorah stared awkwardly at each other while they waited for Pope to return. Hedorah was about as interested in the Iiite underworld as Max was in spherical trigonometry, so there wasn't much to talk about. When Max started making baby noises at his chubby little friend, Hedorah quickly became despondent and joined the new guy staring blankly at his beverage.

"Bourbon, neat." Pope set Max's drink in front of him. He took the remaining seat and slid Hedorah's beer across the table.

"Ladies." Pope raised his glass to the women. They continued to ignore him.

Max filled his mouth, swished it around, and swallowed. Warmth flowed out from his trachea, softening his muscles. "Not bad." He took another sip and returned his drink to the coaster.

Pope pointed to the catatonic man beside him. "That's Merlin, by the way. Not that it matters. He'll be like that for a while."

"What's wrong with him?"

"He's Blissed."

Max raised his eyebrows.

"Bliss is a beverage concocted by Timothy Leering; it contains absinthe, THC, salvia extract, ginkgo biloba, and DHA Omega 3. It's excellent for tripping off into your head to solve especially tricky problems, but, as you can see, it isn't so great for social situations.

"You already know Hedorah and Asphyxia. I'm not sure who those chicks are. For now, let's call them slut one and slut two."

Three birdies were produced, but their tongues mingled on. Max wondered whether the girls were getting off more on each other or from knowing they were the only girls in a room full of horny Nrrds who would go home alone and jerk off thinking about them. He could see why the Nrrds never dated each other. The jocks were probably better in the sack, and the girl with "bitch" tits was a lot less likely to drive them to suicide.

Pope asked Max what tortures he had undergone during his time with the enemy. Max did his best to entertain, he couldn't compete with the show the girls were offering. The only notable interruption was when Merlin snapped awake, shouted eureka, and ran out of the bar as if pursued by a school of laser-mounted, flying barracudas.

Many drinks flowed through them as their man-stares grew more intense. The rest was a kaleidoscopic blur.

SHORT NIGHT OF THE SPOOKS

Liquid sickles slid in swervy patterns darkening the darkness with apocryphal intent.

Max was paralyzed, floating before their--eyes?

They moved like the children of cartoon jackals. With a creepy innocence reminiscent of childlike curiosity, they swam and swarmed across his flesh, poking and pinching. He felt like a table of fruit, but in truth, he was just a vegetable.

His thinky bits had toddled off to somewhere more realistic, and his feely bits had followed. Lolling his head back and forth in waves and particles, he examined his examiners and wondered how, if this was a dream, was he aware yet powerless to change his circumstances. He focused, willing their sooty mass to become soft dreamy flesh, a sexier shade to bounce him into better bedtime, but to no avail.

He could barely feel the impact as he was bounced slowly around the room like a screensaver.

How were these living ideographs, these night noodles, holding him prostrate without any sign of restraints? Were they aliens? Surely aliens would have something better to do than frolic around an inverted levitating stranger.

Max felt like a mouse in the hands of a child. What would happen to him? Did it matter? At least if they killed him, he wouldn't have to deal with the hangover he so rightly deserved. His head drooped across the hand of one of his playmates and sucked itself to sleep.

FROM ZOMBIE WITH LOVE

The next day, Max was roused by his impatient bladder. He rolled into an upright position and coughed until he was fully conscious. Cheeky was curled at the foot of the bed, pretending to sleep but studying him with one narrowed eye. Max suspected Cheeky's hangover might have been worse than his own.

Poor little guy, he must have drunk his weight in Irish cream. He'd tried to stop him, but their time apart had inspired something akin to teen angst. Max couldn't tell if his having been away from Cheeky his whole life had earned him the role of the apologetic, estranged father or if Cheeky was just a belligerent drunk. He'd have to wait and see.

Cheeky needed to sleep it off, so Max pretended not to notice his little friend watching him stagger to the stairs. Hazy waves of memory sloshed in his brainpan in much the same way the previous night's muck sloshed in his stomach. He looked at his arm.

"Aww, come on! Seriously?" His pilcrow was crooked.

He half-remembered a flashy little box that put the mark on his arm without hurting it and the feeling of riding a roller coaster backward. He'd blacked out again. At least he made it home this time.

His clothes were glued to his flesh by something unidentifiable and rank. He stripped them away, loosing a cloud of stinking dust and a series of disturbing flashes from the night before: Siamese twins, a clown, blood in his underwear, blood on the walls, something about a chalupa. It was all jumbled and full of impossibilities. He was sure some of it was from a dream, but there was no way to tell which parts.

Last I checked I can't breathe fire. So, that's something.

He stared at his face in the bathroom mirror, and his heart fell into his stomach. His skin had a greenish glow about it. Smeared greasepaint circled his cheeks, mostly in red and white swirls, but with the occasional ripple of blue.

"That's not good." The lid below his right eye shivered.

Looking closer, he found that his face was covered in tiny cuts. He stared into his bloodshot eyes.

"What the fuck happened last night?"

His reflection responded with a look of tired confusion.

Max relieved himself and stepped into the shower. Tentacles of warmth caressed his nerves as they stretched to tickle his assorted crevices. As the ick dissolved, he was reminded of a toy he'd had as a kid, a mafia playset where he could make gangsters with a mold then dissolve them in a tank of "acid," leaving only the plastic skeleton behind. If only it were that simple.

The phone rang.

They'll call back.

He ignored it and allowed himself to be hypnotized by the orange-tinted water spiraling down the drain.

He tried to make out the message being left on the answering machine in the kitchen. It sounded like the Count. Could the news of his escape already have reached the Owls?

"Great, he probably wants me to be a quadruple agent or something. Next thing you know, I'll be working for the Jengists."

When he was once again shiny with clean, he dried, dressed, and returned the call. Someone had apparently spotted him stumbling drunkenly down the parkway pushing a screaming, disabled sex-clown in a shopping cart. While the Count lectured him about various nuances of public perception, he searched the room for clues. No balloons, no grease paint, no body. He must have misplaced her before arriving home.

"There is a time and place for public acts of depravity. However, you are not yet famous enough for that type of publicity. If you had happened upon a news crew, your career as a hero would be finished. We would be most disappointed to see that happen since we have gone to so much trouble to promote you even in your absence. Where have you been, anyway?"

"I was captured by the Iiites and tortured in an underground base," Max replied flatly.

"Oh, how delightful. You escaped, I assume?"

"Yeah."

"Excellent, I will arrange a press conference post haste. Everyone will want to hear your latest act of heroism. There may even be a movie deal in this. Do practice your delivery this time. Your debut was rather flat. I shall call you later with the details. Good day."

"Do you think you could stock an extra jet pack for me this time? That really sucked."

"I will see what I can do."

Max hung up and glanced at the clock. It was after three, so he returned to his room. Cheeky roused easily, rolling onto his back for a belly rub almost as soon as Max sat down. His floppy tongue curled like a party favor as he yawned and stared lovingly at Max through big black eyes like engorged baby leeches.

"You're so cute when you look like shit." Max cooed and rubbed his belly.

Cheeky stretched and flopped listlessly.

"You know what we need? Fresh air and waffles. How's that sound?"

Cheeky perked up and rolled over onto his suckers. "All right then, let's go drown our troubles in grease. Operation Waffle, hoo-ha!" He picked Cheeky up, draped him across his shoulders, and jogged down the steps.

Lately, even hung-over, he felt better than his old usual.

It was a beautiful day, so he decided to walk the three blocks to Das Waffle. The emerald horizon wore a necklace of ruby diamonds. Crossing slanted arches trailed to the horizon, letting him know the terrorists were done for the day. His sinuses hadn't readjusted to the surface yet, so the air smelled crisp and wonderful. Everything was unusually pleasant until he turned the corner and saw them.

He tried to dart back to safety, but it was too late. He'd already been spotted by the Abel Cultists. He ran, but his hangover made him easy prey for their souped-up Segways. They were upon him in seconds, howling and beating their chests, screaming, "Nude is rude! Nude is rude!"

He tried to push his way through the crowd, but the circle tightened around him. Cheeky clung to Max's head and whined as they pinned them to the wall of a defunct office supply store. Max raised his hands to block the spit and tried to reason with them.

"Hey, stop that. Everybody shut up, and let me explain."

The crowd was in a better mood than usual. They quieted down and confined their indignation to the realm of glaring and sign shaking.

"Okay, look, this is a cheekworm. They don't even have genitalia." He grabbed the back end of his little friend and waggled it at the apparent leader.

Everyone gasped and averted their eyes.

"See, there's nothing to be exposed. Therefore, it is not rude."

"How do they reproduce?" asked the leader, skeptically.

"They're worms. They reproduce by getting cut in half."

The leader, looking like Abe Lincoln, if Abe had been ritualistically abused by snake handlers as a child, stood tall and smiled victoriously. "In that case, the beast's whole body is a reproductive member."

The mob gasped again and put their hands over their eyes.

"Get a jilbab on that thing ASAP. This is your only warning. If we see it naked again, you will wish you had stayed home."

"Where the fuck am I supposed to find a jilbab that fits a cheekworm?" The image of Cakey in that hotdog costume popped into his head, bringing with it a hurricane of emotion. He was so cute and so dead. Luckily the rage helped him focus. "He wouldn't even be able to walk in one. He uses little sucker things to move around. See." He lifted Cheeky's underside into view and pointed out the little suction cups.

Their leader glared at the sidewalk and growled angrily. "That's your problem. We're here to enforce the rules of society, not sell clothing.

"Look asshole, I don't know what your problem is or why you go around staring at and obsessing about animal genitalia, but you're the fucking pervert. Not me. Not him. You can put clothes on every animal in the goddamn world, but you're still gonna be a crazy dog-fucker."

"Is it perverse to see animals and humans as equals? Or to believe that, as equals, the rules of society should apply to both? Public nudity is indecent and vile. If you were naked, the police would be dragging you away as we speak. For some reason, some people don't think the rules of society apply to non-humans. As God is my witness, I'll set that record straight once and for all."

"Amen," said the crowd.

"If you think an animal in its natural state is rude and indecent, I suggest you take it up with God. They're not born with cute little outfits on. Nor did he make them want to put clothes on later. It's God's design you have a problem with, so go spit on him and leave me the fuck alone."

Abe attempted a retort but only managed to sputter. The crowd was so shocked by Max's outburst they forgot to stop him as he pushed through. Abe threw his cowboy hat on the ground and stomped on it in a comic gesture of rage. "Don't let him leave. Get that sinner back here. I'm not finished."

But Max had already stolen one of the Segways and disappeared around the corner. The mob attempted to follow him, but he and Cheeky had already ducked inside Das Waffle and locked themselves in the bathroom.

Segways make a lot of noise when you get fifty or so in one place, so he knew when the Cult had gone. He waited a few more minutes then came out and approached the counter.

Everyone in the restaurant was staring at him like he had just French kissed a camel. He assumed it was because of the Segway. The customers were probably confused, thinking him to be a member of the Cult and yet seeing a naked animal on his shoulders. They probably thought he was going to kill it as some sort of protest. He wasn't one to enjoy attention, but it was nice to be the one in the know for a change.

After procuring a triple fat stack for himself and a double for Cheeky, they sat relishing their sugar and fried bread. It was a fine day, even with a fibbing sky. Cheeky was so adorable trilling and dripping with syrup that even the cluster-fuck of lies he had to figure out seemed distant and trivial.

Pleasantly stuffed and high on sugar, the evil spirits had been exorcised. They decided to throw caution to the wind and go to the park to school some college students in Frisbee football. The Cult had gained partial control of the park during the Pet Wars, but Max was unafraid. He hoped they'd all gone home to microwave their heads. If not, he would gladly pummel them with logic until their worldview collapsed.

The Igor Stanislavski Commemorative Park was almost as unusual as its history. Giant bonsai trees overgrown with Russian sage shaded weather-beaten picnic tables. The path was lined with Moroccan star lamps that made even the most brutal rape glow with the beauty of the rainbow. Heavily graffitied remains of stone lanterns and Tanuki statues were scattered throughout.

Where were all the students? Usually, he couldn't stand still for thirty seconds without being hit with a hacky sack and a couple of Frisbees. Today the zombies outnumbered the living two to one.

They were about to give up and try another park when Max noticed a note fastened to the lapel of a nearby zombie with a rose-shaped pin. He snatched it off, opened it, and smiled.

"Hey, look at that." He smiled at the bombastic elegance of Addy's handwriting. Deciphering coded messages was one of the primary focuses of his training. The code was in the style of the letters rather than the words. He read the letter effortlessly.

I miss you, and hope you are doing well. I hate having to communicate with you this way. Look in the zombie's right back pocket and take the ring. The stone is a tracking device. Rotate it 180 degrees to turn the tracker off. When you have something to tell me, turn it on and put it and your message in the pocket of any zombie. I'll have it within the hour. Keep an eye out for zombies wearing red rose pins. Be discreet. Someone is almost always watching.

I heard you were marked with a pilcrow. That's too bad. The ink is infused with nanotechnology that works as a bug, a tracking device, and a lie detector. Be very careful what you say from now on. They may not be listening, but you are being recorded twenty-four hours a day. If they suspect anything, they will go back and listen to everything you've ever said.

Get in good with the Order of the Owl. They're a lot more important than you know.

There will be another attempt on your life at your next press conference. Be prepared and take them out on live television. They won't know you're working for us. Their orders are to kill you. Hopefully, it will spark a visible war between the Nrrds and the Iiites, which will make the Normals take action. With any luck, a new governing body will form to step in when the rest of society falls into anarchy.

That's all for now. Good luck. Be careful. Hurry.

I miss you.

A.

Max lit the edge of the note and watched carbon creep across its surface. When there was nothing left but ash, he crushed the ash to dust and stomped it into the ground. Slapping his hands together, he glanced over at Cheeky and said, "Those Thai restaurants sure are getting imaginative with their spam, but I only eat at Phuket Thai. I like the name. Let's see what else this guy has on him."

He retrieved a silver amethyst ring, which fit perfectly on his pinky finger. "Hey, that's kind of nice. I think I'll take it."

He rotated the stone as per his instructions and knelt down to scratch his little friend behind the ears. "Aww, don't look at me like that. He doesn't need it anymore. Zombies don't care about worldly possessions. They're very Zen that way."

Cheeky continued to stare incredulously, so Max scooped him up and tickled him until the memory was erased. He wished somebody would be kind enough to do the same for him. More than anything, he wanted to believe Addy was telling the truth, but how could he? She was a professional liar.

She's probably doing this so she can seize the throne for herself, but would that be so bad? The Iiites were already pumping poison into the world's FÜD supply and using various underhanded methods to control people's minds. Both sides were developing more and more dangerous weapons, and Normals were caught in the crossfire. Maybe the world would be better off if it was ruled by one group with total control and no opposition. Addy might not be much better than the other candidates, but she couldn't possibly be worse.

Cheeky and Max tried to salvage the rest of their day by going to see the remake of "The Man From U.N.K.L.E." The plot was stale, and the twists and action were blasé. Nothing he saw compared to his own experiences. All it did was kick his brain into overdrive trying to figure out which way his own plot was going to twist. Max left feeling that he had been robbed of fifty bucks and two hours of his life.

WHERE HAWKS DARE

Max had always thought the only way he would appear live on the 6 o'clock news would be to run up and stab a pundit.

He was wrong.

The devil works in mysterious ways.

Max sat in his trailer watching the organized chaos of the Media© Circus on a live feed provided by a multitude of security cameras, most of which were leftover biometric units from the second American revolution. The Nrrds had spared no expense in refurbishing the system after Max gave an impassioned speech regarding the likelihood of a second attempt on his life. A small army of Nrrds was placed strategically in the surrounding buildings watching every possible entrance from the sewer and surrounding streets through scopes sensitive enough to count the pseudopods on an amoeba a mile away. Autonomous Thor drones had been deployed to patrol the streets and the sewers. If there were threats in the vicinity, the bots would find them and encase them in an electromagnetic field.

Max, was beginning to worry the Nrrds were too thorough. The war couldn't start without an attack? Even as he watched the incognito Nrrds circulate in the crowd, he had faith Addy would find a way. Any disbelief he could possibly have suspended regarding her good intentions had been thoroughly purged from his mind by a series of debriefings he had been given on her history over the last few days. She was the sneakiest, most manipulative, devious sociopath he'd ever met, and God help him, he loved her.

The Media© Circus was bigger than last time. They had added an extra dunking booth, a rollercoaster, and a catapult that propelled scratchy Velcro-suited idiots into the large fuzzy wall of a neighboring building. The Sav-cops had set up a perimeter to keep zombies out, but there hadn't been many, to begin with. They spent most of their time in the lines of various attractions or to get baskets of fried treats for their comrades.

Max shifted uncomfortably in his famous-person getup. His jeans were so oversized it gave the sensation of being naked under denim sheets, and his Corporate Raiders football jersey was basically a man-dress. He hated popular fashion almost as much as he hated sports. He'd felt less silly when the zoo made him dress like a furry and dance beside the road. At least this time, he was making more than minimum wage.

The Count's walking stick tapped out the secret knock on the door. A cruel smile played across Max's lips as he motioned for Hawk to let him in. Hawk's eyes narrowed resentfully, but he did as he was told. Max felt like a kid who had been put in charge of his siblings while the adults were away.

As the Count stepped in, his tophat bumped the doorframe and tumbled backward into the street. He scowled and left it there. "Really Max, I don't see why you insist on using these security trailers instead of our five-star luxury units. Leave security to the security guards and enjoy yourself, for God's sake. You're defeating the purpose of being famous."

Every word stoked the fires of Hawk's paranoia. It was his job to keep Max safe. "Decadence pods" were like giant, neon, bulls-eyes. You might as well sell discounted tickets to anyone with a gun. His nostrils flared, and before you could say professional wrestling Greystoke was on the floor in a chokehold finding out what ripping cartilage feels like in slow motion.

It was intensely amusing to watch the two personalities interact. Max wondered if any other clash in history had been so immediate and complete.

"Which side you working for, you little cunt? You know damn well the Iiites want him dead. You'd probably like for 'im to die, wouldn't you? A national hero dies on live TV. Imagine the ratings. Whaddaya think Max? What should I do with this piece of shit, kill him or kill him slow?"

Max exhaled deeply and shook his head. "Let him go, man. He's just trying to make me comfortable. This is Count Greystoke. He's my contact with the Order."

"I know who he is. I know plenty not to trust him, too."

"You don't trust anybody. It's your job. Now, let him go."

Hawk grunted his disappointment and pushed him away roughly.

Greystoke scuttled to the wall and tried to rub his damaged windpipe back into shape. He rasped, "Really Max, people who can't keep their trained gorillas in check tend to have exceedingly brief excursions into the world of show business."

"I'm sorry about that. He's my bodyguard. With all the people that want me dead, I need somebody like him to keep my head on my shoulders. Hawk, apologize to Count Greystoke. He's a friend." Max smiled and stroked the swatch of cat ear in his pocket.

"Sorry." Hawk grumbled his apology like a naughty child. A lifetime of military service had conditioned him to follow orders regardless of his own thoughts or emotions. He had applied to and been accepted by every offensive or defensive company in existence in search of information that would lead to a perfect military strategy. He had studied violence the way physicists study particles. Unfortunately, one side effect of a lifetime devoted to the study of violence and destruction was a whopping case of paranoia. Max had spent most of the day with him. At this point, death seemed preferable to another of Hawk's survival strategies.

Greystoke stood and cleared his throat. "I decline his apology. People like him belong in cages along with the other primates."

Hawk growled but didn't move.

Greystoke's lip curled cruelly. "I was only going to tell you that they are ready for you to take your position backstage. You had five minutes, but now you will have to hurry. This is live television. It's rather awkward when they cut to a live feed, and there's no one there."

On the stage monitor, Chaz Lightbeard was doing the, "I want to talk about my mother-in-law, so I'm gonna need my corkscrew," bit. He pulled out a pocket pussy painted like a cork and pretended to fuck it while making farting noises with his mouth.

"Shit, that's his big finish. We need to hurry."

Max stood and followed Greystoke out of the trailer. As he passed the fuming General, he stopped and patted him on the shoulder. "Buck up, man, everything's going to be fine. Just try not to kill anybody who can't crush your head in the palm of his hand."

A nervous little man with a clipboard dragged Max up the stairs and thrust him onto an X just outside the audience's view. Lightbeard was doing Max's intro because Han-dog had added a no-politics clause to his contract after what happened at the last press conference. It came as no surprise that a pundit running for CEO would seize the opportunity to associate himself with a real-life action hero who had mentioned him by name in his last press conference. This was an opportunity for Max to make a valuable ally. He couldn't predict what favor he might need from the CEO of Agrocorp, but it certainly couldn't hurt to have one.

The crowd had been lulled to sleep by a long string of punny items Chaz had brought with him, but when Max was introduced, they snapped awake, screaming and pumping their fists. Rather than walk out to the traditional commercial rock, he had demanded they play "Alabama Song." Years ago, a different version had been used in a commercial, so he could play it off as a remix if the crowd went sour. The Owls had not been happy about his decision, but he was adamant. If everything else failed miserably, at least he could say he got the mainstream Media© to play a non-commercial rock song.

The crowd didn't notice.

With three energy shots worth of enthusiasm, Max ran out, clapped Chaz on the back, and shook his hand. They embraced like old friends. Max grabbed the microphone and screamed, "Hey, everybody! Thanks for comin' out to support the good guys. Chaz, thank you so much for being here. You're great. Everybody vote for this guy. He's not corrupt. No, really."

Chaz grinned and dragged his props off stage.

"All right! It's great to be with you all again! Thanks so much for coming out. Who wants to hear about how I broke out of a heavily guarded Iiite compound?!"

The crowd made lots of affirmative noises. This time, three women flashed their breasts, and two of them seemed halfway sober.

"Cool. Last time you saw me, I was on a stage being pushed down the street by a crowd that was being ripped apart by zombies. The cameras got knocked over before I had a chance to do anything, so I'll start there. So I'm getting carried along, and I'm, like, 'I have to do something. What can I do to stop this?'

He the hammer out of his jacket pocket. "I carry this in case of emergencies. You can't ask for a better zombie deterrent. I'm sorry, I know it's not PC, but it's saved me more than once."

He reared back like he was about to swing it. "I was all ready to bash some heads when the stage tipped over, dumping me in the middle of hundreds of freakin' out dead people. When I hit the ground, my hammer got knocked out of my hand and kicked away by the horde, but I knew I couldn't give up. I used my fists, but I was way outnumbered. It really looked like I was gonna be zombie chow.

"Then, all of a sudden, the zombies just chilled out. I was standing there on a huge pile of mashed up zombies like, 'Come and get it, bitches.' I felt a sharp pain in my neck. 'Oh crap, one of them got me.'

He paused for dramatic effect. The crowd was silent. "Next thing I know, I'm disoriented and everything's pitch black. My mouth is dry, my whole body hurts, and somewhere in the darkness, I hear something breathing.

"I thought I was in hell." He paused again to let that sink in.

"When the drugs wore off, I was gagged, blindfolded, and tied to a chair. That sucked, but not as much as what came next."

He pointed at the ground. "The Iiites held me in the sewer for two months. They starved me, tortured me, deprived me of sleep, you name it, all because I made them look bad on TV. I mean, goddamn, vindictive much?"

The crowd erupted with laughter.

"Probably the only reason I'm still alive is that I have such a big mouth. I'd provoke the hell out of them every time the gag came off, and the sadistic jerks elected to hurt me more instead of putting me out of my misery. Luckily, the Riot Nrrds attacked the base where they were holding me. While the Iiites were distracted, I grabbed a fire extinguisher and bashed my guard's head in. It still surprises me how easily those fuckers die. I've killed bugs with more stamina."

The crowd laughed even as green fire rained from the sky. Iiites wearing jetpacks zigzagged over the unsuspecting fans, strafing them with plasma cannons. The Nrrds hadn't anticipated this many attackers, much less that they would come from the sky. Several buildings were leveled by their panicked response.

There went my snipers.

One of the ugliest bastards he'd ever seen dropped down right in front of Max. He looked like an inbred troglodyte who'd grown up near a toxic waste disposal site eating nothing but crack and steroids. Grinning hideously with a yellow-green tangle ripped straight from a dentist's wet dream, the beast raised his plasma cannon and let out a helpless gurgle as his torso curled into a smoldering meat pie. Max's plas-mini looked like a keychain, but it was more than capable of turning people into shadowboxes. The Nrrds even made him a spring-mounted sleeve thingy.

Adhra warned me these guys would mean business, but damn!

The few Nrrds left on the ground were blinded by a mixture of debris and their own tears. They screamed like frightened children and fired randomly at the sky, missing the Iiites and frequently blowing chunks out of the withering buildings where their backup was hiding. The police were all dead, so the convicts were free to trample or be trampled by civilians in a frenzied attempt to find shelter.

"For fuck's sake," Max cried from his podium, "it's only been like forty-five seconds!"

Miraculously, the sound system had remained undamaged. Everyone stopped firing. All eyes were on him.

"Shit!"

He jumped off the stage and ran for cover. The stage collapsed, its metal singing songs in falsetto to the splintering wood. Nobody had trained him to run in rapper-jeans, but the molten jersey dripping down his back kept him moving.

Inside the dunking booth, the redneck hooted and cheered like he was watching an action movie. As Max ran towards him, the convict got so excited he slipped on a puddle of gore and slid into the machinery. Max had to jump to keep from getting splashed as he dashed into the neighborhood Sav-Mart.

Several of the prisoners had taken cover inside the store. As Max ran in, a burly skinhead pushed him down.

"Get the fuck out of here. You're gonna get us all killed." Green fire splashed through a nearby window, missing Max, but withering the convict's right side. His leg slid out of his hip with a greasy pop. He toppled and landed on his face.

The other refugees screamed and ran for the back.

Max forced himself to his feet, ripped off what was left of his jersey, and took stock of the situation. The store's walls were holier than a Mormon's underwear and quickly moving towards the knickers of nuns and bishops, the mortar acquiescing meekly to the plasmatic downpour. With no hope of cover and under constant threat of being squished by chunks of debris, Max ran hither and thither searching for anything that could prove useful and praying the Nrrds were taking advantage of the diversion.

Live wires dangled menacingly from the ceiling, starting small fires all around him. The burning displays were billowing thick, black smoke, making it hard to breathe.

135

He could see the majority of the remaining Iiites were collecting on the sidewalk in front of the store to take potshots at him through its ever-widening entrance. Occasionally, one of them exploded, so there was still backup out there somewhere. Unfortunately, at the current rate of attrition, he'd be dead long before the Iiites were.

Behind the Iiites, a fire hydrant exploded, giving them an unwanted shower. The onslaught stopped for a moment as the Iiites turned and obliterated the final Nrrd who was responsible for their sudden soppiness.

Max searched desperately for a way out and smiled when he spotted a power line through a hole in the wall. He took aim and incinerated the top of the pole. Live wires swooped into the spray like a giant electric squid of doom; 44,000 volts of electricity ended the siege as abruptly as it had begun.

"Yahooooooo!" Max clicked his heels joyously, barely noticing when the front of the building collapsed, trapping him inside the crumbling inferno. His head was spinning out of control. He wondered if it was possible to overdose on adrenaline as he vomited onto a burning pile of cereal. The acrid steam of breakfast and stomach acid hit his nose.

Time to go.

The electric lake was seeping through the rubble. The side walls were so decimated a stiff breeze could bring the roof down. Max's best option was to run through the flaming obstacle course and hope the back door was unlocked.

Dodging flaming ceiling tiles and dangling electric cords, he hopped and dashed through consumerist hell. He ran past melting computers, burning magazine racks, and smoking toilet paper. Once through the stockroom doors, he spotted a fire exit sign mounted high against the back wall. He went for it, but halfway there, the right wall began to collapse. The ceiling toppled a large shelf, sending the store's entire back stock rushing toward him like a Rube Goldberg machine. His leg muscles burned. His side felt like it was caught on a meat hook, but he turned pain into rage, and rage into speed.

He saw the door. It was open, but on the other side of a pallet of propane tanks that lay in flagrante with a crate of flaming sweatpants.

"Goddammit, I hate today!" he screamed as he ran toward the sound of expanding metal. He passed the pallet and was only a few feet from the door when the first tank was compromised. The explosion launched tanks in every direction and turned the air into fire. The others exploded a second later, propelling him through the open doorway as if the entire building were a potato gun. Time slowed as he flew. As he drifted towards the enormous skinhead with a skull tattooed over his face, the only thing going through his head was DEVO's "Secret Agent Man."

Max hit the convict, and together they traveled twenty feet to leave a small dent in the concrete wall that ran along the road. When he regained his senses, he stood shakily and eyed the ruined husk of the second convict who had inadvertently saved his life that day. He was built like a tank, more muscle than fat, but luckily cushy enough to absorb most of the impact on both sides. His chest was caved in, his eyes rested on embellished cheekbones, and blood trickled from his mouth and nose like a cheesy special effect.

"Thanks, buddy."

Behind him, rubble shifted as the dead man's cohorts dug their way out from under piles of exploded cinderblocks. The fact that they were all skinheads made him question the randomness of the dunking booth selection process.

Stunned and angry, the skinheads stumbled toward each other. One of them railed back and punched another in the throat. Soon all four of them were throwing knuckles and kneecaps, spitting teeth and cursing as they hurled chunks of concrete at each other's heads.

Max wondered why anyone who'd just narrowly averted death would be so eager to kill. Then it dawned on him. Their blurry eyes must have misinterpreted their sooty friends as members of a different breed. Did they think their friends were an attacking gang, or were they each so stupid and twisted by hatred that they attacked everyone with a different skin tone? Before long, they were all dead or dying.

"Darwin be praised."

Max's ironic smugness was interrupted by the howl of approaching sirens. At this point, he'd gotten cops killed from every company, and none of them were particularly prone to accept apologies. In his shirtless, filthy state, he looked more like a crack dealer than a TV personality, so he decided to play it cool.

Using the pile of dead skins as a stepping stool, Max scaled the wall and jogged across the street to a gas station. Hawk was over by the coin-operated vacuums, chugging a bottle of hobo juice and muttering angrily.

"Son of a bitch."

Max expected him to run, but Hawk was off in his own little world. Max kicked his leg. "Hey, dipshit, good job today. Thanks for all the help."

The General raised his head then shrank as if he'd seen a ghost, "Holy fuck!" he said as he backpedaled into the carwash.

Max followed him. "Yeah, I'm still alive, no thanks to you. Where the fuck were you? Everybody's dead. I mean everybody; the Nrrds, the Iiites, the Media©, police, spectators—the fucking bugs in the walls are all dead! I thought you said you had it covered."

Hawk switched from terror to defense mode. He stopped swimming, stood, removed his jacket, and tossed it to the ground. "Our calculations said the possibility of an attack from the sky was so unlikely our resources would be more useful distributed among the lower levels."

"You put me through hell with all those security measures, and none of it did any good. I could have predicted they might use jetpacks. They could also have dropped bombs out of hot air balloons, planes, or goddamn zeppelins. They could have come from the skies all kinds of ways, and it didn't even occur to you to have eyes on the roofs?"

"The calculations said..."

"Yeah, that's probably why they did it. They know how your head works, jackass! You guys are predictable as fuck. No wonder this was a disaster. I could have mounted an effective attack against you with twenty-five bucks and a kindergarten class."

"Sorry."

"Sorry for what, for being incompetent? For torturing me all day long with pointless security measures? For letting all those people die?"

"Yeah, okay. All that stuff. Plus, sorry for abandoning you. I figured you was dead. I pulled out when the burning building you were in started to collapse from all the Iiite gunfire. There were only two of us left. We were shooting 'em from behind while they were shooting at you. They noticed what was going on and shot Blackenstein into so many pieces there's not enough of him left for a DNA swab. They didn't see me, so I aborted the mission. Not much I could have done anyway."

"Bullshit! You're a fucking coward. A Nrrd shot a bunch of them in the back while they were firing on me. When they fired back, I shot out a power line, which fell into the spray of a busted hydrant and fried them. You'd know that if you'd stuck around. When did you really run away?"

Tears welled in the General's eyes. "Look, just don't tell anybody. I'll do anything you ask. The guys can't know about this."

"How the fuck did you get to be a general? I thought you had some huge history of combat experience."

Hawk laughed bitterly. "Same as all the other ones—by hiding. The brave guys all get killed in combat. In the military, it's the cowards that get the medals and give speeches about bravery. Everybody else is dead."

"I think most military personnel would take issue with that statement."

"Damn it, I've trained with every military group in the world. I know over a thousand ways to kill a man with one finger. I'm an excellent strategist. In a simulation, I win one hundred percent of the time with an average .05 percent collateral damage. I'm just not so great when the shit hits the fan."

"You don't say."

"Look, I don't want to die, that's all. Not wanting to die's what got me interested in war in the first place. I figured that if I got enough training, nobody could kill me. If I got powerful enough, I could put an end to war once and for all. Thing is, to be good at war, you have to see it as a game. You can't think about all the people you're killing and sending to die. All that matters is winning the game. That shit back there was way too vivid. Game over. How the hell did you survive, anyway?"

"Pure fucking adrenaline—and luck." Max shook his head in disgust. "Whatever. A well-trained wuss is still a wuss. I've barely had any training, but I survived, I am not the athletic type. My idea of exercise is curling my TV remote." He pointed an imaginary remote at Hawk and pretended to try to change the channel.

"Somebody said you need me to give your team the passion, instinct, and unpredictability you need to win. So, why the fuck didn't you involve me? You said, 'Sit back and relax. We'll handle everything. Don't worry.' Well, this shit has me worried now."

Hawk, apparently speechless, offered the bit of crayon red hobo juice that had not yet been dumped down his throat or uniform. Max shot him an incredulous look and walked into the store. A few minutes later, he returned with one bottle of Juicetastic pressed against his lips and another in his pocket. He drained the first, then opened the second and gestured for the General to follow him.

"Come on, general Tso. We can't hang around here. Pope's going to pick us up at the Tweak and Creep on Elm Street."

Hawk sniffled at Max's heels like an ashamed puppy. Max wondered if he should tell the others. No. A coward he could control was better than another coward he couldn't. With a little effort, he might forge this arrangement into a friendship and access to privileged information. His inner spy could hardly wait, but the longer Hawk worried, the more grateful he would be.

They walked in silence past apartments and businesses full of drones that had no idea what was going on right down the street. Max felt like a god compared to them.

He had a vision of himself sitting on the throne of the world with Cheeky and Addy by his side, making all those tough self-condemning decisions he hated others for. It was way too vivid. He could feel himself becoming capable of wide-scale damage. He'd been easily swept up in all this spy business because it seemed too absurd to be real.

But it was real.

All those people who died today were really dead, and it was mostly his fault.

He didn't want to be responsible for death. He didn't want to be like the douche bags that had dragged him into this mess. Something was opening up within him that he couldn't quite understand. He felt a responsibility to save people from the assholes that wanted to save them from themselves. He was swept up by a big pink tsunami of compassion for his fellow man. He wanted to give the cows machine guns.

His tummy grumbled at the thought of cows.

Max glanced back at the plume of smoke swaying in the forest green sky and thought of all those dead fans. He had to blink back a tear before he lost his advantage.

If I'm destined to be a god, I'm going to be a merciful one. I'll act in will and will in love to make the world a paradise. Or something like that.

But what would he do, and how would he do it? Love, being inherently submissive, was generally trampled under the heels of selfishness. He couldn't make people love, but he could remove things that generate vast quantities of hate.

The need for power comes with a lack of compassion, which leads to slavery and war, which leads to revolution, at which point some other asshole with an inferiority complex lies to enough people to take the throne and start the cycle over. To break the cycle by introducing a leader who was only interested in the betterment of the world through kindness would solve most major problems by ceasing to manufacture. Without abuse, power is simply responsibility.

He didn't want control over anyone. He only wanted to be left alone, but somebody had to weed the garden of humanity. Success had turned many good men into monsters. Hopefully, being a monster, to begin with, he would have a different result.

A Superbus honked three times and pulled up next to them. The passenger side window rolled down, and Pope screamed, "Get in before somebody sees you! Every cop within twenty miles is looking for you guys.

As Max entered the car, he glimpsed the constipated look of terror in Hawk's eyes and felt terrible.

He's suffered enough.

Max winked conspiratorially at his new friend. Hawk looked like he might jump for joy and scream, "Whoopee!" Instead, he climbed into the back and shut the door.

"You bring me that change of clothes?"

Pope pointed to the glove compartment and peeled away. "All I had time to grab was a shirt."

Max opened the door and removed a small black t-shirt that said, "Free Ambulance Rides" in bold white letters. "This isn't one of mine."

"No, it's mine. Try not to stretch it out."

Max glanced at Pope's eleven-year-old-boy-physique.

"I wear it ironically. Don't start. Now what the fudge happened back there?"

"You didn't see it on TV?"

"I was otherwise engaged. Hawk was supposed to have this under control."

Hawk chewed his lip while Max indulged Pope with an idealized version of the day's events. By the time he finished, Pope was wearing an evil grin that would make any villain proud.

"Excellent! Your mission was to make the public more aware of the nature of things. The televised destruction of a city block should do nicely. Onward, to drinks and levity!"

THE SAFEHOUSE IS NOT ENOUGH

It was early, so the Nrrds had Pins and Needles all to themselves. Max felt weird being in a bar with the lights up, like he was sneaking a peek in the Tabernacle. Hawk sat next to him in a corner booth drinking Malaysian beer while Pope embellished their story for Newton. He liked the bump in status Max had afforded him and was trying to leverage even more.

Max didn't care. He had beer.

When it got to the part where Max turned Hawk's cowardly abandonment into chest-pounding badassery, Hawk looked as though he might try to kiss him. His eyes were big and moist. He alternated between chewing his lips and parting them as if to speak, but never made a sound.

Cheeky came to Max's defense, leaving his spot on the table and pouring himself into the gap between them. The general didn't seem to notice, so Max draped Cheeky across his shoulders with the toothy end facing Hawk and scooted as far away as he could without falling out of the booth. Then it occurred to him. This wasn't a romantic stare. It was the kind a dog gives its master after a game of fetch.

Oh God, I'm blackmailing him, and he loves me for it. Am I a douchebag? I'm used to feeling like an asshole, but this is the first time I've felt douchey.

When Pope finished, Newton waved them over. "Wonderful job, Max. This is the best news since the invention of the molecular laser! Any misgivings we had about you are forever banished."

This is how they react to the deaths of sixty some-odd geniuses? How fucked does that make me? I don't even have a Bachelor's degree. They probably look at me the way they do a chicken that can play tic-tac-toe.

Max forced a smile and nodded, though he wasn't sure why.

Newton lifted his big, shiny head. "As a reward for winning our biggest victory to date, I will grant you one wish. Make any demand within my power, and it is yours."

Rather than taking the time to consider the possibilities or generate a quip worthy of Newton's level of conceit, Max gave him an immediate, almost knee jerk response. "I want my own apartment."

Newton blinked, looking puzzled, "That is your wish? I said you could have anything. If you don't like Rusty, there are plenty of other safe houses."

"Rusty's fine. I like him. He's a little weird, but a good guy. Granted, it's the noisiest place I've ever lived, but that's not why I want to move out."

"Why then?"

"You didn't say I had to explain my wish."

"I'm just curious."

"Lots of reasons. I am a very solitary person. I hate having to share a space with anybody. I don't have any privacy. I don't like the décor. I feel like I'm imposing on him. It would be nice to walk around naked and piss with the bathroom door open without having to listen to catcalls. Also, the quiet would help me think, which would increase my chances of staying alive. Also again, the Iiites could find out where your safe houses are and attack them. They're less likely to find me in a random apartment only you and I know about. Is that good enough or should I keep going?"

"We would have to find a place off the books. Do you have anything in mind?"

"Hmm, I hadn't really thought about it. What would be the last place they would think to look for me?"

"I'm not responsible if you get yourself killed. If you're going to do this, you have to decide where to go. Only Hawk and I will know where you live, and we will keep in touch with this."

He pulled a phone out of his pocket but pulled it back when Max reached for it. "Let me know when you think of something. In the meantime, there's someone I would like you to meet."

"Hold on, I have an idea." Max motioned for Newton to come closer, then leaned forward and whispered, "What about Scarlet's place? They would never expect you to put me somewhere that was on their radar. Sometimes the best hiding place is right out in the open. It's close to several of our bases. It's more remote than Rusty Nails, so there's less chance of me being spotted, and I already feel at home there. What do you think?"

Newton stood up straight and half-smiled. "Well, it could work. It's ultimately up to you, though. Are you sure you wouldn't rather have unlimited credits for upgrades? There's some pretty cool stuff you can do with superpowers."

"Nah, privacy is more valuable to me than heat vision or super hearing or whatever. Give me the apartment."

"You know, we can do a lot better than heat vision. We can ramp up your whole nervous system so you can move and perceive everything several times faster. It's costly, though. You'll never earn enough to have it done on your own."

"Dude, I said I wanted the apartment."

"Fine, it's your funeral. I'll make the arrangements. Now there's someone I'd like you to meet. This is Emma; she's our best spy and your new best friend."

A figure stepped from behind Newton and put out a hand. Cheeky's suckers tightened on Max's shoulder. Subconsciously, he'd felt someone there the whole time, but she—Max was fairly sure it was a she—hadn't registered until she was right in front of him. Even then, it was difficult to notice her. Her face was remarkably bland. It had no distinguishing characteristics. Looking at it was like trying to focus on static. After a few moments, his eyes ached from the effort of trying to decode her face. He shut his eyes and tried to picture her, but nothing solidified. She might have had dark skin.

"Nice to meet you." He tried to blink away the blur.

She responded pleasantly. "You too! I've heard wonderful things."

"Thanks. So what exactly do you do?"

"I observe and report. I underwent a procedure to mute my features, making me difficult for the brain to register. I can go anywhere."

"You let them do this to you?"

"No, I had them do this to me." She exhaled as though she was already tired of explaining. "I developed the procedure. We measured the brain waves of a few hundred people as they flipped through high school yearbooks. Then we took all the photos that got the least response and extrapolated which individual features they had in common. We compiled some faces with those features and did it again. After a few rounds, we refined the geometry of this face.

"The surgery worked well enough, but then I developed a perfume that cancels out human pheromones. You'd be surprised how much your olfactory senses affect the way you see the world. Finally, I designed this necklace that puts out Fnordian waves, which cancel out any residual interest. Check this out."

She touched her neck, and Max felt an uncontrollable compulsion to look anywhere else.

"Now, I'm a walking blind spot. I can go wherever I want without anyone noticing me. Isn't it cool?"

I can see this becoming a problem. I'll have to find a way to keep her out of my hair.

She turned it off, and the compulsion subsided.

"That's fucking crazy. I'm impressed. What did you look like before?" Max was flabbergasted that anyone could be so dedicated to a cause.

"Everybody asks me that." She pulled a picture up on her phone.

Max could feel his eyes bugging out. The girl in the picture was a knockout. She had the quiet, smoldering beauty of an old-time movie star. Her eyes sparkled, and her rotund love mounds seemed to be reaching out to motor-boat him.

"This was you. What the hell were you thinking?"

Her tone grew more irritable. "Everyone asks that too. A few weeks after that picture was taken, two men grabbed me as I was leaving Sav-

Mart. They threw me in the back of a van and sexually tortured me for three days. They cut every part of me, then tossed me in a dumpster to die. I'd been saving myself for my one true love."

Max wasn't sure how to respond. "Uh, I'm sorry. I shouldn't have asked."

"Don't worry about it. Everybody asks. My psychiatrist helped me come to terms with it, and now I see it as a good thing. Being damaged allowed me to give up a lot of distractions. I got real interested in the functionality of the human brain, and now I'm doing something that matters."

Max wanted to change the subject. He turned to Newton. "Uh, okay."

Newton smiled and put his arm around her. "Isn't she great?"

"Yeah."

"And she's all yours. Use her in any way you like." Newton withdrew his arm. "That came out wrong. You know what I mean. She works for you now. Anything you want to know, just ask her. She's a walking encyclopedia of Iiite gossip."

He handed the phone to Max. "She's speed dial one, I'm speed dial two, Hawk is three, and the rest of the people you might need are in your contact list. I fully expect you to have the Lobsters on their knees within the month. All of our resources are at your disposal. Also, I was bluffing before about the upgrades. Whatever you want is on the house. We need you to be as effective as possible."

"I'm still not sure I want my nervous system rewired."

"Just think about it."

Emma chimed in from across the room. "I had it done, and I'm loving it. It doesn't hurt, if that's that you're afraid of."

Cheeky and Max's heads jerked towards the direction her voice had come. "I'll take that under advisement. So, you mind if I go get settled into my new digs?"

Newton scowled. "Yes, I mind. There is celebrating to be done. Plus, I haven't made the arrangements yet. You would be trespassing if you went right now."

"That doesn't concern me." He leaned closer to whisper, "I have a key, and the people there keep to themselves. Her bills are automatically debited, so I doubt anybody's noticed she's gone. All you need to do is keep some money in her bank account."

"I still have to make sure it's not under surveillance. You can go there tonight, but in the meantime, we drink!" Newton punctuated his statement by slapping Max hard in the stomach.

Pope and Emma appeared on either side of him, each holding two glasses of Bliss.

If I can't get rest, I might as well get trashed.

He took a glass from Pope and downed it in one gulp.

Pope stared at him like he was crazy.

Emma laughed. "Thirsty, huh? You want these too?"

Never one to back down from a drinking challenge, Max chugged them both.

"She was being facetious!" Pope grimaced and tried to take the glass away from him, but Max jerked away, determined to teach the Nrrds a thing or two.

As he set down glass number three, reality turned into a still shot that slowly rotated sideways, allowing him to see behind the façade to the molecular workings of the universe. Space-time revealed itself as a great, spinning wheel grinding against his forehead and shooting little sparks of his brain to the farthest reaches of space. And then came the light.

THE LIVING NIGHTLIGHTS

The onslaught of nine-dimensional colors faded back into the identifiable spectrum as tiny pinpricks of the grand illusion reclaimed Max's mind, one molecule at a time. The pressure propelling him through the cosmos was letting up. The subsequent decrease in velocity crumbled his footing in the multiverse. Soon he was collapsing back into himself. The metallic white noise of everything decreased to a rumbling growl, gently vibrating his waking framework. With sensation came his individual will, which adamantly disagreed with the stream in which it was caught. He knew what had to be done, but he wasn't happy about it.

He cracked an eyelid and immediately regretted it. The goddamned night noodles were at it again. The sudden jolt of recognition and fear was a bullet to the head for his altered state of consciousness. Suddenly sober and hovering three feet in the air above Scarlet's befuddled Bio-Bed, Max was once again in the grip of those strange prodding shapes.

Damn it, I thought that was a nightmare. Maybe I'm still asleep?

He tried to wish them into beautiful nymphets.

It didn't work.

Had he landed in some other part of the multiverse? He tried to speak. He wanted to scream, to shoo them away like the pests they were, but his voice box was as paralyzed as the rest of him.

At least they weren't poking at him as much as last time. When he was fully awake, the black, squiggly creatures formed a circle around him. Hovering a few feet away, they struck strange poses, which made them look even more like pictograms. They were back-lit with a pulsing purple light from an unidentifiable source. He got the impression he was supposed to read them, but he couldn't read Japanese, let alone alien. They were definitely trying to tell him something, but whether it was imperative or declarative, he couldn't tell. They rotated him slowly, as if to show the proper order of words, but all he learned was that Cheeky was still sound asleep. At least he would be spared the indignity of being someone's toy.

They floated him to the living room and pressed his face against the window. Outside, a couple of vagrants were going car to car, trying door handles in the half-empty parking lot. The tower of the Jengists swayed slightly in the distance, scraping the night sky with irregular fingernails. The dull glow of a bonfire illuminated robed figures moving slowly among the beams.

He floated backward and rotated vertically, then turned towards the kitchen. One of the things hurled a bag of coffee at him. It exploded against his face, but the beans hovered around his head as if caught in a gravitational field.

The things resumed their positions around him as he spun.

This went on for a good twenty minutes. Max was about to doze off when the beans exploded into ground coffee, which infiltrated his clothes and scraped across his flesh, violating every orifice. Not even his belly button was safe.

The things took a break bouncing around the room like bored children.

I really hate these things.

A few minutes later, the coffee fell away as ineffectually as it should have to begin with. The largest one, possibly their leader, inflated as it floated toward him. It stopped by a lamp about four feet away and twisted into a ridiculously complex three-dimensional shape. It rotated slowly in the lamplight, projecting a series of figures on the wall.

You can do that, but you can't write in English.

As if in response to Max's unspoken hostility, the wriggling mass burst into flame. Seconds later, all that was left was a black spot on the ceiling. The others faded into the shadows, and Max was dropped on his ass.

"Goddammit, stop doing that! If there's something you want to tell me, tell me in fucking English."

He pushed himself to his feet and glanced around to make sure he was really alone. How could he be sure when the things were barely there to begin with? He couldn't defend himself, so he shifted his focus to something more productive.

The steady flow of profanity continued even as he spit the thick mixture of saliva and coffee dust into the sink. He splashed water on his face and wondered if he would ever be able to enjoy coffee again. It was doubtful.

Squeezing a couple of brown tears from his burning eyes, he stomped over to the window and peered out at the night sky. He half expected to see a spaceship disappearing into the atmosphere. Instead, he found only the workaday trappings of modern civilization.

What had they been trying to show him? The bums had already scuttled off into the darkness. Everything was still and quiet. Well, not quite everything. The Jengists were still standing around the fire, sharing coffee from a thermos.

"Coffee? Great beings of untold power are trying to get me to join the stupidest religion ever? Goddammit!"

Talking to a bunch of suicidal fanatics was the last thing he wanted to do at five o'clock in the morning, but he was afraid the things might return if he didn't. At least he wasn't tired. The coffee enema had seen to that.

He threw on a coat and was almost out the door when Cheeky slithered out of the bedroom, bleary-eyed and irritated. Max scratched him behind the ears.

"Sorry, did I wake you?"

Cheeky bit his fingers gently and tugged him toward the bed.

"Oww, fuck, don't do that. Your teeth are like needles." Max scooped him up and cradled him on his back. "I'm sorry, but I have to step out for a minute. Some aliens molested me, and now I have to go talk to a suicide cult. I have no idea why, but I don't think I have a choice. You can go back to bed if you want."

Cheeky pursed his lips and glared through uneven slits. His blinking was irregular, and his breath stank of chocolate and vodka.

They rubbed noses. "You're so cute when you're drunk."

Max set him down. "So, you're coming?"

Cheeky frowned, then shook his head like a wet dog and stood at attention. It almost disturbed him how perceptive Cheeky was. Max assumed he didn't comprehend English, but he always seemed to understand what was going on.

They crept silently down the stairs and across the parking lot to the field where two wackos slouched on benches. They were perfectly relaxed despite being at the base of a ten-story monument to mankind's self-destructive nature that could collapse on them at any moment. Every creak and falling board thundered in Max's head like a gunshot.

They were talking about the newest Max Spielberger film and how strange it was that Vappo was the villain instead of Zappo, which was a much cheaper detergent and, therefore, inherently undesirable. Max hadn't watched any of Spielberger's films since the one where the giant bag of Crunchy Puffs attacked Tokyo only to be thwarted by a giant carrot with laser beam eyes. He hated directors that used heavy-handed metaphors to shove their agendas down viewers' throats. It made him feel like he was being talked down to.

Max wasn't sure how to insinuate himself into the conversation without coming across as rude or crazy. He had no idea how to talk to a Jengist. What if he said or did something taboo?

The red-robed wacko startled him out of his quandary. "Hey, what's up?"

The white-robed guy—who turned out to be a heavyset woman with a mullet—added, "If you came to build, you're out of luck. The crane's fried. Bobby's coming out to fix it, but he's driving all the way from K-236. It might be a while. You can wait with us if you like."

"Uh, okay, why not? How are you guys doing?"

The red-robed guy took a slug of coffee and responded, "Oh, you know, same old shit. The name's Guido. This is Cadence."

"Max."

Cadence offered him a cup of coffee.

He waved it away a little too fervently but accepted a seat beside Guido. "Nice to meet you."

"And who's this little guy?" Cadence said, reaching for Cheeky, who flashed his teeth and shot her a look that dared her to touch him. She quickly withdrew her hand.

"Don't mind him. He's just grumpy because he's tired."

She eyed the little creature nervously. "So Max, is this your first time at a Jengist church? You look kind of nervous."

"Why would you say that? I'm not nervous, but yeah, it is," Max admitted, running his fingers through his hair. A mist of brown powder floated away on the cool night breeze.

He half expected her to comment about him smelling more like coffee that what she was drinking. Instead, she laughed. "Everybody's nervous their first time. Jengism sounds crazy as shit. My first time, I came expecting a bunch of complete loons with no regard for common sense. I came to laugh at them, but I ended up talking to some of them and found out it made a lot of sense."

"So, what inspired your interest in spirituality at," Guido checked the time on his phone, "five-ten in the morning?"

Max's laugh was a little too hard and bitter for him to play off. "I'm having a weird night."

"How's that?"

"You wouldn't believe me if I told you."

"Try me. I've seen some weird shit in my time."

"Fuck it, why not? Earlier I got drunk and passed out. When I woke up, I was floating around the room being tormented by weird squiggly beings that pointed my face out the window and then raped me with coffee."

"Were the squiggles sort of glowin' purple?"

Max cocked an eyebrow and nodded.

"Yeah, the Night Noodles. I know them. They turned me onto Jengism too."

"Night noodles?"

"Yeah, they were black swooshy things, right? Prone to frolicking?"

"They would be the ones. What's weird is I've been thinking of them as Night Noodles too. Is that their real name?"

"That's what they call themselves."

Cadence was staring at Max in disbelief. "Bullshit. I get it. This is Guido getting me back for convincing him that mole was cancer."

Max shook his head. "I wish. Those guys suck."

Guido's face hardened. "You'll fuckin' know when I get you back for that. That was fucked up." He scratched his side in a manly way and asked, "Is that all they did? The coffee thing?"

"Not exactly. They kept making these shapes like they were trying to tell me something. It was bizarre. I didn't understand any of it. Also, at the end, one of them burst into flames."

"Ooh, that's not good. Not good at all. They only do that when they get really frustrated. You must have gotten something out of it, though. You know their name."

"How do you know so much about them?"

"I come from a long line of mystics. I'm not really interested in it myself, but I've been around weird shit my whole life. When the Night Noodles first appeared to me, I freaked the fuck out and called my sister. She didn't know anything about them, so she took me to this place where all the hardcore shit goes down and introduced me to the twins. They explained it to me. Those are some fucked-up little kids, but they know their shit."

Cadence snorted. "So, little kids explained them to you. Great."

Guido turned to Cadence. "Yeah, I don't blame you for calling bullshit. I still have trouble believing it, and it happened to me."

"How many times did they appear to you?"

He smiled like he was proud. "I think about six, but it's been a while. I actually kind of miss the little guys. They make ya feel special, ya know? Like, they could be anywhere, but they're not. There're in my room, lookin' at me."

Guido sobered when he caught a glimpse of Max's face. "But, it sounds like they're trying to tell you something important. It's rare they do that, but it does happen. If they sent you here, it's probably so

I'd take you to see the twins. They might be able to tell you what the message was. Fucking Noodles probably broke the crane so I'd be bored enough to take you. I should warn you, though, no matter how weird things get, don't freak out. I'm not saying it's safe, but you'll be a lot better off if you stay calm."

"Sounds nifty. Just out of curiosity, what would happen if I declined your offer?"

"If it's important, the Noodles'll keep trying. They're incessant like that. My truck's over there." He pointed to the edge of the field. "You coming or what?"

"Do you ever get the feeling free will is a crock of shit?" Max asked rhetorically as he followed the stranger to an old yellow truck with a thick brown stripe down the side.

"Yeah, totally. The universe is a math problem, and everything in it is a variable. At least that's what my sister says. According to her, there are two ways to come close to having free will. One is to go completely bat-shit crazy. The other is to know the truth. She explained that part, but I didn't really get it."

Guido tore off his robe, wadded it up, and tossed it behind his seat before reaching across and unlocking Max's side. "How do you like my ride?"

He opened the door and tried not to choke on the mildew. "Nice," he said as he scooted his posterior across a roll and a half of duct tape interior. It smells like a sock full of cum that fell behind the washer got pissed on by a dog and played host to a colony of black mold. "I can't tell you the last time I saw one of these on the road."

"Yeah, my car's in the shop. This is my dad's. He's a survivalist, so he keeps this thing running in case of an EMP. No computers, you know?"

Cheeky scrambled into his lap. "Oh yeah, this thing probably predates computers."

"Dude, this thing predates calculators." The mighty V8 roared to life and peeled out onto the road. "But there's nothing like it."

Max screamed over the engine. "But, doesn't it drink gas?"

"My dad's also loaded. He made a fuck-ton off of the economic crash because he knew it was coming. When the value of silver shot up to more than gold, his little ten-thousand-dollar investment made him a multimillionaire."

"That must be nice."

"Yeah."

"So, tell me everything you know about Night Noodles. Are they aliens or what?"

"Kinda. They're extra-dimensional beings that exist in the quantum plane. The twins said they were like pure being and potentiality had a baby. You noticed how childlike they were, right?"

"Yeah, lately, I've been their favorite toy."

"You hit the nail on the head. We're just toys to them. Our reality's like a lake, and they like making ripples. Every so often, they'll get it in their heads to do something big. That's probably what's going on here. They see a way you would be very entertaining for them, and they're pushing you in that direction. They want to play a game with you, and if you don't take your place on the field, they'll use you as the ball instead."

"Lovely."

The rest of the trip passed in awkward silence. Guido was a talker, but Max's obvious irritation kept him at bay. Every thirty seconds, Cheeky would snort to remind Max that he would rather be asleep. The businesses rolled by for what felt like hours but must have only been about fifteen minutes. He recognized the block where the truck began to slow. His dentist used to have his office in the north corner.

Guido parked the truck across two parallel spots in front of a small, square building with no windows. It looked more like a big block of potter's clay with a door stuck to it than a center for hoodoo. Still, after all the secret hideouts he'd been in recently, he'd learned not to judge a book by its cover. This was a building he had passed hundreds of times in his life and never noticed, but he was learning those were the ones to watch out for.

As they walked to the door, Max asked, "This is a house?"

"Who said anything about a house?"

"I don't know, I just assumed since we were going to see a pair of twins before six in the morning that we wouldn't be going to a business."

"It's not your ordinary business."

Guido opened the door and shoved him onto a foggy, rustic, dirt road. Max turned and cocked an eyebrow at him.

Guido looked disappointed as he followed him in. "Really? Nothing? This place freaked my shit the first time I saw it."

Cheeky stayed on the sidewalk, growling through the doorway.

"Come on, Cheeky, don't be a wuss."

Cheeky hissed.

Max followed his guide down the road. When he was about twenty feet in, Cheeky let out an exasperated snort and rushed to his side.

"There's my big boy." He scooped Cheeky up and scratched the flubber under his chin, but Cheeky remained tense.

"Come on, man. We've been in a lot more fucked up situations than this. Well, I have, anyway. I guess you've been lucky enough to skip most of that. Just relax. It'll be fine."

Trees lined the road on either side; their spindly fingers scraped across the starless, chalkboard sky. He wished he'd brought a flashlight. The darkness forced him to follow his new friend a little too closely for either of their comfort. If anything there was capable of creeping him out, it would have been the strange noises coming from the woods around him. It sounded like insects and demons swapping recipes. He felt like he'd stepped into a horror movie, but all he could think about was how long this was taking.

"You'd think they'd keep that door locked. What if a vagrant wandered in by mistake?"

"Actually, they count on that. People disappear through this door every day. I told you, some hardcore shit goes down here."

"And where exactly is here?"

"It's called Witches-R-Us."

"Sure it is."

"No really, believe it or not, this is a corporate chain. Some captain of industry bought a bunch of run-down buildings and paid a sorceress to make them doorways to wherever this really is."

"How do they make money if they keep the door unlocked?"

"You don't want to know, man. Trust me on that."

A few minutes later, they arrived at a clearing. A wilted domicile slouched against a mountain as though, after a lengthy pursuit, it had been cornered by evil sycamores and resigned itself to die. The moon sat off to the right like a bloodstain. The whole scene reminded Max of a cartoon haunted house. It should have been scary, but since nobody was shooting at him, he felt safer than usual. It was nice out, despite the crushing blackness. If he weren't so tired, he might have found it pleasant.

"So, this is what was supposed to freak me out?"

"Nah, this ain't shit. Interesting piece of trivia, though; this used to be a suburb, nice big houses, big yards. It was prime real estate for magic enthusiasts. When everything got weird, it got more and more difficult to get repairmen to come out. Then the forest went dark. Everything's been falling apart since."

"What do you mean, the forest went dark?"

"This place used to look like fuckin' fairyland, all bright and safe, full of flowers and cute little animals. Then somebody fucked up. Nobody knows the specifics. Shit started to get weird. Then it got dark and downright freaky. Everybody with any sense moved away, and the ones who didn't—well, they got weird too. Not to say they started off normal.

"I mean, some people dedicate their lives to this shit. They do stuff to themselves, magic body mods. Now, the twins are what happens when those people fuck. That's why they're so powerful and so fucking creepy. They ain't bad, though. They'll help you out."

"So, they live there?"

"It would be more accurate to say the twins exist in this vicinity. The house is aaaaaaah; I forgot what she called it. It's something metaphysical. Basically, you go in there and get tested somehow. If you come back out, you're smarter or stronger, something like that. Nobody lives there, though."

"So, where are we going?"

"You'll see. We're not far. Somewhere around here, there's an edacious tree with roots that look like tentacles. It has a glowing semicircle on its trunk. Let me know if you find it, but don't get too close. If we walk straight past the tree after seeing the semicircle, we'll bump right into 'em."

Max had given up thinking things couldn't get any worse a long time ago. Things could always get worse. Now, every time he thought things couldn't get any weirder or more contrived, they did. It was like his life was being written by a sadistic drug addict. Any second now, he might find himself wearing a squirrel costume doing an interpretive dance at gunpoint around the lip of a volcano, while mongoloids pelted him with cupcakes filled with scorpions. He wanted to cry.

"There it is," Guido said, pointing to a giant squid-shaped tree.

He counted off ten paces to the left of it and motioned for Max to follow.

The forest got brighter the deeper they went. Max was searching the canopy for the source when he tripped and face-planted in a large patch of mushrooms. Cheeky rolled off his shoulders and darted back and forth, searching for something to kill.

"Oww," said a ghostly voice from behind.

He scrambled to his feet and looked around. All he saw was Cheeky in his battle-stance.

"Why did you kick me?" The voice was strangely hollow.

"I'm sorry, I don't know what you mean." Max was finally getting a little spooked.

Guido stopped and turned, "Dude, come on. I don't have all fucking night here."

"Hold on. Somebody's talking to me."

"That's just Carla."

"Carla? Who the fuck is Carla? I don't see anybody."

A bright light illuminated an area by his feet, where a pale bluish face rose from the dirt. Much to Guido's delight, Max jumped back, fell on his ass, and screamed like a little girl. Cheeky let out a terrified squeak and ran behind a tree. Guido clicked off the flashlight and laughed until he was gasping for breath.

When his breath returned, he declared, "Haha, I finally got you."

Max felt like his heart was going to explode. When his wits returned, he screamed. "What the fuck, man? You had a flashlight this whole time? What the fuck is wrong with you?"

"Just fucking with you. Sorry, Carla. I didn't think he'd step on you."

"That's okay. It happens all the time."

"Why is Carla buried in the middle of the woods?"

"I am a conduit."

Max realized he was being rude, so he addressed her personally, "Oh, all right, I'm not sure what that means, but I'm sorry for kicking you and freaking out like that. I just didn't expect to see anybody down there."

"That's okay. It gets kind of boring out this way sometimes. It's nice to have someone to talk to."

Max turned to Guido. "Turn the fucking light back on. I like to see who I'm talking to."

When Guido complied, Max knelt beside her and hoped she couldn't tell how blatantly he was gawking. Her eyes were sewn shut, so he assumed she couldn't see. Cheeky peeked around the tree. Seeing Max was fine, he let out a sigh of relief and approached cautiously.

"What do you mean, you're a conduit?" He brushed a little of the dirt away from her face, exposing her little root-veins to open air. She began to dry heave and twitch, making sounds like someone was trying to rip her ribcage out through her mouth.

"Sorry, sorry, I didn't know," he said, raking dirt onto her.

"That's all right, but please don't touch. I need constant nourishment, and every little root is necessary."

"Don't worry. I'm just going to sit here for a second if that's all right."

The face in the ground collected itself. "That's fine. To answer your question, a conduit is a pathway between two things. I am a pathway between flora and fauna. I have given myself to the Earth so that she and the creatures that live on her can communicate more easily."

"Huh?"

"The Earth is an organism in the very same way that you are. An organism is a form of life composed of mutually interdependent parts that maintain various vital processes. Like the Earth, you are teeming with tiny life forms, which could not exist without you, nor you they. An average human has ten times as many bacteria cells as they do human cells.

Wouldn't it be nice to communicate with the other life forms that contribute to your functioning? I am a bridge between the Earth and you. Would you like to ask her a question?"

"Uh, that's kind of neat, I guess. Um, what kind of question?"

"I can tell you about the plague that will soon rise and destroy mankind or when and where the next earthquake will be. I know the cure for every disease. I know where the turtles go in the winter. I can tell you the name of the butterfly that died on your windshield last week. I can even tell you how you are going to die."

"As much as it would enrich my life to know those things, I think I'll have to pass. Just tell her that I'm sorry for what we humans have been doing to her for the last few hundred years. We have to be a million times worse than the flu."

"She appreciates that and agrees with you. She also thanks you for allowing your corporations to engineer weaponized bacteria. She is very impressed with how efficient your labs are at turning out plagues with which you will eventually destroy yourselves. Nevertheless, she thinks that you will be blown away by what she is working on." She chuckled at her little pun.

"I'm sure I will be. Well, I think I should get going now. We have to ask some twins why I got molested by a fifteen-dollar bag of coffee."

"Don't go yet. I'll tell you Cakey's last thoughts or the names of the insects that ate him. I can translate for you and Cheeky. Anything you want." She let out a long string of Cheeky noises. He replied with an offended sneeze.

"I'm sorry; I really need to get going. Some other time, though." Max stood to leave.

"The twins won't see you unless you undergo the substantiation of the soul."

Max stopped, and Guido shined the light on her again. "What do you mean? I didn't have to be substantiated."

"Yes, but they made an exception for you because you are a Kana. Your family has been a major player in the spiritual realm for the last three hundred years. This guy doesn't even know what a conduit is."

"Aww, come on. I don't have time to wait around and see if he survives. Can't you make another exception for me?"

"We can't make an exception for everybody. I am sorry, but that is the rule."

"Shit."

"What does she mean?" Max asked nervously.

"It means we have to walk back to the house, and you have to go inside."

"Of course it does. I'm destined to confront every single thing in the fucking universe that has the potential to hurt or kill me. Let's go. I can't believe you didn't tell me you had a fucking flashlight. Douchebag!" Max grumbled, stomping off into the darkness.

Guido rushed to keep up and whispered, "She's lonely. She'll be a lot more helpful if you humor her."

"I'm way too tired to make small talk with planets."

"Imagine giving up your life so people can talk to the Earth, and nobody ever wants to know anything. It's gotta suck."

"Yeah, she shouldn't have done that. I'm just trying to do what I have to do to go home and go to bed, but every time I do what I'm told, somebody tells me I have to do something else. It's fucking annoying, and I'm sick of it."

"That's how mystical experiences always work. You never really know what's going on. It's all dangerous and weird, but there's always a point to it."

The trees began to thin.

"There's no point to anything. Perceived meaning is a projection of your hopes and expectations. Life is painful and unnecessary. That's why people invented drugs."

Guido laughed. "Man, if anybody ever needed a mystical adventure, it's you."

The clearing came into view.

Max took another look at the house. "It doesn't look that bad. This should only take a minute."

He tried to sally forth, but Guido grabbed his shoulder. "Hey, you don't have to do this if you don't want to. I don't want to have you dying on my conscience."

"Is it really that bad?"

"I don't know. I got the impression it was pretty bad."

Cheeky curled himself around Max's right leg and begged him not to go.

"So, it'll either kill me or make me stronger, right?"

"They say that those who emerge will be gods among men, but the souls that fail will be consumed."

"But, the twins can tell me how to get rid of the Night Noodles, right?"

"Probably."

"Well, I'm here. I might as well go in."

Max strolled to the large double doors, twisted the handle, and then jumped back as four of the large knots in the wood rolled back to reveal two pair of blood-red eyes. Cheeky uncoiled and retreated to the bottom of the steps.

"Do you seek substantiation?" asked the doors in perfect synchronization. The left door's voice was deep and gravelly, the right smooth and effeminate.

"Yes, apparently, it's the only way I'm going to rid myself of the Night Noodles."

"What are these Night Noodles of which you speak?" They asked in unison.

"If I knew that I wouldn't be here. Look, don't worry about it. Just please substantiate me quickly. I'm tired."

The left set of eyes narrowed at him. "Your quest does not seem pure, and you admit that you are weak. Are you aware of the consequences should you fail?"

"Yeah, you'll eat my soul. I don't even care anymore. Have you ever had coffee grounds rushing up your pee hole?"

"What is this pee hole of which you speak?"

"I didn't think so. I can pretty much guarantee it's worse than anything you have in there. Please, just let me in."

The right door piped up, "It is your soul, do with it as you like. In order to gain entry, you must first solve an enigma. Are you ready?"

"Sure."

The doors thundered in unison, "Through one door, the answers lie. Choose the other and surely die. Ask one question, but be sly. While one speaks truth, the other lies. Take as much time as you like."

"Really? That's the riddle? That's like the default riddle that's used in kid's movies and shit."

"What are these kid's movies of which you speak?"

"Don't worry about it. Door on the right, which door would the left door tell me led to certain death?"

"The left door would say I lead to certain death."

Max flung the right door open and stepped inside.

"How did you do that so quickly?" asked the door as he slammed it shut behind him.

"Lucky, I guess. Now what?"

"Now, you must pass the test of the vestibule."

Max stepped over at least twenty skeletons in the five feet between him and the next door. He kicked some bones out of the way so he would have a place to stand and asked the tuxedoed barbarian by the door what he was supposed to do.

"None may enter, except by the decree of the substantiator. The substantiator is busy now, but you may wait by the umbrella rack of doom."

"How am I supposed to let the substantiator know I'm here?" he asked, admiring the inlay on the barbarian's massive sword.

"You cannot contact the substantiator. The substantiator will contact you."

"This sounds kind of familiar too. Fuck this," Max said as he grabbed the handle and darted through into a beautiful Victorian drawing room done in red and gold. He slammed the door behind him. The guard didn't move. "I thought so. This place is fucking easy."

A hunchbacked grandmother came around the corner carrying a tray covered with tea paraphernalia. She set the tray on the coffee table and bowed. "Before you may proceed, you must answer one question. What lies between two soldiers?"

"A hunchback?" he said, not really in answer to the question.

"Ah, this one is wise. Indeed, in order to obtain knowledge, one must first ask a question. Every answer brings about more questions in an endless cycle of transcendence. Would you like a cup of tea?"

"No thanks, I want to get through here as quickly as possible."

"Well then, you can follow me."

She led him up the winding staircase and into a bathroom on the second floor. He was surprised to find a modern shower with a glass door amidst all the antiques, but even more surprised when the woman told him to get in. He didn't seem to have a choice, so he ushered her out and undressed.

"I fucking hate it when bathrooms don't have locks on their doors. I guess my next ordeal will be some sort of physical humiliation. I can't think of any other reason she would want me naked. Maybe it'll be one of those things where she makes herself a beautiful woman and comes in to test my virtue. That wouldn't be so bad."

Max used the organic, hemp shampoo to lather away the remaining coffee grounds. He'd just gotten a handful of conditioner when he heard the door creak open. Here she comes. He plumped slightly in sick anticipation.

The door was jerked open, but instead of a beautiful woman, he saw the same old hunchback leering demonically at his chubby. Max covered himself as the range of possibilities formed a nauseating parade down the center of his brain. In either hand, she held a cat by the scruff of the neck. He was almost relieved when she hurled the mangy felines into the shower and slammed the door. Almost.

Upon contact with the water, both cats turned into pint-sized tornados. The calico blurs shredded Max's flesh as they tore up and down his body at breakneck speeds. Blood was spraying in all directions.

The hunchback flung open the door, allowing the infuriated felines to evacuate to more arid climes. One moment longer, and he might have bled to death.

"Help?" Max rasped, reeling from bloodloss.

The hunchback dragged him out of the shower and down the hall to an empty white room where she pushed him to the floor. She then proceeded to kick him around the room as though she were training for the Olympic Soccer team.

I fucked something up. Damnit! I liked my soul.

Rather than screaming or begging for help, he decided to relax and try to enjoy his last few moments of sensation, vexatious though they were, before his soul was eaten by some vicious otherworldly being. His positive attitude did little to improve the experience. He began to look forward to the kind release of oblivion.

Eventually, the woman stopped kicking him and offered him her hand. "All right, sonny, let's see what we've got."

Delirious from blood loss, Max allowed himself to be helped to his feet and sat wearily atop a bar stool, which appeared out of thin air. The woman then raised her spectacles to her eyes and commenced oohing and aahing and mmhmming as she scrutinized him like a work of art. When the entertainment value of his decimated flesh was exhausted, she shifted her attention to the massive splatter painting she'd made on the floor. Inch by inch, she inspected and appraised the meaning of every drop and spurt, making thoughtful noises as Max swooned and tingled atop his perch.

When she finished her inspection, she smiled slyly and pushed a panel on the wall, which popped open to reveal a mini-fridge. She poured a tall glass of something red and offered it to Max in a sweet, grandmotherly fashion.

In his stupor, he forgot what she had done to him only moments before. His head cleared, and his flesh began to tingle as the liquid rushed down his esophagus. It was crisp and fresh, but he could feel it warming him from the inside out like a fine Cognac on a cold winter night. His scratches disappeared, leaving his skin softer and smoother than it had been in years.

He handed her the empty glass. "What the hell was that all about?"

"You did say you wanted this over quickly, did you not?"

"Yeah."

"You passed the first few trials very quickly. That speaks volumes about the maturity of your soul. However, substantiation is not a fast process. It can take anywhere from a few hours to a few years for the process to be complete.

"What you have just experienced is the ancient art of cat scratch divination. Felines are holy creatures, bursting at the seams with mystical powers. However, they only care for themselves and must be persuaded to use them. When the cats were thrown into the shower, their wills were focused but counterbalanced by panic, making them perfect conduits between this plane and the next. The scratches covering your body and the patterns your blood made during the ceremony were coded messages that revealed a single ritual with which you might be substantiated. Unfortunately, in your case, that isn't possible."

" So, there's more?"

"Of course, there's more. You didn't expect this to be easy, did you?"

"Nothing ever is. So, what did you learn?"

"I have performed the ceremony many times, but never have I seen such a remarkable response from the higher plane. You have quite a special destiny. Why do you struggle against it so? What do you find so desirable about mediocrity?"

"I don't believe in destiny. Destiny implies that there's some deity dictating the lives of every living thing. If that's the case, why are so many people stuck in boring ruts? Is he running out of ideas, or is he just lazy? Maybe he put a standard form in the celestial Xerox machine along with a billion dimes and then forgot about us.

"I think life is an ocean full of currents to get caught up in and other creatures to bump into, and it's all random, but mathematically predictable at the same time. There's no meaning and no mission. We're all just fish waiting to be eaten by bigger fish."

The old woman let loose a knowing chuckle, which was neither smug nor cruel. It was the laugh of a drunken uncle when asked by his five-year-old niece why Santa's breath smelled like the cabinet under the kitchen sink. "You are a bigger enigma than anything we have to offer here," she confided, patting his leg tenderly.

"Here's the poop. You are not currently substantiatable. Normally we would be eating your soul right about now, but as I said, you have a very special destiny. We are going to make an exception. You have the potential for a level of illumination that very few people can reach even through a lifetime of intense devotion. To put it another way, you won the spiritual lottery. Your path is set to encounter many currents that will lead to your substantiation, but it must unfold naturally."

"So, this was all a waste of time?"

"No, not really. We were destined to meet. You have learned something here, whether you realize it or not, which will be useful later on."

"Nifty. Well, that was fun. We'll have to do it again sometime. I think I remember the way out." He walked to the door.

"Not so fast, sonny, there's one more thing you have to do before you go."

"Goddammit, didn't you say I didn't need to come here in the first place?"

"You did, and you didn't, but that's not the point. The only way out is through the egress of trepidation. That is your final test. You are destined to succeed, but it is something you must endure to open your third nostril."

"My third nostril?"

"Yes, it is currently clogged with your snotty attitude. Consider the egress of trepidation to be a nasal spray made of Vaporub and ground black pepper. It may not be pleasant, but it will get the job done."

"Fine. Whatever. But before I go, can you tell me anything about the Night Noodles or how to get rid of them?"

"Night Noodles are your friends. You need their help."

"If that's what they call help, I don't want it. Those guys are assholes. How can I tell them I'm not interested?"

"Perhaps benefactors would be a better word. They are servants of Eris, and it is her will that brought them to you. If the physical world is an ocean, and the Night Noodles are children playing on the beach, Eris is the divorce lawyer who brought them there with the money she earned squeezing blood out of turnips. You don't want to get on her bad side. Even if it was possible to escape the riptide you're caught in, the best outcome you could hope for is to be a crab dashed to pieces at their feet by a large wave. I have seen your life unfold, and it is much more than a movie of the week. Be glad, be patient, and go forth unto your destiny with your chin held high, and your balls slung over your shoulder like a continental veteran."

Having grown up coddled by a post-American culture where he was taught all things were possible as long as he worked hard to find the right loopholes, Max was displeased with her response. He knew it was bullshit, but he resented having his helplessness pointed out by someone who had all the power and didn't deserve it.

When Max was a child, his father told him he had to learn to swim. He refused, only to be thrown into a deep lake where he chose to drown to prove his point. His father hadn't even let him have that satisfaction. He fished him out and beat him. That was when young Max had first realized some things were beyond his control. In retrospect, he also learned some things weren't worth dying for and that he would live a longer and happier life if he could learn to be more easygoing. Nevertheless, he was pissed.

"That's easy for you to say, ya big, magnificent, hoodoo balloon. You get to float just outside of the material world in a snug little alternate reality where you make all the rules. But I've got a message for you, Grandma, from all the little people of the lower material plane. Some of us are in this shit for real, and we don't appreciate being toyed with by higher beings. You think you're all high and mighty and all-knowing, and maybe you are, but that doesn't give you the right to torture all the helpless little insects that come within range of your magnifying glass."

"Give it time, and you will come to thank us. It is all for your own good."

"Bullshit! Where is this egress of trepidation thing? And where are my clothes? I want to go home."

She smiled as though he was a kitten who had just done something adorable. "Feisty, aren't you? I see why Eris is attracted to you. If you wish to leave, be my guest. There is a fire escape in the bathroom. Step out the window, and your final ordeal will begin."

"What about my clothes?"

"You do not need them. You will exit in the same physical condition and attire you walked in with, but you will be stronger and wiser."

"Whatever." He stormed into the hall and made for the bathroom.

"One more thing," she called after him.

Max spun around in a huff to see the old lady making jazz hands at him. Her mouth twisted and grew as she spewed guttural gibberish so intense that the walls began to vibrate.

"YROTCIVFOEHCATSUOMEHTFOELKCITEHTERAWEB!"

Her left hand exploded, and then her right. The gibberish swelled as her features melted into something like an insect.

Max let out a little scream and ran for the bathroom. He slammed the door, and the window popped open. Outside, was a wall of darkness. "Fuck this place," he said as he climbed through. His feet hit something soft, but solid. "Well, now what?" He jumped at the window slamming shut and turned to see it had been absorbed by the void.

He stood there for a few moments, drowning in apprehension, his senses wholly deprived, waiting to see what the big bullies would do to him next. After a while, he wondered if he had gone out the wrong window. He kept expecting something big and dramatic to happen, but there was nothing. He felt around with his hands and feet, but level ground was all that was there.

He called out, hoping an echo might give him some clues. He screamed, waited, then screamed again, but nothing came back.

With nothing to stimulate it, his brain amused itself with random images fading in and out of the murk. The images grew brighter and more robust the longer he stared at them. There were trees, but rather than the warped topiary of the cursed forest, he saw the healthy tropical variety standing straight and tall before him like soldiers at attention. The ground appeared warm and brown and sprinkled with black rocks of every shape and size. A warm breeze wafted salty air and hints of spring, drizzling delicious olfactory butter into his nervous system and whisking it lightly. It was all very lovely until he heard the all too familiar chucklunk of a shotgun behind him.

"Well, whadda we have here?" asked the beer keg of a man as he strafed into view.

Max cocked an eyebrow in disbelief as he admired the egress's handiwork. Two hundred and fifty pounds of redneck, straight out of the history books except for the grass skirt and lei, came lumbering into view from his right. Another two hundred pounds appeared at his left. Both wore grease-stained red and white ball caps emblazoned with cheesy come-ons.

If-I-said-you-had-a-beautiful-body-would-you-hold-it-against-me said, "Looks like a city boy to me. Look at 'im, all naked and soft like a girl. I bet he's got one of them buff puffs hangin' in his shower. Don't' cha, pretty boy?

Free-mustache-rides answered, "He prolly ain't never even seen a cow, much less banded one."

"Why ya naked, city boy? You one o' them perverts what can't discriminate as to where your wiener goes?"

Max fearlessly stared into the fat one's eyes. "My clothes were stolen by an old hunchback lady who mutilated my skin and then stomped the shit out of me. But then you know that already. What do I have to do to get out of here?"

Free-mustache-rides had a look of disgust as he responded, "I don't know what's sadder, that he loved up an old hunchback or her beatin' him up afterward. Not much of a lover are ya, boy? Maybe you can't get it up without yer mascot suit. Is that it, city boy? You one a them furry folks?"

"Fuck this, I'm out." Max shook his head as he pushed past them.

"Not so fuckin fast, cream puff."

Max ignored him and continued walking until his left leg was reduced to Manwich by Free-mustache-rides's shotgun. He fell over sideways, screaming as he wrapped his fingers around his bare femur. Next time someone shot at him, he'd try harder to step out of the way.

The rednecks slung their shotguns over their shoulders and ambled closer like they had all the time in the world to watch him bleed.

"Let that be a lesson to ya. I'm the man in this here relationship, and as the man, what I say goes. Now geet up," Free-mustache-rides commanded as he grabbed him by the hair and pulled him to his feet.

Max was surprised to find he was not only once again bipedal but also wearing a big furry squirrel costume. His head fell forward in exasperation as he realized where this was going.

"Well, ain't you a cutie?" If-I-said-you-had-a-beautiful-body-would-you-hold-it-against-me asked rhetorically.

"Whoopee! He's ding dang adorable, and I bet he's talented too. Let's go have us a little fun with our new furry friend up on that hilltop there."

Max pondered the possible meanings of this cruel farce while trudging up the steps coiled around the volcano. The egress was obviously using his previous joke to make a point, but what? It could be a face-your-fears-and-be-free thing, or maybe it was showing him that stuff can always get worse so he'd try to see the good in each moment. He hoped there was more to it than that.

At the top, a Tiki bar and a few deck chairs were set up around the mouth. Max watched the pillar of thick, black smoke belly-dance into the sky. The rednecks set down their shotguns, and each chose two pistols from the impressive gun rack mounted on the right wall of the bar.

"How about I buy you guys a Bahama Mamma?"

hey hadn't invited him there for a Bahama Mamma.

Mustache Rides took a shot at his comically oversized feet. "How 'bout you do an interpretive dance about life as a furry city-boy?"

Dancing around the lip of the volcano, Max did his best to communicate all the emotions and experiences that plagued him these past few months. He felt stupid at first, but given the circumstances, he decided to take it seriously. It wasn't like he could look any sillier.

He was starting to get into it when the mongoloids marched out of the volcano. They pelted him with cupcakes, which exploded on impact covering him in scorpions. Max threw his hands in the air and tried to pirouette the scorpions off, but the cakes kept coming.

Surprisingly, most of the dance consisted of grandiose gestures of triumph rather than the sullen moping of having to do things against his will. In retrospect, this spy stuff was a nice change of pace.

Instead of waiting around for death, he was boldly spitting in its eye, and he felt more alive than ever. The ancient Buddhist concept that life is suffering always seemed like a no-brainer. But maybe there was a deeper meaning than the American adaptation "life is shit." Modern society was a parasite pumping its host full of endorphins to keep it happy while sucking it dry. If all this was planned and implemented by nefarious fuckwads, maybe it could get better.

Life was like dodge-ball. Cowards tried to dodge and ended up covered in welts. The winners were the ones who ran toward the ball, caught it, and took their attackers down. He'd always been the welty kid that wanted to sit by the bleachers. It never occurred to him that the kid who caught the ball might be the smart one.

Inside his furry prison, Max laughed at the irony. A kid who'd tried to drown himself to make a point, ran away from life because he was afraid of getting hurt. He'd been so adamant about not doing things he didn't like, he'd stopped doing anything at all.

With rednecks shooting at his feet and scorpions crawling around inside his squirrel costume, swimming suddenly seemed pretty cool. He danced his way through the line of morbidly obese children, waved goodbye to the rednecks, then did a cannonball into the smoke.

After several minutes of falling through complete blackness, he unbundled himself and assumed a more comfortable position. As soon as he relaxed, he flew out the front door and into his daydreaming accomplice. Both men tumbled head over ass down the stairs and onto the dusty front lawn.

"Oww, fuck. You touch a stripper?" Guido asked as he rolled to his feet.

Cheeky scrambled up and commenced joyously slurping Max's face.

"Take me to those fucking kids. I'm ready to go home."

"Did you get substantiated? You were only in there for like ten seconds."

"Does it look like they ate my soul?"

"No."

"Well then, I must have been substantiated. I guess time works differently in there because that took a hell of a lot longer than ten seconds. The old lady said substantiation can take years in some cases, so that's probably a good thing." He gave Cheeky a hug and set him down.

"What was it like in there?" Guido clicked on his flashlight and led them into the forest.

"I'd rather not talk about it."

"Okay, fine. So, do you feel stronger or wiser or some shit?"

"Actually, yeah. As much as it sucked, it was a pretty enlightening experience. The lady said I have a destiny. So they just did what they could for now. Man, if that was a casual dismissal--."

The trip through the woods went faster the second time. Carla was napping, so they snuck past as quietly as possible. Over the hill and down a bit, they came upon a flat, circular clearing. It was empty except for two small figures standing side by side directly in the center. The only flora in the circle was a tall thin grass, which gave off an azure glow, illuminating the clearing with dusky electricity. Wind spiraled slowly around the figures, making rings in the ankle-tickling grass.

"Max, allow me to introduce you to the twins," Guido said with a bombastic gesture, almost as if the spectacle was his doing. His boastful grin turned down in disappointment when he saw that Max was bored as ever. "You should probably go alone. I'll keep an eye on Cheeky."

Cheeky growled at Guido. He shot Max a 'be careful' look and hunkered down at his feet.

Max offered a reassuring smile and tromped towards the tiny figures that stood with quiet disinterest in the eye of the storm. As he approached with a cool yet cautious swagger, the twin's features or rather lack thereof became more and more pronounced. The girl's high, white pigtails framed pallid flesh, stretched too tight across her sharp Germanic features. Her mouth was a little too small, her lips too dark, but nothing was quite so peculiar as the absence of eyes. High cheekbones framed a fleshy vortex the size of a fist. The girl, face swirling like peach taffy, stood motionless in her dainty strawberry-print dress as he drew closer.

From a distance, the boy's appearance was relatively normal. He shared the taut Germanic qualities of his sister, standing almost at attention in his little blue shorts and suspenders. Though unusually severe, the children somehow leapfrogged the totalitarianism of Hitler youths and instead gave the impression of immutable purpose. They showed no signs of acknowledgment as he approached other than the boy tracking him with an unpleasantly intense gaze.

As much as he wanted to be done with this silly place, he decided to hold his tongue until he was within five feet. He didn't want to commit some sort of faux pas that might prolong his stay in the mystical land of Witches-R-Us. Nodding politely, he closed the gap with his hands clasped behind his back.

"Hello, my name is Max. What's yours?"

The children remained motionless and silent, but the boy's eyes had a look of snide amusement. He'd accidentally used the voice adults use when talking to children despite being unsure whether they were children at all. For all he knew, they were six thousand years old. He decided to revert to his previous strategy of blunt sarcasm.

He looked the boy directly in the eye and continued, "Who needs a name, anyway? Look, I'm tired as hell and a little delirious, so let me jump right in. Everybody seems to know more about what's happening to me than I do. I have some kind of inflamed destiny thing. I keep getting assaulted by Night Noodles, who, apparently, aren't going away until I understand their message. So please answer me this one question. What the fuck?"

"That is not a valid question," said the children in perfect unison. Their voice was small and cold like an old AI voice box sewn inside a dead cat. Max was not impervious to creepiness after all.

Shivering visibly, Max rephrased the question, "Just tell me what I need to know."

Again they spoke in unison. "Come into us, that we might taste your soul,"

The girl's whirlpool spread, swallowing her nose. It spun faster and faster, generating a powerful suction, threatening to draw him in. He braced himself against the rising wind and let out a small gasp as he noticed the boy had little whirlpools where his ears should be. He cocked his head to the left, and Max was no longer able to maintain his footing. He instinctually thrust his hands forward and found himself elbow deep in the girl. The boy's auditory orifice was smaller and tighter, only sucking his hand to the thumb, which was bent painfully back and groping for leverage.

On the verge of panic, Max struggled unsuccessfully to free himself as the wind, now full of brush and inconsequential life, whipped like razors through his hair. It was only due to his close proximity that he heard them chanting over the roar of the tempest, "Come into us. Come into us. Come into us."

Max was so overwhelmed by the experience he didn't notice they weren't eating him until the whirlpools began to slow and loosen their grip. When he was finally free, he stepped back and quickly took inventory of his anatomy.

"What the hell was that?" he demanded angrily.

The boy answered alone this time, as the girl's swirl had swallowed her mouth, "You wanted us to tell you what you need to know. To do that, we must taste your soul. Otherwise, we would not be able to find the true question, let alone the answer."

"So, what's the deal?"

"The deal is coming."

"What?"

A sudden rumbling came from deep within the girl's head, steadily growing louder until, with a deafening bray, a giant llama sprang from her face. Landing majestically, it turned and blinked at Max through a red velvet opera mask.

"Heeeey man," said the llama, sounding sleepy or possibly stoned, "I was beginning to wonder if you were ever gonna call."

"Do I know you?"

"I'm your furry fairy godmother, motherfucker. I'm your fuckin' spirit animal. Recognize!"

"His name is Marvin," added the boy.

Max turned to the boy and asked in a slightly angry voice, "So, what is this exactly? The question? The answer? Is he housebroken?"

"He is the deal."

"What do you mean, the deal?"

"He will answer all of your questions."

"How is he going to answer all of my questions? He's a llama, and I'm pretty sure he's high."

"Hey man, I'm right here. Ya know? It's kinda rude to talk about a guy like he's not there." Marvin sounded hurt. "I mean, you wait your whole afterlife to meet your spirit human, and then he ignores you. That's not cool."

Max sighed and scratched the fur at the base of the llama's gangling head stalk. "I'm sorry. I'm just really tired. My skin's all thick and itchy, my eyes are crawling with fire ants, I've been sliced up, kicked, shot, stung by scorpions and raped with coffee. It's all the Night Noodles' fault. I hate those guys."

"Aww, it's cool. I know how it is."

"So, do you know of a way to get rid of the Night Noodles?"

"Nah, you're stuck with them."

"That's what everybody keeps saying. Is there any way to keep them from torturing me?"

"Well, they're messengers, ya know? So, you'd do well to learn their language. It'll keep 'em from having to rape you with symbolism."

"And how do I learn the language? Is there a 'Noodlese for Dummies' I can buy?"

"Nah, man, they use the universal language, the one that's been spoken since before the dawn of time. Knowing how to read it is like knowing how to run. You just have to know it's possible and open yourself up to understanding it."

"I tried before, and it didn't work."

"That's because your third nostril was clogged, dude. Don't you listen to anybody? That shit's been taken care of."

"So, I can understand them now that I've been assaulted by stinging cupcakes?"

"You could understand them before. You just didn't know you could. What, you think I'm lying? You called them Night Noodles, didn't you? You knew to go talk to what's-his-face over there. Still think I'm lying? You might still have a little clog in there. I could help you with that."

"No, that's all right. I believe you. This is all just a little hard to take in, you know? I could really use a nap. Why don't we go to my place? I'll get some rest, and tomorrow you can tell me all about my destiny and any other cryptic mumbo jumbo you can think of."

"No can do, man. I can't leave this place."

"Why not?"

"I exist on a higher frequency than you. The twins can stabilize me enough to appear here because this place exists halfway between your frequency and mine. I can't go all the way down to the forty-ninth octave. Even if I could, I wouldn't want to. The forty-ninth is a shithole. It's like the Mexico of all existence. There are worse places, but there's still no point going if you don't have to."

"Really? I find that oddly comforting. So, tell me whatever it is I need to hear so I can go home and get some sleep."

"Dude, you have to stop expecting other people to do everything for you. Your question to the twins was 'What the fuck?' and you wonder why the answer's vague? Think about shit and find the answer for yourself. You used to think all the time before you waged war on your brain."

"Said the stoned llama."

"Phht, fuck you, man. I should have just popped out, said forty-two, and jumped right back in."

"Sorry, I'm just in a bad mood. I don't mean to take it out on you."

"You've come about as far as you can tonight. Go home and get some rest. You might not be able to tell, but you really have made a lot of progress. Take my advice and stop kicking against every prick that comes your way. You have nothing to be afraid of. You know why? You have the greatest power in the universe on your side."

168

"What's that?"

"Dumb luck. Some people are destined to come to power. A lot of people aren't, but they try really hard anyway, and that's where a lot of the suffering on your plane comes from. False leaders are like drunken quadriplegics trying to build a ship in a bottle. No matter how much they want to do it, they just can't. You're more like an autistic kid that accidentally builds a functional time machine out of Popsicle sticks."

"All right, I'll try to be more easygoing and proactive and stuff. Anything else before I go? What's it like outside of this shithole octave?"

"The Is is a balanced matrix of complex interdependent systems, which reverberate across all planes and frequencies in an infinite number of dimensions. It's fucking beautiful once you can take it all in as a whole, but the tiny bits that make it up are all too concerned with their own perspectives to appreciate themselves. Your perspective or belief system or whatever you want to call it is like a bridle. The best way to get through this phase of your life is to learn to override your programming and see things as they really are.

"What you think of as you only exists as a kind of psychological splatter painting created by random variables colliding after being projected directly or indirectly by forces beyond your comprehension. To become real, you must first recognize the superficiality of the artistic plane, step back from what you see, and look for meaning in the context of a larger picture."

"Huh?"

"Your ego's like a buggy operating system that's really easy to use, but extremely limited and inefficient in all its designs except the one that keeps you dependent on it. It clings to your hardware like a pissed-off cat, but you can get it off once you understand how its claws work. Then you can install Linux and optimize your shit any way you want. It'll take some time, but you'll love the results."

"So, kill my ego?"

"Yeah."

"Why the hell didn't you say that?"

"It's kind of a cliché, and people don't really understand what it means when you say that. Also, enlightenment takes a lot more work than doing psychotropics. Ten million hipsters can be wrong. It's like they flew to a foreign country, took a four-hour bus tour, then flew back feeling like they know all there is to know about it. They're fuckin' tourists.

"Anyway, I don't really like this guru thing. All these metaphors make me feel kind of pretentious. I mean, it isn't like the information's not out there. The universal truth has been the core of just about every religion since the dawn of man, but you guys would rather kill each other over semantics than accept the gift of enlightenment. I wish I could just tell you the key to the universe is slack and have you really understand, but humans are kinda stupid, well-armed sacks of raging peptides with a god complex. No offense."

"None taken. I can't argue with that. Anything else?"

169

"Man, I appreciate your eagerness, but I don't think you can handle any more tonight."

"Works for me. Stoned llama, creepy children, thank you for your assistance. I'm going to bed."

The boy's eyes briefly flickered with pain, but he seemed to be aware of his creepiness and was simply shocked it had been mentioned. Marvin nodded and waved, then plunked himself down in the field and commenced grazing. Max bowed more out of deliriousness than sarcasm. He returned to the path and found Guido napping against a small mutant redwood, which was slowly opening to swallow him.

"Hey, there's no time for that. Get me home before my brain starts dripping out through my tear ducts," he said as he grabbed his guide by the feet and dragged him out of the tree's mouth. "Cheeky, you were going to let that tree eat him, weren't you? Bad cheekworm."

Cheeky huffed and looked away. Max wondered if he was jealous of him petting Marvin.

Guido clapped Max on the back and led him to the truck, joking merrily about how scared Max had been when he'd stumbled over Carla. Max occasionally grunted to seem attentive while processing everything that happened. It was like trying to catch a bubble in a pot of boiling water.

When they arrived at his apartment, Max thanked Guido and used the last of his energy to crawl up the stairs and into bed. He curled up with Cheeky and lay awake for hours, too tired to sleep.

OPERATION: LIQUIDATOR

Max tapped his pinky toe on the leg of his coffee table and stared at the little blue lines on the sewer map as if they might change positions if he looked away. He'd been obsessing over the plan so long the ants crawling behind his eyes had started whispering nonsense to his brain. The constant reworking had induced strategic dyslexia.

This was his first raid, and he had to do it right. He glanced at the bedroom door. The responsible thing to do would be to get some rest, but there was no time. He wouldn't be able to sleep anyway. Every time he closed his eyes, tactical variations exploded in every direction. Maps and diagrams danced among the accusing gaze of his potential victims.

The plan was based on intel Adhra had passed along via carrier zombie. It seemed okay, but there was no way to tell if Adhra was leading him into a trap. She didn't know the details, so he'd have some element of surprise, but the words Judas cow kept echoing in his head.

It's 3:48. Hawk'll be here any minute for his debriefing. Who'd have ever thought I would debrief somebody? Anyway, best to just use the plan I came up with earlier.

It was a good plan: minimally invasive and simple, but devastating to the enemy. His main concern was to spend as little time as possible in the sewer, thereby lessening the probability of being shot. Secondary concerns were killing a lot of Iiites, damaging their infrastructure, and limiting their ability to retaliate. This plan achieved all those goals, but he was still nervous about showing it to a pro.

What's the worst-case scenario? He laughs at me? No. The worst-case scenario is I get us all killed. Fuck! I hate this shit.

He called on Mr. Booker to calm his nerves, and three fingers later, his old friend had done his job quite well. He was pouring another when the doorbell rang. He grabbed his plasma pistol and hid behind the wall of the kitchen.

"Come in. It's open," Max stared at the front door's reflection in the microwave, ready to spring out.

The door creaked open slowly, but nobody was there. Hawk called from behind the wall, "Beefcake pantyhose."

"I am a termite," Max called back.

"Good job, boy. Just like we rehearsed. "Hawk strode in with a big grin on his face. "Nice place you got here. Where's your hooker roommate?"

"Very funny. I haven't had a chance to redecorate." A fish-hook of remorse caught his guts as he glanced around at Scarlet's kitschy crap. She'd given so much he couldn't bring himself to get rid of her stuff. He'd even kept the plug-in cinnamon air fresheners that irritated his sinuses. This museum of lousy taste was all that was left of her. It was his way of keeping her memory alive and punishing himself for letting it happen. That was none of Hawk's business, so he changed the subject.

"I still don't see why we have to go to all this trouble with stupid passwords and shit. You could say, 'it's me,' and I'd recognize your voice."

"But what if I got captured by the Iiites and they forced me to bring 'em here? The password's so you'll know everything's kosher."

"But a big, brave soldier like you would never do that. You'd die first, right?" Max said sarcastically.

Hawk's forehead wrinkled, and his eyes got shiny. Max felt sorry for him, but it was his own fault for being a big pussy. Unable to find the right words to apologize, Max downed half his drink, returned to the couch and got down to business.

"So, here's what I've come up with. The Iiites live in an underground fortress, right? That seemed like a pain in the ass at first because we'd have to go down there to attack them. They have sensors on all the manholes, so there's no element of surprise. Then I realized we can use that to our advantage.

"Drop those foam bomb things down the drains here, here, here, here, and here and you can create a sealed circuit. Drop a couple poison gas bombs in there beforehand, and you can take out as many Iiites as you can pack into that circuit. I figure we can place a bomb in this central room here. When it explodes, all the nearby soldiers will rush in. Then we detonate the foam bombs, creating an airtight circuit. Detonate the gas bombs and kill everybody inside. Then, while all the other nearby soldiers are trying to save their friends, we'll be sneaking into this area, where the next generation of soldiers is being trained. They'll be on lockdown because they haven't been cleared for battle. They'll be unarmed and scared, so it should be easy to blast through the street and wipe them out before they can regroup. We should be long gone by the time they figure out what's going on. What do you think?"

Hawk had a big, blue-ribbon grin on his face. "Shock and awe, my boy. Shock and awe. I love it. It's so damn simple it'd never have occurred to me. Trap 'em like rats and exterminate 'em. Damn fine work. Them

Mitton boys ain't gonna know what hit 'em. I'll run it through the simulator to work out the bugs. We should be good to go in about a week."

"Really? It's good?" Max asked, genuinely surprised.

"No need to fish for compliments. I done told ya, ya did good. Now, have you had a chance to peruse the catalog?"

Max sighed. "I'm not really comfortable with the whole elective surgery thing. I mean, there's some really cool stuff in there, and I could see how it could come in handy, but the thought of having my eyes replaced makes my skin crawl."

"Who's bein' a coward now? Hell, even I had that done. It's one of the best decisions I ever made. No more eyelashes, infections, irritation, astigmatism, etcetera. Plus I have night vision, heat vision, I can see magnetic fields, read over somebody's shoulder from a mile away, take pictures and video, and to top it all off I can turn the fuckers off when I need to get some sleep in the middle of the day. Regular eyes are downright stupid.

"I'm not saying to go full metal or anything. Everybody has a limit to how much of their body they can upgrade before they start feeling like a robot. But you need to take advantage of the program. Get something little for now, like the internal cell phone. It's just a hands-free walkie-talkie. The procedure takes two seconds, and it doesn't even hurt."

"I don't know, man. I'll think about it." He downed the rest of his drink.

"That's all I'm askin'."

"You want a drink? I've got Bookers."

"Nah, some other time. I got to get back to the HQ so I can get this ball a-rollin'. Where's Cheeky? I'd like to say hi before I go."

"He's napping off a bottle of Irish cream. I wouldn't bother him right now. He can be kind of cranky when he wakes up.

"Well, all right then. I guess I better get movin'. Keep up the good work. A few more ideas like this, and we'll win the war in no time."

Hawk scampered out the door like an excited child, leaving Max to relish the befuddlement his approval had inspired. It seemed he might not suck at this after all, but he wouldn't know for sure until he tasted the pudding of his labors in a week or so. He poured himself a celebratory drink.

Moments later, Cheeky slithered out of the bedroom.

"Hey, I thought you were asleep. You just missed Hawk."

Cheeky scaled the back of the couch, slipped down the front, and almost rolled into the floor.

"Still a little tipsy, huh? I told you, you should have quit after that third glass."

He looked at Max then the half-empty bottle of Bookers and then stuck out his tongue.

"Hey, at least I'm over twenty-one. You aren't even one yet."

Cheeky narrowed his eyes then flipped over for a belly rub.

"Also, you don't have to plan the deaths of thousands of strangers. Nobody wants you dead. I'm probably going to hell for this. Which ring was for traitors? It's been a while since I read epic poetry."

Cheeky stretched and squirmed as Max scratched around his suckers.

"It's not like I want to kill them. They're making me. If they'd all just stop being dicks, I could go back to drinking for fun."

That lumpy little mouth opened as wide as it could, like the yawn was so big it might take the top of his head off if he didn't give it all he had.

"You're so cute." Max leaned over and rubbed noses with him, then nuzzled into his side and fell asleep.

THE GREAT ESCEPADE

Six days later, the dispersant drones were in place, and the troops were waiting. Max only had to give the signal for the attack to begin. Too bad his guts had twisted themselves into balloon animals, and his head was spinning out of control. The only thing he could focus on was the bar down the street. It took everything he had not to run for those big inviting doors. He forced himself to turn away and noticed the other team leaders— Hawk, Neo, and Gandalf— staring at him.

This all came together so fast. What if I missed something?

No, stop that. This will be easy. We kill a bunch of Iiites, Dr. Manhattan's happy. The Iiites kill some of us, Jacob and the Iiites are happy. As long as I don't get my ass blown off, I'm happy. All I have to do is push a few buttons.

Adhra told me about this weakness. The simulator showed a 100% likelihood of victory. It should be like taking candy from a baby, then killing it. So why do I feel like I'm about to die?

The troops stood nearby, fidgeting with their weapons. Aside from Hawk, the only one he'd seen before was Excel, and he only knew her as the girl Asphyxia had made out with that night at the bar. Earlier, in an awkward conversation, he'd asked her to be on his team. She seemed nice, and he thought it would be good to have a familiar face down there. The others were all faceless war-fodder, but he honestly hoped she wouldn't die, and not just because he was hoping for victory sex.

"Come on, Max, stop posin' like a constipated marmoset and give the signal already. It's time to make it rain."

Max was too freaked-out to glare. He could feel his eyes vibrating with terror. He'd been fine until they handed him the plasma cannon. Somehow that triggered the realization that this was actually happening. He really was about to go into the sewer and kill a bunch of strangers. Inside his head, one idea played on an endless loop.

I might die. I might actually fucking die.

The previous battles had all seemed like something he was doing in a video game. He'd been thrown into them without time to think or get freaked out. Shit exploded. He ran. Simple. This felt totally different.

"I haven't got all day. You ready or not?"

"No," Max said as he squeezed his eyes shut and pushed the first button.

The ground grumbled as smoke and dust billowed from the sewer drains. Hawk started the stopwatch. When the minute and forty-nine seconds recommended by the simulator had passed, he gave Max the signal to press the second button. This would seal in the responders and start the timer for the gas. Max was officially a cold-blooded murderer.

Max didn't like killing kids, but he was too afraid of dying to take on anything more daunting. He kept reminding himself the plan was strategically solid. He was killing them now rather than later. No big deal, right? But he couldn't help but feel he no longer had the right to make fun of Hawk.

He forced himself into character and pushed a button on his phone. "Wharghoul" played in the tiny speakers in his helmet. Hawk had suggested it, and Max couldn't resist the irony.

Max blew a hole in the middle of the street and shot the few cadets who weren't killed by the blast before they could get to their feet.

Hawk slapped Max on the back. "Like shootin' lobsters in a barrel."

"If you're done coining phrases..." Max playfully shoved him into the hole.

Hawk tumbled down a pile of wreckage, rolled onto his feet, and shot Max a bird. "That could have fuckin' hurt."

"Quit your bitching. That armor could stop a cannonball." Max hopped down, landing easily with the aid of his hydraulic knee braces. Unlike the other areas he'd seen, the room was furnished in the drab minimalism the military was famous for. Thick gray paint clung to the cinderblock walls like powdered-sugar icing, reminding Max of his high school gym.

They broke into four teams of five. Hawk, being the greatest coward, went north to the mess-hall and classrooms. Gandalf went east to the firing ranges, and Neo went west towards administration. Max's team went south to raid the sleeping quarters. There would be more cadets, but it was less likely they'd be armed.

The first room was simple: twenty sixteen-year-olds who'd shit themselves before the real attack had even begun. The Nrrds burst in to find them hiding behind their beds or in their lockers. Nobody fought back. It was a massacre. Four seconds in, every one of them was spattered, sizzling like fish-fat, across the dull gray walls or dribbling onto the concrete floors to pool and congeal into mutant pancakes.

The next room was easy, too; more sleeping quarters and terrified recruits. They tried to attack, but the cadets' personal items bounced off of the armored Nrrds like, well... personal items off an armored Nrrd. Max was starting to calm down, or at least his adrenaline levels were high enough he no longer felt he was going to vomit.

They blew through the third door, but all they saw were empty beds. Max carefully strafed from side to side, but the room seemed empty. The Iiites had probably run away, but he wanted to be sure.

Max gave Excel the signal to check it out. When she stepped through, two cadets snatched her around the corner and pulled her apart like cheesy-bread.

"Assholes!" Max screamed as he and the Nrrds reduced the wall and everything behind it to ash.

I would have to go and get her killed first. What the fuck was I thinking?

Max didn't see anybody, so he gave the signal to proceed. As soon as they were all in, Iiites rained down, pummeling the Nrrds with their bare hands while backup spewed in from all directions.

Damn it, this wasn't supposed to happen—stupid simulator. Max blasted everything that moved. He couldn't tell how many Nrrds he hit, but by the time he was done, he was the only one standing.

Oops, I guess these things are a little too powerful to use in teams. Oh well, Addy'll be happy.

Retreating to the entry point, he saw that Hawk, Gandalf, and five others were back, but Neo's team was missing. He listened for sounds of battle, but everything was quiet.

"Beta team, where the fuck are you?"

The little chip in his ear didn't respond.

"Well, it looks like Beta fucked-up. Everybody point your guns that way and blast a path. Don't let them get between you. If they come in from behind, form a circle with all your backs so we don't shoot each other. Okay, go!"

The remaining seven Nrrds did as he asked. Seconds later, they had a path half a mile long and twenty feet wide with nothing in view but smoldering piles of unidentifiable ick. Max was about to give the "good enough, let's go home" signal when the Nrrd beside him flew backward and exploded against a pile of rubble.

"Fuck! We went too far. Backs together! Blast everything! Retreat! Retreat!" Max screamed over the roar of bullets and screaming Iiites as they poured through every door and hole.

"It's like we stepped on a fucking ant bed."

He knew they were screwed. The whole attack was supposed to have taken four minutes, but they'd more than doubled that. The Nrrds' formation made them one big, easy-to-hit target for anyone brave enough to stick their arm around a corner. Their bio-armor was strong, but it was never intended to be put to so extreme a test. The blender of bullets and shrapnel was bad enough, but one of the Iiites had a rocket launcher. When they arrived at the entrance, only Max, Hawk, and Gandalf were left.

"Extraction for three! Now!" Max screamed as they reached the hole.

Three extraction drones appeared above them. Max watched with dread as the bays on the bottom opened and dropped rope ladders. They were no bigger than a child's tricycle. How could this five-pound toy carry a man that weighed one-hundred-and-fifty?

Nevertheless, the men grabbed hold and were lifted out with jarring swiftness. The drones were fast and hard to hit from the ground. But were they a match for the squadron of Iiites they found waiting for them above?

Gandalf's drone exploded. He fell fifteen feet and was impaled on a fire hydrant.

"Who keeps giving these fuckers jetpacks?"

Max and Hawk blasted away as their drones weaved through the city with Iiites in hot pursuit.

"Aw crap, looks like we screwed the hornet nest on this one."

Max called to HQ, "Emma, what are we doing about this?"

"Attack drones are on the way. They should be there any second now."

"I told you those mods were handy."

The drones whizzed into a tight alley and let loose a thick cloud of black smoke. Max could hear the Iiites choking and wrecking into each other as they sprayed plasma like drunks writing in the snow. After two blocks, the smoke ran out. Max waited with his finger tight on the trigger, but no Iiites came out of the cloud.

Hawk hooted his approval. "Nice one! I think we're in the clear."

Max breathed a sigh of relief and turned around. "Well, that could have gone better."

"Oh, don't beat yourself up about it. You did great. We lost eighteen brave soldiers today, but took out a few hundred of the enemy and did massive damage to their base. I'd call that a resounding victory."

"I'll have to take your word on that." Hawk was right, though. He felt a lot less guilty about the Nrrds dying this way than he would for sending them into a trap. The only way it could have worked out better would be for Excel to have survived.

As they approached the next street, gunfire and explosions erupted just around the corner. The extraction drones did a quick one-eighty.

"What the fuck was that?"

Emma replied, "The drones just caught up to you. Iiites were trailing you from above. You're being diverted to a secondary base."

"How about you set us down and let us catch a cab? It'd be a lot less conspicuous than a couple of guys being carried around by tiny helicopters."

"There are still too many Iiites in the area. You're a much harder target this way."

"Yeah, but this fucking rope's about cut my hand off. I'm not sure how much longer I can hold on."

Hawk and Emma responded in unison. "Don't be a wuss."

Max gritted his teeth. He had promised himself he would be more assertive, and here he was falling into old habits.

They whipped around a corner to find yet more Iiites waiting for them. They fired wildly while the choppers did another one-eighty and headed down a side alley. Seconds later, the Iiites were closing in. The choppers made a weird whirring noise as a blue flash illuminated the alley. The Iiites fell to their deaths, looking confused.

"What the fuck was that?"

Hawk giggled again. "That, my boy, was an acute EMP. It fries everything with a wire for fifty feet."

"And why didn't it go off before now?"

"We only had the one. You rather we'd wasted it?"

"Why didn't you put more on there?"

"These things are designed to be light and fast. The designer didn't think we'd need any weapons at all, but I got him to put a couple light ones on there just in case. You're welcome."

Max smiled sarcastically and pulled out his phone. "Hey Emma, patch me into the weather-cam. I want to see how bad it is for myself."

Emma responded, "They have every Iiite in the state out looking for you."

The screen lit up with a view of the city. It looked like an anthill somebody had smashed a hornet's nest on. Hundreds of Iiites zipped around like angry wasps while squadrons of soldiers patrolled the streets below.

"Shit, I think we need a change of plan." Max noticed he was in his old neighborhood. "I have an idea. Take a right here and drop us off at the third building."

"You know somebody that lives there?"

"I did, when I was a kid. The basement has sewer access. Some of the other kids in the building used to think it was fun to throw me down there and stand on the grate. I'm pretty sure we can take the tunnels to The Cartridge Which Cannot Be Named. We should be safe there."

Hawk cocked an eyebrow. "You been snacking on lead-paint chips or something?"

Max showed him the screen. "There are more of them up here than there are down there."

Emma chimed in. "That's not what he meant. When the Iiites developed the sewer, they diverted almost all of the city's sewage to a few high-flow areas, and this is one of them."

"Well, that doesn't sound pleasant, but it's not all bad news. We probably won't run into any Iiites. Why don't we see if it's plausible?"

Hawk scowled. "It's your mission. You make the call."

The drones set them down and sped away. Max and Hawk ducked into the building and headed for the basement.

Max pointed up ahead. "There should be a grate right--over--here!. This should get us home. Give me a hand. It's rusty."

They stuck their fingers through the holes and yanked as hard as they could. After a couple of tries, it came off and nearly crushed Max's toes as it clanged against the cement.

"Holy fuck that stinks." Max gagged and stumbled back, pulling his shirt over his nose. The body armor helped keep it in place.

"You surprised? It's the goddamn sewer."

"It's worse than when I was a kid. The shit didn't even touch the walkway. Now, there's a few feet of muck flowing over it. This is going to suck."

"Hold your horses there. I'm not jumping into--."

Max cracked an I-can't-believe-I'm-about-to-do-this smile, held his nose, and jumped in. The feculent liquid came up to his nipples. It would have been impossible to push against its flow. Luckily it was going his way. He hopped along, letting the current do most of the work.

"Come on, don't be a pussy." The taunt wasn't worth the mouthful of poo particles, but he couldn't help but laugh as he heard Hawk sputter and curse behind him.

He navigated by the tiny streams of light that slipped through the vents of manholes and dissolved into the oily dreck. The smell got worse the further he went. He felt like he was going to pass out, but he projectile-vomited instead. After that final protest, his olfactory workers went on strike, making the trip significantly less unpleasant.

"This should be it. If I'm right, The Cartridge Which Cannot Be Named should be right across the street. My GPS is under a couple feet of shit. Could you verify that, Emma."

"Yep, you're there. Give me a second before you go to the surface, though. I'm working on a distraction."

Hawk caught up to Max and sputtered, "Hurry it up, sister. I'm dyin' down here."

A few seconds later, they heard a rash of explosions break out in the distance.

"All right, that should buy you guys a few seconds, get a move on."

Max forced the manhole cover up with his head and peeked at the street. He didn't see anything coming, so he opened it further only to be knocked back into the shit by a passing car. Hawk laughed so hard he puked. Max bobbed to the surface, puked, and punched Hawk in the face. It was his turn to go under.

When they had both regained their footing, they ascended the ladder and emerged right in front of a small group of children. "Poo monsters!" They shrieked as they ran away.

Max and Hawk ignored them and ran for the door, leaving a feculent trail that would likely give birth to a new urban legend. They crashed through the doors, threw the lock, and began stripping away their body armor, much to the dismay of the fifth annual Omnisphere competition taking place to their left. Startled, the Nrrds broke character and cried out in terror as their hand-crafted vestments were spattered with ordure.

One of the cashiers screamed, "Dude, not in the store," while the other jumped over the counter and dove to protect a nearby display of collectible carded figures. The Iiite soldier, who had been checking out, snapped out of his daze a second too late. Max and Hawk dove for their guns and clicked

180

their triggers furiously while everyone around them screamed, "Not in the store!"

Luckily for all concerned, the plasma cannons failed to produce anything more destructive than a dribble of putrid liquid. The Iiite turned to the cashier and saw a small pistol leveled at his head.

Max dropped his gun and exhaled with great vigor.

"Nice going, soldier," Hawk said to the Nrrd with the gun. "Sorry about the mess. You think it smells bad on the floor, try swimming in it."

The second cashier lay at his feet, sobbing into an armful of previously-mint Firefly toys.

"Oh, quit whining. I did it too. You should be thanking me. Your pores are going to look great tomorrow."

"Really? Is shit good for the complexion?"

"I don't know. Probably. Cum is. There's a ton of that down there too."

Hawk gagged again, stripped off his shirt, and used the cleanest spot to scour his face and neck. The gamers concerned themselves with giving and receiving advice on how to get stains out of felt and whether the game should be relocated to a less malodorous venue.

The Iiite glanced back and forth between the cashier and the six-feet of spattered merchandise. "So, I'm going to go out on a limb and say you're the guys everybody's looking for. Is this like a secret base or something?"

"Oh, we bagged us a smart 'un. That big ol' brain you got must make it awful easy to rule the world and all," the Nrrd behind the counter quipped in his best idiot voice.

"Dude, I've been shopping here for years. Be nice. I just meant it's kind of funny. I mean, it totally makes sense now that I think about it. I knew you guys were nerds, but I thought you were a nerd like I'm a nerd, not like Riot Nrrds."

Hawk glared at the guy behind the register, a fat Nrrd of indiscriminate age with a choppy brown mustache and a bowl cut that looked like he did it himself without a bowl or a mirror. The Nrrd adjusted his gold wireframes and responded, "What kind of cover operation would this be if we refused to sell to Iiites?"

Hawk shrugged his eyebrows and glanced over at the band of less-than-merry gentlemen. "All right, everybody out. We're experiencing technical difficulties. This shindig's officially rescheduled."

"What is this tomfoolery? A quest cannot be rescheduled. You burst in spewing filth and demand we leave without so much as an apology! Have at you, sir."

The gamer pulled a long wooden sword from the rope cinched around his waist and swung it at Hawk's head. Hawk stopped the sword with one hand and grabbed the wrist with the other. Twisting the arm around, he crumpled him like a paper cup and hurled him out the door.

"My name is General Hawk, and I outrank the shit out of you. We are in a war-time situation. I will not ask nicely again. Anybody have a problem with that?"

He stared with practiced fury, making eye-contact with each and every one of them as they cowered against the comics. The gamers averted their eyes and made themselves as small as possible.

"You're still here!" he screamed, jarring them into motion. As they skittered out the door like frightened cats, he added, "Act casual!"

When the last gamer was out, he locked the door and strode mightily toward his prisoner. "You picked the wrong time to beef up your game collection." He dumped Resident Evil Fifteen out onto the counter and smiled. "Hey, now that's a good one. Too bad you won't get to play it."

Hawk's previous display had jostled the familiarity out of the Iiite's voice. "Hey, dude, it's cool. I won't tell anybody. This is my favorite store. Where else can I find sealed decks of Fright Flix trading cards?"

Hawk laughed. "Oh, all right then. Off you go."

"Really?"

"No. You think this is my first hoedown?"

"No, obviously not, but I was serious. I'm more nerd than Iiite. Look at me. I abandoned the hunt to buy a video game. You think I want to wear this uniform? I was born into this bullshit. You want information? I'll tell you anything you want to know. Fuck those guys. Keep me here if you want. I always said I could spend the rest of my life in a comic shop. Hold me for ransom if you want, but don't kill me." He turned to the cashier and began to cry. "Come on, man, you know me. You know my name. You kick my ass at Tekken every Saturday. Don't let them do this."

Hawk shot the cashier another glare.

"He does have a point. He's either the best spy ever or king of the otaku. He even has a nickname. We call him Al after the little kid from Fullmetal Alchemist whose soul gets stuck in a big suit of armor."

"Well, if that's the case, then I apologize, but I can't let you live. Get rid of him."

"Just a minute." Max put his hand on Hawk's shoulder and pulled him to the side. "This isn't a race war, it's political. I don't see a reason why he can't switch sides."

"Are you crazy? We can't let him live. First chance he gets, he'll run and tattle everything he's seen."

"Not necessarily. I'm not saying we don't take precautions, but off the top of my head, I can think of at least five better plans for him. We need somebody on the inside. You could put a little bomb in him that we can remotely detonate if he steps out of line. Whether he's a double agent, a hostage, or a janitor, he's worth more to us alive than dead."

"I understand you're new to this, but do I have to remind you there are lives at stake?"

"Yes, there are—lots of ours and lots of theirs. I'll get Emma to look after him. If he tries anything, she'll take care of him." And she'll finally be out of my way. "Think about this; do you want to go down in the history books like George Washington or Adolph Hitler? Why are you fighting this war? Was all that stuff about freeing the downtrodden masses a load of shit?"

Hawk gritted his teeth and exhaled through his nose. "Goddammit, I'm starting to see why you got this job." He spun around and rushed towards the Iiite. Getting right in his face, he growled, "What's your name, boy?"

"Al, I mean Spencer. My real name's Spencer."

"Well, Al, or Spencer or whatever the fuck else people call you, I want you to do something for me."

"Anything!"

"See that guy over there?" He jerked his thumb to indicate Max.

"Yeah."

"I want you to crawl over there on your hands and knees and thank that man for extending your shitty little life."

When the shock wore off, he crawled like a baby with a flaming diaper, clung to Max's shit-caked boots, and commenced washing them with tears of joy.

Max cried out in surprise and mild disgust, "Hey, don't. Stop that. He wasn't serious."

Al's face twisted into a mask of pain as he fell away and landed in a puddle of ick.

"No, I meant you didn't have to crawl over here. I did talk him out of killing you."

"Bullshit! I gave an order. He followed it. That's how it works." Hawk returned his attention to Al. "He didn't talk me out of killing you. He talked me into letting you live a little longer, and that's contingent on a long string of conditions. Consider yourself on probation. You will learn to love your probation. You will do any and every thing we ask up to and including dying to keep from breaking any and all conditions of that probation. Am I clear?"

"Yes."

"What was that?"

"Sir, yes, sir! I love probation, sir! Thank you from the bottom of my heart, sir!" He hugged Max's leg again.

"That's better."

"Damn it, get off. You're getting more shit on me."

Al snapped to attention. "Sir, my deepest apologies, sir. May I please have the honor of cleaning that up for you, sir?"

Hawk cracked a smile. "He's good."

"Sir, I have extensive military training, sir. I hope that you will continue to mold me like an unworthy piece of dirty clay with bits of hair and grit all over it that you found under the couch, sir."

"Now he's just being facetious. Did you like your military training, boy?"

"Sir, no, sir. However, I am absolutely positive that I will enjoy every second of your wise and merciful tutelage, sir."

Max laughed so hard he had to sit down. "All right, man, that's enough of the screaming sir bullshit. We have a different approach than the Fist. You'll probably like it better here."

"Sir…"

"I said to knock that off. We're supposed to be hiding in here."

"Okay. I just wasn't sure if that was a test."

Max shook his head.

The cashier lowered his gun. "So, we're really not killing him?"

Max sighed. "No. We're really not going to kill him. What's your name again?"

"They call me Doctor Feelgood," he sang as he returned his pistol to its shelf below the register.

"Really? I don't even want to know." Max walked over and whispered, "Fit him with a black-light reactive pilcrow and one of those remote bomb implants in case he fucks up. Don't tell him what it is until afterward. He's your responsibility. If he gets loose or anything goes wrong, it's on you."

Feelgood made anime eyes. "Why me?"

"Because you vouched for him. Also, I outrank you. Get a few of the guys from the back to hang out with you and keep an eye on him. Pour some Bliss down his throat and see if he babbles anything useful. Say, does this place have a shower?"

"I'm afraid not."

"Damn. What's the fastest way I can get to one?"

"There's a hotel down the street."

"Can I get there without being seen?"

"No"

"Damn it, man, don't fuck with me."

"I'd like nothing more than to get you out of my face and hosed off. I mean that with utmost sincerity. Unfortunately, the best I can offer you is a sink and or an olfactory block."

"Better than nothing. I'll take both. The block is reversible, right?"

"Everything that can be done can be undone given the proper level of intelligence and a roll of duct tape."

Max glowered menacingly at him.

"Sorry."

Max turned to Al. "I'll get with you later and figure out how you can pay us back. For now, go with," he cringed, "Doctor Feelgood."

Feelgood opened the secret door and gestured for Al to follow. Al followed like a giddy child. As they shut the door, Max could hear Feelgood's whispered apologies.

"Sorry about that stuff I said. I had to make it look good for the boss. I was hoping they wouldn't make me shoot you…"

"And get somebody to clean this up." Max glanced at the second cashier, who was still sobbing into his armful of toys. "You, blubbery guy! Hey, clean this shit up."

The man on the floor looked up at him. His eyes were confused at first but soon shifted to puffy rage. Screaming, he sprang to his feet, grabbed a Bat' leth from a nearby display case, and charged. Hawk stepped in and flipped him onto his own blade. He died moments later, mumbling something about Mylar.

"Wow." Max stepped away from the blood as though his shoes could get any dirtier. "There was something seriously wrong with that guy."

"Yes, I do believe Elvis left that building some time ago. He's in a better place now. You, on the other hand, are still in the shit. Shit, which literally and figuratively... there are just too damn many puns in my head right now. I can't pick one."

"Do they have a colonic machine here? I need to do my sinuses."

"That actually sounds nice. Seriously though, you did real good today. Anybody can plan a mission. Under the right circumstances, anybody can go on or even lead one, but I've only known a handful of people who can keep their shit together when everything goes to... well... shit. Sorry, I think the smell's starting to affect my brain.

"What I mean to say is you showed true leadership today, both in here and out there, and you have earned my utmost respect and gratitude. We may well have died if you hadn't come up with that plan to use the sewer. As a token of my gratitude, you can have the first olfactory block."

"Aww, shucks. That's sweet."

"That said, if you ever make me do that again, I will tear out your lungs and beat you with 'em."

"That's less sweet, but I promise to do my very best."

"I anticipate a long and glorious career for you. Now, let's get our noses plugged so we can get a drink."

THE HAWK AND THE
BAD SHEPPARD

The tension in the air was denser than a stale bagel. The clop of Hawk's heels on the factory's floor ricocheted off the cinderblock walls, hitting the ears of the troops like stray bullets. They cringed with every step. For Hawk, it was soothing, metronomic. It linked him to the moment. It kept him from losing himself, from being crushed under the weight of his thoughts as they rolled through his head like enemy tanks.

Poor shell-shocked bastards jump at quiet farts these days. And who can blame 'em? Everything's gone. They've lost their homes, their friends, their work. I'm the only one that gets to work in my field, and I'd trade it for a job at Big Burger if it wouldn't get us all killed.

The past six months have been more Fundoshi Corps than Marine Corps. The brutality and weirdness were downright Biblical. The appropriateness of that last word made him crack a bitter smile. War is my religion, but what do you do when you meet God and find out he's an asshole? Can't really run back to Buddha, all, "Sorry about that man. I got confused. Let's discuss abstractions over a cup of tea." He'd be like, "Too late, it is. Made your bed, you have. Now, lie in it, you must." Or was that Yoda? Fuck...Yoda. Poor bastard. Nobody should have to die like that.

Hawk had spent the last hour pacing like a lab-rat in a cocaine study, scouring his brain for something he could say to improve morale. Nothing came to mind. He stopped and looked around the room at the miserable husks of his last thirty-seven soldiers.

Damn near everybody's dead now, and the leftovers are all fuckin' crazy. I baptized 'em in blood and adrenaline. They survived through a combination of survival instinct, pent-up rage, and good luck. Well, luck anyway. Hard to say anything's good about what they are.

He scratched his temple then wiped the oily grit on his pants.

Hundreds of thousands dead on either side, cities reduced to Swiss cheese, and we got nothin' to show for it. Some places the Nrrds got lucky, or gone way overboard and killed everybody that looked like they could win an arm-wrestling match. Others got stamped out faster than a stale cigarette in a Klipsch cigar shop. Either way was fine with normals. Worthless bunch a...

We try to be considerate. The strikes are surgical. We try not to fuck up more than a few blocks at a time, but do they appreciate it? Hell no! All they can do is whine about how they're out of a job or how much worse we've made traffic.

Worst thing is, we're still even. It's like we're trading licks, going back and forth taking turns dying. Nobody ever gets ahead. Most frustrating war ever.

There was something he wasn't seeing, and it was driving him nuts. Even the troops smelled something fishy. They'd tried to come up with a formula to explain what they called the see-saw anomaly. But that was before things got bad.

A giant rat scuttled out of an air-duct, picked up a discarded bit of sandwich, and nibbled it like he'd just arrived at a party. Without changing his expression, a nearby Nrrd snatched it up and broke its neck with his thumb. He used to give money to PITA -4.

Half a year doesn't sound like much, but it was enough to turn a bunch of brilliant Nrrds into hollow-eyed monsters. With only three laptops left, there wasn't much to connect them to their previous lives. They'd have probably all killed themselves by now if they hadn't found that closet full of old pencils and notebooks. None of them really believed they'd get to resume work on their projects. Still, scribbling in those notebooks provided a much-needed distraction.

They had been damn lucky to find a small factory where they could spread out a little. It wasn't much more than four walls, a roof, and an elevated office, but they were happy to have it. Even the turf war they were having with the rats was kind of fun.

Hawk's eyes climbed the rusty staircase to the office. Max was up there now, planning their next attack. Max had seized the office with the gusto and decisiveness Hawk had come to expect from him. Who'd have guessed all those months ago that whiny, smug, lazy little shit-smear would develop into the unshakable juggernaut he was today? If I were that cool under pressure, this war would have been over by now.

I do wish he'd share the office more. We're supposed to be partners. Who am I kidding? Max is the leader. He should have the chair. Leaders deserve a little something extra. We can't have the person whose decisions determine whether we live or die being affected by unnecessary discomfort.

If it wasn't for Max, I'd have cut and run months ago. I still might. I sure think about it enough, but Max's bravery is contagious. It's like he has a big bubble of cojones energy around him that can top off your piss and vinegar tanks the second you step into it.

Goddammit, if Max can stay positive through all this shit, I can too.

Hawk resumed his pacing, intent on finding that secret phrase that could slay the dragon weltschmerz.

"If I could just get 'em to laugh. Shit, I can't remember the last time I heard a chuckle. I mean, they weren't the most jovial bunch, to begin with, but..."

"Damnit, pipe down over there. I'm trying to solve for Y in Wilson's paradox of quantum podge," screamed one of the troops.

Hawk was startled. Had he been talking to himself? It scared him that he wasn't sure. Looking in the direction of the complaint, all he saw was a bunch of skinny, oblivious scientists who needed a bath. A grimace hardened on his face as he noticed one of the laptops was being used to generate alien porn.

"Feelgood, don't you have anything more important to do?"

Dr. Feelgood continued to try out various degrees of curl on the blue woman's nipples. "In times such as these, it is more important than ever to keep up morale. The troops need every bit of escapism they can get. To that end, I made my website free and open source. Pornography makes people happy, and happy troops are less likely to shatter under pressure. You're welcome."

Makes sense. A wallop of dopamine might be just what the doctor ordered. I could sure use one right about now. Maybe if I instated mandatory masturbation... No, they'll think I went and snapped on 'em. Things are weird enough as they are. The last thing we need is to spiral into a suicidal circle-jerk. We'd probably invoke Humwawa or something. Then again, Humwawa might be just what the doctor...

Bang! Bang! Bang!

Hawk hit the floor with his weapon drawn, then realized he'd fallen prey to the factory's wonky acoustics. All around him, Nrrds were tripping over each other, trying to find cover in the empty room. Troops were trampled, and weapons were discharged, just because Max had knocked on the office window. Hawk could see him through the grime, laughing at the slapstick he had inspired.

Hawk screamed over their shrieks of terror, "Attention!" It took a few moments for the word to register, but they eventually stopped. He pointed to the office window, and Max banged on it three more times to set them at ease. Instead of laughing or showing signs of relief, the troops went blandly back to their spots on the floor and resumed their scribbling. Things were worse than he'd thought.

He glanced around to take inventory of the damage: nothing major, just a few new holes in the walls. I guess I was right to keep the big guns locked up. You can't say I don't learn from my mistakes.

He felt a little better as he climbed the steps. It was nice to be reminded that not every loud noise was somebody trying to kill him. This was the sort of thing that made Max such a great leader. He would always do the right thing at the right time, whether he meant to or not. It was almost like he was guided by a superior intelligence.

Max sat in the mangled office chair, sipping coffee out of a cracked Styrofoam cup and drumming on the table with his fingers. Rats had chewed the leather to confetti and used most of the stuffing for nests. Rusty springs poked him every time he shifted his weight. Still, it was their only chair, and he was honored to have it at his disposal.

He felt bad about killing the people who depended on him, but it wasn't his fault they had chosen to be violent terrorists. He never forced anyone to do anything. They could leave any time they wanted, and he would prefer it if they did.

The door creaked open, and Hawk came in. He walked over to the desk where Cheeky lay napping and scratched him on the head, rousing him momentarily from his nap. Cheeky lay his head back down and did his maybe-if-I-pretend-to-sleep-this-asshole-will-go-away thing.

"So, how're the troops doing?" Max asked with a smirk.

Hawk glanced sadly out the window. "You saw. They can't take a piss without shooting at the tinkle."

"Yeah, that was pretty funny." Max motioned for him to have a seat.

"I'm getting too old for this no furniture shit." Hawk sat on the stack of pallets, which was the closest thing they had to another piece of furniture, and groaned. "It'd probably be best if you found some other way of getting my attention. We can't afford to lose any more to friendly fire."

Max nodded solemnly. "I hate to think what might have happened if I'd opened the door instead. Maybe I should leave it open."

"Fuck the door. We've got to do something about our people. This war ate their souls and shit what's left into the husks. I know the answer's out there, but it's not slipperier than a beauty queen with daddy issues on oil wrestling night. We won the last battle, so nobody wants to go to the next one."

"Why's that?"

Hawk raised his voice. "You know damn well. We're taking turns dying. It's like the battles are being decided by some snooty artistic type trying to make a point."

Max smiled and set his cup down on the desk. "Sounds like the war's getting to you, man."

"Shit's not false just 'cause it's crazy."

"That very well may be, but come on; do you really think somebody's rigging the battles? A war is made of sides. One is against the other. The object is to win. You of all people should know that."

"Yeah, but if we don't figure this shit out soon, I'm going to have to go on a suicide mission myself."

Max sat up and put on his lecturing face. "They're losing every other battle because they expect to. Here's what probably happened. A random series of events led to the wins flip-flopping for a short time. The pattern was noticed by a bunch of scientists who overestimated its significance because of the stress they were under while observing it.

"You're an expert at calculating probability. What's more likely, obsessive geniuses freaking out over a misinterpretation of facts and getting themselves killed or some kind of mysterious x-factor, hand-of-God scenario? Given the stress of war and the nature of the soldiers, we probably should have seen this coming." Max aped thoughtfulness. "I wonder why the computer didn't warn us?"

Hmm, why didn't the computer see this coming? I mean, common sense, nerds are going to suck at war. It seems like the second they put the statistics into the computer, "Ha, ha, ha. You are joking, right?" should have popped up on the screen.

Hawk grinned for the first time in months. "Well, shit my underpants, you just might be a Nrrd after all. That's a damn fine hypothesis. Even if you're wrong, it'll get 'em to suspend their disbelief long enough to go on a mission. If we win, we win. If we lose, it'll just prove their theory, and they'll all want to go on the next one because it's a sure thing. I can't wait to tell 'em." Hawk stood to leave.

"Not so fast, we need to talk about the next raid."

The General's smile faded, but his eyes still twinkled with excitement. He sat down and waited for his orders.

"The leaders of the Fist have gone into hiding. We've destroyed all the really nice areas of their city except for this one." Max stood and pointed to a group of green push pins that freckled the sewer map on the wall behind him. "It's a resort sector with a lot of areas around it for troops to camp. I checked, and the manhole covers in that area have all been welded shut."

"No chance in hell the Fist is there. Maybe some M.I.L.F.s, but nobody important. Looks like bait to me."

"No shit. They've obviously fled to the surface. The question is where." He removed his phone from the drawer and projected an aerial photo of the city onto the wall. "They're probably in one or more of the buildings above the resort where they can keep an eye out for us, but to know which ones we'll have to figure out who's still loyal to them above ground."

Hawk put on his thinkin'-hard face. "Nobody seems to be supporting 'em anymore. Maybe they are in those resorts. Hell, at this point, we're so beaten down we could win and not even know."

Max laughed and took another sip of his coffee. "True. I assume Al would let us know if we'd won, but I haven't heard from him in a while. Last I heard, he was guarding the M.I.L.F."

"Goddamned freak probably went back to the dark side."

"I doubt it. It's more likely they found him out and killed him. Either way, he doesn't know anything that can hurt us."

Hawk's face darkened. "Yeah, all the stuff he knew about got blowed up."

"Everything got blown up." Exasperated, Max popped into his chair a little too hard. He gritted his teeth, shifted his ass to remove the spring, and continued. "Look, I'm tired of having this argument with you. There's nothing to make me think he turned on us. I made a call. I think it was the right call. Either way, there's nothing we can do about it now. I'm more worried that we haven't heard from Emma. She should be able to come and go as she pleases. If they turned her, we could be in some real trouble."

Max took another sip of coffee. "Get Feelgood to hack into the Fist's bank accounts again. Find where their money is going, and you find them. They don't have enough troops to be spread out, so I'm pretty sure this next attack will finish them off. Be happy, a little more ass-kicking, and it'll all be over."

Hawk let out a little snort and smiled. "Whatever you say, boss." He stood to leave.

"By the way, have you heard from Manhattan lately?"

"Nope, last I heard he was working on a new weapon, but that was before we lost most of our resources. He's probably dead or in hiding."

"If he's half as smart as everybody says, he's probably sitting on a beach somewhere licking pina colada out from between the breasts of a nubile native girl."

Hawk laughed. "Damn right. To fight, one must be brave. To be brave, one must be stupid. I forget who said that, but it's the God's honest truth."

Max cocked an eyebrow. "Quite, so remind me why we're doing this again."

Hawk stood at attention, saluted, and belted out, "Because the Iiites are a menace to the world and the enemies of liberty, sir!"

Max took another sip of coffee. *My sense of humor must be rubbing off. About time he got one.* "And by that you mean they were killing you and making the world suck, and there didn't seem to be another option, and now it's too late to pull out. Point of no return and all that."

"Yessiree, we were fucked either way, and we still are. I tell myself that whenever I feel down."

Max grew deadly serious and motioned for Hawk to come closer. "You know, we could disband; get Feelgood to hack us up some money and Marx to make some chips with new identities. The truth is out. Things are never going to go back to the way they were."

Looking shocked and a little confused, Hawk responded, "As tempting as that is, doing that would mean most of the greatest minds of our time gave their lives for nothing. I may be a coward at heart, but I couldn't live with myself if I quit while there was still a glimmer of hope."

Max stared him down.

Hawk shifted his eyes to the floor and added, "That said, I already have Marx working on the chips in a secret location. I told him it was our last resort and to only make five. He said he'd keep quiet as long as one of the five was for him. Sorry I didn't tell you sooner. One is for you. I was just hoping it wouldn't come to that."

Max sometimes wondered if Hawk didn't come up with his exit strategy before the plan. "No biggie, it's good to know we have a plan. Now get going. I want this over with one way or another."

"Yes sir," the General said with a cheery salute.

Max watched him march down the stairs and give a stirring adaptation the motivational speech from Braveheart. The troops responded enthusiastically. Max carefully nestled in his chair and took another sip of stale coffee, too sad to notice it had lost the last traces of heat and now tasted like the floor of a quick-e-lube.

This time next week, most of them would be dead. Max knew where the Fist was hiding. He no longer needed to arrange traps for his own people. Every remaining Iiite soldier was on guarding one of the seven Fist leaders. Each leader was in the penthouse of a different skyscraper, but they were all in the same area of the city. Each building had a small army on every floor, and they were close enough to provide backup within minutes.

The Nrrds could win, assuming Addy's information was accurate. If she was going to betray him, this would be when. He was about to find out if he was as good a spy as he pretended to be.

He set up his chess set, then scooped Cheeky off the desk and smothered him with kisses. They rubbed noses and stared into each other's eyes for a few moments before Max set him down in front of the board.

Cheeky let out a series of displeased snorts. He wasn't as fond of chess as Cakey, but he was twice as good. Max had been using him to improve his strategies. The endgame was always where he had his ass handed to him. All he could do was hope that if Addy was planning to betray him, she wasn't as good at chess as his pet.

,

A DEADLY AFFAIR

Max pressed into the shadows of a hidey-hole at the base of building seven. All around him, his targets prodded the sky like holy wangs of yore, taunting him to whip it out. He was sweating like a conspiracy theorist at a roadblock. His stomach felt like a pressure cooker full of motor oil. Pointless similes were scurrying around in his brain like...

Ahhh, stop that! Am I making a mistake? Wouldn't it make more sense to storm one of the other buildings and blow up the one with the big boss? Why am I not doing that? Why am I torturing myself? I mean, sure, part of me wants to put a bullet between that bitch's eyes for using me, but the other part, the bigger part... Fuck! This would all be so much easier if we had a few more pounds of C6.

He tugged on the scraggly mess that had taken over his face. It helped him focus, like he was pulling the thoughts back down into his head, reining them in. It had been hard to stay rational while the gorgeous nymphet was pawing at his crotch, but now she was just a twisted memory. All that remained of their romance was a habit of pleasuring himself to the photos in her file.

At first, his fantasies were about making love. Over time, they grew increasingly perverse and abusive. Some of his most recent fantasies were downright hateful. How would he feel when confronted with the real Addy?

Damn it, she's the enemy. Why can't I get her out of my head?

What if I'm wrong? This wouldn't be the first time somebody used Occam's Razor to cut their own throat.

Don't be stupid. Addy gave us a plan that depends on knockout gas and then bought a fuck-ton of gas masks. What other explanation can there be? We were supposed to get massacred so she could get a promotion. If Feelgood hadn't found that invoice, we'd all be dead right now. Fuck her!

Damn, I miss fucking her.

Hawk's voice came over the radio. "Team A in position. How we lookin'?"

195

Feelgood responded. "Just a couple more to go."

Hawk sounded impatient. "You guys were supposed to be done five minutes ago. We're sittin' ducks."

"Yeah, well, maybe if you'd given us more time to prepare, we wouldn't have to keep taping the detonators back together."

Max was thankful for the interruption. The silence was driving him crazy. Still, those two were going to blow the mission if he didn't step in. "Can you stop posturing for five minutes? Hawk, return to cover and wait for my signal. Feelgood, take your time. Doing this right is way more important than doing it fast."

Also, I could use a little more time to prepare myself. If I go in there like this... Ugh.

Anyway, she's not going to have much time to come up with a story. I guess I should give her a chance to explain, if it's convenient. I have a plan for either scenario. The strategy's solid, the enemy's unaware, and the troops are pumped up and growling in Klingon. All I have to do is survive the next thirty minutes.

"Payload is good to go."

"Team A, move into position." Max pulled the jetpack out of his bag, buckled up, and gnawed his lip. Sensing his distress, Cheeky wound himself tightly around his leg, blinking and humming Max's favorite Korpiklaani song. The performance only managed to make him more nervous. Every second felt like an hour.

"Team A is in position. Again."

Max was shocked to find himself shooting up the cleft. He was so nervous that Hawk's voice had made him accidentally engage his jetpack.

Crap!

"B team, go. Ten seconds to detonation."

He'd expected fireworks and loud explosions and Iiites coming from out of nowhere, guns blazing as they zipped around on jetpacks screaming for blood. Instead, there was a low rumble like distant thunder as the monoliths sank into rising clouds of powdered cement. Had he been tricked?

Then he saw them. Hundreds of terror-twisted faces pressed against bulletproof windows as they rushed to meet the rising dust. It reminded him of an old movie he'd seen about the holocaust. He looked away and told himself it's not genocide if they're soldiers.

The adrenaline wore off, and the pain rushed in. Cheeky was twisted around his leg so tight it felt like his calf muscle might shoot out the bottom of his foot. The poor little guy was crying and shitting all over his shoe. Max couldn't hum over the jetpack, so he blinked really fast and prayed they made it to the roof before Cheeky unwrapped his tibia like a birthday present.

He landed and peeled Cheeky off his leg. Fuck! I should have seen this coming. Oww, I'm a fucking idiot. I deserve this. I should have worn body-armor or brought a carrier. Hopefully, this is the dumbest thing I do all day. His pant leg was shredded, but he only had a few minor lacerations and a lot of bruises. He gritted his teeth and put on a brave face for the troops.

A gust of wind nearly blew him off the edge. "Fuck, why is it so cold up here?"

The ledge around the outside of the roof was about three feet tall. He braced against it and looked out over the patchwork of civilization and rubble. With the towers gone, he could see for miles. Traffic scuttled around the destruction like war's finger had poked holes in an anthill.

His new eyes could focus on the little workers staring back, pointing at his latest handiwork. They looked horrified, but Max knew he'd done them a favor. Evil people were dead. Construction workers were rich. Dilapidated structures were being replaced with shiny new ones. Best of all, insurance covered everything. It served them right. They charged extra for terrorism insurance then made deals with the Iiites to exploit loopholes. Now, they were going broke.

Pope overshot the roof, face white, mouth open in a silent scream. He tried to turn around, but lost control and nearly flew into the side of the building. At the last moment, he spun around and skidded to safety about five feet from Max.

While Pope was emptying his inhaler, Magog and Hedorah arrived. They looked like shit, but their eyes were alive with hope for the first time in ages. Nine more Nrrds shot over the ledge, grinning victoriously and whooping like a glee club that had just won sectionals.

Hedorah threw off his pack and screamed around his cigarette, "Shut the fuck up. You want them to hear us?" His greasy locks were whipping around like snakes, attacking his mouth and eyes.

His demands were met with boos and rude gestures.

Finally, Dr. Feelgood appeared, looking like a morbidly obese cat held by its scruff. He was panicking, kicking his feet as the jetpack beeped that it was almost out of juice. He made it over the ledge just as the pack switched off, dropping him on his belly.

I bet a dollar somebody heard that.

Max stepped forward and motioned for everyone to quiet down and come closer. "He's right. We haven't won yet. I told you you'd be further briefed when it was time, so shut up and listen. Also, keep an eye on that." He jerked his thumb towards the door. "Shoot anything that comes through it."

"I have a contact on the inside. She's the leader of a small group of rebels who are fighting to overthrow the Fist. They've infiltrated the central command and should be taking over as we speak. Thing is, I'm not sure we can trust them. They're probably just using us, and there's a really good chance they're going to kill us as soon as we drop our guard."

Max slid his fingers into his greasy cheek scraggle, taking comfort in the frizzy fluff. "Thing is, if they don't double-cross us, they're our golden ticket to the M.I.L.F.'s underground base. So stay sharp, but don't do anything stupid. Follow my lead, and we'll all live to play Blood Gears 8 when it comes out next month. Cool?"

Feelgood screamed, "You had a spy on the inside this whole time? Why didn't you tell us?"

"Would you have worked as hard to find out what was going on if you thought we already knew? I couldn't take the chance we'd miss something." Max bent down and scratched Cheeky behind the ears. The poor thing's muscles were still tense, but the terror was draining from his eyes.

"Getting back to the matter at hand, they think we're working up from the bottom, which we are, but those guys are a decoy. The majority of the guards on the upper floors are rebels who know we're coming, but this isn't how or when they expect us. Hopefully, the rebels have taken the initiative and started the coup. If all goes well, we won't have to fight anybody. We just walk in and make sure the plan worked. Hawk should be up momentarily with the rest of the insurgents, and we'll be one big happy family, assuming they don't turn on us. We'll see what happens."

Hedorah raged like a carcinogenic storm front. "That's your plan? We'll see what happens? Why don't we all just pull down our pants, grab our ankles and walk in backward? Maybe they'll think we're aliens and start worshiping us."

Max waved the smoke away dismissively. "Don't be grumpy. Now, I have to warn you, the leader of the coup is a gorgeous woman with hypnotic tits and eyes and lips and well... everything else. She's a master of manipulation, very dangerous if she's not on our side. Do not get close to her. Do not trust her. Don't even make eye contact. One glance from Adhra can turn a man's brain inside out. Next thing you know, you'll be jerking off fantasizing about eating out of her garbage. Also, don't take any drugs from her. It's mind control shit."

Pope broke out his spare inhaler. "Did you just say you've been working with Adhra? As in Adhra Duke, the most dangerous, manipulative bitch since Cleopatra?"

"Yeah, what of it?"

"I warned you about her."

"Yes, you did. And I took that into account." Max checked his watch. "It's been about five minutes since the walls came tumbling down. If she hasn't taken over, there's been a glitch in the plan, and we have a mess to clean up. We're going to go in through that door, down two flights of steps, and in through the first door you see. Blow the door and storm in, but not with your guns blazing. If you encounter hostile Iiites, shoot to kill. If not, follow my lead."

"I'm amazed you haven't gotten us killed yet." Hedorah looked disgustedly at his cigarette and thumped it away.

"Yeah, me too. Now let's get this over with."

There was a shudder of shrugs and wagging heads, but they did as they were told. Pope pouted while Feelgood sprayed the door down with a generous helping of insta-hole. Seconds later, a steaming orifice began to dilate, birthing the echoed screams of those dying below.

Hedorah muttered something in Japanese then went down first to make sure there wasn't an ambush. He gave the all-clear, so Max motioned for the troops to advance, but held back, expecting a cloud of Nrrd smoke to billow out any second. None came.

Every quark in his body wanted to run, but he managed to put one foot in front of the other. Cheeky followed close behind. The Iiite on the landing smiled and waved with his gun pointed at the ground. Why is he so relaxed? He doesn't know us. He should expect us to try to kill him. He has the confidence of a man with a foolproof plan. Stay cool. I have thirteen guys who are all more paranoid than me watching my back. Everything's going to be okay.

The door to the executive suite was open. The interior was done in reds and blacks, like a Nazi bordello. The left wall was a bar where expensive booze lined mirrored shelves all the way to the ceiling. A dozen Iiites were doing shots. Another dozen or so were scattered about the plush velvet furniture, toasting and slapping each other on the back. To his right, the bulletproof glass was spattered with blood. A few Iiite corpses were heaped in the corner. Aside from the gore, the room was in good shape, implying the coup had been over in seconds.

"Hey, Max!" Al waved from behind the bar.

Addy was sprawled on a divan looking like Aphrodite seen through the eyes of a thirty-seven-year-old virgin who recently washed down a handful of ecstasy with a gallon of Spanish fly. She smiled at him with those lips of hers, and his pants grew tighter.

As he had feared, a tempest of doubt swept over his mind the moment they made eye contact. Maybe she's not going to betray me. Maybe the leader ordered the gas masks, and she wasn't able to get a message to me because of how tight security was. That's probably it. These guys all seem friendly enough. I'm sure somebody would be nervous if their plan was to knock me off.

Max crossed the room cautiously, but couldn't keep the dopey grin off his face. Addy smiled and jumped up to greet him. His eyes flashed over her again, partially in search of hidden weapons. Her dress clung to the contours of her torso like lingerie--red-on-red blood-spattered lingerie. Her flesh hummed with desire. He knew there was a good chance she would betray him, but the closer she got, the less he cared.

✶✶✶✶✶

Cheeky could hear the blood rushing to Max's underwear. Uh-oh, here we go.

"Max, what's the hold-up? Didn't you miss me?"

Max broke into a run. They met and embraced, kissing pornographically, much to the chagrin of everyone else.

Really?

Cheeky circled them like a shark, analyzing every crevice, every movement for signs of betrayal. He didn't detect any, which was good, because he wouldn't have had time to do anything about it.

"I've spent the last seven months on the run with a bunch of weaponized scientists. What do you think?"

Their second kiss was slower, more passionate. The Iiites and the Nrrds stood in oafish silence, occasionally glancing at each other with pitiful questioning eyes. Cheeky was mortified. Cheeky is two parts Max. Must be dumbest cheekworm ever.

When hands began to wander, Cheeky was the only one brave enough to intervene. He scaled Max's leg and wormed his way between them, managing to come off as sweet and adorable. Max appeared to regain his senses and glanced around at the thirty-odd slack-jawed spectators, making confident and unapologetic eye contact with every third person. "I apologize for the PDA, but come on, can you blame me?"

No one responded. Any monkey would eat its grandmother for a chance to dust her crops. The only whiff of hostility came from a couple of jealous Iiites who probably thought they had a chance with her.

"So, this is Cheeky," Addy said, scratching his chin gently. "He's even cuter than I imagined. Can I hold him?"

Cheeky was uncomfortable with the idea of clinging to the enemy without tearing her to bits but decided to play nice. It couldn't hurt to get a closer look for future reference. For whatever reason, Max wanted her alive, and he had learned not to go against his father's wishes.

Cheeky rolled into her arms and felt around for concealed weapons or likely places she might hide them later. She was the softest thing he'd ever felt. Her DNA was remarkable. He could see why Max's brain had turned to pudding.

While she was giggling and cooing over him, Cheeky formed a full 3-D map of her body in his head. Concealing a weapon would be next to impossible. He could sense she was not one to do her own killing, so he shifted his attention to the rest of her crew. He slithered down her leg and scanned the crowd for signs of dishonesty.

"He's adorable. Do you think he'd mind if I reproduced with him?"

Images of their gorgeous offspring tearing Max apart flashed through Cheeky's mind. Bad idea.

"Hey now, if anybody's going to be reproducing with you, it's me." He laughed and smooched her forehead.

"So, you want me to cut off your ass and fondle it until it grows into another you?"

Max leered and pulled her closer. "You might have to get me drunk first for that one. Seriously though, that's up to Cheeky. He does have a mind of his own, you know."

"He does? Aww, that's so cute. I think he likes me."

Cheeky is a master of deception.

"I assume the coup went smoothly?"

Adhra pulled away. "Yeah, considering. You could have mentioned that you completely changed the plan."

"You could have mentioned that all the troops in this building were equipped with gas masks."

"I tried to tell you, but security was too tight. It wouldn't have mattered, anyway. The gas in this building was just a diversion so my guys could take out the others. Your plan was better than mine, though. You really know how to make an entrance."

Max blushed. "Thanks. So, where is he? Is he as fucked-up looking as I've heard?"

"He's tied up in the supply closet. I saved him for you."

"Huh? You didn't kill him when you had the chance? What the fuck? What if he gets loose? Haven't you ever seen Batman?"

Adhra put her arm around him. "Relax. He's not going anywhere. We stunned him and tied him up with SC1G7. I thought it would be a nice treat for your guys to pull the trigger."

"What the hell is SC1G7?"

Addy smiled in a way that would look smug on a lesser face. "It's a new synthetic rope God himself can't get out of. Seriously, we tried it. He was pissed."

"Uh, okay. I guess we should wait for the others to get here before we do it, though."

Hawk and his men stormed the room, dripping with the blood of the fallen. Max held up a hand to let them know everything was okay.

"All good, sir?" Hawk asked suspiciously.

The Iiites tensed at the intrusion and reached for their weapons, but Max was quick and loud. "Yeah, man, it's cool. Chill." *God, I hope I'm not committing suicide right now.* The troops who didn't collapse twitching with nervous exhaustion shifted their focus from the soldiers to the comfy chairs, rushing in to conquer them with mighty plops and great sighs of relief. Many of their faces were completely red except for the trails left by their tears. Max's Nrrds rushed to fill them in while the Iiites lapsed into their previous conversations.

"Next time somebody has to fight their way up sixty flights of steps, it's your turn. My legs are screamin' like a couple teenyboppers at a boy band bonanza."

Max poured him a glass of champagne. "Hopefully, we won't have to worry about that. I have some news I think you'll like. First, let me introduce you to Adhra," he said, wrapping his arm around her and pulling her close. "She's my girl on the inside."

She smiled and offered her slender hand. Hawk stared at it in befuddlement as if the options to kiss it or shoot it off had stalemated his brain.

Max continued, "Mitton is tied up in the closet. She was nice enough to gift wrap him for us."

Hawk's eyes might have exploded. "What! Haven't they ever seen Batman?"

Max and Addy shared a smirk. Hawk raised an eyebrow and took a step back.

"Chill, he's not going anywhere. All that's left is to figure out who gets to pull the trigger. We can all do it together, or we could flip coins or whatever. It's up to you. In the meantime, I should probably go see if I can get anything useful out of him." He turned to Adhra and smiled. "Did you get anything good lately?"

"Oh yeah, tons, but I doubt you'll get anything out of him now." She slinked onto the couch where Cheeky was perched and patted the seats beside her. "I think we might have broken his head when we tied him up. He started drooling and muttering nonsense."

Cheeky stared at the back of her head like he was hungry, so Max reached over and gently squeezed the fat lumps behind Cheeky's ears to distract him. "Hmm, that sucks. Could it be a trick?"

"I don't know, maybe. We haven't tortured him or anything. He was pretty forthcoming before the attack. The only thing he wouldn't talk about was the secret weapon the M.I.L.F. is hiding behind. I've never seen anything so hush-hush."

Max took the spot to her left and put his arm around her. "I'm not too worried. It could even be a bluff."

Adhra and Hawk responded in unison, "I wouldn't bet on it." They shared a weird smile, and some of the tension went out of Hawk's posture.

Max smiled. Everything was working out so much better than he had expected. "Well, we'll figure something out. I have a plan I think will work as long as they don't know you've turned on them. By the way, where's Jacob?"

"He's keeping an eye on the M.I.L.F. We've been out of contact for a while, but I think he's still alive."

"Cool. I have a spy there too." *Damn it, I probably shouldn't have said that. Eh, it won't matter. She's probably about to kill me anyway.*

Addy grinned. "Really? I didn't know about that one."

"Well, we world-class spies can be rather sneaky."

She ran her hand up his inner thigh. "Let's get business out of the way so we can celebrate. I have something special planned that I think you're going to like."

Max leered and ran his hand up her side, stopping just below the breast. "Works for me."

He kissed her, then stood and addressed the Nrrds. "Hey everybody, great job today. The war's not quite over, but we're really close. Adhra was nice enough to save Felix Mitton for us. We need to question him, but then he's all yours. You just need to decide as a group what you want to do with him."

Happy to have something to draw them back into their element, each Nrrd attempted to prove the logic of their individual scheme.

Max glanced toward the door. "Can I see him?"

"You don't need my permission."

Hawk pulled off his shoes and gave himself a foot rub. "You go on. I'll be there in a minute."

Max opened the door, screamed like a little girl, slammed it shut, and commenced dry-heaving in the comforting squish of Addy's chipper rib-muffins. Hawk tried to spin around to see what was going on but slipped off the couch instead. His knees hit the floor with a thud.

Addy pulled him out of her cleavage. "What's wrong? Did he get loose?"

"How the hell is that thing even alive?" he asked, swallowing in an attempt to suppress his lunch.

Addy cocked her head. "Oh, that? You knew he was a super-mutant. What the hell did you expect?"

"Not that! Where the fuck does he keep his brain?"

"It's in his chest, actually." Addy whispered, "I know he's funny looking, but you're embarrassing me."

"His head is a hand, and it was drooling! That's not right! That's not right at all."

Max's reaction distracted the Nrrds from their debates. Their scientific curiosity drew them like cats to lobster bisque. They crowded around the open door, jostling for a better position. Once they had taken him in as a whole, they closed in, groping and prodding every part of him. Each tried to talk over the others, speculating how he might look on the inside.

"Interesting, his grey matter has migrated to the thoracic cage. Given the extra room, said tissue could expand and develop more freely, which could account for his legendary IQ."

"What efficient usage of space. The metacarpals are totally unaffected by the ancillary adipose, which constitutes the sole bulwark for the optic nerve. This most likely caused glaucoma, which would explain the unusual size and shape of the eyes as well as their abnormal movements. The specimen's eyes and mouth are in a relatively normal configuration but mirrored on the back. Check if his limbs are double-jointed."

"It appears to be able to straighten its phalanges and crane its neck to create a protective wall of bone and flesh around its vital organs."

"I wonder where his nose is. Oh. Wow, that's cool."

Max collected himself and joined them, but medical enigma notwithstanding, all he saw was a big fucking monster. Mitton's sides were bumpy and oozing a clear liquid from a series of orifices, which Feelgood hypothesized were nostrils. His chest was abnormally large and lumpy. The most noticeable and disgusting feature was the giant hand. It sat squarely on his shoulders and had a frenzied drooling face in the center of the palm. Two more sets of arms, each twice the size of the biggest he'd ever seen, sprang from his shoulders and back, making him look like a bug-monster out of an especially perverse hentai.

Max had a feeling akin to vertigo. *Fuck, I hope that SG-whatsisfuck is as strong as Addy says.*

The horror with which Max observed the creature didn't so much recede as acquiesce to share his brainpan with further observations and emotions. The great Felix Mitton sat before him helpless and mad, like a mouse that's shared a cage with a python for too long.

I've won. I did my thing, and the Earth shook. I'm the hero with my enemy at my feet and the girl by my side. Sure, the war isn't technically over. There's still the M.I.L.F. to deal with, but how hard can it be to take down a few stuffy intellectuals and a handful of bodyguards?

"So, who gets to pull the trigger?"

The Nrrds looked at each other and nodded in agreement, but Pope was the first to speak. "Given the creature's unique physiology, it would be a crime against science to simply kill him."

"What, you want to study him? I don't think that's a good idea."

"No, of course not. We don't have the means to do that anymore. We want to vivisect him and see how he works."

The casual pragmatism of his tone sent a shiver down Max's spine. Nevertheless, this was a bad guy, and the Nrrds deserved to have their fun. "Whaddaya say, Felix? You mind if these boys take you apart to see how you work?"

The Iiite leader showed no reaction. If he was faking it, he was doing a remarkable job. Max nodded his consent and left the room. The Iiite rebels shrank in horror at the sounds of the Nrrds indulging themselves, but Addy remained fastened to his arm.

Soon, they would raid the M.I.L.F. together and reshape the world in love and beauty, but first, he had an itch to scratch. They hardly noticed the screams as they walked out the door and down the stairs to the empty office where Addy had prepared her special surprise.

End of Part 1

To be continued in:

APPENDIX

The Baptastic Party

The Baptastic Party formed when the Republican political party merged with the Southern Baptist sect of Christianity. Initially, the American government feigned separation of church and state, making it necessary for politicians to pretend that their religious views were separate from their political views. No one believed them, but without laws limiting religious rights, it was impossible to keep them from manipulating politics to coincide with their religious beliefs. After the government fell, there was no longer any reason to pretend they were separate.

Membership fell off steeply during the period of adjustment. They now function as a secret society, using the you-scratch-my-back-and-I'll-scratch-yours method of back-room manipulation to encourage laissez-faire consumerism; hinder other ideologies; and wage their war on abortion, gambling, gay marriage, and recreational drugs. Though they discuss morality ad-nauseum, very little can be observed in their actions.

At best, the Baptastic Party can be seen as an amusing anachronism, at worst a bunch of rich crackpots who hate everything enjoyable. Still, they strive to impose their religious beliefs on as many people as possible, in any way possible. Mostly they fund radical terrorist sects, but they have had some success in convincing a few prominent physicians to come out with an official stance that drugs, abortion, gambling, and sex are all unhealthy practices.

Bio-Bed

The Bio-Bed is one of Bio-Corp's greatest achievements. When Dr. Gus Mengela was a child, he observed that nothing was softer than a big fat cat. He wanted to use his cat as a pillow, but it would never cooperate. As an adult, Mengela discovered a solution.

He started by removing the genetic codes for limbs and bones so the cats would be born quadriplegic and unable to roll over onto their owners. Then he adjusted the metabolic rate so they would grow ten feet long and eight feet wide with a sleep radius of seven by eight feet. They were hypoallergenic, shed about ten hairs per day, and their endocrine glands were modified to keep them in a state of perpetual bliss. The result was a huge lump of furry fat, which purrs its owner to sleep.

Bio-Beds are cheap to grow and easy to maintain. They rarely have to be replaced, and upkeep is as simple as changing out the convenient IN and OUT bags once a week. The IN bag is an IV filled with nutrients and sedatives. The OUT bag collects the waste. Best of all, the Baby-Bio® grows at the perfect rate to complement a human. A well-maintained bed can be a companion throughout most of your life. Mattresses or "dead beds" are obsolete and rarely seen outside of low-income guest rooms and prisons.

The Cult of Abel

Many years ago, a conceptual artist named Alan Abel formed a fake activist group who tried to convince the population that, "A nude horse is a rude horse." This group, The Society for Indecency to Naked Animals or SINA, strove to clothe every animal in the world. Despite the initial support of the religious right, SINA quickly died out when it was exposed as a hoax.

One hundred and sixty years later, Bob Crane, the Pastor of a small Baptastic church, ran across an old pamphlet and heard the call of the lord. He quickly introduced his new philosophy to his parishioners and stoked the fires of controversy with weekly protests in dog parks, pet shops, and outside theaters showing children's films featuring "exhibitionist" animals. Many Baptastics embraced the philosophy, making SINA one of the world's most influential activist groups. As of March 5, 2135, eight states had adopted ordinances regarding nude animals. The Cult of Abel continues to harass, lobby, and threaten supporters of animal nudity.

Districts: Economy and Security

After the fall of the world's governments, all cities were divided into new economy-based corporate districts, each with its own security firm. K. Co. develops and manages middle-class areas known as K-Districts and provides security through their world-famous K-Squads. I-Force (a division of IMD) handles security for high-end I-Districts. Low-end S-Districts use Sav-Cops (a division of Sav-Mart).

S-Districts

Inhabitants of S-Districts are known as Savanians, taken from Sav-Mart, which manages the district. These are the poorest of America's communities and the most plentiful. They have service-based economies and provide unskilled labor to other areas. The educational system has six grades, but successful Savanian families often send their children to K-Districts for further education.

Sav-Mart began as one man's vision of a friendly place to purchase almost anything at a reasonable price and quickly grew into an untouchable financial juggernaut. By the time the major political and economic turmoil began, Sav-Mart was so large that it benefited from the rise in global calamities. Sixty-seven percent of the population couldn't afford to shop anywhere else.

Crime is rampant in S-Districts because Sav-Cops are not paid enough to risk their lives in combat. Sav-Cops are more likely to run away than they are to help, but the consensus is that they are better than nothing. They are paid minimum wage and wear basic blue uniforms. They service two-thirds of the population. The only way for an officer to get in trouble is to cross another security firm, so corruption is rampant.

K-Districts

Inhabitants of K-Districts are known as Sonians, taken from the Soni Corporation (a subsidiary of K Co.), which is the prime manufacturer of the goods they sell. Sonians are middle class with a decent standard of living. Their educational system has fourteen grades. The economy is based on research and development, but it also provides middle management to other districts.

Crime is rare in K-Districts. K-Squad offers dependable security at affordable prices to roughly twenty-five percent of the population. They have access to most modern weapons and surveillance equipment. Perks of belonging to K-Squad include above-average pay, full benefits, the respect of the general populace, and the potential to be purchased by I-Force. Some of the more well-to-do S-Districts buy K-Squad security for their neighborhoods

At one time, K Co. was roughly on par with Sav-Mart in regards to prices, quality of service, and products, but they were only a fraction of the size. A decade before the government collapse, K Co. was bought by a large Japanese conglomerate run by Kenji Sono, a notorious samurai enthusiast.

When the unemployment rate reached twenty-five percent, Mr. Sono used the desperation of the masses to leverage several unreasonable stipulations in K Co.'s employment contracts. One of which was the seppuku clause, an agreement that a member of K-Squad who failed to protect a client would have to commit ritualistic suicide to atone. Every new hire had to accept this condition to get the job. The seppuku clause encouraged faith in his product, which allowed him to charge more and pay better. Sono trademarked all reasonable variations of the seppuku clause. One year later, he received a Nobel Peace Prize.

I-Districts

Inhabitants of I-Districts are referred to as Klipsch and have the highest standard of living in the country. Their name comes from the high-end electronics company Klipsch, because they are the only people who can afford their products. Unlike Savanians and Sonians, their name was foisted upon them by the lower classes. They refer to themselves simply as People.

People are the economy. They own and or run all of the businesses and make decisions on behalf of the other classes. Their extravagant displays of wealth determine their place in the Klipsch hierarchy. Rather than an educational institution, every child is brought up with a small army of tutors who groom them for their roles as world leaders.

I-Districts are hardly managed, but what little is needed is provided by IMD a division of Macrosoft (a.k.a. International Monetary Divestures, a.k.a. the Bank). In the early 2000s, IMD was the first bank declared too big to prosecute. Despite stealing, insider trading, money laundering, collusion with terrorists, and a long list of other major offenses, governments publicly acknowledged they were above the law. With their new power, IMD executed a series of schemes that ultimately led to their acquisition of all other banks. Ironically, several years later, their software/communications provider, Macrosoft, shut down IMD's systems and transferred all of its employees' funds into their own account. Macrosoft, now too big to prosecute, replaced all the bankers with their people and continued business as usual.

I-Force offers air-tight security to the five percent that can afford them. I-Districts have an average of two and a half officers per block. Their clients, tiny pockets of gated communities and high-end shops, are guarded by highly trained police equipped with body armor, machine guns, tanks, helicopters, and every other state-of-the-art gadget money can buy. I-Force boasts five million officers worldwide (half as many as K-Squad).

Once purchased, an officer becomes the property of I-Force. Most live on-site in emergency facilities or surveillance plazas. Though technically slaves, desertion is nonexistent due to the work-hard-play-hard lifestyle. Officers have the option to retire after age sixty. However, it rarely happens as the retirement package (a house in K-District with utilities paid and a monthly stipend of $2000) is unthinkable after prolonged exposure to Klipsch decadence. To keep their elite forces young and fit, I-Force requires officers to take part in bare-handed death matches for the amusement of their owners. To decline an invitation to participate is grounds for immediate retirement, or worse, but most consider it an honor.

The Divine Disturbance

Also known as "the day everything happened at once," the Divine Disturbance was arguably the most significant event in mankind's history. April 12, 2148, the hair band Poison Candy got tired of being underappreciated. After countless failed attempts at comeback tours, they finally decided to give up the charade. They went to Bryant Park on a busy night and reverted to their alien form, melding into a giant glowing Heavy Metal God. The psychic energy released from their melding shot out over the world at just the right frequency to raise the consciousness of every human being to a state of enlightenment for about ten minutes. It also killed all the batteries.

Everyone experienced the entire circle of life timelessly; giving birth, being born, dying, having sex as male and female, struggling, failing, and achieving, experiencing the entire spectrum of emotion and sensations all at once. Their perspectives were both detached and involved as though it was happening to them, but they also saw it happen from outside. Concepts, freed from language, fit together in layer after layer of dualistic truth and beauty in even the simplest of minds.

Many believe that Poison Candy is God come to Earth to free them from their muddle. Poison Candy knows better but is happy to finally be appreciated. He sits on a giant throne in the center of Bryant Park, granting wishes to those who compliment his hair.

Of the many bizarre side effects the Divine Disturbance had on humanity, perhaps the most puzzling were the sudden changes to human biology. The rising of the dead was strange enough, but the horror industry had prepared people for that eventuality. Stranger still, certain lucky people (whether that luck is good or bad is a matter of hot debate) began to heal at an amazing rate. Some could even survive without functioning organs. Scientists were unsure if it was an evolutionary leap, a miracle, or a curse. Extensive studies were done, but the data stymied the world's greatest minds. All they could agree on was that these anomalies were somehow connected to the Divine Disturbance. Many rules changed that day, leaving humanity floundering in a spooky new reality-tunnel.

Fnordian Necklace

A Fnordian Wave transmitter generates an ultra-low frequency EM field that the human brain is incapable of interpreting. The mind immediately tries to regain its bearings by focusing on something that it can understand. The Fnordian Necklace works at any distance. From far away, the wearer is camouflaged as the observer's brain edits them out of the picture. Up close, it inspires a strong urge to look away and nausea in those who don't. The wearer is protected from its effects because they are within the electromagnetic bubble.

FÜD

Just before the collapse of the world's governments, The U.N. passed a law that required all non-nutritional foodstuffs labeled as FÜD. This was part of a health initiative to point out the amount of high-fat-low-nutrition garbage that the masses were consuming. Overall, it was considered a joke. The masses didn't care what they were eating as long as it tasted good. A hand gesture denoting the umlaut became a popular pop-culture joke, making the term so popular that it stuck around even after the law was defunct.

Igor Stanislavski Commemorative Park

Founded in 2014 to honor the sole survivor of a survivalist cult who had lived for a year and a half trapped underground after an earthquake had crushed the exits of his subterranean compound, the Igor Stanislavski Commemorative Park has retained its name despite a multitude of bizarre events. The controversy started when it came to light that Stanislavski had not only survived by cannibalizing his followers but also planned on doing so from the beginning. Mayor Earnest "Stay the Course" Pickle refused to admit his mistake even when it threatened to end his career. However, this was the kind of move that had endeared him to his supporters in the first place. He kept his job, and the park kept its name, but funding dried up completely.

A sympathetic Japanese suicide cult stepped in and turned it into a kaiyū-shiki homage to Stanislavski, shaping bonsai trees into representations of major events from his life. After the cult committed suicide by impaling themselves on long spikes that lined the sidewalk, the Park was once again without funding. With no one to maintain it for over a year, its beauty gave way to vagrancy and violence.

It was unexpectedly snatched from the jaws of urban sprawl by PITA -4, which was only recently coming into its own thanks to donations from the eccentric heir to the Snuggie fortune. Ironically, PITA -4 was unaware of the park's historical link to cannibalism. They bought it at a pittance to use for promotional barbecues and yearly muzik festivals.

Being associated with PITA, it predictably became a prominent dog park. When the Cult of Abel heard about the takeover, they tried to establish a permanent presence and spread their message in what they considered the most belligerent and vital public sector. Soon after they put their plan into action, PITA -4 heard of their animal-oppressive proselytizing and decided to stop it. Push came to shove, and soon the Pet

Wars were underway. These dark times provided some of the most absurd moments of human history.

When the war ended, the local HOA decided to end the violence by funding the repairs themselves. People eventually started to straggle in, but most left their pets at home. Today, the Igor Stanislavski Commemorative Park is considered a national treasure and a symbol of human perseverance in the face of unimaginable stupidity.

Iiites

The Iiites (pronounced E-Ites) are a violent race of sewer-dwelling mutants who are notorious for committing random brutal attacks on surface institutions. Many call them Lobsters because of their disproportionately massive right arms. They are deeply entrenched in a long-term war with their nemesis, the Riot Nrrds.

Before the release of the Blacktooth chip, people played video games on consoles. These consoles were primitive computers with specialized handheld controllers. In the beginning, these controllers were connected to the consoles by long cords, but over time they progressed to lasers and eventually PANs.

One of the first groups to utilize this new technology was a Japanese gaming company by the name of Genki-Suki. In the early part of this century, Genki-Suki came out with a new platform called the ii (pronounced E), which revolutionized the gaming industry. Despite the pronounced lack of quality games, it met with immediate success because of its unique controller system, which consisted of two sticks, one for each hand, which were covered in buttons and connected to the console by way of a primitive PAN.

Unlike previous controllers, players now had to move their limbs while playing. Ii games quickly became one of the most popular forms of exercise. The movements were more natural and accessible than the previous button-only configuration. Within a year, there was an Ii in one-third of the homes averaged over the whole planet.

Soon after the system became successful, the Ii was linked to a new disease caused by the constant spasming necessary to play the games. Quickly dubbed Iiitis (pronounced E-I-tis), the number of reported cases increased dramatically as the systems began to break. Doctors' offices were overrun by sufferers of inflamed joints, carpal tunnel syndrome, and the decimation of cartilaginous tissue in one arm. In the worst cases, the victims suffered a mutation of muscle tissue, resulting in a disproportionately massive appendage.

Grandmothers frequently broke their grandchildren's backs while hugging them with their new gargantuan appendage. The children adapted much more easily, excelling in sports and other physical activities. Pets suffered enormous casualties. Then they discovered the cancers.

No one knew at the time that the CIA had signed a contract with Genki-Suki's mother company, the Bakemono Corporation, to dispose of toxic waste left over from American nuclear power plants. When the shareholder's union got wind of the deal, they sent a representative to the CEO with a note explaining their dissatisfaction and threatening him with removal should he not immediately find a way to sell the waste back to the U.S. at a considerable mark-up.

Ii was the solution. They used the toxic sludge in batteries for Ii and its controllers. After a while, the lead electroplating flaked off leaking free radicals into the player's bloodstreams. One-third of Ii users died of an aggressive form of cancer. Another third were either immune or lucky enough to ditch their systems before they leaked. The last third adapted. Their bodies used the radiation as an evolutionary catalyst, metamorphosing frayed ligaments and torn muscle tissue into meaty hydraulic presses.

At first, many unaffected people poured their bleeding hearts into charity, volunteering their time and money, and otherwise demonstrating their ability to pity the less fortunate. Things went downhill when it became apparent the mutants were stronger and healthier than regular folk. No one minded when the mutants flooded the hard labor market as ditch diggers and factory workers. However, when they found a home in professional sports, Normals began to envy their handy-capable brothers. They grew tired of watching "Lobsters" take over their favorite teams. It got to a point where a regular Joe with a fanny-pack full of steroids couldn't even join a junior-high Frisbee team.

Complaints were screamed, bills were passed, and segregation became the norm. Those affected lost their jobs. They were denied business loans, and what businesses they already had were boycotted. Normals called them Lobsters to their face, and anyone who had a problem with that was ostracized. Adopting the name Iiite, the affected banded together to survive.

Regular folks would never consider dating much less fucking a Lobster, so they were forced to interbreed, transferring Iiitis to their offspring. Soon the shadows were teeming with Loblets.

This new generation grew up seeing nothing but hatred and abuse from Normals. Reverse racism turned militant when the new generation reached adolescence. Teen angst grew into guerilla warfare.

With every generation, the Iiites became stronger and more organized. Chase Quincy, a blogger known for his impassioned rants on everything from civil rights to sci-fi movies, was carried into the spotlight by a riptide of discontent. His website, I.com, became the central hub of the burgeoning Iiite rights movement, but a series of flubbed interviews convinced him that Normals were not interested in doing the right thing.

At his suggestion, Iiites began to meet underground to make a new home in the sewers and subway tunnels. Quincy believed that, due to social media's alienating nature, the only way to create a real and lasting bond was for Iiites to gather in-person to come up with a plan for the future. The meetings grew radical. Before long, they embraced a new philosophy, "If you can't join them, beat 'em."

The Iiites were forced to educate themselves, which allowed them to disseminate vast quantities of information without the hindrance of the public education system. Before long, Project Prometheus was put into action. Their children became much more intelligent than their surface-dwelling counterparts who were only taught enough to make them smart shoppers and competent workers. Individualism and imagination flourished, creating a cultural renaissance, out of which developed a multitude of scientific advances and, subsequently, a higher standard of living.

Currently, the Iiite government consists of two branches. Felix Mitton is the head of the Iron Fist, which exists to spread disinformation and fear through terrorism. His brother, Xavier Mitton, oversees the Meta-Intellectual Liberty Foundation, or M.I.L.F., which decides policy and focuses on the advancement of the race. The Mitton brothers are super-mutants, genetically engineered to increase the qualities the Iiites find amiable. Hyper-intelligent, super-strong, and notoriously ugly, the Mitton brothers rule from the shadows, hidden even from the Iiites by a veil of secrecy and misdirection. Using manipulation and underground explosives, they toppled the infrastructure of the world's governments, allowing handpicked corporations to step in and supply relief while restructuring civilization to fit a more profitable and efficient paradigm.

Today, these two agencies control every aspect of government above and below ground. Between manipulating the Normal elite and calculated terrorist acts, the population lives in a state of constant fear.

The necessity for guerrilla activity has diminished due to the Riot Nrrds's bungled attempts to gain attention. It is easier and cheaper to spin the Nrrds' actions into gold than it is to scare people themselves.

Jengists

Jengism is a construction-based religion focusing on the purification of the soul through the act of creation. In his book, The Holy Manual of Structure, Jim Jenga outlined the cycles of creation and destruction as apparent in nature and societies since the dawn of time, saying that anything that has structure must be built in some way and everything that has been built will someday collapse. Focusing on the beauty of the cycle rather than individual creations, it teaches that destruction and creation are the same holy act because nothing can be created in a world that is already full.

Jengists believe that, since God is timeless, the amount of time any given thing exists is inconsequential. It is more important to create a wide variety of things than it is to keep them in working order. Life and death are inconsequential because people are part of the natural cycle and therefore bound by its rules. Death is seen as a transformative gift from God, even an honor since that is God's way of saying you achieved perfection. Jengists live for the day they will be transformed into something new.

People flocked to Jenga's new religion, happy to finally have a simple explanation for the meaning of life they could observe in concrete terms. Blind faith was not required since the application of the scientific method could prove the principles of Jengism conclusively. Thousands of Jengist churches sprung up all over the world in parks, sports fields, and elsewhere with enough room.

Whereas most religions see church as a place to pray, sleep, and listen to their leader speak, Jengists show their devotion in a more corporeal fashion. Rather than choosing one or two times a week to meet, Jengist churches are open twenty-four hours a day, seven days a week. To join a church, one must donate two thousand dollars to the building fund, which is used to buy large metal and wooden beams and pay for the construction equipment needed to put them in place.

Most churches begin as a four-level structure consisting of thirty-two beams stacked on top of each other to form an octagonal base. Once the base is completed, the congregation is free to add beams to the structure using any resource necessary. Since the structures are not meant to last, the builders do not bother with blueprints or nails. The only thing a Jengist is encouraged to do is stack the beams symmetrically so the balance can be maintained a little longer and provide more geometric possibilities. Once the building materials have all been used, they begin to create variations on their church by pulling beams out and inserting them or stacking them somewhere else in or on the structure. As building progresses, the structure becomes more unstable and eventually collapses, sending the builders on to glory. Those who are chosen by the structure are recorded in the Jengist Book of Saints.

NAADP

The National Association for the Advancement of Dead People was founded almost immediately upon the first zombie's appearance. People quickly fell into two categories, those who saw reanimated humans, and those who saw monsters. Virtually everyone was affected. Those who saw their friends and family mistreated by fearful mobs were angry enough to launch the NAADP into an overnight success.

Neo-hippie founder, Teddy Pushpin, decided to take a less violent approach than other special interest groups and teamed up with the budding Order of the Owl. Together they created a fecund Media© campaign to manipulate the masses into acceptance of the deceased up-and-comers. No art-form was forsaken as the growing bohemian horde sank their tendrils into the superconscious mind-field. In everything from prop comedy to major motion pictures, they portrayed Zombies as innocent, harmless, and even friendly. Before long, it was more common for a person to tell a cute story about a zombie than a scary one.

The efforts of the NAADP did nothing to reduce the number of zombie attacks, but they were mostly successful in creating an equilibrium in which zombies were allowed to mind their own business. Zombie legislation flip-flopped more frequently than abortion had in the past, but people's attention to the matter—as well as anti-zombie violence—began to dwindle on its own once people got used to them. Despite being unnecessary, the NAADP is still inundated by cash from the newly affected.

The Neo-Catholistic Church

Formerly a Christian religious sect known as Catholicism, the Neo-Catholistic Church is one of the largest and most powerful corporations in the world. The Catholic Church grew from a monotheistic religion based around the teachings of Jesus Christ, whom the members believed to be the son of God. Jesus performed magic and taught his followers to reach their spiritual potential through love, forgiveness, experience of the divine, and the control of base instincts. One of the core beliefs was that human souls are consigned to one of two places after death. Good Christians would go to a paradise called Heaven, and everyone else went to a very unpleasant place called Hell.

Those in power did not like Jesus's message of personal liberation, so they executed him. He could have used his magic to escape, but as a sacrifice to his father, he allowed himself to be nailed to a T-shaped piece of wood and put on display. In return, his father broke down the barrier between God and man, granting the repentant forgiveness for their sins without further sacrifice. Three days later, Jesus rose from the dead, reassured his followers, and passed into the afterlife of his own volition.

After his departure, his disciples converted as many people as they could. Those followers would meet to talk about Jesus and his teachings. As their numbers grew, a complex hierarchy emerged to protect them and keep them organized. Their strategy of evangelism and adaptivity helped their religion to spread quickly, and soon it was among the most widely practiced in the world.

As their power grew, so did their ambition. The Church launched a series of holy wars against Muslims, Pagans, Slavs, Orthodox Christians, Mongols, Hussites, Cathars, and political enemies of the Popes. Crusaders took vows and were granted all-inclusive spiritual pardons allowing them to rape and murder the unfaithful as well as plunder their possessions.

The Church launched Inquisitions to prosecute Christians who publicly dissented from the Catholic faith's doctrines. Believing that the souls of those deemed to be heretics were in danger of being consigned to hell, the authorities used whatever means they considered necessary to make the sinner recant. Although the Church initially condoned these proceedings, abuses eventually forced the Pope to withdraw support.

In 2002, priestly pedophilia got so out of hand that it was impossible to conceal. Officials of various Catholic dioceses were aware of some of the abusive priests, and shuffled them from parish to parish (sometimes after psychotherapy), sometimes allowing contact with children. A survey of the ten largest U.S. dioceses found that 234 priests out of 25,616 had allegations of sexual abuse made against them in their careers.

In response, the United States Conference of Catholic Bishops initiated strict new guidelines for the protection of children in Catholic institutions. However, it was too little, too late. Nothing could stop their numbers from dwindling.

After many unsuccessful attempts to repair the Church's public image, Pope John Paul III looked objectively at the Church. He saw a massive non-profit organization made up mostly of homosexual atheists. The Church owned more than half of the world's land, art, and wealth. They no longer needed God to frighten the people into submission.

The Church spent two percent of its wealth to produce the most extensive ad campaign in history. They wanted to distance themselves from the Church that was best known for torture, manipulation, hypocrisy, etc. Trillions went into market research. Among other things, they found that people are most likely to have positive associations with words ending in the letters' ic'. After testing over five-thousand variations, they settled on the name Catholistic.

Soon after the initial changes, they removed themselves one step further by staging another schism. The most respected clergy members split off in protest of the Catholistic's use of funds. Neo-Catholisticism was so popular that no one noticed when regular Catholistics disappeared.

The Neo-Catholistics framed themselves as the world's biggest charity. Rather than alienating their followers who believed in a God, the shift of focus was sly and gradual. Severe dogmas softened into cheery slogans. "God wants you to do good works" became "why should we need a God to make us help each other" and then "people helping people." "Birth control is against the will of God" became "the more people there are, the more helpers we have," and finally, "the more, the merrier." Perhaps their most inspired action was to make the Church "Cool" by coming out against chastity, even going so far as to claim that it was a satanic conspiracy meant to limit the numbers of the priesthood and drive them mad. Virtually the only thing that stayed the same was the Catholic tradition of ornate regalia and over-the-top showmanship.

Without the judgmental airs and religious dogma, the Church was free to accept tithes from atheists and members of other religions. Membership quadrupled in the first year. There were so many grand gestures of charity and good-will that no one noticed they were only using three percent of their income. Today, Pope Benny II is the best-loved TV personality in the world.

The Pet Wars

Though little-known outside of Southern California, thousands died on either side as PITA -4 faced off against the Cult of Abel in one of the most brutal conflicts in recent history. PITA -4, a cannibalistic sect of fanatical animal rights activists, purchased and restored the Igor Stanislavski Commemorative Park. A few months later, the Cult of Abel chose the newly founded dog park as their base of operations in the war against animal nudity. They would get in people's faces and scream things like, "a nude dog is a rude dog."

PITA -4 thought clothing animals was cruel and ridiculous, so they barred the cult from the premises.

In the beginning, fighting was primitive, with rocks and sticks being the primary weapons. Both sides adopted increasingly sophisticated tactics as the battles escalated into war. PITA -4 members concealed themselves in the trees and dropped like silent tornados of steel at the first sign of cultist presence. As a warning, the skins of fallen cultists were fashioned into clothing and placed on animal statues throughout the garden. Cultists then brought in heavy artillery, which damaged the park to the extent that no one wanted to go there anymore.

Since the fighting never spilled over into the surrounding area, no one paid much attention. Those who did, viewed it as a good thing since two fanatical groups were killing each other off. Eventually, the war ended the same way as any other; both sides were losing too much money and too many converts to make it worth their while. They reached a truce, and the cult was allowed on the premises three times a week with no repercussions. The public has learned not to go on a Monday, Wednesday, or Friday.

PITA

PITA, or People for Improving the Treatment of Animals, is an animal rights group with about thirty-thousand members worldwide. They believe that "Animals are not ours to eat, wear, experiment on, use for entertainment, or abuse in any way." It began as a group of animal lovers hoping to prevent the abuse of non-human organisms. They lobbied, petitioned boycotted, investigated the treatment of animals, and reported their findings to the public through graphic propaganda films.

Some believed PITA's protests and propaganda were not accomplishing enough. They broke off and formed PITA-2, which focuses on recruiting passionate young people to take to the streets with flyers, stickers, and bullhorns. Some still did not think enough was being done, so PITA-3 formed around the slogan, "Shut up and do something." This new group raids businesses known to experiment on animals, sabotages entertainment that exploits animals, and kills people they deem guilty of crimes against animal kind. PITA-3 keeps a low profile with the help of their sister-groups.

Then came PITA-4, who defend their furry brethren by promoting cannibalism among humans. Their logic is that there are too many people already, and the ones who victimize the helpless creatures of the world know how it feels to be rationalized onto a plate. None of their members have ever been arrested. The police turn a blind eye, and the rest of society tolerates them because of their ingenious ad campaigns. On average, four of the top ten hits at any given time are written by PITA-4, and their contributions to film and art are rivaled only by the NAADP.

Project Prometheus

Citing the high probability of Iiite children devolving into a race of violent uneducated monsters, Dr. Hugh Gasol convinced Iiite parents to send their children to a separate educational facility that would save them from their hopeless future. Rather than hiring teachers, he recruited specialists from various fields and allowed students to choose the courses that most appealed to them. He designed a tiered reward system in which good test scores earned prizes.

Grade 1:
A- candy bag – big plush
B- choco-pop – medium plush
C- starlight mint – small plush
D- nothing
F- nothing

Grade 2:
A- candy bag deluxe – big toy
B- candy bag –medium toy
C- piece of candy – small toy
D- nothing
F- nothing

Grade 3:
A- slice of cake - board game
B- snack cake – large toy
C- piece of candy – medium toy
D- nothing
F- extra chores

Grade 4:
A- favorite dessert - computer game C

B- slice of cake or pie – board game
C- nothing
D- extra chores
F- extra chores

Grade 5:
A- favorite meal- accessory D - computer game B
B- favorite dessert – computer game A
C- nothing
D- extra chores
F- extra chores

Grade 6:
A- favorite meal - accessory C - computer game A
B- favorite dessert- computer game B
C- extra chores
D- extra chores
F- remedial class and extra chores

Grade 7:
A- favorite meal - accessory B - computer game A - vice C
B- favorite dessert - game time - accessory C
C- remedial class and extra chores
D- lose a class
F- lose a class

Grade 8:
A- favorite meal – accessory B – computer game A – vice B
B- favorite dessert – accessory C – game time - vice C
C- remedial class and extra chores
D- lose a class
F- Lose a class

Grade 9:
A- dining card B - accessory A – computer game A – vice B
B- accessory B - game time - vice C
C- remedial class and extra chores
D- lose a class
F- lose a class

Grade 10:
A- dining card B - accessory A - computer game A - vice A
B- accessory B - game time B - vice A
C- remedial class and extra chores
D- lose a class
F- lose a class

Grade 11:
A- gift card A - game time A - vice A+ dining card A
B- accessory A - game time B - vice B
C- remedial class and extra chores
D- lose a class
F- lose a class

Grade 12:
A- gift card A - game time A - Vice A+ - dining card A
B- accessory A - game time A - vice B
C- remedial class and extra chores
D- lose a class
F- lose a class

Dr. Gasol knew he could buy a first grader's attention with candy, but more complex subjects would require better rewards. To that end, he created a tier-based catalog, each tier having several subsets for children with different interests. There are currently thousands of available rewards. Above are a few examples to provide a basic idea. For foodies, the prizes ranged from a starlight mint to a dining card, which granted the used one month of unlimited credit to purchase food (or FÜD) in any form from anywhere. Accessories might range from a plastic bracelet to an item of clothing, a gadget, or body modification. Vices might range from cigarettes or lingerie catalogs in class C to cocaine or prostitutes in class A+.

In addition to a top tier prize, A students always had the option to take on another class. Students who worked the hardest also played the hardest, which conditioned them to associate being cool with doing well in class. Since more courses meant more rewards, students wanted to take as many as possible.

The children's knowledge grew at a remarkable rate. By the time the second generation was graduating, the first had developed better ways of teaching. Inventions became more common than acne. Breakthroughs in genetic engineering yielded smarter and smarter children who went on to learn more, faster. IQ and information transfer methods doubled with every subsequent generation. Classes evolved from time with a teacher to subconscious info-dumps. Instead of standardized tests, students were given real-world problems to solve and were graded on their solution's ingenuity, effectiveness, and efficiency.

Though hugely successful, the program didn't work for everyone. In utero modifications did not always take. Occasionally children would be born with normal levels of intelligence and heightened endocrine production, making it extremely difficult for them to function in the educational system. Typically, by third-grade students with this affliction had become so violent and distracting to their fellow students that they had to be reassigned to ROTC classes where they learned to defend their homes and go on surface raids. The ROTC class eventually grew into the Iron Fist, and the rest formed the Meta-Intellectual Liberty Foundation.

Riot Nrrds

The Riot Nrrd movement is a train wreck of punk ideology and classical nerdiness. In the 1970s, those in power decided to lower the overall IQ of the masses. American pop culture presented stupidity as the new cool, and the youths of that time were grateful for an excuse to tune out, drop out of society, and spend their time getting turned on by an overdose of sex and drugs. Those who didn't buy into the decline of western civilization were wedgied, swirlied, mocked, and beaten. Dubbed nerds, loonies, paranoids, radicals, revolutionaries, extremists, terrorists, conspiracy theorists, kooks, weirdos, fanatics, and many other hateful monikers, disenfranchised thinkers the world over grew tired of watching humanity dig its own grave.

Nerds discovered the radioactive vials in the Ii and tried to warn people, but no one would listen to them until it was too late. In fact, no one listened to them about anything. The masses were unwilling to admit how out-of-control governmental corruption had gotten, let alone take responsibility for letting it get so bad. They didn't want to switch to renewable energy or make an effort to solve the world's problems. While Iiites were being persecuted for differences in physiology, nerds were persecuted for variations in lifestyle and social awareness.

The Nrrd revolution was born on September 21st, 2128, when a political joke turned into a semantic argument in a bookstore between Laslow Huggins and an unknown Normal (Normal is the term both Riot Nrrds and Iiites used to describe the sedated masses). Several strangers chimed in with their opinions. The Normal threw his cookbook at one of them, and a full-scale riot ensued. Laslow died in the riot, but remains an icon of intellectualism and conviction.

WWLD (What Would Laslow Do) memorabilia was in trendy stores within the week. Soon after, copycat riots sprang up all over the country as Nrrds began to stand up for truth. They formed groups and adopted the pilcrow as their banner. Nrrds tattooed the mark on themselves, using it as a key to gain access to meetings.

Now that the isolated intellectuals of the world had a reason to band together, they quickly organized into powerful anti-establishment groups.

Using the recently formed mythology of Laslow as a prototype, Hubert Selby V created an ideological platform that united all of the smaller groups under a single agenda, the overthrowing of the global elite and deprogramming of the masses. Despite the Nrrds' best efforts at waging an information war, the Iiites had the lead in the race for power. As it turned out, it was much easier to subjugate the masses than to free them. Today, the Riot Nrrds continue to destabilize Iiite control by hacking and Guerilla warfare. However, the Media© (controlled by the M.I.L.F.) continuously spins their actions in the Iiites favor.

Scrap Cookers

Designed by Bio-Corp, the Scrap Cooker (better known as the crap cooker) was the perfect solution to the steady decline of the waste disposal service. Recycling was time-consuming and frequently created more pollution than it prevented, and landfills were getting full, so Dr. Gustav Mulagatani designed a machine that would solve all the waste issues.

How they work: People with items they would like to get rid of will open the door and place the objects on the disposal platform. With the door closed and fee paid, jets of gas incinerate those objects. The smoke and ash are sucked through a series of liquid filters that reclaim useful substances and compress the rest into sheets of light non-toxic waste, which is spooled and resold as packing material or fused to make high-density plastic.

Coin-operated waste disposal units are cheap to franchise and easy to transport, so they are a prime investment for Savanians who want to move up in the world. They are available in a range of shapes and sizes. The most popular are about the size of a vending machine and dispose of objects up to 25" square. They cost around $20.00 a day to rent and $1.00 to use.

Victory

Developed by Adhra Duke, Victory is a designer mind-control drug that combines the worst elements of cocaine, crystal meth, heroin, PCP, and pure adrenaline to create a highly addictive, high-biological impact drug indistinguishable from regular cocaine. A sort of conditioner catalyst, Victory tunes the decision-making parts of the brain to be super-susceptible to suggestion. The speaker's voice, entering the mind at a time of such extreme pleasure, will destroy associations that contradict it by hardwiring whatever is said to be associated with pleasure. It essentially wrings out the dopamine gland so that the user won't notice the damage to their Basal Ganglia.

ABOUT THE AUTHOR

S.T. Gulik is a magical cockroach.

He started life as a common wood roach in 1681, living in a small castle outside of Dublin. One day, a human alchemist blew himself up while trying to brew the elixir of life. S.T. survived the blast, but the fumes cursed him with self-awareness and immortality. A lot has happened in three-hundred-thirty-five years. Everyone he knew and loved has died. Vampire movies make him cry.

On the upside, he's had countless adventures and learned many things. He worked for the goddess of chaos for one-hundred-twenty-three years. About thirty years ago, she turned him human and disappeared, which is fine because humans are smart and likable.

Oh, and he writes absurdist fiction. That's important. Gotta mention that.

Discover more at Sausage-Press.com

Stalk me at Facebook, Google+, Spotify, and Twitter

Read more S.T. Gulik:
Muffy or a Transmigration of Selves
Dead Bait 3
Killpoet Issue 9
Pussy
Dolphin Cock Massacre
The Final Draft
Sex or Busier Than a Three-Legged Cat Trying to Squeeze Blood from the Tip of an Iceberg

Need some Karma? Paypal Fnord33@gmail.com literally any amount of money. This is a great option for people who read this book for free, but don't want the author to starve.